Limerick County Library
30012
D1142395

TURNCOAT

Also by Aaron Elkins

Skeleton Dance
Loot
Twenty Blue Devils
Dead Men's Hearts
Old Scores
Make No Bones
A Glancing Light
Icy Clutches
Curses!
Old Bones
A Deceptive Clarity
Murder in the Queen's Armes
The Dark Place
Fellowship of Fear

With Charlotte Elkins

A Wicked Slice
Rotten Lies
Nasty Breaks

TURNCOAT

Aaron Elkins

ROBERT HALE · LONDON

First published in Great Britain 2003

ISBN 0 7090 7352 6

Robert Hale Limited
Clerkenwell House
Clerkenwell Green
London EC1R 0HT

2 4 6 8 10 9 7 5 3 1

Typeset in 11/13pt Goudy by
Derek Doyle & Associates, Liverpool.
Printed in Great Britain by
St Edmundsbury Press, Bury St Edmunds, Suffolk.
Bound by Woolnough Bookbinding Ltd.

Chapter One

For everybody else in America it was the day JFK was killed in Dallas. For me, it would always be the day Lily's father turned up on our doorstep.

But first things first. . . .

SOMETHING WAS WRONG with my eyes. I could make out the peeling white farmhouse and the ramshackle outbuildings, I could see the sheep nuzzling the grass in the dappled shade of a clearing about twenty yards from where I lay in the thicket, flat on my stomach; I could see the slender, unnaturally still woman in the apron and the long blue dress, holding a basket propped against her hip and peering – or at least facing – in my direction. But it was all wavery and fuzzed over, as if I were looking through misted glass. I couldn't make out her face, or whether she was young or old, or what was in the basket, or whether or not she'd spotted me.

I knew that all I could do was lie there – my legs didn't seem to be working right either – and pray that I was hidden by the vines and brambles. I tried to remember how I'd come to be there, but couldn't quite put it together. We'd taken off from England that morning on another bombing run, headed for the benzol plant near Linz; I remembered that much. We'd completed the mission and made our turnaround. And then at about the Austrian border the flak had started popping, and then the Focke-Wulfs had shown up, and we were in big trouble. Three of them slipped through our escort of P-51s and screamed straight up at us, homing in as if they'd decided from the beginning that out of the whole 350th Bombardment Group – two dozen B-17s, plus three hundred additional bombers filling the skies around us – it was us alone, the *Betty G*, they were after; nobody but us.

The next thing I knew . . . well, the next thing I knew, there I was lying on my stomach in the thicket, injured and frightened, looking at the woman without a face and trying to figure out what I was supposed to do next. I didn't remember our getting hit, I didn't remember Captain Slocum ordering us to bail out, and I didn't remember jumping, or getting rid of my parachute when I landed, or anything. I was starboard waist gunner. Had I even had a chance to fire? I couldn't remember that either.

I realized with a start – probably it was the look of the farmhouse and the soft, rolling countryside – that I'd come down in France, not Germany. She was a Frenchwoman! My heart came near to bursting with relief. Not only was I likely to be in friendly territory, I was in my native land. I'd been born in Lyon and spent most of my childhood there before my father brought us to the States.

'*Madame!*' I called, surprised to hear how feeble my voice was. '*Au secours! Je suis un aviateur Américain. Mon avion a été démoli par les Boches.*'

Nothing. She just stood there without saying anything, without moving, as impassive as a statue, for a long time, and when she did begin to speak it was in a weird monotone, a chant, nothing like normal speech. The individual words were French, all right, but the sentences were gibberish, and I began to get a scary, queasy feeling that something was terribly wrong – even more terribly wrong than it obviously was, I mean.

If only I could get out of these clothes, I thought. I was roasting. The waist gunners' slots were the coldest places in the plane – no glassed-in turrets, just a couple of big rectangular open holes in the fuselage, and at twenty thousand feet oxygen was the least of our problems. The temperature could get to twenty below zero, with a freezing wind that could crack your bones. So we had to dress accordingly, and I was still in my heavy leather flight jacket, over-pants, and boots, and my heavy cap with the ear flaps pulled tight. I felt as if I were liquefying inside my casing of fleece-lined leather. No, I *was* liquefying. My ribs had begun to melt into a soft mush. I could feel them running out from under . . .

I'm hallucinating, I thought with a jolt. *None of this is happening.*

I'm strapped into my bed in the mental ward at Kings County General, writhing and sweating, and dreaming the whole thing up. And not for the first time either. No, I've been here before: the same thicket, the same stony, faceless figure, the same torpid, dopey sheep. In another minute, the rest of the cast will come marching out from around the corner of the farmhouse.

And out they came. Sometimes they were rustic farm people, or soldiers, or policemen, but most of the time, as now, they were fussy-looking village functionaries of some kind in pince-nez, wing collars, and rusty black suits. They filed out two by two, six of them, muttering and wringing their hands, while some of them banged pots and pans together. Hallucination or not, the whole thing was scaring the hell out of me, and when the woman in blue began to move toward me – to glide as if on rollers, not to walk – I screamed. For a moment the scene shimmered, struggling to hold itself together. Then it fell apart into ragged pieces and I was staring at the light fixture on my ceiling, with the tattered, long-dead moth inside that I never seemed to get around to removing.

I WAS SWEATING, all right, and the twisted bedclothes proved I'd been doing plenty of writhing, but I wasn't strapped into any bed in the mental ward, and in fact I never had been. In a mental ward, that is. It was all part of the Dream. I'd been having it once a month or so for two or three years now, or maybe more; I'm not sure when it started – and Kings County General and everything else was part of it. It wasn't always exactly the same; sometimes the woman in blue was a statue, a literal statue – a sphinx, perhaps, or a Greek goddess with her face worn off. And I never knew quite what to expect from those characters who popped up at the end. The pots and pans this time were a new wrinkle. But it always had more or less the same elements, and it was one of those nightmare fantasies that was inexpressibly more eerie and frightening than it had any right to be.

The interesting thing is, I'd actually been a waist gunner in a B-17 and had flown a couple of sorties against German railroad depots in 1945 as an extremely green nineteen-year-old, but nothing remotely like this had ever happened to me. So why did I keep having the damn dream?

What I know about the psychology of dreams doesn't amount to much. And most of what little I do know has struck me as . . . well, pretty soft-headed. Pretty wacky, if you want the unvarnished truth. But I have this friend, Louis Winkleman, who's on the psychology faculty at Brooklyn College (where I'm an associate professor of history), and so after I'd had the dream a few times I told him about it on the off chance that he might be able to shed some light. After all, when a dream keeps repeating itself like that, there has to be *some* reason, doesn't there?

As always, Louis had a theory in his hip pocket. As usual, it struck me as pretty wacky. The likely root of the problem, he explained, was a guilt complex. (Louis is first and foremost a Freudian, which means, so I'm coming to understand, that most problems seem to boil down to guilt, generally repressed.) In my particular case, he suggested, I was troubled by the memory – presumably the repressed memory – of having let my buddies down on one of my missions. Perhaps, through momentary panic or misjudgment, with antiaircraft shells exploding around my ears, I had put my companions at risk, or even caused, or rather *believed* I had caused, someone's death or injury.

The statuelike, faceless woman represented my superego, righteous and unforgiving (which was why I was so terrified of her), and what else could my own strangely blank mind during the dream be but a manifestation of my refusal to admit even to myself what I'd done?

He'd been so taken with his analysis that I almost hated to tell him it wouldn't work. There hadn't been any exploding shells within a mile of my ears. I'd never been under fire, I'd never even seen anyone wounded. Other than practice and training, I'd never had occasion to fire my own .50-caliber Brownings, and when I had it'd been fun. On the two missions I'd flown, our squadron had never been seriously threatened, let alone hit or shot down; nothing worse than a few puffs of harmless-looking flak off to the side and way below us. It had been the very end of the war and the German Luftwaffe was out of business. If there were still any Focke-Wulfs or Me-109s in the air, we sure didn't see them. Both our missions had been as smooth as anyone could hope for: fly over, unload the bombs, and fly home. As far as I knew, the only crew member who'd required medical attention was my buddy Al Maloff, the port gunner, who'd gotten frostbite on one cheek because he hadn't properly secured his earflaps.

And, as I told Louis, I categorically refused to accept responsibility for that.

Besides, this was 1963. The war had been over for eighteen years. I was thirty-seven, for God's sake. It was half a lifetime ago, and I'd never spent a lot of time thinking about my tiny part in it even back then. So what was I doing dreaming about it now? I continued to lie there musing for a while, heavy with sleep, before I realized that somewhere in the distance the dream-shouting was still going on, and the banging of the pans too. I frowned, trying to focus my hearing, and was able to make out a few words.

'Tu ne comprends pas!'

'Va-t'en!'

French? On Eighty-third Street and Bay Parkway in Brooklyn?

I don't happen to be one of those annoying people who spring from sleep with batteries fully charged, so it was another few seconds before it got through to me that I was listening to two real people in a real argument, seemingly at my front door, and that the higher voice – a choked screech, really – belonged to my wife, Lily. This was astounding: in seventeen years of marriage I'd rarely heard Lily raise her voice, and I'd certainly never heard her *screech* before. And while French was also her native tongue, she'd long ago made it clear that she'd left it behind, good riddance, when I'd married her and brought her to the United States.

I got into my robe and stumbled downstairs and through the living room to the entrance foyer. There was Lily in her flowered housecoat, standing at the open door, her back toward me, head held high on her slender, graceful neck, as it always was, but from ten feet away I could see that she was shaking. Beyond her, on the stoop, was the apparent source of it, an old man I'd never seen before, hollow-cheeked and yellowish, with a meager, tobacco-stained white goatee and a heavy black overcoat. With his disordered white hair, and the tendons standing out like ropes on either side of his neck, and a wild-eyed look behind round gold-wire-framed glasses, he was, if anything, more agitated than Lily was. He was thrusting what seemed to be a film canister at her, a big gray one, the kind you see in movie theaters, and as he spoke he struck it for emphasis with the flat of his hand. (Ah, there was my banging of pots and pans.)

'*Regarde-le*,' he was pleading in a strained, urgent voice, '*c'est tout que je te demande*.'

'*Vas à l'enfer, fiche-moi la paix, va-t'en!*' Lily was shouting back at him.

In other words:

'Just look at it, that's all I ask!'

'Go to hell, leave me alone, get out of here!' And as she spat the words she was trying to close the door on him while he struggled to keep it open.

It was so unlike Lily, so totally, impossibly out of character, that for a moment I thought I must surely still be sleeping, that this had to be some new little fillip the Dream had worked up for my entertainment. But no, it was real enough; I could feel the crisp November air on my face and the cold linoleum under my bare feet; I could smell mothballs from the old man's coat.

'What's going on here?' I said curtly, directing it at the man on the doorstep. 'What do you want?'

It startled him enough that he took a half step backward and Lily managed to get the door slammed in his face. And locked, although her fingers were trembling so much she had trouble doing it. Then she braced her back against it as if she thought he might try to hammer it down and stared at me – or rather through me – so fiercely, so unseeingly, that I could feel the hairs standing up on the back of my neck. She was like someone I'd never seen before.

I took a step closer. 'Honey, what is it? Who is that guy? What—'

'Shh.' She jerked a finger to her mouth, listening intently. 'Wait.'

He was still out there on the stoop, ranting in French about mistakes made, and death, and forgiveness, and St George, and things not being what they seemed. It went on for a while, an incomprehensible muddle, then subsided into a singsong moan and stopped altogether. Lily waited a minute more before she opened the door an inch.

'He's gone,' she breathed. And then flung herself into my arms. 'Pete . . .'

I stood there holding her close. She was pulling herself against me as hard as she could. I could feel her heart thumping almost like a bird's, and her breath coming in shallow little gasps.

I found that my own heart was racing too. 'Lily—'

'Just hold me for a minute, will you?' she said into my shoulder. 'Tight.'

I gathered her even closer, so that my arms went all the way around her. 'Shh,' I said, stroking her hair. 'It's okay, sweetheart, shh.' After a while, when she'd quieted down enough to take a couple of deep breaths (me too), I spoke gently. 'Honey, what *is* it? Who was that?'

'A salesman,' she said into my shoulder. 'I don't know. A peddler.'

'A peddler? It's not even seven-thirty in the morning. I don't— What was he selling?'

'I don't know.'

'How can you not—'

'A movie, I think. Some kind of movie. Oh, Pete.'

'A *movie*?' I was growing increasingly confused. 'Why would anyone come here trying to sell a movie? At this time of the morning?'

'I don't know, I don't understand either.' She was starting to tremble again. 'I heard a knock at the door, you were still sleeping, I didn't want to wake you up, I came down . . .'

'But he was speaking French. How did he know to speak French?'

She drew her head back to look into my eyes. 'Pete, why are you asking me all these questions? Who cares what he wanted? He's gone, that's all that's important. Can't we just forget it? Brrr.'

I was getting a bad feeling here. I'd never known her to lie to me, not about anything important. 'But honey, why are you so upset? Did he—'

'He was so . . . rude, that's all. You saw him, he kept pushing, pushing. He just gave me the creeps.' She shuddered, genuinely enough.

'And you never saw him before?'

She stepped back and with one hand drew the housecoat around her neck, as if I'd become the enemy. 'Of course I never saw him before. What are you driving at? I told you, I heard a knock at the door, I came—'

'Lily,' I said quietly, 'he called you *tu*, not *vous*. I don't see a stranger doing that.'

She closed her eyes. 'My God, my God,' she said in a low moan, and a shiver crawled down my spine. 'Oh, oh, oh . . .'

'Baby,' I said gently, 'I'm only trying—'

But her smooth, lovely face – even at thirty-five, even without makeup, she had skin like a Coty girl's – had gone all pink and blotchy. Still clutching her collar, she slid slowly to the floor with her back against the wall, and, weakly beating her fist on the linoleum, dissolved into a fit of weeping and, it seemed to me, helpless rage.

FOR A MOMENT I couldn't move. Lily is, and always was, anything but emotional. She is the calmest, most level-headed person I know. Serene. Things don't get under her skin. Insert her into an overwrought situation – sudden grief, say, or dashed hopes, or a bitter quarrel – and it's as if somebody put Valium in the drinking water. She smiles in that knowing, soothing way; she speaks softly, and sensibly, and warmly – 'Let's sit down and talk about it a little,' 'Let's think it through,' 'Why don't we go back and start at the beginning?' – and the frenzy, or anger, or turbulence swirls away like water down the drain. You can actually see people take deep breaths and settle down when she gets into the act.

Oh, she gets a little cranky from time to time; who doesn't? But by and large she's great to have around in a crisis. And as it happens, I'm not exactly the world's most temperamental person either (aside, of course, from the occasional blue funk of my own), so as you can imagine, our life together has been pretty quiet, which is fine, just the way I like it.

So to see her the way she was now, collapsed into jelly, her eyes puffy with crying, was enough to make me feel as if the floor had just come out from under my feet. Lily was my rock, my rudder.

I got down beside her on my knees and took her hand, the one she was banging on the floor with. I was shaking a little too. 'Honey . . . please . . . can't you tell me . . .'

She wouldn't unclench her fist. She wouldn't look at me either, and when I tried to embrace her again she twisted away, wrapping her arms around her knees and burying her head in them.

'Lily, Lily, don't do that, don't pull away from me. Whatever it is, I'm right here, I love you, just tell me what's the matter.'

Her face came up with a jerk, tear-stained and frightened. She peered at me for a long time without saying anything, then seemed to collect herself and, with a sigh, come to a decision. Whatever this was about, here it came. My heart continued to sink.

She looked down and murmured something.

'What?'

'I said he's my father.'

'Your . . . your . . .'

'Father.' She managed a wan smile. 'Marcel Vercier. *Mon cher père*.'

I was stunned. 'But . . . and you sent him away like that? I mean, he looked so—'

She waved me quiet, took in a quivery breath, let it slowly out of her mouth, and visibly got herself in hand. 'Pete, it's getting late. I have to go to work, I have to get dressed. I'm all right now. I'll tell you all about it over breakfast, all right? I promise.'

She kissed me on the cheek – as always a real kiss, warm and generous, not a peck – and scrambled to her feet, wiping away the marks of her tears with a Kleenex. 'I'm really embarrassed. This is so ridiculous. I'd better go put on my face. I must look like death warmed over.'

I watched her go, wondering what in the hell this was all about. Even at the time, knowing as little as I did – knowing nothing, really – I had the unwelcome sensation that some critical balance in our lives had just shifted, that a vital, unseen underpinning had snapped. That things were never going to be the same.

Chapter Two

YOU SEE THE thing is, Lily wasn't supposed to have a father. We'd been married for almost seventeen years, and from the beginning I'd understood that she was an orphan. Her father had been a barber who'd been shot by the Nazis in 1943, one of six local civilians executed in reprisal for the assassination of a German colonel just outside their town. Her mother, always unwell, had lived just long enough to see the Liberation, dying of a lung infection in 1944. That's what she'd told me on our first date, in a London pub, back in 1945, and I'd never doubted it.

I mean, why would I?

I jerked my head to get my mind back on track. It was past seven-thirty and I had a class to teach at nine, so I had to get myself dressed too. Lily had said she'd explain over breakfast. That was good enough for me.

BUT SHE DIDN'T. Breakfast was a rushed affair, and over my juice, scrambled eggs, and coffee and Lily's espresso, brioches, and jam (a proteinless French breakfast was one of the few Gallic traditions she retained, while I, having been here since childhood, was as all-American in my eating habits as in everything else), I learned nothing. Softly and reasonably, she turned aside all my questions. It was far too complicated to try to explain now; it would be better if I heard the story all at once, but that couldn't be done in fifteen minutes; she was sorry she'd misled me for so long about her father – it had weighed on her from the beginning – but, really, there was a good reason, as I would understand once I heard the whole story. In a way, as upsetting as it was, she was glad that she'd finally be able to set the record straight. Tonight we'd have a simple, quiet dinner, perhaps roast chicken and salad, and a couple of glasses of Chablis, and she'd lay everything out for me and answer all my questions, every single one. Would I mind waiting till then? Would that be all right?

Well, no, not really – I wanted to know right then – but I didn't see what else I could do, so I said all right.

'Oh, Pete, you look so solemn,' she said, laughing. 'Cheer up, it's not as bad as all that. I overreacted, that's all. Seeing him standing there was a bit of a surprise.'

'You're telling me,' I said.

She stood up and put the dishes in the sink. 'I'd better go or I'll be late. Drop me off?'

'Sure,' I said, getting up to find the car keys.

Lily put a hand on my arm. 'Kiss?' she said, closing her eyes and putting out her lips in that childlike, expectant way she had, still so sweetly affecting after all these years. I kissed her willingly, tasting cherry jam and brushing the backs of my fingers along her cheek, now back to its usual satin. Her face was 'on,' and she was wearing a powder-blue woolen two-piece suit with a high-collared, boxy little jacket that made her look more elegant and beautiful than ever. Friends are always saying she looks like Leslie Caron, but I could never see it; I think it's just that they know she's French and that she's always worn her hair in this really cute, boyish bob, as short and thick as velvet nap. In any case, there's certainly no argument about her being slim and beautiful and pert, and right now, with the red gone from those wonderful cornflower-blue eyes, she looked terrific.

Me, I felt lousy.

She touched a finger to my upper lip, just under my nose. 'You're not mad at me?'

'Come on, you know I'm not mad at you. Just . . . I don't know . . .'

'Mixed up?'

'Yes. And concerned.' And unsettled. And apprehensive, although I didn't know about what.

She gave me one more lip-smacking kiss and grabbed her purse from the counter as we headed out the door. 'There's absolutely no reason for concern. You'll see, I promise. All will be clear.'

MY NINE-O'CLOCK Survey of European History class went smoothly enough (it should have, after ten years of teaching it), after which I spent a couple of hours in my office working up an outline for a promising new upper-division seminar on the later Renaissance in Italy, occasionally stopping to commiserate with students who came by to express disappointment or concern (or in one case 'utter confoundment') over their midterm grades. Then cheeseburgers in the faculty cafeteria with Louis Winkleman, who had a new hypothesis about the Dream. This one was the fourth, actually. Number two had been something about repressed guilt (what else?) stemming from the searing moral ambiguity of dropping bombs on human beings, no matter how worthwhile the end, but while I wasn't crazy about having done it I was pretty sure I wasn't suffering any searing moral ambiguity either, repressed or otherwise. So theory number two bit the dust too.

For number three he'd gone back to his Freudian roots and come up with a B-17-as-phallic-symbol-faceless-woman-as-sexually-desirable-mother-German-planes-as-avenging-father guilt trip, but I wasn't about to touch that one with a ten-foot pole. Look, I'm the first one to admit that Sigmund Freud was a smart guy, but the Oedipus complex? Every kid can't wait to have sex with his mother? Every kid is afraid his father's going to get upset about it (and why wouldn't he, I ask you) and cut off his penis? Please, give me a break.

No sale, I told him.

'Okey-doke, scratch that' had been his amiable response. There were, after all, always more where that came from.

Frankly, my pal Louis Winkleman is a somewhat weird-looking bird with a spiky mop of ginger-colored hair, a tendency to jabber when he gets excited, and a goofy, manic, Marx Brothers kind of grin that can make people who don't know him wonder about his sanity. But he's also intelligent, good-hearted, and upbeat, and he's certainly never at a loss for an interesting theory for very long. So the moment he plopped into the seat across from me I knew from the look on his face that he was all ready with number four.

He didn't waste any time getting down to it. 'I should have seen this years ago,' he said cheerfully, using the flat of his knife to lift the top half of the bun off his hamburger in order to position the sliced onion in a more centered position. 'It was staring us right in the face. Okay, are you ready? Here we go. You were never wounded during the war, correct?'

'Right.'

'Never even shot at, never even—'

'Right, right, you know that.'

He had gotten the onion adjusted to his satisfaction and now, with the tip of his tongue protruding to assist his accuracy, he set about surgically dissecting the sandwich into four perfectly equal pie-shaped segments, which he would then – as I knew all too well – eat in counterclockwise order, starting at the pointy end of each as if they were slices of pizza, up to and including leaving the crusty edges. Like many of his kind, Louis has some pretty queer habits. Then again, I've known him a long time and know that he often makes sense in spite of himself. He also has three teenagers, none of whom are visibly screwed-up, and how many psychologists can you say that about? How many *anybodies* can you say that about?

'But some of your friends were,' he said.

'Were what?'

'Wounded, wounded. Pay attention.'

'Well, yes, if you mean the guys I grew up with,' I said. 'Two of them were killed. A few more were wounded.' I paused. 'Some badly.' Morty Berger, my best friend as a kid, had come back from the Pacific without his legs.

'But not you.'

'No, I just told you—' I saw what he was getting at and paused in my chewing. 'You mean I might feel guilty because I wasn't hurt? That I *should* have been wounded?'

He waggled his eyebrows.

I sipped my Coke and thought about it. 'There just might be something to that, Louis.'

He lit up. 'Well, it took a while, but when it finally dawned on me . . .' He wiped his mouth with a paper napkin and set the remaining three-quarters of his sandwich off to the side, an infallible sign that he was shifting into lecture mode. '. . . that almost every dream element could be seen as a form of ego-defense against feelings of self-condemnation—'

'Louis, this is really interesting,' I said, glancing at my watch, 'but I'm afraid I've got to run. One-o'clock appointment.'

His mobile face fell. 'Too bad. Another time, then.'

I didn't doubt it. I thanked him, finished the coffee, and left. There really wasn't any appointment. I just didn't want to talk anymore. Maybe Louis had finally put his finger on the source of the dream, but it was Lily that was on my mind, not my dreams, and I needed to be by myself somewhere and think about things. This was the most awkwardly scheduled day of the week for me, with one class at nine and the next one not until four, but for once I appreciated having all that time in between. I sat bundled up in my coat for a while on a bench near the lily pond, in the sunken gardens that flanked the library, but that wasn't isolated enough, and besides, I needed to walk as well as think, so, leaving my car in the campus lot, I caught the BMT at the nearby Avenue H station and took it to Stillwell Avenue, the end of the line, the Coney island stop.

Possibly Coney Island doesn't strike you as the place to go when you want to be by yourself and think about things, but that's because you haven't seen it in the wintertime when the place is virtually shut down. Crossing Surf Avenue is like crossing Main Street in some windblown ghost town, with every little souvenir store and hot dog stand and frozen custard counter and weight-and-fortune penny scale locked up and battened down till summer. Nathan's Famous stays open, mostly for form's sake, I suppose, but it doesn't do much business. On days as dreary as this particular rain-spattered November one, the men behind the counter stand around drinking coffee out of cardboard cups to keep warm and talking to each other to stay awake.

Then, when you cross under the boardwalk and come out on the beach, it's spookier yet. All the things that make Coney Island Coney Island – the Cyclone, the Wonder Wheel, the parachute jump – are stilled and skeletal against the gray sky. The enormous beach itself is bare of everything but the empty steel-mesh trash cans placed every fifty yards or so in rows that seem to extend forever. Here and there a sheet of newspaper blows over the sand, and one or two hunched-over, solitary walkers with troubles of their own are usually moving along the water's edge, keeping to themselves. The whole thing is kind of creepy, really, but if it's a reflective, inward-turning ambience you're looking for, you couldn't do any better than Coney Island in winter.

And so I went down to the shore, breathed in the salt air, turned up the collar of my coat, pulled down the brim of my hat, and plodded into the wind, with nothing but the rumble of the surf in my ears and only the occasional crab shell for company. Plodded and thought.

Lily and I had met in the spring of 1945, in London. She was going on eighteen, a typist at the Free French headquarters in Carlton Gardens, and I was that nineteen-year-old flier I was telling you about, except by then the fighting was in its final stages and I'd been transferred to administrative duties at a SHAEF administrative bureau in Grosvenor Square, acting as a clerk to a Captain Hendricks.

I'd been working at the files out front one day, and in came this heart-stoppingly beautiful girl with a manila envelope for the captain. Not beautiful in the movie-star sense, I suppose – not with that long, coltish face, and a nose to match, and those wide, flat cheekbones, and those very slightly (but delightfully) crossed eyes – but she sure bowled me over. You have to understand: the place was a madhouse – negotiations between de Gaulle and the rest of the Allies had broken down for the hundredth time and everyone had been running around screaming at everyone else for days. We were all going nuts. So when I irritably rolled my eyes up from an impossible mess of paperwork, ready to do battle with whoever it was that had come to bother me, and saw instead this composed, lovely girl standing patiently at my desk and looking at me with eyes as blue and clear and calm as a glacial pool, it was as if a cool, damp cloth had been laid across my forehead. I felt time slow down from breathless-fast to nice, easy-going normal. From the very first, that was the effect she had on me.

'Allo? Ey 'ave 'ere sumzing for your Capitaine Ahngdreeks,' she'd said, smiling, with the most charming French accent imaginable, and that finished the job; I was a goner. I invited her out for drinks on the spot. (Well, I didn't know she was seventeen. I thought she was nineteen, maybe even twenty. Yes, really.)

We talked for six hours straight, mostly in a noisy, beery, smoke-filled pub off Parliament Square that was full of horny GIs and local English girls. Language was no problem. Lily – she was 'Lili' then, Lili Vercier – was well into the process of learning English, and I spoke fluent, idiomatic French. Naturally enough; my father didn't bring the family to the United States until 1935, when I was nine. I told her about that, and about Brooklyn, and the Dodgers, and America, and life in the Army Air Force. She talked about her girlhood in Veaudry, and the glorious prewar summer vacations she'd taken with her parents in Corsica at her grandfather's chestnut farm in the green hills above the Mediterranean, and, of course, about the deprivations, and scarcities, and humiliations of the Occupation years.

And about the tragic death of her unfortunate father.

'Ee was keel by ze Boches. Zey shoot eem in ze strheet,' she'd told me sadly. 'Wiz five uzzers.'

All right, I'll be perfectly frank here. I was more engrossed in watching that red, luscious mouth form the words than I was in the words themselves. (Look, I'd just turned nineteen. You want to tell me about your priorities at nineteen?) Still, my heart honestly went out to her; she was like some tender, soft-petaled flower that had miraculously survived the muddy, bloody hell that Europe had just been through. I'd asked questions about what had happened to her father and she'd gone into some detail: about the German colonel (bald, scar-faced), about the other hostages (the tobacconist, the baker, the baker's assistant, the pharmacist, and the butcher), and about the executions themselves. The townspeople, including Lili, had been herded together and forced to watch. The victims had been placed against a sinister, heavily pitted wooden wall made of thick planks and brought in by truck for the purpose, then shot one at a time by a three-man firing squad. Her father had been third, dying bravely, without a word. Afterward, the body had been turned over to her mother and then buried in the churchyard with the others in a stirring ceremony.

Sure, except that six hours ago he'd been standing on my stoop banging on a film can and yelling about things not being what they seemed (I'll say!), and money, and forgiveness, and who knew what else.

I came to a halt. St George. He'd said something about St George. What had that meant? My specialty is medieval and Renaissance history, so my mind naturally enough turned to the St George of *The Faerie Queene*, the St George of the dragon, the patron saint of England and Portugal (and in Greece, of lunatics), the mythical figure probably derived from the eighth-century Anglo-Saxon Beowulf legend. But that line of thinking wasn't likely to get me anywhere. Whatever Lily's father had been raving about, I was pretty sure it hadn't had anything to do with eighth-century Anglo-Saxon literature. Dead end. The only other St George that came to mind was the St George Hotel in Brooklyn Heights, the one with 'the world's largest indoor saltwater pool.'

The light was fading and a thin rain had begun to mist down, not enough to bother me. I started plodding again, occasionally turning over a shell from one of the big, menacing-looking (but harmless, they tell me) horseshoe crabs with my toe. My mind began to drift, as it usually does after an hour or two at the beach. I hadn't thought about the St George Hotel in a long time. The grand old pile – it had been built in the 1880s, the largest hotel in New York at the time – was as exclusive as hotels got in Brooklyn, but its celebrated ornate, glass-ceilinged swimming pool was open to the public for a small fee and I'd spent a lot of memorable hours there with Morty when I was fifteen or sixteen, either in the water trying to pick up girls or upstairs on the balcony that overlooked it, trying to see down the tops of their bathing suits. Neither effort had ever been met by what you'd call wild success, as I recall, but that hadn't stopped us from trying.

I was smiling to myself now. Memories of the St George pool, of the chubby, baby-faced Morty, and – I stopped short again. Christ, what was the matter with me? I turned and jogged over the damp sand back out to Surf Avenue. There was a telephone kitty-corner across the street from Nathan's. I found a dime in my pocket, located the number of the St George, and dialed. Was there a Mr Marcel Vercier staying there?

There was, I was told, but he didn't answer his telephone. Did I wish to leave a message?

'Yes,' I said, and then, quickly, 'No.' I hadn't really figured out how I wanted to go about this. Or even if. I wasn't comfortable with the idea of doing it behind Lily's back, and I was hopeful that I still might not have to. After all, we were going to talk it out that evening over dinner. Right?

'Look, is he going to be staying there awhile?' Just in case we didn't get around to it at dinner.

'Well, I'm not permitted . . .'

'Please, it's extremely important.'

'Well . . . all right. Apparently, yes. He's booked his suite through next Wednesday.'

Suite? At the St George? For a *week*? Wow.

'Er . . . good, thanks very much.'

I hung up thoughtfully, and headed for the elevated station. On the way I passed a General Electric appliance store where a knot of people was huddled in front of a window display of television consoles. I stopped to see what it was that was engrossing enough to keep them standing out there in the cold rain, expecting a sports event, but all four sets were tuned to a strangely haggard-looking Walter Cronkite.

'What's going on?' I asked the rapt older man beside me.

'Shh!' He shook his head without taking his eyes from the TV screens.

The woman in front of me was more helpful. 'The guy that killed him. They got him,' she said over his shoulder. 'Lee Harvey Oswald.'

'Who's Lee Harvey Oswald?' I asked. 'Killed who?'

Chapter Three

THAT DID IT for our discussion of Lily's father over a quiet dinner of roast chicken and salad. Instead, like everyone else, we had whatever leftovers were in the refrigerator and sat, devastated, in front of the television set, hour after hour, focused on the events of that terrible day. The same on Saturday. Like the rest of America.

There were times during those days when I might have raised the subject of her father, but I was as heartsick and disoriented as everybody else, and I just didn't have the emotional energy to bring it up. And then on Sunday horror was piled on top of grief when a squat, hatted Jack Ruby jumped from a crowd and shot Oswald point-blank in the stomach in full frontal view of the rolling cameras. Monday it was back to grief. With the schools closed – with everything closed – we watched the funeral march: the riderless black horse, the veiled, slender young widow walking behind, the bare-legged young son's salute . . .

By late afternoon I'd had all I could stand. I was ready to move on to something else: our own life, for example.

'Lily,' I said when she was in the kitchen brewing us some coffee after dinner, 'I think it's time we sat down and talked about your father, don't you?'

She jerked her head. 'Pete, I just couldn't. Not now. It's such a horrible time.'

'We're going to have to talk about him sometime, you know that.'

'Yes, I know. But not now. I need a little time, that's all.'

The funny thing is, she'd often talked willingly enough about him in the past; not about his supposed execution – she'd steered clear of that after the early days – but about the idyllic August vacations she'd taken with him in the prewar days at his family's chestnut farm in Corsica (*castagna*, 'chestnut,' was the only Corsican word I knew), where Vercier himself had grown up before heading to the French mainland at fifteen to seek his fortune. She would tell me about the mustachioed old rustic that had been her grandfather, and about the glorious country walks she and her father had taken in the close-by hills overlooking the harbor of Calvi, and their picnics on the beach, in the shadow of the ancient citadel, and about the secret, spooky, earthy-smelling, stone-walled root cellar on the farm, where they'd go when it rained, and eat crusty bread with olive oil and salt while her father told her romantic stories about Corsican vendettas that always ended with the lovers dying in each other's arms. And always, her voice would soften when we talked about him.

Well, it was anything but soft now. In fact, I noticed that her accent had thickened a little, which it did in times of stress. Ordinarily it's hardly there at all, almost as nonexistent as mine. Strangers sometimes hear something when she speaks, but they think perhaps she's from the South or the Midwest, once in a while even England. They rarely guess France.

Later, at about seven-thirty, when we were browsing through magazines side by side in the living-room armchairs after dinner, the telephone rang. I picked it up.

'Is it BE 6-2122?' an elderly voice asked, very French.

'Yes.'

'Lily Simon, please,' he said. *Lee-lee Seemawng.*

I handed the receiver to her. 'For you.'

She hesitated, took it from me, listened for maybe two seconds, and slammed it down into its cradle. 'Damn him.'

'Lily—'

She headed me off. 'Pete, I'm not going to talk to him. I'm not.' She was on the verge of tears. 'I'm sorry, but I don't care what you think.'

'Honey, I hate to see you like this. Isn't there something I can do to help?'

'No.' She closed her eyes.

I put my *Time* magazine aside, reached across the little table between us to grasp her hand, and tugged her gently from her chair. She held back for a second but then came, settling on my lap and leaning her head on my shoulder with a sigh. I rubbed her back.

'Pete, my darling, I love you so much,' she murmured into my neck. 'I can't begin to tell you.'

I stroked her hair, her beautiful, boyish auburn hair. 'I love you.' It had been almost two decades, and I still honestly couldn't figure out what she saw in me.

Her head came up. 'Everything is still all right between us, isn't it? I couldn't stand for anything to come between us.'

'Between *us*? God, things couldn't be any better.' It was true too, if you discounted the last few days. If anything, I loved her more than I had when I married her. I sure needed her more. And I didn't want anything to come between us either.

We sat like that for a while, nuzzling and stroking like the old, affectionate married couple we were. Once the telephone rang again, making her jump. 'No, I can't talk to him,' she said quickly, looking as if she was about to break and run.

I kept her on my lap while I picked it up.

'Lee-lee—'

'*N'appelez plus ce numéro, s'il vous plaît,*' I said sharply and hung up. Don't call this number again.

'Thank you,' Lily breathed, and snuggled in again.

'Honey?' I said when we had just about fallen asleep in the chair. 'I just want you to know that there isn't anything that you can tell me that could possibly make me love you less.'

'Mmm.'

'I mean – look, if he . . . if he did anything to you as a child, or took advantage of you, or convinced you to do something you didn't want to do, it doesn't mean—'

Her head came up. 'Are you asking me if he molested me? If there was – if there was incest between us?'

'Well – yes.' I was thinking about those long, rainy days in the root cellar, I guess.

'No,' she said, making a face. 'Of course not.' Her head settled against my shoulder again. 'Good gosh.'

That made me feel a little better: not only the reply itself, but the fact that I'd actually gotten an unambiguous answer from her. Encouraged, I pushed on.

'Well, then, how about telling me what *is* going on?' I asked softly. 'I think it's time, don't you?'

She surprised me with the violence with which she pushed herself off my lap and stood up. 'Damn you! Can't you leave me alone for a single minute?' She was suddenly furious. 'Can we please get something straight? I don't ever want to see that man, I don't want to talk to him, and I don't want to talk *about* him!' She started to say more, but turned and stalked off toward the stairs and the bedroom.

I sat there, astonished. Astonished and wounded. Lily had never thrown a 'damn you' at me before, or anything like it. In seventeen years, not once. It just wasn't the way we talked to each other. It took me a few seconds to find my voice. 'Well, *I* damn well want to talk about him,' I called sourly after her. Not my usual m.o. either.

Lily yelled something down at me from the top of the stairs and I yelled something back. We shouted a few more clipped, angry words at each other. I forget who got the last word in, whatever it was, and then the bedroom door slammed and put an end to it.

I turned off the light and sat there muttering to myself in the dark, licking my wounds and coming up with some snappy after-the-fact ripostes.

NOW BY NATURE I'm a pretty peaceable person. Like Lily, I try to steer clear of squabbles, grudges, and general hysterics of any sort. Of course, my good pal Louis, being a psychologist, sees this as something to worry about and has explained it to me as a withdrawal mechanism, a shying away from meaningful dyadic interaction (I'm quoting here), preferring to accept people's surface, ceremonial words and actions rather than to take the chance of delving to a deeper, more authentic level and thereby risking a more challenging, demanding relationship. Generally speaking, I have to admit the guy has a point. Who wants to 'delve' into a relationship that's doing just fine as it is? Who needs relationships that are more challenging and demanding than they already are?

Not me.

Naturally, Louis ascribes this 'defensive' attitude to my early childhood experiences, and there I'm inclined to agree with him. I had all the anger, frustration, and emotion I'll ever need watching my driven, tortured father make himself – and my mother and me – miserable while I was growing up. You know those tattoos – *Born to Love? Born to be Bad?* Dad should have had one that read *Born to be Unhappy*. He was endlessly striving, endlessly embittered and boiling inside, constitutionally unable to settle for what we had, which was more than a lot of our neighbors had. The kind of man who took little joy in his achievements but suffered agonies over his failures, he never stopped struggling for something more, something better. But nothing (and no one, including and especially himself) ever lived up to his hopes. His idea for a fabric business failed, his several investment schemes flopped, his French-style bakery chain never got off the ground. Always he lost whatever hard-earned money he put in. Always it led to noisy squabbling with my mother.

Not that they got along that well at the best of times. Mom had married beneath her, and neither of them could ever forget it. Mom's family owned an industrial chemicals plant near Lyon; Dad's father had a little grocery store in the city, where Dad had worked as a clerk. When they got married, her family disowned her. A few years later, and largely in retribution for that, or so I've always believed, Dad pulled up stakes and took Mom and me to Brooklyn, New York. That was in 1934, the black heart of the Great Depression. But Dad was a hard worker, willing to take on anything, there was no taking that away from him, and he did manage to support us by carving out a niche for himself as a fruit-and-vegetable supplier to grocery stores all over Brooklyn.

We ourselves settled in a tenement in the Brownsville section, because Dad had heard that's where the Jews went. He was right too; at that time Brownsville was known as the Jerusalem of America, with a larger population of Jews than any city in the world. It's changed since then, with the decrepit old tenements, the ones I and Morty and the rest of my friends all lived in, being gradually replaced with decrepit new tenements, otherwise known as 'the projects,' and the beaten-down Jewish and Eastern European faces gradually being replaced with beaten-down black and brown ones. But its essence hasn't changed; it was a slum then and it's a slum still.

Like everyone else, we lived in one of those six-story walk-up apartment buildings with fancy marble entries giving way to gloomy hallways with embossed-tin ceilings painted algae-brown (whose idea was that?), and apartment front doors that usually opened directly into the kitchen. Aside from us, however, none of the tenants seemed to be French. Every family we knew had its roots in Russia or Poland, Lithuania or Estonia.

With Dad's sweaty, six-day-a-week, up-at-three-in-the-morning business and the smell of rotting vegetables that always clung to him, we were as solidly working-class as any of them, but our Frenchified speech and manners gave us a toney quality in the eyes of our neighbors, who regarded us as the patricians of Hopkinson Avenue. Unfortunately, my father started believing it, which made him more frustrated with our lot than ever, and even more haplessly upward-striving. While most of my friends' at-home language was Yiddish, ours was French. I'd even heard him imply to strangers that he wasn't Jewish at all, that the apparent Yiddishness in his accent was actually Alsatian, by way of his grandmother.

Oh, I got bar-mitzvahed when the time came, but that was more for the sake of propriety than conviction. Nobody in our circle was what you'd call Orthodox, but if you were a kid on Hopkinson Avenue, you got bar-mitzvahed when you hit thirteen, period. As for the religious responsibilities that went along with becoming a man, Dad very conspicuously didn't care about them or push them on me. Not for him were the ways of the *tallis* and the *tfillen*. On the other hand, such was the complex man who was my father, he was the one who went into a male version of hysterics a few years later when I told my folks that I wanted to marry a Gentile (and a Frenchwoman at that). Not that Lily didn't eventually win him over, of course.

Anyway, back in the thirties, by the time Hitler began to openly covet France we'd been living in Brooklyn for six or seven years and I was already more American than French. Punch ball, stoop ball, stick ball, the Dodgers . . . your everyday all-American first-generation kid. I was fourteen or so and Europe seemed very far away, but I remember how appalled Dad was at what was happening to France. At first, oddly enough, he'd mainly been angry at the anti-Nazi movement – 'bastard Communist agitators' – who in his view were more interested in spewing upheaval and anarchy than in trying to resist the inevitable. Then he was furious at the appeasers and the collaborationists, with the once-sanctified Marshal Petain at their head, who were selling the country down the river and willingly rounding up every Jew they could find for deportation to the camps. Then it was de Gaulle and the Resistance that he couldn't stomach, for bringing so much retribution on innocent French men and women, and for screwing things up in general. That he hated the Nazis themselves went without saying. Also the Vichy government, for so cravenly and enthusiastically doing their bidding.

And that was my father in a nutshell: raging at every side there was, straining toward some impossible end, something he probably couldn't have put into words himself. '*Tire pour les étoiles*,' he used to drum into my head when the subject of my eventual career came up. '*Tu pourras arriver à la lune*.' His own philosophy: shoot for the stars, maybe you'll hit the moon. Me, I saw it the other way around, not that I'd ever said it to his face: *Tire pour la lune. Tu pourras arriver aux étoiles.*

For years, right up until the day he keeled over onto his face with a massive coronary, I'd watched him bang his head against stone walls and then fume and seethe and drive Mom nuts when they wouldn't budge. And Mom gave as good as she got, believe me. Four times she walked out on him, twice dragging me with her, one time for a full month, but in the end she always came back. Once my father ran away too, but he came back after a couple of days as well, looking sheepish for once in his life.

As a reaction, I suppose, my own approach to living has been the opposite of what his was, more along the lines of take-things-as-they-come, don't-overreach, and – especially – don't-take-a-chance-on-making-the-gods-angry-by-expecting-too-much. As a result, I haven't been the kind of person who makes things happen. Things happen to me, and I make the best of them. And as far as I'm concerned, it's worked. Life has been good. Unlike Dad, I'm not consumed with envy or resentment. I live in a nice neighborhood. I took advantage of the GI Bill to go to college, and my academic career, if not spectacular, has been fulfilling and secure; I'll be up for associate professor next year. Lily, the one star I aimed for and got, has been everything I could hope for. Our marriage is (or has been until lately) tranquil, loving, and settled, with few bumps in the road.

I suppose a lot of people would say my life has been on the uneventful side, even boring. Well, that's okay with me. I like uneventful. Uneventful is good. If you'd grown up with my mother and father you'd like it too.

So what had just happened between Lily and me – that brief, exasperated blowup, which probably wouldn't have qualified as anything more than a minor skirmish in most households – was for us a full-scale battle that had left both of us bloodied.

For an hour I sat there in the dark getting more depressed. When I went up to bed, Lily was lying on her back, pretending to be asleep. I figured it had gone far enough and I was ready to make up. But when I crawled in beside her and reached out to touch her face she twisted away, with much rustling of bedclothes. *The hell with it*, I thought. *What did* she *have to be mad about?* I turned away too, heaving a disgusted sigh through my nostrils, just to let her know that she wasn't the only one who knew how to be crabby.

Chapter Four

THAT WAS MONDAY night. Tuesday was a chilly day at the Simons'. We were civil enough, we had breakfast and dinner together and chatted about this and that. But no olive branches, no kiss-and-make-up, and no further discussion of Marcel Vercier, the Undead. A really, really lousy day. Another not-so-great night either. Aside from everything else, I had the Dream again.

Wednesday morning started off much the same, and neither of us seemed able to do anything about it. We'd had off-days before, sure, but two in a row was rare and upsetting. And this business of pussy-footing around something that we both knew was on our minds was something new. I could see that Lily was as miserable about it as I was, and as powerless to turn things around.

So on my way to the college for my back-to-back Wednesday-morning classes I went to the St George to find her father. Something bad, something I didn't understand, had come down on us out of nowhere, and if I was going to deal with it I needed some sort of handle on it. Whatever it was, it was Marcel Vercier who had brought it to us with him.

In the marble lobby the desk clerk rang the old man's room. 'Sorry, Mr Vercier doesn't answer. Would you care to leave a message?'

I didn't want him trying to get in touch with me at home because I didn't want Lily involved at this point – if ever. I'd thrashed it over with her as much as I intended to, with no result beyond screwing up our lives, and now it was her father I wanted to talk to, not Lily. So I left an anonymous note in French, saying that I wished to talk to him about something of importance to him and that I would return at noon.

Which I did. Again, he wasn't there, and the clerk told me that he hadn't picked up my note. I went home, planning to telephone him hourly until I got him. Conveniently, I had the house to myself until about five; Lily works as a counselor at a junior high school and Wednesday is after-school-staff-meeting day. I got out of my sport coat and tie and into a sweater and heated up a can of pea soup for lunch, and at one o'clock I tried Vercier's room at the St George. No response, but a second after I hung up the phone it rang. I snatched it up.

'Monsieur Vercier?' I said without thinking.

There was a hesitation on the other end. 'What name did you say?'

'I'm sorry, I was thinking of something else. Who is this, please?'

'Can I speak to Mr Peter Simon, please?' A bass voice, slow talking and authoritative and a little world-weary.

'Speaking. Who's this?'

'Mr Simon, this is Detective Sergeant Ivan Kovalski. I'm over here at the Sixty-first Precinct house in Sheepshead Bay. I'm afraid I may have some bad news for you.'

I'd been in the act of sitting down, but I froze halfway to the chair. *Oh, my God. Lily.* My heart turned to water.

'Yes?' I managed.

'We found the body of a man this morning, and he had your—'

A man. Thank God. I sank bonelessly into the chair, lightheaded with relief.

'—name and address on him. I was hoping you could help us identify him. In his sixties or seventies, on the small side—'

'White goatee? Glasses?'

'I don't know about the glasses, but goatee, yes.'

'I think it could be my wife's father. I mean, I don't know, but—'

'Well, we'd appreciate it if you or your wife could come take a look and make sure.'

'Yes, uh . . . sure.' Lily's father dead? Despite how quick I'd been to think it, it had only now registered. 'How . . . what happened to him?'

'I'll explain when I see you. You know where the morgue is?'

'The *morgue*? No!'

I guess something about the way I said it made him feel I couldn't be trusted to find my way around the city unaided. 'Sir, you're at home, right? 2017 Eighty-third Street? You just stay right there, and someone will be along for you in five minutes.'

Someone was, and not long afterward I was standing in a carpeted, purposefully cozy room, much like a doctor's or dentist's waiting room, complete with out-of-date magazines, except that one wall had an oversized window, on the other side of which was a 'viewing room' with walls of white-glazed brick tile that brought to mind the gorilla cage at the Prospect Park Zoo. Into this room an attendant wheeled a gurney with a sheet-covered form that didn't look substantial enough to be a human body.

It was, however. When the attendant bent over it and delicately lifted one end of the sheet, watching my reaction like a waiter displaying the contents of a chafing dish, I saw the old man's face. Aside from the blue-gray, waxy cast to his skin, I can't honestly say that he looked any worse than he had when he'd stood on our stoop; even then he'd had the look of a man with one foot in the grave. If anything, I'd have to say he looked better. His eyes were closed, his facial muscles relaxed. He looked peaceful.

'That's him,' I said.

Sergeant Kovalski nodded to the attendant, who gently replaced the sheet. Kovalski then led me to a small office a few yards down the hall.

He didn't bother to shut the door. 'Have a seat.'

It was the kind of charmless, all-purpose room that was there for the use of whatever cop or assistant district attorney was passing through: gray metal desk, matching Naugahyde armchair and side chair, a telephone, and an old Royal manual typewriter. No mementos, no knickknacks, nothing but a few shreds of Scotch tape on the pale-green walls.

And Kovalski looked like the kind of person who was as much at home there as anywhere else, a baggy-faced, old-shoe kind of guy in his late forties in a poorly fitting black wool suit, with dark rings under heavy-lidded eyes and a slightly fed-up but not truly unkind expression that said he'd seen just about everything, so don't even think about trying to pull anything on him.

'Name?' he said.

'Pete Simon. Well, Pierre on my birth certificate, but—'

'No, his.'

'Oh. Marcel Vercier.' I spelled it for him.

'No middle name?'

'Uh . . . no, I don't believe so. Well, I don't actually know for sure.'

'Uh-huh. Age?' He was ignoring the typewriter and writing in a notebook, block-printing his letters.

'I, uh, don't know that either. Mid-seventies, wouldn't you say?'

He shrugged. 'Address?'

'I'm afraid I don't know.'

'But he lived here? In New York?'

'I don't think so. I'm not really positive.'

His eyes rolled up just a little – what kind of twit was he dealing with here? – as he passed across a transparent plastic envelope with a card inside. On the card was my name, address, and telephone number in pencil, in a European hand.

'Other side,' he said.

I turned it over. It was a business card, expensively engraved on thick stock, but dog-eared and stained: *Galería Metropolitana. Antigüedades superiores.* There was a telephone number and an address in Barcelona, Spain.

'Mean anything to you?' he asked. 'It was in the breast pocket of his coat, the only thing he had on him.'

I shook my head. 'No. Sounds like an antiques shop.'

'Yeah, so why would he be carrying their card? Was he an art collector or something?'

'I have no idea.'

'Huh.' He rooted around for another question. 'So what did he do for a living?'

Another shrug. 'Sorry.'

He put down his mechanical pencil and swiveled his armchair to look at me, his mouth pursed. 'How long you and your wife been married, Mr Simon? You mind if I ask?'

I was starting to get uncomfortable. For one thing, he was looking increasingly dubious. For another, being interrogated by a cop was a new experience for me. Let alone in a morgue.

'Seventeen years,' I told him.

'You been married seventeen years and you don't know where your wife's father lives? You don't know what he does? You don't know if he has a middle name?'

'I've only seen him once – last week. I thought he was dead.'

'Yeah, well, he's dead, all right.'

'I mean already dead. Twenty years ago.'

That took some explaining, and by the time I finished I was sweating and jittery, and making dumb remarks. *I'd make a hell of a criminal*, I thought. I was practically ready to hold out my wrists and let him put the cuffs on me.

Kovalski jotted in the notebook while I spoke, then snapped it shut and slipped it into a pocket. 'Well, under the circumstances, I think we better get your wife to come in too. You know, to confirm the identification and fill us in a little more on the old guy.'

'You mean here? To the morgue?' Lily had been so tightly strung, so . . . fragile all week that it worried me to think of her being hauled out here to look at her father's corpse. I shook my head without meaning to. Using *Lily* and *tightly strung* in the same sentence was something I wasn't used to.

Kovalski, God bless him, must have sensed what I was feeling. 'No, I don't think she needs to view the body itself. We'll use a nice photograph from the neck up, nothing too terrible, and we can do it at the station house. Coney Island Avenue, just above Avenue W. That'd be easier to get to. Today would be good.'

I looked at my watch. It was three-thirty. 'She'll be out of school in an hour. It's not far. I could have her there by five.'

'Good enough.' He got up and extended his hand. 'Okay, Mr Simon, thanks a lot for coming in. We'll get you back home now.'

'What did he die of, do you know?' I asked on the way back down the hallway.

'I wouldn't put it this way to your wife,' Kovalski said, 'but he died of getting the shit kicked out of him.'

I stopped short. 'He was *murdered*?'

'With a baseball bat, a lead pipe, something like that.'

'But his face – it wasn't – there weren't any—'

'He took it in the stomach; the stomach and the back, down

here.' He put his hand on his hip, about where his kidney was. 'Busted ribs, cracked pelvis, internal injuries.'

'Well . . . but . . .'

I was stunned. He'd looked so ill when I'd seen him before that I'd assumed he'd died of whatever it was that was eating him up. And now this, coming out of the blue on top of everything else. It just seemed like too much to deal with. How was Lily going to handle it?

'It didn't take much,' Kovalski said. 'The doc said he was on his last legs anyway. Panactic cancer, something like that.'

'Pancreatic?'

'Yeah, pancreatic. Anyway, they dumped him in a marsh down by the bay.'

'What was it, robbery? You said he had nothing on him but the card.'

'Yeah, probably.'

I shook my head. 'But why would they need to beat him up like that? What kind of fight could he put up, that they'd have to do that to him?'

Kovalski snorted, blowing out his lips. 'What, they need a reason? Look, I don't suppose you'd know if he carried a lot of cash on him?'

'No, I don't. He was staying in a suite at the St George, so I suppose he must have— No, I don't.'

'No. I didn't think so.'

He swung the front door open for me. 'Listen, buddy, don't worry about your wife. We'll be as gentle as we can. You can come in with her if you want.'

But of course I did worry. On the way home in the squad car I kept wondering how she'd react. If seeing him on the doorstep had unhinged her the way it had, what would happen when I told her he'd been killed? I wasn't even sure whether it would be bad news or good news. I simply had no idea what to expect, and that was one more strangeness added to all the rest. If someone had told me a month ago that I'd ever think of Lily's behavior as unpredictable, I would have laughed. But things had changed and I wasn't laughing now.

*

MY WIFE WORKS three days a week as a counselor at a junior high school on Kings Highway, six or seven blocks from our house, where she counsels handicapped kids. On most days she likes to walk there and back, but occasionally I drop her off or pick her up. Since she wasn't expecting me today, I parked smack in front of the main entrance, where I could see her come out, instead of in the parking lot.

While I waited I suddenly became aware that the muscles at the base of my skull, which had been tense for going on a week, had unknotted, and that I was actually feeling . . . what?

It took a minute to admit to myself that it was relief, plain and simple. Whatever discord and trouble that unhappy old man had brought with him and dropped into our laps, it was ended now, already in the past and telescoping backward. Sure, I had some distressing news (at least I thought it would be distressing) to break to Lily, but after that it would be over, done. We would be as we were before.

When the doors opened and she emerged chatting with some friends, I waved to her from the car. She came smiling, thinking that I was picking her up as a peace offering and eager to accept it. I did my best to return the smile – I wished it had been a simple peace offering too and nothing more – but something in my face must have been off-key. Her smile faltered as she got into the car.

'Pete, is anything wrong?'

I wasn't sure what the answer to that was, so I borrowed Kovalski's approach. 'Lily, I'm afraid I have some bad news.'

A muscle twitched near her mouth but she didn't say anything, just stared at me with wary eyes.

'Your father's dead. The police found him this morning.'

She turned away and looked at the sidewalk. 'I see.'

'Someone . . . he was murdered.'

Her head spun back. 'Murdered? He was *murdered?*' I could see that her mind was whirling, but I couldn't tell what she was thinking. Or feeling. Surprise, of course, and maybe consternation, or even horror. I was pretty sure it wasn't grief.

'Why? Who did it?'

'They don't know.'

'How was he – how did it happen?'

I told her as much as I knew, editing Kovalski's description into something a little more tolerable. 'The police would like you to come in this afternoon. I told them I'd bring you.'

'You mean this afternoon? Right now?' She was sitting straight up on the front of the seat. Her knuckles were white on the dashboard. '*Why?*'

'Well, to confirm the identification—'

'No, I'm not looking at his body.'

'No, you won't have to. I already did that. They want you to come to the police station, not the morgue. They'll show you a picture of his face, that's all. It isn't bad to look at, there aren't any – they didn't hurt his face. And I guess they want to ask you some questions. A Sergeant Kovalski. Not a bad guy, you'll see.'

She shook her head slowly back and forth. 'I never, never thought . . .' She didn't tell me what she never thought; she just let the sentence drift away and sank back against the seat. 'All right,' she said quietly.

'I'll go in with you, if you want.'

She didn't say anything.

'Or not,' I said. 'Either way. Whatever you want.'

'I'd rather do it alone.' She glanced at me. 'Do you mind?'

'No, of course not.' Like hell I didn't. Was I supposed to not mind being kept out of her life? I needed to help her, to offer whatever support I could.

We drove without saying anything for a few minutes, until I turned south off Kings Highway. 'Honey, you'll have to tell them the truth, you know. Whatever it is.'

'I know that.'

'Aside from whatever was wrong between you and your father, this is a murder investigation we're talking about.'

'Pete, I said I know,' she said and went back to looking stolidly out the window on her side.

Me, I sulked on mine, but when I parked a few yards down the street from the station and turned off the engine she didn't get out right away. Instead, she reached out tentatively to touch my hand. 'Pete . . .'

I looked at her. Her expression had softened, become uncertain. 'Pete, I know I haven't been fair and I'm sorry. You've been fantastically patient with me.'

I waited.

Her eyes dropped to our hands. 'Do you remember what you asked me a couple of nights ago? Did my father ever . . . did he—'

'Take advantage of you?'

She nodded, still looking down. 'I said no, but I wasn't telling the truth. When I was seven years old he started to . . . to. . .' She cleared her throat and waited a few moments with her eyes closed. 'It went on for weeks – at least I think it was weeks, I can't really remember, but it was horrible, I can't tell you. . . . When I finally found the nerve to tell my mother, there was a huge explosion and she threw him out. I never saw him again. Not till last week.'

She looked up savagely. 'I hope to God he rots in hell,' she said through clenched teeth.

I leaned across and gently kissed her forehead. 'You could have told me, baby, you should have known that. Did you really think it could make any difference in the way I feel about you?'

She squeezed my hand. 'I know, I should have told you in the first place, years and years ago, but I so much wanted you to like me. There'd been so much ugliness during the war, so much filth. I wanted you to think of me as *clean*. I was so young, Pete . . . I made up that story about the executions, and after that I couldn't bring myself to tell you the truth. And the longer it went on, the more impossible it got. I guess I convinced myself that it was all dead and buried, but then when he showed up, it all came back. I just couldn't – I didn't know what to do, I was so afraid you'd be—'

'Well, I'm not; of course I'm not. I'm glad you finally told me.' I pressed the tip of her nose with my finger, which made her laugh, the way it always did. 'Okay,' I said happily, 'now that that's out of the way, you go and tell the sergeant about it too. And that'll be the end of it. I'll wait here for you.'

She nodded, her pretty eyes brimming, and reached for the door handle. 'My gosh, I love you.'

I touched my fingers to my lips and blew her a kiss.

NOT FOR A second did I believe her. Oh, I don't mean about loving me, I believed that, all right; I'd *really* have been in bad shape if I didn't believe that. But the story about her father: that hadn't rung true. When I'd suggested something of the sort the other night her shocked, disgusted denial had been a hundred-percent genuine, I was sure of it. (Considering the fact that she'd successfully flummoxed me for seventeen years about his being dead, I suppose I shouldn't have been so certain, but I was.) And something about this new story, or rather about the way she told it, convinced me that it had been contrived on the way to the police station, concocted to get her out of a jam.

I didn't believe it, but that didn't do anything to affect that overwhelming sense of relief. Whatever it was, whatever nastiness or imagined nastiness had taken place between her and her father, it was over now, and if she wanted to let the past lie and go back to being my good-humored girl, I was more than ready to go along. What did I care about what might have happened twenty years ago or more? Could it change what I felt about this woman I knew so well, or what she felt about me? Of course not – not unless we let it, which we'd been doing since he'd appeared. But that was it; no more.

Did I give any thought to the idea that she was in there, in the Sixty-first Precinct house, lying to Detective Sergeant Ivan Kovalski in connection with a murder investigation? That what she told him – or failed to tell him – might send him down the wrong path? That because of her, some brutal thug who'd beaten a sick old man to death might conceivably get away with it?

Frankly, no.

Not then.

Chapter Five

LILY WAS THE first to notice anything.

'Did you pull down the shades?' she asked from the foot of the stairs while I was hanging our coats in the hall closet. We'd just gotten back from her interview with Sergeant Kovalski.

'The shades?' I closed the closet door and stuck my head into the living room to look at the front windows. Three of them, and all with the shades pulled right down to the sills, something we didn't usually bother to do because the eight-step front stoop put us out of sight of passersby.

'No, I didn't,' I said, frowning. 'That's—'

I heard her intake of breath and turned. A figure in a black woolen ski mask was coming down the stairs from the second floor. I got the impression that he was in his early twenties, fit and lithe. Loose-fitting jeans folded up at the cuffs, old gray-blue sweater, blunt-toed, steel-tipped workman's shoes, dirty cotton work gloves, a two-foot length of metal pipe in his right hand. But it was less the pipe that alarmed me than the way he moved – a confident tough-guy amble, arms held out slightly from his body, James Cagney-style, as if he owned the place. I wasn't looking at some surprised burglar caught *in flagrante delicto* and trying to make his getaway. He'd been sitting in the dark in one of the upstairs bedrooms with his pipe, sitting and waiting for us to come home; this guy had business with us.

Lily looked at me, her face white. 'Pete . . .'

I didn't say anything. I just grabbed her hand and pulled her toward the front door.

We didn't make it because it turned out that there were two of them, not one, and the second, wider-bodied, longer-armed, and seemingly the older of the two, maybe in his forties, was blocking the door, standing in front of it with his thick legs planted and his broad back against it. This one, dressed much like the other, including the ski mask, was holding what looked like a three-quarter-size baseball bat in one hand, cradling the heavy end in the palm of the other.

If you've ever walked unsuspecting into your house, your own inviolable house, and found a couple of masked thugs armed with clubs waiting for you, then you know what it feels like. If you haven't, count your blessings. Suffice it to say it was not pleasant. And having Lily there and at risk didn't make it any easier for me.

People's thoughts are funny at moments like that. The first thing that jumped through my mind was the perception that this latest dream theory of Louis's had been close, but not quite on the mark. If anything from the war was eating at me it wasn't guilt about never having been wounded, it was guilt about never having been *tested.* I'd fought in a war, I'd flown combat missions, but I'd never learned whether or not I was brave. The big question had never been answered, never even come up: when the chips were down, would I bear up and hold my own, or would I fail myself and those who depended on me? I had a hunch I was about to find out.

Lily moved closer. I put a sheltering, not-so-manly arm around her. I couldn't remember ever feeling so wretchedly powerless, so thoroughly at the mercy of others in the most literal, physical sense. There I was, in my own house, 'protecting' my wife, trying to keep my knees from knocking, submissively waiting for whatever was going to happen – whatever these two brutes decided was going to happen – next.

No, it wouldn't do. I straightened my shoulders.

'Okay, what do you want in this house?' I said harshly. The 'in this house' was tacked on as a not-so-subtle implication from which they were supposed to infer that this was my turf we were standing on, not theirs, and thus obliquely change the balance of power a little.

But inference wasn't their long suit. 'Hey – you – shut your mouth,' the younger one said.

'No, you listen to me. You've broken into my house—' I had no idea where I was going with this. 'And I damn well have a right to know, uh, to know—'

'Hey!' he said again, jerking the end of the pipe at me.

The older one cut him off with a gesture. 'Calm down, pal,' he said to me. 'Don't get so excited.' (Excited? I'd thought I'd brought it off with determined, don't-mess-with-me fortitude.) 'If everybody takes it easy, nobody has to get hurt.'

'I don't like this guy,' the other one said.

'Yeah, well, I'm not too keen on you either,' I said recklessly. I was showing off for Lily and I knew it. I also knew it was stupid, but I barreled ahead anyway. My hormones had kicked in. 'I think maybe—'

He smashed the pipe suddenly and ferociously down on the telephone we kept on a chest near the base of the stairs. Lily and I both jumped about a foot. There was a shower of black plastic shards and sprung telephone innards, and a squarish polished-stone flower vase that shared the top of the chest fell over on its side. Water slopped onto the floor.

It was a show of violence meant to cow us, of course, and did it ever. I decided to leave my thought, whatever it was, unexpressed. As far as the bravery question went: so far, not so good. I was mad, but I was also scared. My mouth was bone-dry.

'So if you just tell us where it is,' the older one said, coming nearer, 'we'll get out of your hair. No harm done, you know?' He was on my right, about three feet away, the other one about the same distance from Lily's left. For the second time that day I thought of the monkey house at the zoo. The young one, the one that didn't like me, was like an oversized rhesus monkey, wiry and tightly wound, and maybe a little nuts. The other one was more the gorilla type, calm, slow, thick-limbed, and big-bellied, but heavy with latent menace. The young one stood an athletic five-nine or five-ten. The older one was huge up close, looming a good four inches over my five-eleven and outweighing me by seventy pounds.

'We don't know what you're talking about,' Lily said in a small voice, pressing herself closer to me. 'I have a little jewelry in the bedr—'

The young one, the rhesus, grabbed her arm and spun her around to face him. Lily gasped.

'If I was you, lady—'

I balled my hand into a fist and smashed him in the face.

My thought processes weren't exactly explicit at that moment, but I think it was seeing that filthy glove on Lily's arm that did it, and then, especially, hearing the little cry when he dug in his fingers and twisted. It was the first punch I'd thrown at anyone since I was a teenager, possibly the first ever that I'd thrown in sheer, blind anger, but apparently I got the mechanics right, because I managed to put my shoulder and legs behind it. It caught him over the right eye and it must have hurt. I felt the impact all the way up my arm, felt his head snap back, heard his bark of pain and surprise. It felt great.

'What the fuck!' he said, shoving Lily off to the side and squaring off to face me. He touched his hand to his forehead, looking for blood but finding none on his gloved fingertips. I used the half-second it took him to do it to get hold of the stone vase, thumb inside the lip and fingers outside, and when he came at me with the pipe I was ready. I swung it straight at his bared teeth.

This time, no luck. The big one, a bit slow to get started but quick enough once the message from his brain worked its way down his neural pathways, grabbed my wrist in a grip that felt like a giant blood-pressure cuff clamping down. I twisted, getting my other hand on his face, or rather on the rough wool of his mask, and leaned into him, trying to push him off balance, with about as much success as I would have had trying to push a refrigerator truck off balance. I felt his warm, damp breath on my palm, felt his powerful neck muscles resist and hold firm. In the meantime the young one had gotten behind me and swung the pipe in a low, concise arc. It caught me behind the knees, sweeping both legs out from under me. I sprawled onto my back; the vase went skidding across the floor.

They were on me before I came to a full stop on the smooth linoleum. There was nothing I could do but curl up into a ball and try to protect myself, hands and arms over my head, knees drawn up to cover my midsection. I felt heavy blows on my thigh, my arm, and a dreadful one that made me cry out in the fleshy area between my ribs and my right hip. I could smell their sour sweat, hear their grunts as they laid into me.

Lily's father had been killed 'with a baseball bat, a lead pipe, something like that,' Kovalski had said. *How about both?* I thought now. 'Busted ribs, cracked pelvis, internal injuries . . .'

'It's in the closet, it's in the closet!' Lily was screaming, clawing at their backs. 'Stop!'

They stopped, although the younger guy got in an extra kick to my chest with his steel-toed shoe. It momentarily knocked the breath out of me. I did my best to avoid giving him the satisfaction of hearing me gasp, but I couldn't stop my eyes from bulging.

'What closet?' one of them asked. I had my eyes squeezed shut now, using all my concentration in trying to get my breathing started again.

'This one, right here.' I heard her run to the hall closet and open it. 'See? Here it is, it's right here.' Her voice was an octave higher than usual, her accent marked.

By now I'd managed to suck some air back into my lungs and to pull myself to a semierect position against the wall, both arms pressed hard to my sides. I couldn't tell if I was hurt inside or not. Lily was up on her toes, rummaging under the spare hats and mufflers on the shelf above the hanger rod. In a few seconds she came up with the big gray film can. In her nervousness it slipped through her fingers, popping open when it hit the floor. The celluloid reel inside unwound a loop or two but stayed put, and all of us just remained where we were, looking at it. I could see heavy sheens of sweat on the brows of the two thugs. It was warm in the house and they were heavily clothed, and they'd worked hard beating me up.

The older one was the first to speak. 'Schmuck,' he said to his partner. 'All we had to do was open the fuckin' closet door.'

'So? Who stopped you?'

The older guy shook his heavy head. 'Just pick it up, huh?' He wiped sweat from his forehead and nose, flicking it onto the floor, and turned to Lily. 'Where's the other one?'

She shrank back, shaking her head. 'I . . .'

'The other one, the copy, where is it? Come on!'

She shook her head some more, her eyes wide. 'I don't know.'

'Don't bullshit us, lady,' the young one said. 'You're his kid, aren't you?' He took one slow, menacing step toward her.

'It's true, there was only one,' I said, or croaked. 'That's all he had with him.'

He turned angrily on me. 'We know that, ass-face. The question is, what'd he do with the other one?'

'And how the hell is she supposed to know that, you goddamn pinhead? She hasn't seen him in twenty years.'

Considering that the wall was the only thing holding me up and that for all I knew my arms clutched against my sides were all that was keeping my insides in, it was interesting to see that at least my hormones were still working fine.

He shook his head. 'I'm telling you,' he said to his partner, 'this guy is a real piece of work.'

When he slapped the pipe against his leg and started for me I straightened up as much as I could and glanced around for a weapon. Nothing within reach, but I sure as hell wasn't going to just stand there and take another beating. And what would happen to Lily if they got me out of the way? I braced myself, but at that point Lily heaved something (the vase, I found out later) through the middle front window. It stopped us in our tracks. A tremendous rattling crash as the vase hit first the window shade and then the window itself, then a tinkling rain of glass on the ground outside, and finally a hysterical *whapwhapwhapwhap* as the shade went spinning around on its roller.

Somewhere else a window opened. 'What the hell is going on down there? Is everybody all right?'

The two of them looked at each other and made for the back door, taking the film with them. We heard the door open, heard their heavy steps on the wooden stairs that led to the alley running down the center of the block behind the houses.

I let myself sink slowly to the floor, sliding down with my back against the wall. I felt like absolute hell.

Lily's face was sharp with concern. 'Pete, are you—'

The doorbell rang. Lily started. 'Should I answer it?'

'Well, I'm sure not going to get there anytime in the near future,' I said, my hand to my side.

She nodded and went to the door. 'Who is it?' she called from a few feet away.

I heard the voice of Sal Gianini, who lived next door – actually, in the same building, this section of Bensonhurst consisting of block-long rows of 'semidetached' houses, that is, of buildings made up of two mirror-image, two-story houses each, with a driveway leading back to the garages between every two buildings. With Sal literally right on the other side of our walls, he had probably gotten an earful.

'Lily, is something wrong?' He was whispering. It was going on midnight.

'No, Sal, it's nothing,' she said with an easy, embarrassed laugh. 'God, I'm sorry if we woke you up.' He was probably in the terrycloth robe and shuffly leather slippers he wore to pick up his *Daily News* in the morning.

'It sounded as if – well, we didn't know what it sounded like. Wasn't that your window that broke?'

'I'm afraid so,' she said sheepishly. 'We were feeling silly – we had a few glasses of wine with dinner, and we were just sort of fooling around like a couple of idiots. We were playing this kind of touch-football game we have, and we actually used this heavy vase we have for a ball, if you can believe it. It was really stupid—'

'Mary tried to call you on the telephone. We couldn't get through.'

'Yes, we've been having trouble with it all day. We told the phone company.'

Pause. 'You're sure you're okay?'

'Oh, sure, absolutely, except for feeling so stupid. Apologize to Mary for us, will you? Tell her we promise to try to act our ages from now on.'

He laughed. 'You'd better get that window taken care of. Getting cold.'

'We will. Good night. Oh, tell Mary I'll see her at Bebe's on Sunday.'

She came quickly back to me and got down on her knees beside me, peering anxiously into my eyes. 'Pete, are you all right? Are you hurt?'

'No, I'm okay.' I'd used the time she was talking to Sal to check myself over. No broken bones and, as far as I could tell, nothing inside felt any squishier than usual. I was sick to my stomach, however, and every place that I'd been whacked hurt like hell, with one of my arms, where I'd been hit above the elbow, beginning to puff up. 'I'll probably be stiff as a board tomorrow,' I said, 'and black-

and-blue all over, but I'm all right. I think.'

She looked as if she didn't know whether to believe me or not. 'You don't look all right,' she said. Her hand came tentatively out to brush some hair back from my temples. I shivered, as I almost always did at her touch. 'Pete, you were so . . . so incredibly brave. I was so scared myself. I thought they were going to . . . I couldn't believe the way you . . .' She shook her head, laughing and crying, then put her lips against my forehead and gently pressed my face between her breasts. 'Pete, Pete. Foolish man.'

It should have been like manna from heaven. I was brave. I had stood up like a man and defended my woman the best I could against overwhelming odds, and now I was reaping my reward. That's the way it *should* have been, but all I could think of was how easily she'd just lied to Sal, how readily, how convincingly, she'd come up with a ridiculous story and made it seem the most natural thing in the world.

I hadn't known she could do that. And if she could, how did I know that I could trust these tears, this concern for me, or anything else, as genuine? God help me, I was beginning to wonder if I knew her at all.

'Lily, what was on that film?'

She drew back. 'I don't know. I don't have any idea.'

'Why didn't you tell me you kept it?'

'Pete, don't look at me like that. There was nothing to tell. He left it behind on the stoop. I didn't want to deal with it. I just put it in the closet until I could throw it away.'

'You had it hidden underneath those things.'

'It wasn't "hidden". What's the matter with you? I hate it when you sound like that. It was just on the shelf. Things got tossed on top of it, that's all. You could have seen it anytime. You just didn't look.'

That was true enough. I rarely looked into the hall closet in the sense of seeing what was in it, I just reached in for what I wanted or, as she said, flung a pair of gloves or a scarf up on top.

'Anyway,' she said, 'if I wanted to hide something from you, would I hide it in the hall closet?'

But hiding it wasn't the point. Why had she kept it at all? Given the way she felt about her father, you'd think she wouldn't have been able to wait to get it out of the house and into the garbage. And the garbage cans were out back, in the garage.

'Yeah, I'm sorry.' I sighed. 'Maybe I'm getting paranoid. Well, here goes . . .' With her help and the wall's support, I pulled myself to my feet, wincing as I bumped my arm. '*Ow!* Damn.'

She cringed right along with me. 'Do you want me to get you to a hospital? Should I call a doctor?'

'No, it was only a twinge,' I said as the wave of pain and nausea passed. 'We'd better call the police, though.'

'The police?' She stared at me. *Here comes another story*, I thought, angry at myself for thinking it. *I know the look now. She's coming up with reasons why we shouldn't call them.* 'What would be the point?' she said. 'Those men are gone, they got what they wanted, they're not coming back.'

'They think there's another copy of the film. They seem to think you know where it is.'

'But I don't! They'll realize that. Look, what can the police do? We can't describe them, they didn't leave fingerprints—'

'Goddammit, Lily, I don't believe this. When two guys break into our house like that, and all the rest of it, I'm calling the police.' Now it was Lily I was mad at. 'Besides, they're probably the same ones that killed your father, have you thought about that?'

Her face stiffened. 'I don't care—'

'But I do. They're murderers. And they could damn well come back.' I pushed myself away from the wall. I was feeling steadier now. That's what anger does for you. 'I'm going to use Sal's phone. I want you to come with me; I don't want you here alone.'

'Sal's phone! But I just told him there was nothing the matter. I can't—'

'That's your problem,' I said. My chest was rigid. I felt as if something in me had come unhooked. 'Put on a coat, it's cold.'

She looked at me with narrowed eyes. 'You've changed, Pete. You're different.'

'*I've* changed! Lily, what the hell is—'

This was an exchange that wasn't headed anywhere promising, so I was glad when we were interrupted by the front buzzer again, followed by hammering on the door. 'Police! Open the door, please.'

We continued to stare balefully at each other. When had we both become so volatile, so ready to be angry with one another? 'Pete, please,' she said, squeezing my forearm. We went to the door together, me trying not to hobble.

Two rumpled police officers who looked as if they were at the end of their shift stood there looking us over, ready not to believe whatever we were going to say. Behind them, down at the curb, their car was pulled up crookedly. 'We have a report of a disturbance here. What exactly is the trouble?'

Both of us were suddenly tongue-tied. 'Uh—'

'What happened to your window?'

Lily glanced at me, pleading. *Please*.

'We've had a break-in,' I said, looking away from her eyes. 'Two men in ski masks. They were after a can of film.'

Chapter Six

THE POLICE DIDN'T leave until 1 A.M., and when they did, they took us with them, dropping us off at the Kings County General emergency room, me for X-rays, and Lily along with me because neither of us wanted her to spend the night alone at home. The X-rays came up negative, but they kept me there till morning anyway, to poke and prod at their leisure. Happily, they didn't find whatever they were looking for, and by 9 A.M. we were back at home.

But home was hectic. We had barely showered and changed clothes when the police were back with more questions. Kovalski got into the act too, stopping in a little later to ask questions of his own and look dubious when we answered. He'd come to the not unreasonable conclusion that the murder and the break-in were related: that Vercier had been battered in an effort to get out of him the whereabouts of the film, and that the effort had been successful. That, he said, must have been how the two thugs knew where to come looking. Whether or not Vercier had been killed intentionally or had just succumbed to the beating he'd taken was still up in the air. As to our situation, Kovalski offered to have the local beat cops keep a particularly sharp eye on our house, a suggestion I gratefully accepted, although Lily grumbled that it was silly, that she wasn't in any danger, that they certainly weren't going to come back and try again, and that on reflection they'd realize she couldn't possibly know anything they wanted to know.

'Actually, I think you're right, Mrs Simon,' Kovalski said pleasantly. 'I wouldn't think you're in any danger, but it's no trouble, so let's just go ahead and do it.' Which settled it.

Just before leaving he asked Lily if she'd been aware that her father had been a partner in the Galería Metropolitana, a prosperous Barcelona dealership in antique jewelry and silver.

She colored slightly. 'I told you, I don't know anything about him. I haven't seen him since I was seven. I didn't even know he was in Spain.'

'A partner?' I put in, surprised.

The reason I was surprised (aside from the fact that the last I'd heard he'd been a barber) was that he'd hardly struck me as a cosmopolitan art-world type, or a well-to-do guy either. On the other hand, a partnership in a big Barcelona gallery would explain the suite at the St George.

He nodded absently. 'Yeah, I called Barcelona – well, I didn't, Officer Ramirez did – and talked to the other partner, a guy named Lebrun. He filled us in. The reason I bring this up, Mrs Simon, is that when we asked what he was doing in the States, they told me he'd come to see you; they didn't know about what. I thought you might want to take a guess.'

'Other than to make me take that film of his, I don't have any idea.'

He accepted this with an unsurprised shrug. 'Also, it occurred to me you might want to talk to them, find out the name of his attorney and so on, because you might have something substantial coming to you. I mean, it's none of my business—'

'Thank you, Sergeant,' she said. 'I appreciate what you're trying to do, but I have no interest in anything that's "coming to" me from him. I think I've explained why.'

He didn't answer, just looked at her steadily with his sad, sleepy eyes. *He doesn't believe her either*, I thought.

THE NEXT NIGHT, after years of watching next to nothing on television, she suddenly turned into a fanatical TV addict. As soon as dinner was done she flicked on the set, plumped herself down in front of it, and stayed right there, with a closed, frozen look on her face, for the next four hours. She sat through *You Asked for It*, *The Donna Reed Show*, *The Best of Groucho*, *The Real* McCoys – whatever happened to be on, things she'd never have thought of looking at before. If I said something to her, I got back a monosyllabic reply, except once, when I pointed out that it was eleven o'clock, late for us. That got me a complete sentence.

'You can go to bed if you want,' she said.

Even I – I with my shying away from meaningful dyadic interaction – couldn't help seeing what all this TV-watching really meant. Not to put too fine a point on it, she was avoiding having anything to do with me. Even *The Real McCoys* was preferable.

I was doing my best to be understanding and give her the room she seemed to need, but I was really starting to worry about us. I felt as if I were carrying a huge stone in my chest. It hurt me to be excluded like this, to be kept at a distance from the only person in the world I deeply cared about. At midnight, at the end of a half-hour special on bird life in Antarctica, I turned off the set.

'*Million Dollar Movie* is coming on,' she said. 'It's a Sonja Henie. I wanted to watch it. Will you turn it back on, please?'

'No.' I came back and took the chair beside her. 'Lily, this is no good. What's happening to us? We used to talk about everything, we used to trust each other—'

'I trust you, Pete, it's not that. Don't think that.'

'Tell me what to think, then.'

She hunched her shoulders. 'Oh, it's everything together, really. President Kennedy, my father, that detective and his questions, questions . . . so many memories I thought I'd put behind me. It's hard to put into words. I just feel as if my world's suddenly turned kind of black. I don't want to think about anything right now.'

'Lily, honey, this is just not—'

She smiled a little. 'It's just temporary, darling; don't worry, I'll get over it. Just give me a day or two, all right? Just give me a little time.'

When I started to say something more she put a finger against my lips. 'Pete, please don't press me right now. That detective is bad enough. I already told you what happened with my father – what he did. Don't make me go into the details.'

That stone in my chest got heavier. *You already told me, but I don't believe you.* 'Okay,' I said with an inward sigh, 'I won't press you.' Not yet.

THE NEXT NIGHT it got worse. Going to the closet to get her coat after dinner, she abruptly declared that she was going to the movies and that, if it was all the same to me, would I mind if she went by herself because it wasn't the kind of picture I liked and I'd just spoil things by sitting there grousing about it.

This generated one of the mild but painfully repetitive little disputes we'd been having for days about her going out alone, which ended, as usual, with her declaring that, first of all, Kovalski himself had said there was little danger, and second, she wasn't going to have her life dictated by what a couple of rotten thugs might or might not do.

Inasmuch as I agreed with her on the second point (I was less sure about the first), I just nodded and told her to have a good time. But watching her go, I felt as if I'd come unmoored. In just these few days I could sense her slipping away from me, receding into the distance, growing ever smaller, fainter, less real. Already the calm, lovely, uncomplicated years of our marriage seemed like a dream, like a not-quite-real memory of some fresh, clear brook that had run for a wonderfully long time but had finally flowed on by, dried up, and disappeared. I began to wonder if we could ever put it together again. I was scared.

I was also a little paranoid. Was she really going to a movie by herself – something she just about never did? Was she really alone? Was there something else going on? She was going to the Benson, she'd told me, just a few blocks from home. So half an hour after she left, I walked there, bought a ticket, entered, and looked for her in the darkness. There she was, all right, and alone, sitting motionless in the tenth row, her usual row, with flickering gray-blue lights and shadows from the screen playing over her face. She was watching Jerry Lewis in *The Nutty Professor*. From a seat at the far end of the last row, feeling like some kind of pervert, I watched her for forty solid minutes. Her face never turned even fractionally from the screen. She never once laughed, never moved. She looked like the statue-lady in my dream.

I slunk home in a wet, sticky snowfall, brimming with doubts and anxieties I couldn't name and unable to bring up the subject when she did come home. Like a couple of considerate roommates we chatted a little about nothing and then went to bed, each keeping carefully to our own side.

*

I KNEW I had to talk to someone before this went much further, and it was to Louis that my mind turned. Despite the overlay of gobbledygook (mostly acquired during a year's sabbatical at the Institute for Analytico-transformative Psychotherapy in London, before which he'd made sense a majority of the time, or pretty close), there was a perceptive and intelligent guy there, and, more important, an old friend with my interests at heart. But it was hard to go to an outsider, even Louis. About my dreams, sure – I only half believed they meant anything anyway, and even if they did, so what? Talking to him about them was more fun than anything else, a mental diversion for us both. But about Lily and me? About the very core of my life? No, that was hard.

But now, in the single week that had passed since her father had shown up it had reached the stage where I was so unable to communicate with her that I was actually sneaking around spying on her. When I wasn't feeling resentful or put-upon I was feeling rudderless and empty. What Lily was feeling I couldn't tell. We were in trouble and I was no longer sure we could find our way back.

So the next day, after lunch, I asked Louis if he would meet me on campus, even though it was a Sunday. I didn't want to go to his house with his family around. I didn't want to talk in his office either – too close to a professional consultation – or in my cluttered little cubby-hole, so we found an empty classroom in Boylan Hall and pulled a couple of desk-arm chairs around to face each other.

'This is really hard for me, Louis.'

He nodded, doing his best to suppress his natural, slightly maniacal look in favor of a thoughtful, judicious restraint that didn't suit him at all. 'Okay, shoot. I'm at your service.'

I took a breath – chalk dust, steam heat, and floor polish – and laid it out for him, right from the morning Marcel Vercier had returned from the dead. It took me half an hour. Mostly he listened quietly, with his head down, tracing with one finger over the old names and initials that had been carved into the wood long ago and darkened over the years by layer on layer of Waterman's blueblack ink. After I'd finished he was silent for a few seconds, then looked out through the window at the campus, where a few students trudged through the thin layer of snow on their way to or from the library.

'I gather you're not in need of any theoretical constructs at this point.'

'What I'm in need of is help, Louis. Lily and I, we . . . well, dammit, I just don't understand what's going on. Last week I knew everything there was to know about her, I understood her better than I understand myself. Seriously. You know, she'd start a sentence and I could finish it. Half the time she wouldn't even have to start it. Now, it's as if . . .' I shook my head. 'I don't know what's in her mind, she's like a different person, a stranger. I can't get close.'

'No, I don't buy that, Pete.'

'You don't buy what?'

'I don't think you knew everything there was to know about her.'

'Well, everything important, everything that mattered.'

'Really? Let me ask you something.' He looked hard into my face. 'You've always thought it would be nice to have kids, right? But Lily doesn't.'

'So?' I said. 'A lot of women don't. What's that got to do with anything?'

'And what career does she choose?'

'She's a junior high counselor, you know that. What's the point?'

'The point is that this woman who's not interested in having children picks a career of working with kids, and handicapped kids at that – kids who need a lot of attention. Does that make sense to you?'

That stopped me for a moment. 'Well, she's interested in helping others, Louis. She always has been.'

'Oh, please, that's lame, and you know it. All right, how much do you know about her life before she met you?'

'Well, when she was a little girl—'

'No, I mean after she was a little kid, her life during the war.'

I shrugged. 'She doesn't like to talk about it, and I don't blame her. I haven't pressed her.'

'You haven't pressed her,' he repeated. 'For what – twenty years, you haven't pressed? You never asked what her life during the Occupation was like day to day? It must have been a tremendously formative time for her. Was she in the Resistance? Did she—'

'Pete, she still was a kid, for Christ's sake. She was twelve in 1940, when the Germans came. She was barely seventeen when it ended. She's put it behind her, and as far as I'm—'

'Did she go without food? Was she ever in trouble with the Nazis? Did she spend the whole time at home? What happened to her relatives? Did—'

'She went hungry, just like everyone else, but no, she was never in trouble, and, yes, she spent the whole Occupation in Veaudry with her mother, and . . . and . . .' And that was about all I knew. Aside from the never-happened execution of her father, of course, on that fateful day on the village square in Veaudry.

I grumbled something. This wasn't the way I'd intended the conversation to go. 'Look, Louis, I know you find it hard to believe when someone prefers not to go around sharing all her innermost feelings, but . . .' I waved my hand to cancel out the rest of the sentence. 'Oh, hell, I'm sorry. But you see, Lily—'

'No, no, you miss my point. I'm not talking about Lily, I'm talking about you.'

'I don't want to talk—'

'Tell me about *your* career.'

'I don't see what—'

'Just answer; humor me. For Christ's sake, you ask me to leave the bosom of my family on a Sunday to help you, and then you won't shut up. What's your profession? Come on.'

'I'm a historian, okay?'

'Exactly. Now, you don't suppose that could be because you like things cut and dried?'

'History isn't cut and dried, Louis.'

'Trust me on this, Pete. When you've been dead four or five hundred years, things are cut and dried. Remember that war you were getting so excited about last week, the War of the Three Andrews in whatever it was, 650?'

'The War of the Three Henrys, 1585. *So*?'

'So this: here you are; you were alive at the time of the greatest conflict in the history of the world – you were *in* it, for Christ's sake; a participant. Your wife was *really* in it; right in the middle of it. Am I right or am I right?'

'Louis, I've really got a big problem here. I wish you'd—'

'And after you get back from defending your country you go to school for eight long years so you can spend the rest of your life studying stuff like, what? The famous, seminally important War of the Three Henrys.' He stuck his face out at me, the better to fix me with that goofy stare, then tapped his temple. 'Could this be part of a pattern, I ask myself. Is this – I mean, just possibly – a man that works overtime to avoid problems that just might turn out, God forbid, to be *relevant?*'

I sighed. I'd heard this kind of thing from him before. 'I don't know, Louis. At this point, I don't really care. Where does it get us?'

'It gets us to the root of the problem, Pete. You've been married twenty years—'

'Seventeen.'

'And you've been content to accept everything about her at face value, avoiding anything that might be problematic, never probing beneath the surface, never curious enough to—'

'Delve to a deeper, more authentic level. Okay, I admit it. I happen to believe people should be allowed their private space. So does Lily.'

He didn't return the smile. 'Yes, exactly. You're both big believers in private space. Well, I'm sorry to tell you, but that's not exactly the best way to maintain a close relationship.'

'But it's worked for us, Louis. We've been really happy, I think you know that. Do you know anybody who's got a better marriage than we do? It's just that—'

'It's just that now you're finally faced with a problem that you can't solve your usual way – by not dealing with it. And don't forget, it's dangerous to just let this go on. Lily's father's been murdered, you guys got your house broken into. Who knows what's coming next?'

'Believe me, I'm not forgetting.' I stood up and walked to the window. Outside, a few pallid rays of sun had broken through. The dusting of snow on the paths was starting to evaporate. 'Yeah, you're right,' I said with another sigh. With my finger I drew curving lines through the crescents of condensation that had collected in the corners of the panes, then suddenly banged the windowsill with the side of my fist. 'Dammit, what is she *doing*, Louis? What would make her change like this?'

'I wouldn't presume to say, Pete. I don't know the details.'

I laughed. 'I don't remember that stopping you before.'

'Yes, but this is serious. Look, assuming that what you've been telling me is accurate – that is, that none of this behavior has anything to do with you, which, may I point out, is something you can't really know for certain – then it's pretty obvious that there's some sort of trauma she associates with her father. That's clear even to you, right? She's been repressing it, maybe even unconsciously suppressing it, all this time, and her father's return has kicked it off. Brought it to the surface, you know? Now, from the sound of it, and from the way she's been avoiding you, especially at night, if I were to take a not-so-wild guess—'

'You'd be wrong,' I said. 'He never fooled with her sexually.'

He rolled his eyes. 'How can you know that, Pete?'

'Because I raised the question and she said there *was* something like that, but she was lying. I do know her *that* well, Louis.'

I was on the receiving end of a skeptical stare, but to my surprise he didn't argue. 'All right, then, we'll say it was something else. Considering what precipitated it, almost certainly it goes back to Europe. Probably to the war. Whatever it is, it's going to have to be exposed – brought to the surface – and dealt with. Otherwise it'll just fester, which is bad, or get buried again, which is worse.'

'Is that analytico-transformative psychotherapy?'

'It's common sense, buddy.'

I returned to the chair and dropped heavily into it. 'Yeah, okay, you're right, of course, only how do I deal with it? Do I keep after her, do I just let her be until she gets ready to tell me about it, do I just sit back and hope it passes, because, let me tell you—'

'None of the above. You *can't* deal with it yourself. You need some outside help – both of you. I can give you a couple of recommendations.'

I made a face. 'A therapist? Boy, I don't think so. I don't think Lily is the type for that. I know I'm not.'

'You don't say! Well, now, you don't suppose that might have something to do with why you find yourself in the situation you're in, do you?'

I shook my head. 'Louis, I just don't see us—'

'Look, I'm not talking about psychoanalysis here—'

'That's a good thing, because if you were—'

'I'm talking about a simple third-party intercession; someone to facilitate the framing of fresh communication modes—'

'Whoa, this is starting to sound an awful lot like theoretical constructs. Louis, I really need some practical help here.'

'Which is exactly what I'm trying to give you. Look at it this way.' With his eyes shut he paused to scratch purposefully at his scalp under the mop of spiky ginger hair, almost the way a dog goes after a flea. 'Now, then. Any two people that have been together for a long time naturally establish certain ways of interacting. They identify certain things that are referred to only in a certain way, certain subjects that are fit for joking or teasing and certain ones that aren't, other subjects that aren't raised at all, and so on. This helps make the relationship more predictable and continuous and is, at least on the surface, generally helpful. Are you with me so far? Does it sound like you and Lily?'

'I guess so, yes.'

'Yes.' He leaned earnestly forward. 'The trouble is that it doesn't take long for these ways of interacting to become rules – agreeable, comfortable rules, but rules all the same, see? And then, when a problem arises that can't be resolved within those rules of interaction, the people that are having the problem have no way of coping with it. So you have to bring in a third party, someone who isn't bound by those particular rules, who can help you come at the issue from angles that neither of you is able to by yourselves. That's what I'm suggesting.'

Finished, he sat back. I could see that he'd really put himself into this. 'Does that make sense to you?'

I thought about it. I thought about what Lily's and my 'interaction' had been like lately. For a while the only sound was the splutter of the radiator. Then I nodded slowly. 'You know, Louis, it surely does.'

I DROVE HOME thinking hard. What Louis had said about a third party made eminent sense to me; God knows we weren't getting anywhere on our own. The big problem would be getting Lily to go along with it. Louis was right about both of us being overly private people. I thought briefly about asking him to come over to the house to go through his spiel again for Lily's benefit but discarded the idea. For one thing, Lily would resent my telling our secrets to him. For another, Louis and Lily had never exactly hit it off, although they were friendly enough when they met at college functions. Lily hadn't taken to Louis because she thought he spouted an awful lot of claptrap (which was true), and Louis hadn't taken to Lily, so I thought, because she seemed to be so much on the surface (which was also true). What you saw was what you got – until now, anyway – and Louis preferred complexity and covert, preferably murky, motives.

So it was up to me to convince her, and I was having trouble hitting on the best, the most delicate and unthreatening, way to broach it.

As it turned out, the question was moot.

THE MOMENT I walked through the front door, I knew that the house was empty. It was chilly; Lily liked the house warmer than I did and usually turned the heat way up when I wasn't around. It was almost five – where was she?

'Lily?' I called from the foyer. No answer.

Deep down in my belly I could feel the first sickish stirrings of panic. God, what had I been thinking when I let her go everywhere on her own, wander around all over the place? Why hadn't I put my foot down, how could I—

The white envelope propped against the bud vase on the dining-room table caught my eye. 'Pete,' I read in Lily's smooth, looping handwriting as I snatched it up. I let out my breath with relief, but my hands were still shaky as I opened it. Inside the envelope was a sheet of E-Z Erase typewriter paper, folded in thirds.

My Darling Pete, it began. Not scrawled in a hurry, but written with care.

I have to go away for a while. Don't worry, I won't do anything foolish. My father's coming back has opened a lot of old wounds that I thought were healed, and I need to be by myself to sort things out in my own mind. I'll be back, I promise, and things will be the way they were before. I know you're going to worry about me anyway, and I know I'm going to miss you terribly, but I also know that in the long run this is for the best, for both of us.

I'm sorry I've been such a mess lately. None of this has anything to do with you, my dear, dear Pete. I hope you know that. You've been an angel. It's my mess and it's only right that I take it away with me. You shouldn't have to get caught up in whatever might happen yet. But the main thing is, I'm the only one who can work this out and I have to do it alone.

I know you're going to want to try to find me – I know I would if it were the other way around – but please, please don't. Even if you did – and you never could – the last thing I want is advice, or support, or help, or anything else from anyone – even you, my darling. Not now, anyway; maybe later. All I need at this minute, and I need it desperately, is some space, some room to try and make sense of what's going on in my own head. I'll be in touch with you the minute I can, I promise. Please bear with me.

Oh, sweetheart, sweetheart, I'm already heartsick at the thought of being away from you. . . .

I love you!

Lily

P.S. I took $1,000 out of the savings account. I hope that doesn't make a problem. There's still $3,550 left.

P.P.S. I just remembered, I'm supposed to be at school tomorrow morning. Will you please call them before eight-thirty for me? Just tell Sharon in the principal's office that I couldn't come in and to put me on the unavailable list temporarily.

Chapter Seven

It was like being walloped in the chest with a sledgehammer. I mean, obviously, things between us had been strained ever since her damn father, who should have had the decency to get himself shot in 1943 the way he was supposed to, had walked up to our front door. She'd been keeping her distance since then, turning steadily inward and away from me. But that she'd feel the need to *physically* get away from me, to spend her days and nights apart from me . . .

I threw the note on the table and ran through the house searching for her; the garage too. Sure it was silly, but it seemed impossible that she'd really left. I just couldn't get it through my head; I thought that maybe she'd just . . . well, I'm not sure what I thought. In any case, she was gone, all right.

So was one of the suitcases, a medium-size Samsonite, and her everyday winter coat, a mackinawlike affair. Her long, more formal winter coat was still in the closet. As for clothing, there were a couple of dresses that weren't where I assumed they usually hung, and a few pairs of slacks that didn't seem to be there, although who knew for sure? The dresser drawers where she kept her underwear and things didn't tell me anything either. They were half full, so at least I knew she hadn't taken every single thing with her, but how full were they usually? Had she taken anything at all? Again, who knew?

I returned to the table and sat down. I reread the letter word by word, trying to squeeze out nuances, looking for clues to her frame of mind, to her plans, to anything.

'I'll be in touch with you the minute I can, I promise,' she'd said.

That 'I promise' bothered me. She'd 'promised' to fill me in on her father at breakfast the day he appeared. She hadn't. She'd 'promised' to make everything clear at dinner the same night. She hadn't. And now this. It worried me. Besides, why 'I'll be *in touch with you* the minute I can'? Why not '*I'll be back* the minute I can'? Getting in touch with me sounded remote and long-term, the kind of thing you did through a lawyer. Good God, was that in the cards?

And she'd taken a thousand dollars from our joint savings account. That was bad too. You could live for a month on a thousand dollars, even staying in a hotel. Did she plan to be away for a *month*? How long could it take to figure out what was going on in your own head? It seemed to me that it'd take maybe a couple of days, and if it didn't make sense to you by then, another month or another year wasn't likely to help. So was there another purpose to her leaving, something beyond sorting out her feelings?

And what about 'You shouldn't have to get caught up in whatever might happen yet'? *What* might happen yet? Was there, despite what she maintained, something she was afraid of, some danger she knew about? And was she really carrying it away with her? Was she protecting me?

The longer I stared at the note and the longer I thought about the last week, the more half-formed questions went skittering through my mind. But no answers. I didn't have the basic information to start from. I didn't know why her father had come to find her; I didn't understand the immense significance to her of his return; I didn't know what the 'wounds' were that it had opened; I couldn't even guess at what was on that film, or why he was so eager for her to have it, or why it was important enough – important enough to someone else – to have gotten him killed. All I knew was that Marcel Vercier was at the heart of it, but Marcel Vercier was dead, so where did I go with that?

I went to the telephone and called Sergeant Kovalski, hoping he might be in his office and that he might have come up with something new on Vercier. He was there, but no, there was nothing, he told me in his usual weary manner; no progress since the last time we'd spoken. He heaved a sigh. 'I haven't been getting a whole lot of help on this, you know.'

From us, he meant. I understood his irritation. 'Did you ever find out anything more about Vercier himself?' I asked.

'Well, he lived in a good section of Barcelona, we found that out,' he told me grudgingly; he preferred getting information, not giving it. 'Unmarried, lived alone, no legal or financial problems anybody could tell me about. No known enemies. That's about it. Who knows what it's worth?'

'Any clues as to what was on that film?'

'Nup.' Pause. 'You got any for me?'

'No, of course not.'

He waited a second to see if I was going to have any second thoughts. 'Well, give my best to your missus.'

I didn't, as they say, know whether to laugh or to cry. 'I'll tell her when I see her,' I said. There seemed no reason to tell him about Lily's leaving; he already knew more than I was comfortable with about my personal life.

'If she thinks of anything, tell her to give me a call.'

'Right.' Right. 'Well, thank—'

'Mr Simon?' He hesitated. 'Look, I don't want to butt into your personal affairs here – I mean, Mrs Simon already told me where to get off once – but if you and your wife are having any trouble over this thing and there's any way I can help, well . . .'

I was speechless. Was my voice that much of a giveaway? I was aware of how my throat had tightened up on me, but I had no idea it was as obvious as that. And Kovalski had sounded as if he was honestly concerned, not just a cop on a case but a rough, kindly uncle who really wanted to help.

'Actually, we are having a little trouble,' I mumbled, surprising myself. That unexpected show of human sympathy must have unmanned me, because out tumbled the whole story.

There was nothing he could do, of course. There wasn't any direct connection to his murder investigation, and Lily, having willingly left under her own steam, hardly qualified as a 'missing person.' And even if she had, would I have wanted the police to hunt her down for me? Of course not; not if she didn't want to be found. So what was the point?

Embarrassed, I thanked him stiffly for listening and for being reassuring ('That "whatever might happen yet" could mean just about anything, Mr Simon; it was pretty unlikely that it referred to physical danger. If it had, wouldn't she have just come out and said so more clearly?'), and promised to let him know if I heard anything. Then I went looking for the bourbon.

By the time I crept to my chill and lonely bed that night, having stayed up until 2:30 A.M. hoping for a call, I'd decided to honor Lily's request to be left on her own, but only up to a point. I would give her three days to get 'in touch.' If I hadn't heard from her by then, I wouldn't wait any longer. Whether she knew it or not, Lily needed me, and if I had to, I'd take things into my own hands. Admittedly, I was a little fuzzy on what precisely that might mean, probably on account of the three stiff bourbons I'd downed in increasingly gloomy solitude.

Or maybe it was five.

'THIS IS SHARON Wayne at PS 252. Is Mrs Simon there, please?'

The telephone hadn't caught me at my best. It had rung a little after eight-thirty the next morning, about two minutes after I'd crawled out of bed. I'd awakened in about the shape you'd expect: downhearted, worried, stiff (the results of the beating I'd taken were worst first thing in the morning), and hungover – the first time since New Year's Eve 1959 I'd had a hangover. I'd been in the bathroom sticking my tongue out at myself in the mirror and not much liking the look of it, or for that matter of anything else I saw in the glass, when I heard the jangle. I sprang back to the bedroom and snatched it up on the second ring, pretending to myself that I didn't think it might be Lily, thereby (a) fooling the gods, and (b) avoiding disappointment if it didn't turn out to be her.

But it hadn't worked on either count.

'She's, um, not in. Uh, right now.' Lord, my tongue felt like burlap, my head was stuffed with feathers.

'Oh. Well, do you know if she's on her way to school?'

'School? I—' Oh, Christ, wasn't I supposed to call them and tell them something? 'No, she won't be coming in,' I mumbled. 'She . . . she wants to be put on the temporary list. I mean the unavailable list, temporarily. I was supposed to call you, but it slipped my mind.'

I'd met Sharon Wayne once or twice when I'd picked Lily up from work; a determinedly old-school type who regarded the staff, up to and including the principal, as extensions of her own grandkids and subject to the same no-nonsense rules. I could practically hear her brows knit with suspicion. 'Is something wrong there? Is this Mr Simon?'

Wrong? No, what could possibly be wrong? 'Yes, it's Mr Simon, and there's nothing – well, yes, there is, in a way. She . . . she has a sick cousin, I mean a cousin who's having a baby, and she's gone to help out, you see.'

'Really? I didn't know Lily had any relatives she was still in touch with.'

'Oh, well, you see, they're not really cousins, just friends. The French do that, you know. Call their close friends cousins. The words are interchangeable.'

'They are? I never heard that before.'

Neither had I. 'Well, thank you for calling. I'm sorry I didn't—'

'So when exactly can we expect her back? I need to put down an "expected-back" date.'

'I don't see how I can tell you that, Mrs Wayne. There might be complications and she might be needed. You see, her friend lives alone. Far from the nearest hospital. In the woods, in fact. The doctor's a long way off.' *Shut up, Simon, enough already.*

'In the *woods*? Do you mean, as in a log cabin?'

I was beginning to think that Sharon Wayne had too much time on her hands. 'Well, yes, as a matter of fact, a cabin made of logs.'

'Huh,' she said. 'Where is she, exactly? Upstate? I could pop up over Christmas vacation and give her a hand if she's still there. I don't imagine Lily knows much about such things.'

'No, no, it's in . . . North Dakota, near . . . near Minot.' I hoped Minot was in North Dakota. I hoped there were woods.

'Well, when you speak with her—'

'Gosh, will you look at the time! Mrs Wayne, excuse me, I have to run. Sorry I forgot to let you know about this. I'll tell her you called. Bye.'

'I—'

I banged the phone down. Good gosh, there was a lot more to having your wife run off than I'd realized. The emotional upheaval was easy enough to anticipate, but I hadn't considered the logistical complications. Naturally I'd planned to keep it to myself as much as possible – especially after having blurted it out to Kovalski without meaning to – but all the same I knew that situations might pop up where I'd have to fabricate something. My plan had been to keep it simple, offhand, and uncluttered.

You bet. So now, after one telephone call, I had everybody at her school thinking she was with her nonexistent cousin/friend, midwifing in a log cabin, deep in the woods in Minot, North Dakota.

Simple. Uncluttered.

THAT WAS MONDAY, December 2. Except for running off for my classes and a trip to the grocery store, I spent the day at home, staying close to the telephone in hopes that she'd call, but she didn't. Ditto Tuesday and Wednesday, long, slow, down-in-the-mouth days, relieved only by occasional telephone calls, but none from Lily. On those few occasions when I had to come up with an explanation for her absence I stuck with the Minot, North Dakota, story, figuring that it'd be simplest to have only one fabrication to work around after she returned.

If she returned. As the days passed I found myself growing less certain that she would, or that, if she did, we could ever find our way back to what we'd had before. My feelings were a mess: at night they were mostly a sick, hollow-chested grieving mixed with worry for her. I hoped she was with old friends somewhere. I hated to think of her in some unfamiliar hotel room trying to come to grips with whatever was chewing away at her. I imagined her sitting on a narrow bed with cheesy neon lights blinking on and off outside her gauze-curtained window. *H-O-T-E-L.*

She needed me. She wouldn't admit it, but she did, and it gnawed at me. I could feel her reaching out to me the way twins are supposed to sense what the other is feeling. Whatever it was she was trying to deal with, she was obviously going through hell, and it tore me apart to think of her doing it alone. If she didn't need someone to lean on, at least she needed someone just to be there, and if not me, then whom? And was she, all by herself, facing some actual danger? Was that pair of thugs, or their like, hunting her down? *Why wouldn't she let me help?*

But during the day my feelings were more self-centered, a grumbling, sorry-for-myself resentment at being ill-used and left alone to fend for myself. Where were the dish towels? How the hell did the washing machine work? Which cleaners were my suits at? What did I do to deserve this?

I spent a lot of time remembering too. I couldn't believe that I'd let all those years – so many shared, joyful memories, so much laughter – flow by like that, as if we had a God-given right to them, as if they'd never come to an end. And I drank too much. There were more hangovers. I'd fall asleep at eight o'clock at night and wake up at one in the morning and just prowl the house for the rest of the long, long night. In the morning I'd feel shattered. I was starting to look like hell. The house wasn't looking too good either.

Wednesday was day three, the end of my self-imposed grace period, so that evening I started hunting for her in earnest. She'd left behind her address book (good sign? bad sign?), and I had already leafed through it looking for people she might be staying with. Lily had a lot of friends, but there were only four that seemed to me to be possibilities: all old friends living in New York or New Jersey. Within a couple of hours I'd gotten hold of all of them and had come away convinced that none of them had seen her. I'd had to tell them something, of course, and I knew Minot wasn't going to fly, so I said that she was dealing with some old personal problems from wartime France and had temporarily gone off to work them through, but I didn't know where and I was worried about her. At least there weren't any lies there, and I suspect they all read between the lines pretty accurately. They promised to let me know if they heard anything, but they were primarily her friends, not mine, so I couldn't be sure. At least I knew they'd tell her I'd called if they saw her.

Over the next couple of days I telephoned almost two hundred hotels in Brooklyn and Manhattan – even the St George on a whim – but came up with nothing besides a blister on my index finger. With every call I grew more discouraged. What made me think she was using her real name? What made me think she was in New York? With a thousand dollars she could easily have flown anyplace in the country (Minot, North Dakota, for example) and still have had money to spare. Even back to France, for that matter, but I knew that was out of the question. She had nobody there, and since I'd brought her to the States in 1945 she'd never once expressed interest in returning. Quite the opposite, in fact; even when I took my occasional history-related trips to Europe these days and wanted her to come along, she chose to stay behind if France was on the agenda.

At any rate, I knew full well that I had little chance of finding her by telephoning around the city and asking for her but kept on with it anyway. It was better than sitting around doing nothing, and what if I stopped after a hundred hotels and she was in the hundred and first? I took a fifteen-minute break every hour in case she was trying to get through to me, and it was during one such break on Friday that I heard the mail come through the slot and plop onto the entryway floor. On top of the little pile I found a business-size envelope with my name and address in Lily's hand. I tore it open, my heart pounding. Another plain white sheet of typing paper, this one dated 2 December, the day after she left.

Dear Pete,
I just wanted to let you know that I am safe and well and I hope you are too. I'm not too sure when I will be in touch with you again. Things are still a little confused, but I'm fine. Please don't worry about me.
Love,
Lily

That was it. Confounded, I stared at it indignantly. What kind of letter was this supposed to be? I turned it over, looking for something more. I tore open the envelope to look at the inside of it. Nothing. I read it again, shaking my head and talking to myself. What was it, some kind of code? Where were all those 'darlings,' the 'sweethearts,' the 'dear, dear Petes' of the day before? This was the kind of letter a ten-year-old might write home from summer camp under proddings from his counselor: *I am fine, how are you?*

I looked again at the front of the envelope. No return address, but the postmark was legible: 4 December, Washington, D.C. I took it to the dinette table in the kitchen and sat down with it, not knowing what to make of this. We'd been to Washington only once in our lives, for three days, to do the usual tourist things. I didn't know anyone there, and I didn't think Lily did either. A quick check showed that there was no one in Washington in her address book. So what was she doing there? Searching through immigration records? Talking to our congressman? Checking something in the National Archives? A hundred possibilities came to mind, but none of them came close to making sense – and none of them could conceivably consume five days.

And what was I supposed to do now, start in on the Washington hotels? No, thank you. For all I knew she wasn't there anymore anyway. Besides, I was convinced by now that looking for her this way was a waste of time, and this cold, superficial letter had convinced me that I was running out of time to waste.

To be honest, it wasn't only Lily's state of mind that worried me; mine did too. Maybe I didn't subscribe to Louis's analytico-transformative theories of behavior, but I knew enough psychology to understand that my feelings were also going to figure in this when it came time for resolution. Not a day passed that I didn't feel hurt, angry, misused, and depressed (frequently at the same time), plus other feelings I can't put a name to. That wasn't good. The longer it went on, the tougher it was going to be to put our lives together when she came back.

If she came back. I was beginning to admit to myself that her eventual return was hardly a certainty. The unsettling change from that first loving, troubled letter – in retrospect it seemed almost charming – to the few careless, enigmatic lines I'd received today was hard to ignore. If I didn't do something soon I wasn't going to have to worry about how to go about putting our lives back together. What I needed was another approach entirely, some new point from which to start, something that might give me a clue to what had precipitated all of the crazy doings of the past couple of weeks.

And that meant her father. Kovalski hadn't been able to help me there, but there was another place to turn. I poured the last cup of coffee out of the percolator, called long-distance information, got the number of the Galeria Metropolitana in Barcelona, and had the call put through. It was 6:30 P.M. there, but I'd been to Madrid a few years before, and I was aware that Spanish businesses stayed open late.

'*Buenos tardes*,' a cultured female voice said, coming through loud and clear. '*La Galería Metropolitana. Aquí es señora Aguilar. En qué puedo servirle?*'

'*Lo siento mucho, señora,*' I said. '*No comprendo español. Habla usted inglés?*' There is only one language besides English that I can actually get along in and that's French, but, world traveler that I am, I can manage those particular two sentences in nine languages, and be understood six out of ten times.

'I speak English. A little.'

'Good, thank you. My name is Pete Simon. I'm calling about Marcel Vercier—'

'Oh, I'm sorry. Mr Vercier, he . . . he is passed on.'

'Yes, I know that. I have some questions about his—'

'One moment, please. Better I give you to Mr Lebrun.'

There were a few rustly noises and a click. '*Sí?*'

I went into my routine again. '*Lo siento mucho, señor Lebrun. . . .*'

'*No hablo inglés,*' he said curtly.

Terrific. Thanks, Mrs Aguilar. '*Parley-vouz français?*' I asked, banking on his name.

A pause, followed by a cautious '*Oui.*'

'My name is Simon, Mr Lebrun,' I said in French. 'I'm calling from New York in reference to Marcel Vercier.'

This was received with a whinny of peevish disbelief. 'For God's sake, I've already talked to your Officer Ramirez twice. Marcel's death has put a great deal of stress on us here, don't you realize that? I have a business to run, I can't come running to the telephone every time you people think of another question.'

You people. He'd jumped to the assumption that I was with the police, and although I wasn't going to lie outright and say that I was, I didn't go out of my way to say that I wasn't either. 'Yes, sir, I understand that,' I said in my best New York police detective manner, courteous but not to be messed with, 'but I'm afraid I do have a few more questions.'

I could feel his reluctance crawling out over the wires all the way from Spain before he gave in. 'Oh . . . yes, well, what is it you want to know?' I heard leather creaking. He was settling back in his chair with a will-they-never-leave-me-in-peace sigh.

'I understand that Mr Vercier came to the United States to see his daughter. Would you happen to know what it was in reference to?'

'I don't know. Why do you keep asking me this? I already explained to Officer What's-his-name.' He had a put-upon way of speaking, the kind of voice that made it clear that he was a man with a thousand things on his mind, and whatever it was you were bothering him with wasn't one of them. There was a faint rapping noise in the background; fingers drumming on his desk. 'I had little knowledge of his personal life. He was a very private man.'

I said nothing.

Another sigh. *If I must, I must.* 'A few weeks before he left he told me he was going to see her; I think it was for the first time since the war. He said he would be gone for a week. There, that's all I know. I explained this already. More than once.'

'He didn't say any more than that? It must have seemed strange to you that after so many years he'd suddenly pick up and go to New York to find her. He must have told you something. You must have asked.'

'He must, you must. You don't seem to understand. Marcel didn't have to explain his actions to me, and I'm not one to go around asking. But in this case, yes, I knew without having to ask. He had cancer, an advanced case. He was dying. He wanted to see his daughter one more time. That much I knew. Does it seem so strange to you? It doesn't to me.'

No, not to me either. 'He had a film of some kind with him. Would you know anything about that?'

'Only what I told the officer – Officer Ramirez – that I knew he'd had some sort of film for years, that he attached great importance to it. He kept it in a safe deposit vault in America, I believe.'

'America? Why would he keep it in America?'

'I have no idea. Perhaps he thought it was safer.'

'And you don't have any idea at all what was on it?'

'I . . . no. I already said so. Now, if you have no other questions, I must get back to my work. Marcel's death has come at the worst possible time for us. Objects are flooding in. Everything is in a state of disorganization.'

But I hadn't missed that stammer at the start. Was I getting close to something?

I spoke quickly, afraid he was going to hang up on me. 'Mr Lebrun, I understand that there may be another copy of that film in existence.'

'Yes, yes,' he said impatiently, 'I've heard the same thing. So?'

'Would you have any idea at all where it might be? It could be of tremendous consequence.'

He paused before answering, and when he did, it was with a tinge of suspicion. 'Is this or is it not in connection with the police investigation of his death?'

Oops – my police cover, such as it was, was blown. Maybe cops didn't go around saying 'of tremendous consequence.' It was hard to imagine it coming out of Kovalski's mouth.

'Ah . . . no,' I said with an airy laugh, 'not at all, but you see, I'm married to his daughter, and—'

'You're married to Marcel's daughter? You're Lily Vercier's husband?' For the first time I'd said something that captured his interest.

'Yes, Lily Simon's.'

'And you want to know where to find the other copy of the film? Is that what you're asking me?'

'Yes, I've been trying to tell you—'

'Why don't you ask your wife?' he said.

My turn to stammer. 'Ask – ask my – what did you say?'

'I said, if you want so much to know where the other copy is, you should go and ask your wife, not me. Goodbye.'

'My—'

Click.

Chapter Eight

ASK MY WIFE.

Whatever I did with that, however many ways I turned it over in my mind, I couldn't make it mean anything. *Lily* knew where the other copy was? Did that mean she knew what was on it as well? Had she been lying to me about that too, along with everything else? She'd been so damn convincing! How much of what I knew – what I thought I knew – about her, about her life, her feelings, was based on anything real? And what about the way she felt about me? Was that also . . .

Wait. Hold it. This was all wrong. I'd fallen in love with Lily practically the minute I saw her and I'd never looked back. I'd never stopped loving her, and I knew her better than I knew anybody else in the world. I'd lived happily with her for seventeen years, never once having reason to doubt her honesty or her constancy. I wasn't about to let the weird happenings of a couple of weeks or the casual insinuations of some stranger in Barcelona undo all that. No. Uh-uh. I had some serious finding out of my own to do. The question was, how?

'I'm going,' I said aloud, and it startled me, almost as if someone else had interrupted my thoughts. I almost answered myself. 'Going where?'

But I knew exactly what I meant. The idea had jumped into my head fully formed. I was going to Barcelona, why not? I could take some emergency leave. There were two or three colleagues who would be able to take over my classes for a while, a favor I'd done for them more than once. If Lebrun chose to be cagey over the phone, by God, I was betting I could get something more out of him face to face.

'Almost certainly it goes back to Europe,' Louis had told me, and I thought he was dead right. 'Probably to the war. Whatever it is, it's going to have to be exposed – brought to the surface – and dealt with.'

Okay, this was a way to start doing that. And it was a whole lot better than hanging around the house like a lump, hoping for a phone call that never came. I stood up, feeling better than I had since I'd come home to find that first letter. At last I was taking things into my own hands, taking control again.

Or so it seemed at the time.

WITH MY PASSPORT good for another two years, it didn't take much preparation beyond arranging for my classes. I did leave a house key with our next-door neighbors the Gianinis, told them I'd be gone a few days, and asked them to pick up the mail; I would call them each evening to find out if anything important was in it. They were curious as hell, of course, and Sal started to ask some questions, but Mary shut him up with one of those wifely not-to-be-disobeyed warning glances.

Other than that, all I had to do was to throw some clothes together, find the passport, get some traveler's checks at the bank, and buy a ticket, which I did with the four hundred dollars we'd set aside for our Christmas vacation in the Catskills. (Had it been only last month that we'd sat down over hot toddies at the kitchen table to plan it? Already it seemed like another lifetime, misted-over and unreal.) It was impossible to fly directly from New York to Barcelona, but for $389 I got a round-trip ticket to Madrid, leaving from Idlewild the next evening on an Icelandic Airways red-eye, then had the agent book me through to Barcelona on an España flight leaving two hours after I arrived in Madrid. Unfortunately, the New York–Madrid leg involved a slightly circuitous route – a long stopover in Reykjavik, to be exact – that brought the total trip to a grindingly long twenty-one hours, but I didn't mind. For one thing, as the agent cheerfully pointed out, it did give me an opportunity to see what Iceland was like, something not many people got to do.

More important from my point of view, it would put me in Barcelona on Sunday night, almost a full day before any other available flight, which meant I could be at the Galeria Metropolitana first thing Monday morning, a day before I otherwise could. And with so many days already wasted, I wasn't about to squander any more.

WITH MY FLIGHT the next day not leaving until 7 P.M., I spent Saturday afternoon in the periodicals room of the Forty-second Street library, researching the Galeria Metropolitana, or rather doing my damnedest to research it, in hopes of finding out something more about Vercier. But other than listings in a couple of art-world business directories, the only mention that I could put my hands on was in a recent *Holiday* magazine article on (of all places) Tegucigalpa, Honduras. It seemed that Honduras, in an effort to lure tourists from the United States, had opened an ambitious museum, and that the pride of the collection was, in the words of the director of the Honduran Museum of Ancient Art, 'a spectacular gold Merovingian pendant known as the Rearing Lamb, dating from the seventh century A.D. and set with rubies, pearls, emeralds, and crystals.' The work, according to the writer of the article, had been purchased for over $100,000 from 'the well-known and highly regarded Galeria Metropolitana in Barcelona.'

Well-known or not, that was it; the only reference. Three hours' work and not a mention of Marcel Vercier. At four-thirty I threw in the towel and caught a taxi to the airport, and a few hours later, as promised, I did indeed get to see for myself what Iceland was like.

It was cold.

WHAT I'D HEARD about Barcelona from the few acquaintances who had been there was that it was a cosmopolitan city, with Las Ramblas, the famous tree-lined boulevard of shops and restaurants, at its heart and with an edgy, pushy, vibrant ambiance in which people walked twice as fast as they needed to, with their heads out ahead of their bodies, as if everybody was late for an appointment. It was the most energetic, least romantic of Spanish cities, they said. As one of them had put it, Barcelona was to Madrid as humming Chicago was to laid-back L.A.

All very true, it seemed to me when I got my first daylight look at the place, but nobody had bothered to tell me the most interesting fact of all, at least to a historian like me: that in the midst of all this twentieth-century pizzazz was a complete city within a city, this one straight out of the Middle Ages – the old Gothic Quarter, a square mile of narrow, twisting streets and dead-end passageways jammed with aged, crumbling buildings mostly built of stone blocks and, judging from appearances, not repaired in five hundred years.

And it was here, in this warren of blind alleys and zigzag back streets, that I found myself at nine-thirty Monday morning, standing on the uneven sidewalk outside the Galeria Metropolitana. I was on Calle d'En Quintana, a street that except for the few enterprises at sidewalk level – dimly lit furniture stores, dusty groceries, cafés consisting of a single table out on the sidewalk and two more inside – would have been perfect as a setting for *The Hunchback of Notre Dame*. Crooked lamps leaned out from walls on corroded metal brackets, iron balconies leaked prodigious rust stains onto the stone, fortresslike casings protected windows that had never been penetrated by a shaft of sunlight.

Under ordinary circumstances, a scene like this would have brought joy to my dry historian's heart, but the thirty-minute walk from my hotel (ten, if you don't count the times I got lost) had left me feeling jangly and frazzled, uninterested in my surroundings. Part of it was merely the usual travel jitters, of course – my body, still on New York time, was griping that it was only 3:30 A.M. and what the hell was it doing out and about at that hour of the night? – but mostly it was the nature of my mission. Now that I was here, about to do battle with Lebrun, I was second-guessing myself, not so sure that coming to Barcelona was the best thing to do. Not that I was worried (much) about anything I might find out about Lily from Lebrun. No, what bothered me was that I might not find out anything at all, and what did I do then?

The gallery was one flight up, above a dingy photography shop. Kovalski had said it was 'prosperous,' and according to *Holiday* it was 'well-known and highly regarded.' Maybe so, but you'd never know it from looking at the street entrance. Only a small, chipped marble plaque beside the heavy old wooden door marked its existence: *Galeria Metropolitana*, it said in age-blackened incised gilt lettering. That was it. Under the plaque was a brass button and a speaker. I pressed it, expecting to hear a voice, but instead the lock on the door clicked open and I pushed my way in.

Flicking on the hallway light did nothing for my doubts. In front of me was a narrow staircase that rose at a formidably steep angle, and to my right a tiny, dubious-looking cage elevator. I chose the staircase as the safer bet and creaked my way up to a closed glass door protected by iron grillework. Through it I could make out a scene of considerable disorder, with opened crates and boxes everywhere, many with their contents of what looked like coins or medallions half in and half out of them, and wads of packing materials – straw, shredded paper, sawdust, matting – strewn in messy heaps over the floor.

At the back of the room a dignified woman sat erectly behind a desk, typing with methodical competence while a stout, short-armed man in folded-back shirtsleeves stamped around in circles, waving his arms and complaining or lamenting, sometimes to the woman (who paid him little attention), sometimes to the walls, and sometimes, with eyes and hands raised, to God, or possibly just to the stuccoed ceiling. It was obvious that his fuming wasn't anything that his companion hadn't seen a hundred times before. Every now and then she would calmly say a few words, not bothering to raise her eyes and barely pausing in her typing.

Mr Lebrun and Mrs Aguilar, I presumed.

I opened the door and walked in. They both stopped what they were doing and looked at me, Lebrun with his hands still spread in exasperation or supplication.

'*Buenos días, señor*,' the lady behind the desk said. Mrs Aguilar, all right; I recognized the cultured voice. '*En qué puedo servirle?*' In the meantime Lebrun was grabbing his suit coat from the back of a chair and slipping into it.

'Mrs Aguilar, I'm Pete Simon. We spoke on the telephone last week. Is Mr Lebrun in?' I had no doubt that the agitated man standing four feet away from me was Lebrun, but I thought I might as well follow protocol.

She cocked her head. 'Mr Simon? But you are not in New York?'

She was a lean, plain-faced woman in a simple white blouse and dark skirt. With her long, homely face and her horsey teeth she looked so much like Miss Doyle, my patient but no-nonsense first-grade teacher – she of blessed memory, having taught me to tie my shoelaces after my mother and everyone else had given up on me – that I took to her instantly.

I smiled. 'I was. I came here specifically to talk to Mr Lebrun.'

Lebrun perfunctorily extended a moist hand. 'How do you do, I'm Charles Lebrun,' he said in English. 'I'm sorry, but you come at an extremely inconvenient time. Two big consignments have just arrived.'

So much for my welcome, but I hadn't expected any better. And I was ready for him. 'So I see. I thought you didn't speak English, Mr Lebrun.'

He dismissed this with a shrug. 'A little. French is easier,' he said, promptly switching to that language. 'Really, I don't know what more I can do for you, Mr Simon. I've already told you everything there is to tell.'

Lebrun, in middle age, looked like a man who had newly put on weight, the fat having settled in for the moment around his chest, not yet around his belly and midsection, so that he was more turnip-shaped than rotund; puffed-up and bloated-looking, like one of those gout-ridden, bewigged Englishmen you see in eighteenth-century cartoons, with one swollen, stockinged leg propped up on a cushion for relief. His splotched, ruddy face might once have been hawklike; now it was owlish and pouchy, with bristling eyebrows, a hooked nose that doubled back down toward his upper lip, a narrow, truculent mouth, and a negligible chin. His thinning brown hair was cut short.

'You can tell me why you told me to ask my wife where to find the copy of Vercier's film,' I said.

He blinked at me. 'You didn't ask her yourself?'

'No.'

'You came all the way here to Barcelona to ask *me* instead of speaking to your own wife?' He looked at Mrs Aguilar as if to share his incredulity, but she kept typing primly away, minding her own business, or at least pretending to, which made me like her all the more.

'Mr Lebrun,' I said firmly, 'how about just answering my questions? The sooner you do, the sooner I'll be out of here.'

That got his hackles up. 'Oh, is that so? Has it occurred to you that I might be getting tired of answering questions? That I might have other matters—'

'Mr Lebrun, if you'd rather I went through my old friend Colonel Zuniaga of the Guardia Civil . . .' A deadpan, flat-out lie, of course, but I'd gone to the trouble of finding out the name of the local police commandant that morning, and it stopped him dead. Nobody in Spain liked the idea of a visit from the Guardia Civil.

He used both hands to push the idea away. 'No, no, no, no, no. That won't be necessary, not at all, why put you to the trouble? Come to my office, it will be better there. Leave your coat with Mrs Aguilar. Leona, my dear, bring us some coffee.'

'You're not supposed to have coffee,' Mrs Aguilar told him, but even as she said it she was getting up to prepare it.

'Come along, sir,' Lebrun said, almost gracious now.

His office was no less a wreck than the showroom, with crates and stuffing all over the place, but at least there were a handsome desk and a couple of comfortable leather chairs. Lebrun swept confetti from the chairs onto the floor and sat in the one behind the desk, in front of a single small, heavily barred window so grime-encrusted that I couldn't tell what it looked out on.

He motioned me into the other chair. 'Now, sir, you wanted to know. . . ?'

'Why you think my wife knows where the film is.'

'Ah. The film.' He settled back to the creaking of his chair. 'Well, the fact is, I heard it from my cleaning woman.'

Whatever I expected, it wasn't that. 'Your—'

'You see, Marcel and I, we have – we had – the same cleaning woman, Mrs Mota; we've had her for years and years. Three times a week to him, three times a week to me. Not the easiest woman in the world to get along with, Mrs Mota, but once you know how to butter her up, she can be a jewel, the best worker in the world.'

I shifted in my chair and cleared my throat again. 'And she told you. . . ?'

But Lebrun, once you got him going, preferred to proceed at his own pace. 'Now, I'll admit to you, I'm as curious as anyone else. For years I've wondered what was so special about that film of his, how could I help it? What could be on it that was so significant? A hundred times I raised the subject with him, but always he'd just shake his head. Once, he gave me one of his sly little smiles and let slip that he'd had an 'insurance copy' made, just in case, but that was all. What was I supposed to make of that?'

An insurance copy, I thought. *So that was what those thugs were after when they wanted to know about the 'other' copy of the film. But insurance for what?*

'Well, the very day you called me – she cleans for me on Fridays – I asked her, Mrs Mota – in a discreet way, of course – if she knew anything about it. She used to cook for him sometimes, you see, and when he was sick she'd look in on him. They had a close relationship.'

'I see.'

He wagged a stubby, admonitory finger at me. His nails were chewed so far down it made me wince to look at them. 'I hope you don't imagine I'm suggesting there was anything—'

'I understand.'

'All right then. In any case I thought that, perhaps, sometime, over the years, he'd told her about it.'

'And?' I said when he stopped. He was proving to be a difficult guy to get anything specific out of. He liked to talk, but he also required coaxing.

'She said . . .' He paused and licked his lips, leaning forward to look at me conspiratorially from under those beetling brows.

I gritted my teeth. 'She said. . . ?'

'That she too had heard about this insurance copy. He'd once told her that if anything should ever happen to the copy in the vault, he had another one as well, and he wasn't telling anybody where it was, even Carmen – Mrs Mota – even me; but when the time came his daughter, Lily, would know where to find it.'

'But he hadn't seen her in twenty years. How would she know? Are you saying he was in touch with her? Why would he tell Lily about it? Wouldn't she—'

'You're asking me these things? How would I know? I haven't seen her since she was a child.'

This was something new. 'You knew Lily as a child?'

'Of course I did. I'm from Veaudry too. Marcel and my uncle Fernand were boyhood friends. Later, I used to see little Lily every day, a delightful child. Uncle Charles, she used to call me. And Marcel was just like every other proud papa, you know?' He shook his head. 'But for the last twenty years, here in Spain, working side by side with the man, not once, not *once*, did I ever hear him speak her name. I didn't know where she lived, I didn't know she was married to you. I barely remembered her name was Lily. What do you want from me?'

'I see. I'm sorry.'

But getting an apology just made him more blustery. 'Well, I don't see. I ask you again: why don't you ask *her* these things? Why come all the way to Barcelona to pester me?' He gestured at the welter of packing material. 'Do I look like a man with nothing to do but answer questions?'

'Mr Lebrun,' I said, 'if I knew where she was I'd ask her, believe me.' It had slipped out without my meaning it to. Chalk it up to travel fatigue; I'm not a very good flier. Or liar.

His eyes narrowed to squints. 'You don't . . .'

What the hell, I thought, *why am I bothering to keep it from him?* 'I'm trying to find her. That's what I'm doing here.'

'Aaah.' He nodded hugely, as if everything now made sense.

'You see,' I told him, 'when she saw her father it really unsettled her. Me too, for that matter. I thought he'd been dead for years. It made Lily . . . well, it doesn't matter. The important thing is that it upset her enough so that she went off somewhere by herself. It's been more than a week now, and—' With an effort I reined myself in. There was no need to spill everything; certainly not to Lebrun.

'All I know is, I have to find her. Where she's gone and why, I don't know, except that it's got to have something to do with her father, and you're about the only person I know that might be able to help me.'

'I understand now.' With his hands folded on his stomach, he looked like a big, well-fed bird – more pigeon than owl, perhaps – settled in its nest. 'I'm sorry for your trouble. I've had my own troubles at home, so I understand better than you think. If I could help you I would, believe me.'

'Well, do you have any idea why his daughter would have hated him so much?'

'No, I – not really, no.'

But his eyes had jumped away and back, and then down to the littered desktop, where they'd stayed. He had an idea, all right. My fingers tightened on the arms of the chair. 'Well, who *was* Vercier?

That would help. What was his background?'

'His background? There's not much to tell. He apprenticed as a silversmith as a young man, or perhaps it was as a jeweler; I'm not sure. In any case he couldn't make a go of it, so in the thirties he became a dealer in fine antiques, a successful one, with clients in Paris and even outside the country. He also earned some income as an appraiser. Everything I know about the antiques market I learned from him.'

'He was never a barber?' I said, feeling like an idiot before the words were out of my mouth.

'A barber? No. Where did you get that idea?' A chuckle rolled from the barrel of his chest. 'A barber.'

'It doesn't matter. It's not important.'

That's what I said, but it wasn't the truth. Not to him, it didn't matter, but it did to me. It really stung me to think that Lily had invented the barber story out of whole cloth, that she'd stuck to it for going on twenty years and had never once broken down and told me that it was made up. Considering all the other evasions and untruths I'd been digging up, you'd think that finding out about another one wouldn't have been any big deal, but it was. I just wouldn't have believed she'd be able to do that, to bring it off so coolly, to take me in so completely for so long. Aside from everything else, I was beginning to feel like a sap. I knew Louis had a point about my tending to accept things at face value, but Jesus, was I really as dim-witted as that?

'Well, I think that's everything,' Lebrun said with a happy air of wrapping things up. 'And now, perhaps . . .'

'Did you work with him in France too?' I asked, to keep him going.

'No, in France I was an official in city government. But the Occupation made a big mess for everybody, and afterward, when things settled down, the two of us ended up here in Barcelona. Marcel first opened a small shop not far from here, but it wasn't successful. He knew antiques inside out, and he could be the most charming of men when he chose to be, but he had no patience with people, you see. To do business with him, a person had to know exactly what he was looking for and how much he was willing to pay. No small talk, no bargaining. That was all right in France, but not here in Spain. Me, I know about negotiating, about buttering up customers, but what did I know about coins, and silver, and jewelry? Well, I remembered him from Veaudry, of course, and I suggested we get together. Since then . . . well, look around you.' He puffed up a little more.

What I saw around me was a mess, but I couldn't deny that it seemed like a thriving operation. 'It's very impressive,' I said.

Mrs Aguilar came in carrying a tray holding two demitasse cups of coffee and set them before us. There was a manila folder under her arm. 'Would you like milk or sugar?' she asked me kindly. 'A pastry?' I got the impression that she'd taken to me, as I had to her.

'No, thanks, this is fine.' I took a sip of the hot, thick brew and made an appreciative noise.

Lebrun was looking at the folder the way a nervous taxpayer looks at an audit notice from the IRS. 'What is that?'

'There are some problems with the invoices from Gottfried and Vilas,' she said to Lebrun in French, not Spanish, presumably as a courtesy to me so that I wouldn't think they were talking in secret.

His trepidation increased. 'What's wrong now, for God's sake?'

Leaning over his shoulder, she spread the manila folder open on his desk, and they went into intense, murmured conversation that I didn't follow. Lebrun was getting more upset. He snatched at forms, jabbed at scraps of paper with a pencil, thumped them with his blunt fingers, finally making a harried, explosive noise, scattering the papers with his hand. 'I don't know, I don't know! Can't it wait? Can't *you* deal with it?'

'If you want me to,' she said tranquilly, retrieving the papers as she spoke, 'but you usually prefer—'

'Then do it, for God's sake,' he cried. 'Do you have to come to me with every little thing? Don't I have enough on my mind as it is?' He waved helplessly at the chaos surrounding us.

Clearly, this kind of tantrum was also something Mrs Aguilar had been through before. 'Fine, I'll take care of it; I simply thought you should know,' she said, and waited while he drained his cup in two quick, grimacing swallows, head thrown back for each one, like a man downing a slug of rotgut rye.

'My God, I have to stop drinking this stuff,' he said, gasping, with a hand pressed to his abdomen. 'My stomach . . .'

Mrs Aguilar looked at him, eyes narrowed and lips compressed in a way that would have done Miss Doyle proud. 'It might help if you followed your doctor's instructions,' she said.

'Him, what does he know?' Lebrun said, still making a face. 'Oh, hell, wait a minute,' he called wearily after her as she began to leave. 'I'll take care of it, I'll take care of it. Show me what we have from the Vilas consignment. Excuse me, Mr Simon.'

I heard him ranting some more and slamming metal file drawers for a minute or two and then he returned, rolling his eyes as he fell back into his chair. 'This business. You have no idea. I can't understand why I don't have two ulcers. Probably I do. With Marcel gone it's nothing but one lousy headache after another. I don't know why I keep on with it. And now, if there's nothing else . . .' He looked encouragingly down at my cup, urging me with his eyes to finish and be gone.

But I had a feeling that I was getting close to something and I didn't want to leave yet. 'Mr Lebrun, if you have any idea at all why Lily and her father didn't get along, I'd really appreciate hearing it. Even a guess. Please. I've come all the way from New York.'

He inflated his cheeks – he might have had an apple in each one and slowly let the air out. 'Well, if you want the truth,' he said uneasily, 'Marcel and Odile – Lily's mother – were not what you'd call a happy couple. Marcel had a roving eye in those days, if you take my meaning. It made for strife in the household. Odile wasn't one to turn the other cheek. And back then he used to gamble too. Cards, racetracks. He made a good income, but they were always in debt, always running from the butcher, the grocer, the landlord. Maybe that was it.'

'Maybe,' I said, but of course it wasn't. Sure, it might explain why Vercier wasn't at the top of Lily's list of favorite people, but not the rest of it. Not the near-hysterics, and certainly not the pulling away from me, the running off to God knew where for God knew how long.

Lebrun stood up. 'Truly, that's all I can think of, and now I must get back to work.'

I got up as well, not seeing any choice, but gave it one more stab. 'Sir, what do you *think* was on that film?'

'I told you, I don't—'

'I know you don't. But you said you asked him a hundred times. Didn't he ever say anything at all?'

He started to say no, but then, with obvious misgiving, changed his mind. 'Yes, once,' he said gravely. 'A single word. "Security." '

'Security?'

Lebrun nodded sadly. 'That's what he said. "Security." '

'What do you think he meant?'

He hesitated, aimlessly shifting some of the clutter on his desk and then, to my surprise, he sank back into his chair. I sat as well, but I was on the edge of my seat. *Here it comes*, I thought. *Whatever it is*.

'I may as well tell you,' he said, toying with the pencil, no longer looking at me. 'At the end of the war, there was some . . . trouble with the Liberation authorities – the so-called authorities. Ever since then, he was afraid they would find some way to come after him, even here in Spain. And I believe Marcel thought this precious film of his would defend him against that.' He looked keenly at me. 'You know what I'm talking about, I think?'

'No, I don't.' But I had a pretty good inkling, and it stopped my breath.

'Marcel had enemies back home, you see – he was never an easy man to like – and when Liberation came, certain . . . accusations were made against him.' He shrugged. 'But you have to understand, the Occupation had lasted five years . . . *five years*! Marcel was not the only person who found it necessary to do business with the Germans so that his family could survive.'

'A collaborator,' I breathed, more to myself than to Lebrun. *Marcel Vercier was a collaborator*.

Chapter Nine

I CAN'T SAY it came as a shock. It had been in my mind as a possibility from the start, and hearing it confirmed now by Lebrun was more reassuring than anything else. Without my quite knowing it, a part of me had been hoping all along that this was what it was about. I'd feared something worse, something even darker, something that involved Lily directly. But this was better, this explained everything. Of course, it was ridiculous of her to think her father's guilt was any reflection on her or that it could make any difference in the way I felt about her, for Christ's sake – ridiculous but completely understandable. That's the way people are.

Even now, almost two decades after the war, the French were still tearing at each other over who did what in the Occupation. Firm numbers will always be hard to come by, but it appears that in the purges that came after the Germans were driven out, Resistance tribunals had executed at least ten thousand of their countrymen, and pronounced death sentences *in absentia* on thousands of others that had fled. Many more thousands were sent to prison. It was, in many ways, the French Revolution all over again. Longtime neighbors denounced one another. Brothers denounced brothers to the justice tribunals, and did it gladly. Was it any wonder that Lily had preferred to think of her collaborationist father as dead all these years, or that her life had seemed to her to come apart at the seams the day he'd come back into it?

All the same, it was hard to accept her having been so uncertain of me that she'd pile lie on lie on lie to keep the truth away from me. Could she really think that I'd—

'Yes, a collaborator!' Lebrun shouted. 'To you, it's the worst word in the world, isn't it? A collaborator! A Quisling! Odious! Despicable! *You* would never do such a thing, would you?' His head had been withdrawn into his shoulders so that he seemed to have no neck. His face had turned purple in spots.

'I'm sorry,' I said, taken aback; I certainly didn't want the guy having apoplexy on me. 'I only meant—' But I didn't know what I'd meant. I'd been thinking about Lily anyway, not Vercier, and not the living hell that Occupied France must have been. 'All I—'

Lebrun steamrolled over me. 'You Americans,' he huffed, 'so righteous, so sanctimonious, oh, it's wonderful. But when was the last time foreign troops set foot uninvited on *your* soil? I'll tell you when – almost two hundred years ago. You've never lived under an occupier, and neither has your father, or your father's father; you don't know what you're talking about; you know nothing! You come over here, and you – and you—' He stopped, having run out either of words or of breath.

He'd gotten under my skin with that lip-curling 'you Americans,' but how could I argue with what he'd said? Vercier had been through it. So had Lebrun and millions of other Frenchmen. All I ever saw of the German military machine was from four miles up.

'Look, I wasn't making any moral observations. You're right, I wasn't there. I'm not condemning anyone.'

That seemed to calm him down. With his eyes closed he waved a hand, signifying the end of the tirade. 'Forgive me. I have strong feelings. We all do. It's only that—'

He collected himself a little more and took a slow, deep breath. The dark streaks of color faded from his face, leaving a few pink smears on his throat, like finger marks. 'What a strange thing it is when you think about it. What if he *had* been a barber? Would anyone have expected him to refuse to cut the hair of a Gestapo corporal who came to his shop? Of course not, unless he wanted to commit suicide. And if he'd been a grocer he would have sold cabbages and radishes to the Boches when they came to buy. The same if he owned a restaurant or ran a laundry. And no one would have criticized him for it. We all did it – what choice was there? You couldn't live without compromising.'

'Then why was he in trouble?'

'Why? Because Marcel sold antiques, fine antiques, not groceries. That was his crime. He sold them before the Occupation, and he sold them during the Occupation, and you don't sell sixteenth-century silver salt cellars to corporals, you sell them to colonels and generals. That was what was so unforgivable. He had to deal, not with the underlings, but with the military commandant of the entire region, even with the chief of the Gestapo. In the eyes of many people, that made him a collaborationist in a way that selling a bunch of carrots to a twenty-year-old private wouldn't have. But I ask you: what is the essential difference?'

'I don't know,' I said truthfully.

'And I ask you again, what choice did he have? When some sneering *Sturmbannführer* walked into his shop wanting to buy something, do you suppose he could just say, "Thank you very much for the honor, but no thank you, please take your business elsewhere," and go about his life? Can you honestly say that you would have done differently than he did?'

No, I couldn't honestly say that. I shook my head. 'And that's why he left France?'

'Yes. He ran from them, from his own people, from the French. Some of them were worse than the Nazis had been, more bloodthirsty. There was no way of knowing what might happen if they actually brought him to trial. You have no idea what it was like. People were using the Liberation as an excuse for settling old grudges, and tell me, who doesn't have enemies? A lot of innocent people went before the firing squads, you can take my word for that. All you had to do was to be suspected, and it was all over, goodbye to you. So when he heard they were after him he ran for the Spanish border, and I don't blame him.'

'And came to Barcelona.'

'Yes, as many others did too. I myself followed not long aft—' He clamped his mouth shut, but the words were already out.

'For the same reason?' I asked.

He stiffened. 'I was the supervisor of the records department in the municipal office, a responsible job that I'd worked hard to get. I'd been there for three years before the Occupation, and when the Germans came they let me keep my job. I was lucky; where else was I supposed to go? But now I had German bosses, and people who were less fortunate began to whisper about me. I don't blame them. I was far from what you would call well-paid, but others had nothing, and they held it against me. But what was I supposed to do, with a wife and child at home? I did my job the same as I had before, that's all. But when the Liberation came at last, there were threats. The atmosphere was poisoned; I thought it better to leave before they got around to putting me in front of a tribunal too.'

He glared at me, his inconsequential chin thrust out as far as it would go: *you want to make something out of it?* I had no doubt that his rendition of events was blatantly self-serving, but it wasn't Lebrun's record that had brought me here.

'The film,' I said. 'How could it possibly have protected him?'

'The—?' He simmered down when he saw that I wasn't interested in what he had or hadn't done during the Occupation. 'Who knows? Maybe it contained something that implicated someone of importance, perhaps even someone in the government—'

'Implicated how?'

'How should I know that? Maybe it recorded an illegal transaction of some kind, an unlawful deal, a conversation with a known criminal; maybe an affair with a minor or with the wife of someone else. It might be anything. And with it hidden safely away, Marcel could well say, "Renew the charges against me, come after me, extradite me – and I'll reveal what I know about you . . . and prove it." What do you think?'

'Mm.'

'Well, it would explain what he meant by "security," wouldn't it?'

'It would seem to, yes.'

'And it would certainly explain why someone might kill him to get it, don't you think so?'

'Yes, I guess it would at that.'

YES, IT WOULD, I thought, walking back to my hotel, but what it didn't explain was why Vercier had been so anxious to show it to Lily, and all I was interested in was things that might lead back to her. I didn't really give a damn about Vercier himself except insofar as he might help me get Lily back.

Still, coming to Barcelona had been worth it. At least now I had some idea of what was going on with her. Her unbending antipathy toward her father was finally comprehensible: he had been a traitor. That wasn't Lebrun's version, of course – according to him, Vercier (like himself) had been a blameless victim of circumstances – but I suspected there was plenty more to it than what he'd said to me, and that, whatever it was, Lily had kept it locked up in her all these years, as if the crimes were hers. Guilt by association, by blood. And in her mind, she had long ago declared him dead and buried, something like the way my father's brother Sol had told him it was his solemn duty to declare me dead – not merely disowned, but literally, officially dead – when I brought Lily back from Europe, a Gentile girl, and married out of the faith. (Dad, in one of his finer moments, had told him to get lost.)

So when Vercier showed up in the flesh so many years later, the careful structure she'd built up for herself (and for me) – how he'd been a simple barber, how he'd been executed – had imploded; her world had come down around her ears. At first she'd tried putting me off, then she'd told me stories of how he'd abused her, but as events dragged on and Kovalski plodded along on the case she'd known that the truth was bound to come out and I would find out this worst of all things about her: that she was the daughter of that most vile of Frenchmen, a wretched turncoat who had collaborated with the hated Gestapo. And so she'd run away out of shame, and fear, and misplaced guilt.

Did that make sense, or had I been hanging around Louis too long? But even if it did, I realized unhappily, even if it gave me some much-needed insight into what was happening inside Lily's head, it didn't get me any closer to finding her. What if she didn't come back on her own? How would I locate her? Where should I go from here?

I got back to my room in a rotten frame of mind, which the hotel itself didn't help. The travel agent in Brooklyn had found it for me in his files. Hotel Carlota, the brochure had said. Inexpensive (true), clean (true, more or less), English spoken (true, sort of), and conveniently located only steps from Las Ramblas (well, yes; about eight hundred of them). But what it didn't say was that the windows looked out on a mean, smelly alley in which gaunt cats skulked among discarded junk and a few parked Vespas double-chained to iron railings, or that the rooms were 'lit' with twenty-five watt lightbulbs and furnished with a disreputable bed, a freestanding wardrobe, a cigarette-scarred round table, a single ashtray, and one wooden chair with a ratty cane seat, all enclosed by four walls coated with two kinds of equally nightmarish 'Oriental' wallpaper. All it needed to be a credible place for a couple of gangsters on the lam was a half-empty bottle of booze and some shot glasses on the table and two holstered guns slung over the backs of the chairs. Bathroom down the hall, of course, and up three dark steps, and around the corner.

Feeling lower than I had since the day she'd left, and worn out as well, I tossed my coat over a chair and fell on my back onto the bed, planning to spend the next half hour feeling sorry for myself, for which the room provided the perfect backdrop. But I fell asleep instead, and, to my surprise, slept heavily for almost four hours, waking up in the same position in which I'd lain down. I sat up feeling a little groggy but better for having slept, and the first thing I did when my brain was functioning again was to figure out the time in New York. It was three-twenty in the afternoon here, which made it nine-twenty in the morning there, and that meant I could call the Gianinis to see if there'd been any mail from Lily, if the delivery had been on the early side.

Calling New York from Spain is no simple affair if you don't speak Spanish, but fortunately the clerk at the long-distance telephone booth in the post office down the block was a helpful, long-suffering type, and eventually I got through, doing my best to keep a sudden, irrational surge of optimism in check. There would be something from her; I could feel it.

Nada, as they say over here. Mary Gianini, who answered the phone, went through the mail item by item: telephone bill, postcard from an aunt in Florida, cookbook for Lily from *Life*, two packets from Brooklyn College, a letter from an acquaintance in the Bronx. I had her open and read the one from the Bronx, just in case, but no go.

That put me right back down in the dumps, and with my tail dragging I stopped at a café right around the comer.

'*Café, por favor*,' I mumbled; another of the essential little phrases I could handle in a lot of languages.

It was a gray, cold day, but the only available table was outside, so that was where I sat, slumped deep into my overcoat, my hands thrust into the pockets, my feet up on the rim of a stone planter, wondering what to do next. Because I'd left a few extra days in my itinerary in case I stumbled on something that needed following up, my flight back to New York wasn't until Thursday, three days from now. But of course there wasn't anything to follow up, and as soon as I'd had my coffee and gotten a little energy back I planned to head over to the España ticket office on Las Ramblas to see if I could fly home tomorrow instead.

What I'd do when I got there I wasn't sure, but I knew I'd damn well rather do it in my own house than at the Hotel Carlota. At the very least, knowing what I now knew, I could think about how best to approach Lily once I was able to talk to her again. I understood now what was at the root of her fears, and surely I could make her see – it might take time, but I could make her see – that her father's behavior, no matter how heinous, had nothing to do with *her* and less than nothing to do with us. I loved her more than ever, there wasn't any doubt about that, and I was equally certain – well, almost – that she felt the same about me; it was impossible that she didn't. Given all that, how could things that had happened twenty years ago, involving other people during a calamitous and aberrant time, damage what she and I had built together? No, I was absolutely confident I could help her see that she was the same terrific person she'd always been, that being a rat wasn't something you carried in your genes, and that nothing had really changed.

There was only one thing missing in this hopeful little script, and that was Lily. Was I ever going to get the chance to tell her these things?

Only gradually did I become aware that the fingers of my right hand, deep in my pocket, had been worrying the corners of a folded sheet of paper, something I was positive hadn't been there when I'd started out that morning. When I took it out and unfolded it, I found four typewritten lines in English, centered on the page.

If you like to learn the truth about Marcel Vercier, you should go to Veaudry and examine at the city hall the record of his trial 11 September 1944 by the People's Justice Tribunal of the Comité Départemental de Libération. Good luck to find your wife.

The waiter set the coffee down at my elbow, but I sat unmoving, staring at the message. It had to be from Mrs Aguilar, Lebrun's assistant; there wasn't much question about that. Who else even knew I was there? Clearly, she had overheard – or listened in on – my session with Lebrun and slipped the note into my coat while I was in with him. But why would she be interested in this? And what was she telling me? According to Lebrun, Vercier had never been tried; he had fled before they got to him. So what was this about a justice tribunal? Had he been tried or not? And why would Mrs Aguilar care whether or not I knew about it? That last sentence, 'Good luck to find your wife' – didn't that imply that there might be a connection to Lily? Why else would she tack it on?

I downed my coffee, paid, and headed for the España office full of welcome new energy fueled by a dose of caffeine and an even more welcome sense of purpose. I was still in the dark, but maybe I was closing in on something. Moreover, I now knew where I was heading next, and it wasn't back to Bensonhurst.

Chapter Ten

VEAUDRY, FRANCE, MY wife's birthplace and the scene of her growing up, lies on the eastern outskirts of Paris. Within easy commuting distance, not much more than thirty minutes by rail from the Gare de l'Est, it hardly seems to be in the same universe as the City of Light. Workaday and nondescript, it is one of the anonymous gray villages that dot northern France. (The pretty ones in the travel books are mostly in the south.) Remember the newsreels of Allied tanks grinding their way over those plain, gray, war-scarred village streets as the Germans retreated? Well, then you know what Veaudry looks like.

No more war-scarring to speak of, but even so no one could call the place high on charm; a cluster of unprettified streets surrounding a central square, the predictably named Place de la République, with the railroad station and the town's one hotel on one side and most of the usual mom-and-pop business enterprises around the other three, and small cafés and restaurants on the streets leading away from the square. The buildings, three stories high at most, are typically mudgray stucco, with a few of the fancier ones decorated with scalloped corner edgings of once-red (now dried-blood-brown) brick.

When I got off the train from Paris at two-thirty Tuesday afternoon, the dismal gray rain that had been falling all morning was turning to sleet, stinging my face and soaking my hair (Lily had always been the one to remind me to pack a hat when I traveled). I humped my suitcase over to the modest Hôtel Mercure next to the station. Not stopping to unpack or to eat lunch, I asked the hotel clerk where the city hall was, and made straight for it across the cobblestoned square (the place of Marcel Vercier's nonexecution, no doubt).

GULP.

That was the response of the teenage clerk when I stepped up to the counter and politely asked to see the record of the trial of Marcel Vercier before the regional justice tribunal on 11 September, 1944. Followed by:

'I'm not supposed to . . . I'll have to get the supervisor.'

And off she ran through a door at the rear of the room, to return a few seconds later trailing a tall, pale, stooped man with hangdog features and a patently distrustful air. 'I am Mr Roche,' he said, drawing out the words. 'I am the head clerk. You wish to see the file of Marcel Vercier?'

For a moment I thought I was back in some new variation of the Dream, because this guy reminded me of nothing so much as one of those characters in pince-nez, rusty black suits, and wing collars, the petty bureaucrats or whatever they were who regularly came trooping out from behind some building or other, wringing their hands, or muttering to one another, or banging their pots. There weren't any pots or pans in sight, and he wasn't wearing a wing collar, but his close-fitting three-button suit was black, all right, and the round wire-rimmed spectacles sitting on his nose were most assuredly pince-nez, something you didn't see every day.

'Ah . . . yes,' I said, hardly able to stop staring at him, 'the file of Marcel Vercier.'

'Why?'

'Well, because . . . isn't it public information?'

He scowled, not much liking the question. 'That's not the point. Are you a relation?'

'No.' Well, sure, I guess I was Vercier's son-in-law, but I didn't feel as if I was, and I wasn't anxious to claim him as a relative. Besides, this character out of my dream had hardly won my goodwill thus far, and I didn't see how it was any of his business.

He sniffed. 'Do you have a valid reason for seeing it?'

Did I ever. 'Yes, I do.'

He waited for more, but I didn't say anything.

'It can't be taken from the room, you understand.'

'All right.' It occurred to me that Roche now held the position that Charles Lebrun had been in during the Occupation: supervisor at the city offices.

'It must be read here, in the presence of the clerks, you understand that?'

'Okay.'

'And you'll be required to sign for it.'

'Fine.' I was certain Roche was pulling things out of his hat. Why, I didn't know.

From under the counter he brought up a ledger, the open page of which had signatures going back six months, then slid over a tray with a built-in inkwell and a stained, cork-handled pen.

'Pierre Simon,' I wrote, and slid the ledger over to him.

He slid it right back, tapping the column next to my signature. 'The date, the date.'

I complied. Mr Roche turned the ledger around and leaned close to the page to peer at my entry. A few yards away, at the other end of the counter, a rangy, weather-beaten man in a grease-stained blue workman's smock, who had been engaged in a whispered, heated argument with another clerk, had stopped in order to gape at us instead.

'Very well,' Roche said grudgingly, apparently unable to come up with any more excuses to put me off. 'You may use the table over there. The young lady will bring the material to you.'

Now what the hell had that been about, I wondered as I sat at one of two library tables in the room, joining a bespectacled, elderly man who was meticulously making notes in the margin of a complex permit of some kind, stopping after every jotting to touch the point of his pencil stub to his tongue. Was Roche giving me in particular a hard time, or was this just one more example of the famous attitude of the French civil servant toward one and all?

When the file came I was surprised at how little there was to it – just four or five pages neatly bound to a brown cardboard folder with a metal fastener. The cover sheet was of cheap, thick paper, no letterhead, and it got to the point in a hurry.

Having been duly tried this day in absentia *on charges of (1) collu-*

sion with a foreign power for the purpose of assisting the acts of that power against France and for his own profit, (2) trafficking in stolen objects, and (3) engaging of his own will in other criminal activities damaging to the welfare of the community and the nation in its time of need, Marcel Vercier, 47, of rue Weller 149, is hereby adjudged guilty of treason and sentenced to death in a manner to be determined at such time as his apprehension may be achieved.

Judgment determined this eleventh day of September 1944, at the Veaudry Palace of Justice, by the People's Tribunal of Veaudry, under authority conferred by the Seine-et-Marne Committee of Liberation.

Antoine Donnadieu, COLONEL, FTP, PRESIDING MEMBER
Claude Goujon, MAJOR, FTP, MEMBER
Henri Lefebvre, CAPTAIN, FTP, MEMBER
Jean-Claude Ribeau, LIEUTENANT, FTP, MEMBER
Robert Lienne, CORPORAL, FTP, MEMBER

Whew. This was just a little different from the story Lebrun had fed me. Clearly, Vercier had done more than sell a picture or two to a German bigwig. And he'd not only been *accused* of collaborating, he'd been tried for it; tried and sentenced to death. My first reaction was anger at Lebrun for misleading me, but then I realized that I hadn't necessarily been lied to by him. If he had left France before the trial he wouldn't have been aware of it. For all I knew, Vercier himself hadn't known of it. After all, it had been conducted in his absence.

But obviously Mrs Aguilar had known. I wondered why that was, and how much else she knew about Vercier. It was beginning to look as if I'd spent my time with the wrong person in Barcelona.

There was something else at the bottom of the cover sheet. Opposite the signatures and just below the round, embossed seal of the commune of Veaudry, slantwise across the page, was a box in which two fragmentary sentences were stamped in uppercase blue letters:

SENTENCE ANNULLED, GENERAL AMNESTY LAW OF 1953. CASE CLOSED 28 JULY 1953 BY ORDER OF THE COMMISSIONER OF THE REPLUBLIC FOR THE DEPARTMENT OF SEINE-ET-MARNE.

Thoughtfully, I ran my fingers over the pale-blue ink. *Case closed.* Yes, that would be right. The French had passed their first amnesty act in 1953 in an effort to heal the festering lesions that had been produced by the Occupation. As of 24 July, 1953, the purge was declared over. Except for those who had committed the most atrocious offenses – the torturers and murderers, the denouncers of partisans, the vermin who had put on the Nazi-supplied uniforms of the despised Milice, the volunteer French militia that eagerly helped the Gestapo in their bloody work – except for these most vile of traitors, those still in prison were released; those convicted *in absentia* were pardoned; those not yet tried had their cases taken off the books. Marcel Vercier was technically no longer under sentence of death.

But 'technically' and 'actually' weren't necessarily the same. I looked again at the names of the judges that had tried him. Antoine Donnadieu, Colonel, FTP; Claude Goujon, Major, FTP . . . all of them were officers of the FTP. This was an organization I knew a little about: the Francs-Tireurs et Partisans. Literally, the name meant Irregulars and Guerrillas, and it was one of the many Resistance outfits that fought the Nazis during the Occupation. More a loosely knit, frequently squabbling association of local fighting units than a single entity, it was nevertheless dedicated, resourceful, and daring, and a source of great concern to the Nazis, who did their best to exterminate it. I had two barely remembered cousins in Lyon who had joined up in 1943. Alfred made it safely through and became a bookbinder after the war. Armand never became anything. As we learned later, he had thrown himself headfirst out of a second-story window after being arrested by the Gestapo, to avoid giving away the names of compatriots under torture. He'd been my age at the time: seventeen.

Although it had originally been organized by French Communists before the war and had been considered by many (my father, for instance) to be an outlaw mob of anarchists, by the end of the Occupation the FTP banner had flown over Jewish refugees, anti-Fascist Italian migrant workers, young Frenchmen who preferred to fight rather than accept deportation to forced labor in Germany, and French men and women of every stripe who chose to fight the Nazis on their own after their government, under Pétain, had chosen to collaborate.

With the coming of the Liberation, the FTP, like other resistance groups, took it on itself to organize *ad hoc* tribunals that tried accused collaborators in a sort of twilight zone between frontier justice and blood revenge. Sometimes there were defense attorneys, sometimes not. Few trials took more than a day, there were no appeals, and when the sentence was death the defendant was usually shot the following morning. Once de Gaulle's new provisional government moved from Algiers to Paris and took firm control of the country, these seat-of-the-pants tribunals were replaced by more orderly courts of law, but that time hadn't yet arrived in September 1944, and the early justice that was meted out was a rough justice indeed. Neither the people's tribunals nor the FTP itself was inclined to forgive and forget. There had been a lot of suffering under the Occupation.

So wasn't it at least possible that Vercier's murder in New York had been the carrying out of that nineteen-year-old sentence of execution by parties who chose not to be bound by the amnesty law? 'Death in a manner to be determined at such time as his apprehension may be achieved,' the formal sentence had read. Who was to say that didn't include death by pipe and baseball bat?

But if so, it raised other questions. Where, for example, did the film figure into it? And why would they choose to kill him in New York when they'd had him practically on their own doorstep in Barcelona all this time, where they would surely have found it easier to arrange his murder? No, the idea didn't seem to hold water. Still, it was something to tuck away, and certainly something to tell Kovalski about.

I turned to the next page, a photostated sheet in German. I couldn't even make it all the way through the letterhead and turned more pages in hopes of a translation, but there were two more sheets in German, one of them an itemization of some kind, and then, I was relieved to see, a page-by-page translation.

THE MILITARY COMMANDER IN BELGIUM AND NORTHERN FRANCE

BUREAU: WORK GROUP NORTHERN FRANCE

19 November 1943

To: The Military Commander in Belgium and Northern France
Head of Military Administration
Bureau: Enemy Property Accounts
Section: Expenditures
To the Hands of Deputy Registrar Dr v. Zeitz

Dear Deputy Registrar!

This office requests your authorization of the allotment of 50,200 francs to be paid to Marcel Vercier of Veaudry, antiques dealer, who has rendered us many services, particularly in regard to the identification, evaluation, and seizure of objects in the hands of Jews and other undesirables. The man Vercier has already been paid 85,000 francs of the 135,200 francs owed him, as previously approved by you. He is now owed the remainder, 50,200 francs, as is shown in the following records. I remind you with respect that prompt payment is always advisable in matters of this kind, although it is my belief that Vercier is rendering his services out of genuine allegiance to the cause of National Socialism, and not merely from a desire for selfish gain.

Heil Hitler!
(Nazi stamp) (Signature)

Well, so much for any lingering thought that Vercier had somehow been railroaded by the tribunal, à la Lebrun's sanitized rendition, and as if it wasn't already bad enough, things got worse on the next page, an itemized account of just what services Vercier had provided during the previous three months and what he was paid for them.

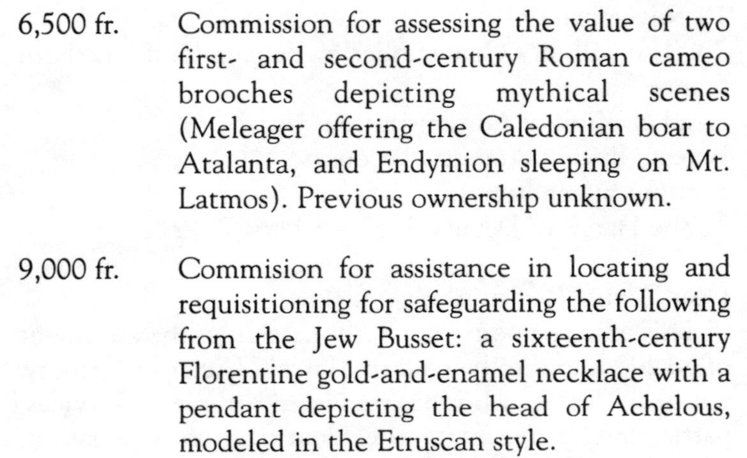

6,500 fr. Commission for assessing the value of two first- and second-century Roman cameo brooches depicting mythical scenes (Meleager offering the Caledonian boar to Atalanta, and Endymion sleeping on Mt. Latmos). Previous ownership unknown.

9,000 fr. Commision for assistance in locating and requisitioning for safeguarding the following from the Jew Busset: a sixteenth-century Florentine gold-and-enamel necklace with a pendant depicting the head of Achelous, modeled in the Etruscan style.

12,100 fr. Commission for assistance in locating and requisitioning for safeguarding the following from the Jewess Denier: a mounted set of three very fine Greek coins from the fifth century B.C., comprising Syracusan decadrachms bearing on their obverse the heads of Mithradates VI of Pontus, Hieron the Tyrant, and the nymph Arethusa. All are signed in relief by the engraver Eukleidas.

I glanced at the rest of the list, then shut the file with something close to a shudder. The itemizing had gone on, a total of seven entries for which he was owed money for his assistance – 'a rowel spur reputedly from the field at Agincourt,' 'an Elizabethan silver-mounted agate tea set,' and so on. All pretty much the same thing; all pretty damning. Well, maybe not the first one, if you wanted to give him the benefit of the doubt; the Germans had paid Vercier

6,500 francs to evaluate three cameos, 'previous ownership unknown.' On the one hand, as Lebrun had pointed out, how much choice would he have had? He was an appraiser. When a Nazi officer came to him with work, and well-paid work at that, was he supposed to tell him to take a walk? Giving him the benefit of the doubt, then, one could say he had only been doing what everyone else had been doing: trying to get along and do the best he could under difficult circumstances.

On the other hand, there was no way he could have failed to understand that these were plundered possessions he was helping out with – what else was 'previous ownership unknown' supposed to mean when applied to art objects in the possession of the German military in the middle of Occupied France in 1943? I'd heard a lot of different things about Vercier, but never that he was stupid.

In any case, when it came to the other eight entries, there wasn't any doubt to give him the benefit of. To anyone at all familiar with what had gone on during the Occupation, his 'assistance in locating and requisitioning' various objects, particularly from Jews, meant that Vercier had joined those other French art and antiques dealers – not a majority, but by no means a tiny minority either – who, to the shame of their country, had crawled out from under their rocks and voluntarily offered to tell the Nazis where Jews and other undesirables had hidden their belongings. For a commission, of course; anywhere from ten to twenty-five percent of the value of the items that were recovered.

This the Nazis were more than happy to fork over, inasmuch as it was their only cost, the Jewish owners being owed nothing at all. Since they were among the groups technically classified as *Untermenschen*, subhumans, Jews were in no position to make legal claim to their own property (only human beings were capable of owning property; anyone could see the logic of that). So, having been given advance information as to where some particular artworks had been hidden, all the Gestapo had to do was to barge in and carry them off. Pardon me, requisition them for safeguarding. All perfectly legal, and with no possibility of recourse available to the victims, most of whom knew better than to object anyway.

I sat staring at the closed file for a minute, not quite willing to open it again yet, and surprised myself with a prolonged, jawstretching yawn, no doubt a tension release. My shoulder muscles had tightened up somewhere along the line, and I shut my eyes and rolled my head around to relax them. Reading this stuff had given me a neck ache, but at least it was a lot easier now to understand why Lily had never told me the truth about her father. In her place I probably would have buried him and everything about him too.

When I opened my eyes I saw that the man in the grease-stained smock who'd been at the counter had taken a chair at my table, directly across from me and not four feet away. Actually, I smelled him before I saw him: gasoline, grease, oil. With a cigarette dangling from the corner of his mouth, he was staring at me with avid, unwavering intensity, not even pretending to be doing anything else. (Watching me do what? Read? Yawn?) Great, I thought, the town nut has taken a personal interest in me.

No, not the town nut. That was animosity in those eyes, not craziness. For whatever reason, he'd decided he didn't like me. Pinioned by the steady glare, I wasn't too crazy about him either. Veaudry, I was beginning to think, was not the friendliest town in the world.

I scowled at him, which had the expected effect (none), pointedly moved my chair a little so that at least I wasn't facing him directly, and opened the folder again. My fingers seemed actually to shrink from it, as if I were touching something putrid, but I made myself turn to the final two pages anyway, with a sense of dread that turned out to be well founded.

First there was a translated memorandum from one Nazi bureaucrat to another proudly reporting that Field Marshal Goering himself had complimented them on the acquisition of the 'superb set of Greek coins' (the one previously 'requisitioned,' with Vercier's able assistance, 'from the Jewess Denier'), which Goering, collector that he was, had purchased after several intermediate negotiations within the Nazi hierarchy, and with which he was supremely pleased. Vercier himself was commended by name.

But it was the final page that was worst of all, the frosting on the cake, so to speak: a copy of a handwritten letter in French from Marcel Vercier to a Polizeimajor vom Steeg.

Dear Major vom Steeg,

On 29 May you were kind enough to ask me to examine a most interesting gold-and-enamel art object at your home in Bobigny. I was deeply flattered by this display of confidence and visited your beautiful home on 1 and 3 June, when I conducted a thorough analysis of the object. It is my great pleasure to tell you that in my considered professional judgment, this piece can confidently be attributed to Hans Mülich, who was at one time goldsmith at the court of Duke Albrecht V. The object in question is almost certainly one of a set of two book covers (the whereabouts of the other is unknown) executed to the order of Anton Fugger of Augsburg in 1555 and depicts the Fountain of Youth and the Creation of Eve. Permit me to congratulate you, sir, on the acquisition of this superb piece and on its rightful return to the Fatherland.

I look forward to the continuation of our mutual esteem and our very amiable association and hope to contact you very soon concerning the location of certain other art objects in which I am sure you will be interested.

In hopes of soon seeing you again, accept, sir, the assurance of my marked admiration and good wishes.

Marcel Vercier

I shut the file again, this time with a full-fledged shudder that crawled from the base of my skull to the base of my spine. I don't really know why Vercier's toadying should have made what he'd done even worse, but it did. Plenty of other Frenchmen had had to associate with the Nazis out of what they perceived as necessity, or fear, or even conviction, but they didn't go burbling on about mutual esteem and marked admiration, or openly lick their chops over the prospect of future dirty business. What loathsome creeps human beings could be when they got the chance. No wonder Lily had slammed the door in the bastard's face, sick old man or not.

According to the wall clock it was ten minutes after four, so I'd been at it for only an hour, but it felt as if I'd been cooped up with that odious file for days. I turned it in at the counter, looking over my shoulder to see that the man who had been observing me so closely was gone, then walked back to my hotel and put in another call to the Gianinis in New York from the telephone in the lobby to see if there'd been anything from Lily. The news was the same as before: nothing.

Once upstairs, I got out of my clothes and into a bathrobe, flip-flopped down the hall in slippers to the bathroom, and stood under the shower spray, as hot as I could make it, until the hot water heater suspended over the tub gave out (a whole six minutes). That made me feel somewhat cleansed, and while I was toweling off and changing clothes in my room, I thought about what I'd learned.

Plenty, but unfortunately not much in terms of what I'd hoped for. I now knew the score on Vercier, even had a good notion as to why he'd been killed, and I sure understood why Lily had reacted to him so violently. But as for the important things – finding some clue as to where she might be, or where to look next – I was no closer than I'd been when I'd left Barcelona. Or when I'd left New York, for that matter.

I was at my second dead end in two days.

Chapter Eleven

I WAS ALSO ravenous, having had only coffee and a *churro*, a deep-fried Spanish breakfast pastry of no known nutritional value, at a bar on the way to the Barcelona airport that morning, and having forgotten altogether about lunch. Reading Vercier's file had effectively killed my appetite for the time being, but now it was lustily, demandingly back, and I went downstairs in search of a restaurant. It was one of the glories of France, in my opinion, that even in a place like Veaudry, even in a hole-in-the wall eatery in some back alley, you had a better than fifty-fifty chance of getting a really fine meal, or at least of not getting an awful one.

As I stepped out onto the pavement in front of the hotel, turning my collar up against what had turned into a freezing rain, my eye was caught by a familiar and unwelcome face among a group of men lounging at the counter of a tobacco shop across the street. It was the grim, intense, weather-beaten guy who'd been so fascinated by me at city hall. Was I getting paranoid, or had he been there watching the door of the hotel, waiting for me to come out?

My route to the street where most of the restaurants were clustered took me past the shop, and I gave him a hard look through the TABAC sign on the window just to let him know I was aware of what he was up to, whatever it was, and he wasn't getting away with anything. He stared stolidly back, swiveling his head to follow me, and when I glanced back over my shoulder as I turned the corner I saw that he had left the shop and was keeping pace with me, across the street and a little behind. Well, if nothing else it was nice to know I wasn't paranoid.

I kept walking and he soon crossed the street diagonally and came abreast on my right, long-armed and sinewy, redolent with his automechanic smells. Like me he was hatless; he was more solidly built and taller than I'd realized, a couple of inches more than my five-eleven. He was younger than I'd thought too. In the city hall I'd taken him for about fifty; now I saw that he was only about my age. Close up his long face was all flat planes and angles, like something carved out of hardwood. Coarse, dark hair, long, crooked, broken nose, a grim cleft of a mouth with an old scar hooking from one corner of it, through a two-day growth of wiry beard, to the lobe of his right ear, or the place where the lobe would have been if he'd still had one. This guy was a rough customer.

'How are things going, my friend?' he asked in French.

The 'my friend' was patently *pro forma*. He had about as much interest in being *mon ami* as I did in being his. And what a voice; a strange, papery, insinuating whisper that made the hair on the back of my neck stand up. I had an image of dead grasshopper husks blowing over a wooden porch.

'Fine, thank you,' I said, 'and with you?' I kept on walking.

'So-so.' We continued on a few steps with him matching my stride. But as we approached a wine café he bumped my arm with a knuckle. I guess I was edgier than I realized, because to my embarrassment it made me jump.

'Come in, I'll buy you a drink,' he said.

'That's nice of you,' I said, 'but why?'

'You're a stranger. We like to be hospitable here in Veaudry.'

After a moment's hesitation I motioned to him to lead the way. Sure, it was clear enough that he had something besides simple hospitality on his mind, but on thinking it over I couldn't see much reason to be nervous. If he had anything nasty in mind, he'd hardly have chosen the Café Grand Luxe. There wasn't anything remotely sinister about this laughably named place, a noisy, no-frills, warehouselike bar (*sans prétentions*, as the French like to say) of the kind you might see in any working-class village, with house wines served from a couple of barrels set up on trestles (takeout service available provided you brought your own jar) and a few aperitif and brandy bottles on a rack above them. There were a dozen or so mismatched tables for customers, most of them occupied either by exhausted-looking laborers in their blue denim work jackets or, in a few cases, by men in conservative dark suits – bank clerks, perhaps, or civil servants – mostly middle-aged or older, and all enjoying their glass or two of *vin ordinaire* before heading home to dinner and family. Not a woman in the house, but that was standard for this kind of place.

I did see one face I recognized: the hangdog visage of Monsieur Roche, the guy who'd given me the hard time over Vercier's file. Oddly enough, his presence made me feel easier too. If the head clerk from city hall was there, how nefarious could things get? And above all, I was interested. If this bird wanted to talk to me about Marcel Vercier (and what else could it be?), fine; I wanted to talk to him too.

He led me through a dense fog of sweat and hanging ribbons of smoke – if there was anyone in the place without a lit cigarette jiggling between his lips, I didn't see him – to a small table with three chairs drawn up to it, on one of which sat an elderly man, well over eighty – possibly over ninety – one of the few in suit and tie, with a glass of cognac in front of him.

'Sit down, please,' the old man said, gesturing to the chair opposite his. In appearance he was pretty far along toward ultimate decrepitude, flaccid and sack-shaped, with a liver-spotted skull on the crown of which sat a silly orange toupee (for the first time I really understood why they call them 'rugs'), thick tortoiseshell glasses, and gnarled, crabbed hands with a steady slow tremble. Wattles hid the rim of his collar on either side. But when he spoke it was with a crackling, unmistakable air of authority. Command presence, we used to call it in the Air Force. Whatever was going on, he was the one running the show. I sat down on the chair he'd pointed to. My new 'friend' took the remaining one.

'A glass of wine?' the old man asked me. 'Cognac?' I have to amend what I said a moment ago: he had no cigarette in sight.

'Coffee, I think.' What I could have used was a sandwich, but this wasn't the time.

He nodded brusquely and got down to business. 'If you don't mind, I should like to know the nature of your interest in Marcel Vercier.'

I didn't mind telling him why I was there, but at the same time I didn't appreciate being shanghaied and then interrogated in semi-military fashion without explanation. It seemed to me a small display of independence was in order. 'If you don't mind, I'd like to know what concern it is of yours.'

His bottle-bottom lenses made it impossible to tell if he took offense. 'My name is Antoine Donnadieu,' he said, both of his hands resting on the table, motionless except for their unrelenting, slow palsy. 'And this' – he indicated the man in the smock – 'is Claude Goujon.' He let the names sink in. 'Do you know who we are?'

It took me a moment. 'You were members of the tribunal that tried Marcel Vercier.'

Donnadieu had been listed as an FTP colonel, I remembered. Goujon had been a major. If he was really my age, it meant that he'd been fighting the Nazis as an officer in the Resistance when he was sixteen or seventeen. It didn't make me feel any warmer toward him, but it sure made me respect him more. When I was sixteen, Morty Berger and I were still fooling around at the St George pool, trying to see down girls' cleavages.

'Colonel Donnadieu was the chairman,' Goujon said in his spooky voice, tugging a cigarette from a pack of Gitanes with his lips and jabbing a matchbook at me. 'And a goddamn good one.'

'I never said he wasn't.' I had no idea if he was perpetually angry at everyone, or if it was just me.

'It was a legitimate trial,' he said, slapping the table as if I were arguing the point. 'All the legalities were observed. Colonel Donnadieu knows the law. He was a regional prosecutor before the war and then a fine judge. He saw to it—'

'Thank you, Claude,' Donnadieu said, effectively cutting him off. It was interesting to note that eighteen years after the Occupation his onetime subordinate was still referring to him by his military title. It was also interesting that it didn't work both ways. 'So you see,' Donnadieu said to me, 'it's natural that we have a continuing interest. And now, may we know who you are?'

That seemed reasonable, and this being France, I told him my name was Pierre Simon, pronouncing it the French way. 'But I assume Mr Goujon has already told you that.' I figured that I might as well let him know that I hadn't been oblivious to Goujon at city hall.

It didn't seem to impress Donnadieu one way or the other, not that I was really able to tell. 'And you're what?' he asked. 'A writer? A lawyer?'

'No, I'm a history professor.'

Goujon uttered a malicious laugh. 'What did I tell you? I knew it as soon as I saw him.'

'Now wait, let's give him a chance,' said Donnadieu. 'It may not be what it seems.'

Ah. I understood now what this was all about. These were men who had suffered under the Germans and had fought them with what few weapons they had. They were worried that I might be one of the new wave of revisionists-writers, attorneys, academics – now poring through town records all over France, rewriting the history of the Occupation, tearing apart the mythical perception of unified, heroic resistance and replacing it with the no less mythical image of France as a nation of servile collaborators, in which all were equally compromised, all equally guilty.

The truth, it was becoming increasingly clear, was, as usual, somewhere in between. Only a small minority of the French – something like two percent – had been active members of the Resistance, but they had been supported by a huge informal network of sympathetic common people, people in every town and village who kept things to themselves, provided food, information, and shelter to the resisters, and hindered the Germans in whatever small ways they could, when they could get away with it. As for willing collaborators, they might also equal about two percent – not a small number by any means – but that was it; there was no great infrastructure of Nazi sympathizers to be found. To the average Frenchman, the Germans were there behind their guns and their threats, unwelcome and disliked. The essential heart of France, as one patriot writer had put it, had always been in the right place.

'Let me explain something,' I said to them. 'If I ever do come up with a reinterpretation of a war, it'll be . . . well, it'll probably be the War of the Three Henrys, 1585 to 1589, all right? As far as I'm concerned, if it's after 1815, it's somebody else's problem.'

That got a perfunctory one-note chuckle from Donnadieu. From the sullen Goujon, nothing.

'Then I ask again,' Donnadieu said, 'what brings you to Veaudry?' He inclined his head and turned the left side of his face toward me;

his good ear, I presumed.

Fair enough. Obviously, I hadn't won over Goujon (or vice versa), but I was ready to go along with the colonel. 'As you know, I'm trying to find out about Marcel Vercier. Now that he's dead—'

An exchange of glances jumped between them like an electric arc. 'What did you say?' Goujon whispered, squinting through the haze from his cigarette.

I sipped from the cup of black coffee that had appeared at my elbow, trying to size them up. There was a queasy feeling in my stomach; I didn't know if it was from hunger or from something else. Had they really not known about Vercier's death, or were they faking? I couldn't tell. Their surprise seemed genuine enough to me, but then you have to take into consideration my well-documented problem with seeing beneath the surface of things.

'He was killed,' I said. 'Murdered. In New York.'

Goujon started to say something, but Donnadieu shut him down with a wave of the hand.

'By whom?'

'The police don't know,' I said. *I wonder if you do.*

'And how do you come to know this?'

'I live in New York. He—'

Donnadieu's chin came up, Goujon's went down. 'New York?' Donnadieu repeated.

'Yes, I'm an American. My French is good because I was born in Lyon, but I was taken to New York when I was a kid, and I've lived there ever since.'

'You there – speak up, stop mumbling!' somebody off to the side shouted, and I realized that the scraping noises that had been going on since I'd sat down were the sounds of the other patrons hauling their chairs over, and in most cases their tables as well, for a better view. Now most of them were in close and straining forward, all ears. Obviously, I was the big attraction of the day in Veaudry. Maybe of the month.

'Forgive me, Mr Simon,' Donnadieu said, 'but there seems to be an element missing somewhere. I'm not sure I follow you.'

'I'm married to his daughter, Lily,' I said. 'I'm trying—'

But this created a wave of exclamations around the room, followed at once by heated conversations and even what sounded like arguments, so that an irritated Donnadieu had to rap on the table like the judge he once was. When it had quieted down sufficiently, he turned to me with a nod: the witness will continue.

I delivered a sketchy explanation, telling him – telling all thirty people or so, I should say – that I'd had no knowledge of Vercier's collaborationist history until an hour ago, that I'd believed until recently that he had been killed during the Occupation – I thought it better, given what I now knew, not to mention that I'd been under the impression that he'd died a hero – and that when he'd shown up at our home he had caused Lily tremendous agitation. I was trying to find out why.

'So why come here?' said Goujon. 'Why not ask your Lily?' The cigarette waggled between his lips in time with the words.

I glowered at him. For one thing I didn't care for the smart-mouthed way he'd said 'your Lily.' For another, I was getting tired of that particular question and I really didn't want to get into my personal life in front of all these strangers. On the other hand, I could understand that it was a reasonable thing to ask, and if I was hoping to get any help from them, I didn't see any way around it.

'Well, you see, I don't know where she is. She's, uh, run off somewhere.'

A knowing, drawn-out 'mmmmm' welled from the audience, followed by a buzz of Gallic, worldly, man-to-man observations: 'Ah, there you have it.' 'You see the way it is.' 'That's life for you.'

This, I thought, was getting increasingly weird. These cigarette-smoking, wine-guzzling, sandpaper-jawed Frenchmen sitting in a dingy bar in a little town in northern France were discussing me. I drank a little coffee, wondering how in the world I'd come to this, but continuing anyway. I had run out of leads to Lily, and I was hoping there might yet be something in this for me. 'I found out that Vercier had been a partner in a Barcelona antiques gallery, so that's where I started. I talked to his partner, a man named Lebrun.'

Donnadieu's eyebrows lifted. 'By any chance, would that be our old friend Charles Lebrun?' he asked, to the accompaniment of more buzzing from the surrounding tables. 'From Veaudry?'

'That's right, Charles Lebrun. He used to be—'

'Ah, we know who Charles Lebrun is, don't we, Claude?' Goujon angrily poured himself a second glass of red wine from a carafe. 'Yes, we know. Another ass-licking parasite who should have been shot when we had the chance.'

'Now, that's enough of that,' Donnadieu said. Every clipped sentence he uttered sounded as if it were being delivered in a command post on the front lines. 'Please, Mr Simon, go ahead.'

The rebuffed Goujon put his head down and jerked it like an angry bull, continuing to mutter wordlessly into his glass. Lebrun, it occurred to me, had been right about getting out of France while he still could. I didn't think Claude Goujon was kidding. If he'd had anything to say about it at the time, Charles Lebrun would have been executed, had he not run off to Spain before the trials started.

'Marcel Vercier was murdered, you said. . . ?' Donnadieu prompted.

'Beaten to death.'

'Good,' said Goujon. 'He got twenty years of living he didn't deserve, didn't he? I hope they made him suffer, the bastard.'

'He was also dying of cancer.'

'Wonderful. That makes me feel even better.'

'Claude!' Donnadieu said sharply.

Goujon grumbled some more and tossed off the rest of his wine. Almost two decades after the Occupation, I thought, and feelings still ran so deep. How must it have been in the early days, with the hated Germans on the run and ten thousand raw wounds to be avenged, ten thousand bereavements to be paid for?

'Well, then, I think we can consider that particular score settled, even if a bit late,' Donnadieu said. 'So, Mr Simon, do I understand that you heard about the trial when you were in Barcelona?'

'Yes.' I saw no reason to go into the business of the anonymous letter that I'd found in my pocket.

'And came here to Veaudry to look into it.'

'That's right.'

'I see.' He had been drinking his cognac extremely slowly. Now he took another minuscule sip, hardly enough to wet his lips. 'But, if I may return to my original question, why, exactly?'

'Well, I thought I explained—'

'No, you didn't.'

No, on second thought, I guessed I hadn't. 'Look, I'm trying to find out what's going on with my wife,' I said, uncomfortable with all those eyes on me, all those ears attuned to every word. I felt like a freak show exhibit at Coney Island: Pierre the Fish-Faced Boy Tells All. 'I don't know where she went – I'm not even sure why she went; I only know that it had something to do with her father, and I was hoping . . . I was hoping that if I could find out more about him, it might help me figure out where she is, or at least it might give me some understanding of what's going on in her mind . . . so I'd know what I ought to do, how I ought to act, when . . .' I clamped my jaws shut to stop babbling. I couldn't have felt more naked if I didn't have any clothes on.

'And now that you've found out more about him, has it helped you?' inquired Donnadieu with the same formal impassivity he'd shown from the beginning.

I sighed. 'Not much, I guess. Maybe a little, but— Wait a minute, there was one thing; when he came to New York, he had a film with him. He was anxious for her to see it, and I can't help thinking – hoping – there might be something there that would help. Do—'

'Film? What sort of film?' Donnadieu asked.

'Well, that's what I was about to ask you. All I know is, it was obviously important to him, and it was important to him for Lily to see it. Would you have any idea of what might have been on it?'

'No,' said Donnadieu.

The thought of telling them what Lebrun had suggested – that it might contain evidence of collusion on the part of some high-level official – crossed my mind but was quickly dismissed. For all I knew, the high-level official was Antoine Donnadieu.

The two men looked at each other, then at me, then shrugged. If they weren't genuinely ignorant of the film, and not very interested to boot, then they were giving a convincing imitation.

'If you're so interested in the way your wife's mind works . . .' Goujon said, and now there was something about the way he said 'your wife,' a knowing, hard-to-pin-down nuance that made my ears prick. It suddenly occurred to me that he might very well have known her, known her quite well, in fact; a thought I found instinctively distasteful. But he was, after all, about her age and Veaudry wasn't a very big place. Lily had told me that she'd had a lover before me. Who was to say it hadn't—

'. . . then you should have asked Lebrun,' he finished.

With my mind off on its own track the way it was, it took a second for the words to penetrate. 'What did you say? I should have what?' It seemed to me that every time I'd tried to find out something these last few weeks, I'd been told to ask someone else. *You want to know about the film? Ask Lily. You want to know about Lily? Ask Lebrun.*

'I said you should have asked Charles Lebrun about her,' he said in that dry-ice hiss of his. 'They're very old friends. Oh, you didn't know?'

At a table near the edge of my vision, a sweat-stained workman with an eye patch puckered up his lips like a chimp's and blew a kiss at a companion. Others laughed, as if to say: 'Ask Lebrun, that's a good one!'

It felt as if someone had poured ice water down my collar. Dear God, what were they telling me? Was it possible that . . . that Lily and the blustery, blubbery, purple-faced Lebrun had been lovers, was that what Goujon was saying, was that what everybody except me knew? Could it be? Lily and *him*? She'd been a teenager; he was old enough to be her father. No, what was I talking about, this was two decades ago. Twenty years ago his body wouldn't have been gross, he would only have been twenty-five or twenty-six – not so weird to imagine consorting with a sixteen-year-old – but still, to think . . . I shook my head. What the hell was wrong with me? Inside of ten seconds, out of nothing close to evidence, I'd concocted two brand-new – that is, old – lovers for my wife. *Take it easy*, I told myself. *Go slow. One step at a time. This could make you crazy.*

Besides, what was I getting upset about? What difference did it make to me what lovers she'd had, as long as they were before I came along? The French were more precocious than we were when it came to sex, everybody knew that. Anyway, who was I to get upset? Had I been a virgin when she'd met me?

Well, okay, so I had been, but that's not the point.

'No, I don't know about that,' I said – reasonably evenly, I thought, although my heart was banging away. 'How about telling me? What are you trying to say?'

'Claude,' Donnadieu cut in, 'this is not your concern. You've said enough.' I began to wonder if these two were playing their own version of good cop, bad cop.

Goujon tipped his head to one side, removed the half-inch butt from his mouth, dropped it in an ashtray, and shrugged. 'It's no matter to me.'

'Now wait a minute,' I said. 'You can't just—'

'I have something to say,' someone shouted from behind me. A thin voice, nervous. I turned in my seat to see that a slender, mustached man at the back of the room had stood up, a dandyish man in his forties, one of the few other than Donnadieu in a suit and tie, with his overcoat neatly folded and placed over the back of his chair.

There was a chorus of catcalls: 'Who asked for your opinion, Chastenet?' 'Sit down and shut up.' 'We're not interested in what you have to say, Chastenet.'

But those at his table, outnumbered though they were, tried to give as good as they got: 'It's a free country now.' 'He'll talk if he wants to.' 'Who are you to say who can speak and who can't?' 'Go ahead, Chastenet, we're listening.'

'The great September resister,' Goujon said sarcastically, speaking to no one in particular, then stuck out his lower lip and spat noisily and sloppily on the floor.

Un résistant de Septembre, the Resistance fighter's term for those who had joined the movement after the Germans were on the run, when the danger was past and it had become safer to be for the Resistance than against it.

Chastenet looked anything but comfortable standing there; indeed, there was a furtive, weasely look to him that seemed to come naturally. Still, he waited it out and when the noise had died down, it was to me that he spoke. 'Marcel Vercier is really dead? It can be proven?'

'Yes, I suppose so,' I said. 'You can get in touch with the police in New York if you want proof.'

He nodded and swallowed, glancing to all sides, as if he expected someone to throw something at him. 'Then I have something to say about him.' He'd had more wine than was good for him. There was a little slur to his speech, a slight sway to his stance.

'No one cares what you have to say, Chastenet,' somebody called. 'You'd better shut up.'

'No, I won't, not any longer. I'll admit it: Marcel was my friend. You think you know everything there is to know about him, but you don't. I know something about this film of yours, Mr Simon, quite a bit, in fact—'

More heckling, and nothing good-humored about it. The atmosphere in the bar had turned dangerous. Some of the more peaceable-minded were restraining their friends. Where Americans would boo, the French hiss, and now a snaky *s-s-s-s-s* seemed to fill the smoky air all around us. Even the bartender was doing it. If you've ever heard the sound, you know it can be more menacing than booing ever could.

It didn't seem as if it was going to stop, and Chastenet had to shout to be heard. 'Did Marcel associate with the Germans? Yes, certainly, he associated with the Germans. Who here can say he never once associated with the Germans?' He was stumbling nervously over his words. 'Have you all forgotten so soon? You couldn't survive back then, you couldn't live, not unless you compromised your precious ideals. Oh, I could tell stories—'

But someone on the other side of the room had also jumped to his feet, a big man in working denims, with a powerful voice, used to being heard in a crowd, and he easily cut Chastenet off. 'You little piece of shit, it wasn't just "associating" with the Germans and you know it. Sure, I worked with them too. I was a waiter's assistant at the Tour d'Argent back then, wasn't I? Would I have refused to clear the table of a German officer? Of course not, it wouldn't have been possible; we all had to do such things. If we didn't like it, we lumped it. But that wasn't the way it was with Vercier.'

The hissing and jeering had stopped when he began speaking, except for an isolated, halfhearted call from Chastenet's table: 'Oh, sit down, we've heard this story before.'

'More than once I saw him there,' the big man continued, 'eating away with his precious Boche friends, laughing it up. Fancy uniforms, colonels, generals, *achtung, heil Hitler*!'

His neighbors attended raptly, many of them open-mouthed. It's true, I thought; they *have* heard his story before, but that didn't mean they didn't want to hear it again.

'Sometimes I worked at his table. I saw everything. *Foie gras*, they ate, and crayfish, and naturally they had to have the fat duck, stuffing themselves, looking down through the big windows at those cold, miserable buildings where everyone else was starving, where the meat allowance was three ounces a week—'

'But only when you could get it,' someone called with a dry laugh.

'—where even the children's skin was cracked and peeling from lack of fat, where, where . . .'

Well rehearsed or not, there was no mistaking the emotion in his voice. He let the sentence die off without finishing it. 'Oh, you couldn't miss what those Nazi bastards and their pal Vercier were thinking, what they were feeling,' he said, staring straight ahead of him. I could see his jaw muscles popping. 'They were feeling like big men, what you get from living high off the hog when everyone else has to fight and scratch to get half a rutabaga to carry home for dinner for four people.'

'And what about the power of being a waiter's assistant at the Tour d'Argent?' somebody in Chastenet's group yelled angrily into the near-total silence. 'That's a job I wouldn't have minded having back then. All that leftover food, all that food in the kitchen . . . What do you think, Maurice, no one used to see you going off to work with an empty knapsack and sneaking home at night from the train station with a bulging one? I don't remember *your* children's skin cracking open. Was that because Papa used to bring home here a little pat or two of butter, there—'

That did it. The room erupted in shouts and name-calling. Now maybe a dozen men at various tables had stood up and were waving their fists and looking as if it wouldn't be long before they started using them. Chastenet, who had shut up when the waiter's assistant had started, walked directly up to me, through the hostile crowd. He looked scared to death, but he kept his eyes straight ahead and open wide like a man in a staring contest, not responding to the catcalls or the fists brandished in his face.

'My name is Armand Chastenet,' he told me, speaking rapidly. 'I take my morning coffee at nine o'clock at the Metropole. If you would care to join me, I think you'll find that what I have to say – ai!'

Someone behind him had hit him in the shoulder with his fist. 'If you know what's good for you, Chastenet—'

'Go to hell, you bastards!' he yipped and made quickly for the front door. The threats and jibes followed him, and this time someone did throw something, a chunk of bread, I think, that bounced off the small of his back. Wisely, he kept going.

Mystified, but definitely intrigued, I turned back to my companions. 'Who—'

There was no point in finishing. Their chairs were empty, pushed neatly back under the table.

Chapter Twelve

THE WEATHER THE next morning was a little better: still the same clay-colored sky and cutting wind, but at least the sleet had tapered off. I got directions to the Brasserie Metropole and found it on a tiny, unexpectedly pretty square around the corner from the city hall, a definite cut up from the Grand Luxe or any place else I'd seen so far in Veaudry. An attempt had been made – not altogether successfully, but the intention was there – to provide a turn-of-the-century Parisian ambience. Scalloped green awning over the sidewalk, swan-necked globe lights inside, flocked red walls, gilt-framed mirror behind the bar, round tables with white linens. It was doing a good business in coffee and wonderful-smelling croissants with customers who looked decidedly middle-class; no denim work smocks or stubbly chins in here. There were even some women.

I took a seat at the back, away from the draft from the door, and ordered *café au lait*, which came in two steaming metal pitchers, a small one of coffee and a bigger one of milk. The breakfast coffee at the Hotel Mercure had been good but a bit meager, and this smelled delicious. While I was pouring the two pitchers together into the cup with my mouth watering, Chastenet came in punctually at nine o'clock. He was wearing an expensive-looking gray topcoat and carrying a cloth bag of groceries in one hand: I could see some vegetable greens poking out the top, and of course the ever-present baguette, without which no self-respecting French grocery bag would feel presentable. Looking at him now, I found that I had the same impression I'd had last night: there was something weasely about him, although I couldn't put my finger on exactly what it was.

Something shifty around the eyes, something sly about the mouth.

He saw me right away and sat down at my table, putting the sack on the seat of the chair beside him and folding his coat over the back. Then he held up a peremptory finger to get the waiter's attention. 'Guillaume! My usual, please.'

Clearly, Chastenet was more at home here than he'd been at the Grand Luxe, but he was pouty, no doubt still stewing over last night's scene there, for which I couldn't blame him. 'So you came,' he said. 'I'm surprised that you're willing to be seen with me in public after what happened yesterday.'

'Well, I wanted to hear what you had to say.'

That wasn't strictly true. At this point I wasn't much interested in Chastenet, or even in Vercier anymore. Whatever Chastenet had to tell me, I was there to hear it, but I was itching to get on to Barcelona to see what Lebrun had to say about Lily. If I caught the 10:05-A.M. train back to Paris, I could make a 12:30 flight to Madrid and be in Barcelona by evening. My bag was packed and waiting in my room.

He blew out a puff of air. 'Puh! Animals! It's easy for them—' He glanced up, irritated. 'Yes, what do you want? What are you looking at?'

It was a man who'd just come in, still bundled up and hunched over from the cold, with his cap jammed down to his ears and his muffler almost up to his eyes, and his hands thrust deep into his coat pockets. 'Mr Chastenet?' he asked.

'Yes—'

I don't know why I saw the gun before Chastenet did. Probably because Chastenet, in speaking to him, was trying to look him in the eye and I wasn't. Maybe because it seemed strange to me that with the Metropole as warm as it was, he hadn't shed some of that winter gear. As a result, I was checking him over out of simple curiosity, and I saw the blue-black muzzle of the handgun come poking out between the buttons of his coat, pointed at Chastenet. Either way, I saw it right as it happened.

In personal accounts of heroic actions, you know how you often hear the person say that he didn't really think, he just acted? Well, I don't know if what I did qualifies as heroic or as just plain dumb, but I can tell you for sure that I acted without thinking. I made a lunge for the gun, trying to shove the barrel aside before the trigger could be pulled. Would I have done the same thing if it had been coming up to aim between my eyes and not Chastenet's? Frankly, I doubt it very much. I think I'd have done the same thing Chastenet did once he saw it, which is to say I'd have given a sick little whimper and ducked under the table.

As it happens, my lunge was successful . . . up to a point. I went sprawling on my belly over the table, splashing through coffee and milk, and managed to get my hand on his wrist, grabbing it through the fabric of the coat pocket and pushing, just as he pulled the trigger, or perhaps it was my action that made him pull it. Things were happening so fast and confusedly that I don't really recall hearing the shot, but I do remember feeling his wrist jerk upward with the recoil. In any case the shot went off to the side somewhere; harmlessly, as it turned out.

That was the high point right there. From then on it was all downhill. The layers of wool between my hand and his wrist made it easy for him to jerk his hand, with the gun, out of my grasp, and then take a whack at my head with the side of the barrel. But I was a difficult target, still sliding on the tabletop from the momentum of the lunge, and writhing onto my back as well, doing my best to twist away from him. As a result, I was able to get my arm up to block most of the impact, although I did take a blow – more of a scrape, really – over my right eye and along the temple. At the same time, my outstretched hand closed around something that I thought was his other sleeve and I yanked, as much to give me some leverage as anything else. But it was only his muffler, which came loose in my hand, and I found myself looking straight up into a pair of wide-spaced, slitlike black nostrils. I got a brief glance – an upside-down glance – at a broad, flattened, toadlike face even as I kept on rolling and fell over the side of the table onto the floor, from where I scuttled on all fours to get behind the table.

Chastenet, having scuttled before me, was already there. We had only a chance to stare dazedly at each other – I must have looked as terror-stricken as he did – before the guy, standing on the other side of the table out of our sight except for his legs, started shooting.

And shooting. *Crakcrakcrakcrak*. I hadn't heard that earlier wild shot, but I sure heard these. All I could do was to wrap my arms around my head and scrunch down to make myself as small as possible. I think Chastenet did the same thing. (What else was there to do?) I was scared absolutely out of my wits. The bullets were spraying everywhere, splintering the table, thunking into the floor, literally whistling past my head. I actually felt the rush of air as one went past an inch from my eye. *I'm going to die*, I thought. *Now, here, under a table in the Brasserie Métropole in Veaudry, France.*

The time involved seemed very short, not much more than a second or two, and yet the firing seemed to go on and on. *Crakcrakcrakcrak*. How many bullets did he have in the damn gun? How many guns did he have? Had I been hit yet? I knew that sometimes you could be shot and not know it, but—

'*Uhh!*' The sound was wrenched out of me by a ripping, searing pain in the upper left side of my chest, like nothing else I'd ever experienced. I felt like a fish being gutted with a single, brutal swipe of the knife, like . . . like . . . I couldn't catch my breath. My eyelids fluttered and rolled up and I started to spiral down into a deep, darkening, slowly spinning tunnel.

Chapter Thirteen

WHEN I OPENED my eyes a severe-looking woman with iron-gray hair was leaning over me, looking into my face.

'Who . . .' I was so thirsty I could barely grind the words out. 'Who are you?'

'*Je m'appelle Docteur Grenier.*'

Ah, that's right, I was in France. I was also in bed, on my back, wearing some kind of flimsy tunic. I was in a quiet room that had three other neatly made beds in it, none of them occupied. A hospital, then. An accident of some kind? A heart attack?

Pieces of the wild scene at the Métropole trickled back into my brain. I shut my eyes briefly against a heaving wave of nausea. I'd been shot, right over the heart, yet I was still – how could this be? My hand went to my chest.

'Don't touch,' she said in French, firmly placing my hand back at my side. She held a cup with a straw in it to my mouth and let me gulp down a few swallows before taking it away. 'That's enough. How do you feel?'

I licked my lips and lay back. 'Not too bad. Woozy, that's all. Dopey. Tired. A little sick to my stomach.'

She shrugged. 'That's all perfectly natural.'

'Where am I?'

'You're in Melun.'

'Um . . . Melun?'

'Melun is the capital of the *département*. You're twelve kilometers from Veaudry. This is the nearest hospital. You were brought here by ambulance. You've been here about five hours.'

'Oh.' Maybe half of it had registered. I became conscious of a pungent smell, or maybe taste, that seemed to be lodged in my nose and throat. 'What is that, ether?'

'Yes. You were given an anesthetic so that we could remove the splinter. I wasn't sure what exactly we might find once we got in, but it wasn't complicated at all. I finished up in half an hour. If I'd known, we could easily have done it with a local anesthetic.'

I was slow processing this too. 'Splinter?'

'Yes.'

'That's what I have? A splinter? I'm not shot?' I snickered, a sure sign that the anesthetic was still coursing merrily through my system.

'You thought it was a bullet?'

'Well, yes . . . I mean, he was shooting at me. . . . Well, sure.'

She shook her head. 'No. Only this.' She went to the tray fixed to the foot of my bed, brought an object back, and placed it in my hand. 'It came from the table, you see.'

'This is a splinter?' I said, staring at it. It looked more like a railroad spike, a good five inches long, almost an inch in diameter at the wide end, and tapering conically to a vicious point. One surface, from the top of the table, apparently, had brown, glossy paint on it; the others were rough, ugly bare wood. There were flecks of blood – *my* blood – caught in the crevices between the fibers. It was hard to believe that thing had pierced my chest and yet I was still alive, and I said as much to Dr Grenier.

'Don't get dramatic with me,' she said. 'You weren't impaled, you know. The point entered laterally, just beneath the outside border of the left clavicle, here' – she demonstrated the location on her own collarbone – 'and continued horizontally across just under the skin, and partially emerged here, near your sternum. You lost perhaps a pint of blood. There was minimal damage to the underlying muscles and no penetration at all of the bony structure of the thorax. It was a simple matter of making a superficial straight-line incision from entry to exit, removing the object, cleaning out the wound, and sewing you up. There was nothing to it, really. But you have about twenty stitches, which should come out in a week or so. Oh, and of course you hit your head on something and suffered a grade-three concussion.'

Twenty-odd stitches and a concussion were nothing? I would have begged to differ if I'd had the energy. Again my hand moved toward the wound, and this time she didn't stop me. What I touched was a thick compress running just under my left collarbone, held in place with gobs of adhesive tape. It felt as if someone had wrapped a hot dog in gauze and pasted it to my chest.

'I want you to stay here tonight,' Dr Grenier said. 'We'll see how you get along and we'll change the dressing and have a look at it in the morning. If it looks all right, and I see no reason that it shouldn't, you can go then, but not before.'

I nodded submissively. Staying right where I was sounded fine to me. I sure wasn't in the mood to get up and go anywhere.

'I'll see that you have something you can take for the pain over the next few days.'

'There isn't any pain.'

'There will be. But you have enough opiate in your system to keep you comfortable for the rest of the day. If not, if you wake up during the night and it hurts, ring for the nurse. I don't believe in pain.'

'I'm glad to hear it.'

She looked importantly at her watch. 'Well, I have to get along now. I'm glad it all worked out.'

'Thank you very much, Doctor . . .' I began, starting to doze off, then blinked. 'Christ, I forgot about Chastened What—'

She shook her head. 'Killed at once. There was nothing to be done.'

'Oh, Lord, that's horrible.' I rubbed my eyes, fighting to keep from drifting off again. 'What . . . what was it about? Who was the guy with the gun? Why—'

'I know nothing about these things, Mr Simon.' She hesitated. 'There's a police inspector, a high-ranking one, I understand, who wants to speak with you. He might still be here. I told him tomorrow would be better, but if you wish . . .'

'Yes, please. I'd like to talk to him.' My eyes felt gritty. I closed them for a second.

'All right,' she said, 'I'll see if he can be found. Bear in mind, you may not be at your sharpest right now.'

That was putting it mildly. I wasn't even conscious. She'd barely left my side before I was far down into a wonderful dream. I was a child again, visiting my Aunt Vivienne – the one great cook my family ever produced – and I was about to sit down to one of her marvelous, fragrant duck cassoulets. I leaned over the table inhaling the steam from the tureen with its enchanting aromas: thyme, garlic, sausage . . .

'. . . call me away from dinner for this,' someone was muttering in a bemused, rueful way, apparently to himself. 'What am I supposed to do, interrogate a corpse?'

The lovely cassoulet shimmered and disappeared and I swam reluctantly back up to reality. 'I am not a corpse,' I said with as much certitude as I could muster. It irritated me to be thought dead. At that point, with some effort, I opened my eyes to see a florid, comfortably overweight, middle-aged man with pepper-and-salt hair leaning over the bed and peering back at me, his face about a foot from mine.

He took my remark under consideration. I could hear the air going in and out of his nostrils while he thought about it. 'You may be right,' he said at length.

Later I would realize this was his offbeat sense of humor at work. At the moment, however, with my own funny bone temporarily rendered inactive, I didn't see the joke. If this was the high-ranking cop Dr Grenier had meant, I thought, then the French justice system was in big-time trouble.

I waved a finger weakly at the bedside table. 'Do you suppose you could give me some of that water?'

He poured a little from the pitcher, handed me the cup, helped prop me up to drink it, and took it back when I'd drained it, studying me good-humoredly all the while.

'I am Inspector Alphonse Juneaux of the Police Nationale's Provincial Department of Criminal Investigation. I shall be responsible for the investigation of this case.'

Too many long words in a row. I stared stupidly at him, my head stuffed with cotton. I'm pretty sure my mouth was hanging open, since I was breathing through it. 'Could you . . . would you mind repeating that? I'm afraid I have this headache.'

'Of course,' he said, and did so, word for word, as far as I could tell, then leaned over to shake hands. Either he was being considerate or he didn't subscribe to hearty handshakes, but his large hand closed on mine as gently as a child's, for which I was grateful. Then he pulled a chair up to the side of the bed, sat down, placed one hand on each plump knee, and smiled upon me like a beneficent Buddha. With that kindly expression and portly form, he didn't look much like a cop to me. He looked, in fact, extraordinarily like Mr Scheidlauer, the nice man at the Thom McAn shoe store on

Pitkin Avenue, who'd always had a friendly word and a Tootsie Pop ready for me whenever Mom brought me in for a new pair of shoes.

'So you're an American, I understand, but born in France, in Lyon. A professor of history.'

'Uh, yes.'

'And you're here to find information on your wife's father?'

'Yes.'

'Marcel Vercier.'

'Right.' The haze was beginning to dissipate a little.

'You went to the Métropole this morning to meet with Armand Chastenet, is that correct?'

'Yes.' So far I liked his style of interrogation. Three questions, three one-syllable replies.

But that promptly changed. 'About what, may I ask?'

Oh, God, was I going to have to go into that whole tired story one more time? I didn't have the strength; not at this point. 'He said he had some information about Vercier. I don't have any idea what it was. Look, Inspector, could I tell you about that another time? I don't feel all that great.'

He acceded with a dip of his head and the French version of a tut-tut sound. 'Certainly, that can wait. However, I must ask you how much you remember of what happened at the Métropole.'

'Actually, I'm afraid I'm a little muddled right now.'

'I understand, but such events have a way of growing more muddled with time. Please, do the best you can.'

I did, but I'm not sure how much sense it made.

After listening for a minute, Juneaux held up his hand. 'You wouldn't have a pencil here?'

'I don't think so.'

'Just a minute,' he said, getting up and heading for the door. 'I'll be right back. Don't go anywhere.' More humor.

He returned with a freshly sharpened pencil and a few blank hospital forms, which he smoothed out over his thigh, preparatory to writing on the backs of them. 'No notebook,' he apologized cheerfully. 'I was called away from dinner. A good dinner too.' A wistful gleam came into his eye. 'A pity. What a cassoulet.'

A cop without a notebook? I thought. *A cop who's more interested in his cassoulet than in the murder investigation he's supposed to be in charge of?* These were not good signs. Besides, Juneaux seemed too easy-going, too open, too good-natured to be a good policeman. Too damn considerate of my feelings. I preferred my cops like Kovalski: tough, laconic, world-weary.

'Yes, I thought it was a cassoulet,' I said, provoking a puzzled expression from him, then went on with my account. Juneaux paid close attention, asking few questions but taking neat, rapid notes on the backs of the sheets. When he ran out of space he wrote sideways and upside down around the margins.

The sheets of paper went into the inside pocket of his blue serge suit, which I now saw was pretty well-worn at the elbows. 'How well did you know Armand Chastenet, Mr Simon?'

'I didn't know him at all. I never saw him before yesterday.'

'At the Grand Luxe?'

'Uh-huh.' My eyes were getting heavy again. I tried to stifle a yawn but didn't quite make it. I wasn't going to last much longer. 'Inspector, do you have any idea what this was about? Why anyone wanted to kill him?' I seemed to myself to be speaking more and more slowly, like a phonograph record running down.

'Oh, it doesn't seem so hard to understand.' He crossed his legs, found it uncomfortable, uncrossed them, and steepled his fingers in front of his mouth, his elbows on the plastic arms of the chair. 'Consider. Here is a crowd drinking wine at a café, absorbed in watching the lively discussion between you and your new acquaintances.'

'You know about that?' I asked stupidly.

He laughed. 'Because you have been taking your ease all day doesn't mean that some of us haven't been busy.' He moved his head so that his ample chin rested on the tips of his fingers. 'So. The subject is wartime collaboration, always a volatile topic. Now: here is Armand Chastenet, an unpopular man who comes forward to speak up for his friend, an even more unpopular man. No one wants to hear what he has to say; they shout him down, they grow angry. He comes up to you and says he will tell you what it is he has to say the next morning, at nine o'clock punctually, at the Métropole. Everyone in the Grand Luxe – what, thirty-five people? – hears him. The next morning, at the Métropole – at nine o'clock punctually – he is shot dead. He carries his secret to his grave.' He gave a Gallic mouth shrug and spread his palms: *Voilà.*

I was floating in and out of a delicious doze, but I was able to track most of what he said, which made perfect sense.

'Mm,' I said. Another yawn. 'Excuse me.'

'But at the moment, you know,' he said casually, 'what I'm most interested in is why anyone would want to kill you. Can you help me there?'

'Why anyone . . . I'm sorry, what did you say?'

'Why anyone would want to kill you.' His affable, ruddy face was wavering and growing blurry.

'Kill me? Nobody *wanted* to kill me. I was just . . . just there.' Yawn. 'I was unlucky, I got in the way.'

'Oh, do you think so?' he said pleasantly. 'No, in my opinion there was more to it than that.'

YOU'D THINK THAT hearing something like that just before your eyes closed wouldn't make for a good night's sleep no matter how much sedative had been pumped into you, but the fact was that I slept soundly from whatever time it was until a nurse woke me absurdly early the next morning – they do that in French hospitals too – to take my temperature, check the dressing, and so forth, and help me with a much-needed general sprucing up. All things considered, I felt pretty good, although I was happy to have the pain pills that Dr Grenier had ordered for me. Not only was the splinter wound sore, but the abrasion on the face that I'd taken from the gun barrel, something that I'd completely forgotten about, was sore now too. It hadn't been bandaged, and there was a little blood on the pillow.

A little later a young male doctor that I hadn't seen before swept in with assistants in tow to snip the dressing from my shoulder, peel away the adhesive tape (taking half the hair on my chest with it), have a cursory look at the incision, mutter that all was well, and sweep off to the next patient, leaving me with one member of his entourage, who rebandaged the wound – I managed a peek at it myself and was reassured. Dr Grenier would never win any sewing bees but the incision was closed up tight with only a minor bead of congealed blood here and there, and I saw no angry red streaks or other signs of infection. The assistant patiently told me how to dress the wound twice a day, cautioned me to keep it dry, and gave me the name of an ointment to apply.

After that it was goodbye and good luck. My clothes were brought to me along with the bill, a ticket good for breakfast in the cafeteria, and a note from Inspector Juneaux asking me to telephone him at his office first thing in the morning. Naturally enough, I was extremely interested in talking to him – had he really implied that the murderer had fully intended to kill me too, or had I already been back in dreamland by then? – but somehow, although I didn't doubt his dedication to his work, I didn't think that 'first thing in the morning' meant 6 A.M. Besides, I was feeling empty; I needed something inside me before facing the world again. So I got dressed in an undersize plaid sport shirt they'd found for me somewhere – my own had been cut off me last night – and in my own blood-spotted trousers. Then I went down to the basement cafeteria for my breakfast, where I learned that it *is* possible to get a lousy meal in France. The rolls were stale, the croissants mushy, the butter suspect. I was gazing into my barely touched cup of black coffee, a sinister goop that could have been used to pack ball bearings, when, to my surprise, in came a smiling, freshly shaven Inspector Juneaux. It wasn't yet 8 A.M.

'Ah, I'm happy to find you up and looking so well.'

Indeed, he did look happy to see me. It almost made me feel as if I had a friend in France. 'Thank you, I'm feeling a lot better. I hope I wasn't too incoherent last night.'

'Not at all, not at all. Oho, coffee, I see. May I join you for a cup?'

'I don't know, how's your stomach lining?'

He responded with a noiseless chuckle, perceptible only in the merry crinkling of his eyes and the shaking of his shoulders. 'You'd be surprised at what a policeman gets used to dealing with.' He was wearing the same blue suit as the day before. The same tie too. About the shirt I couldn't say for certain.

He took off the coat, went to the counter, got a small black coffee, rolls, butter, and jam, paid, and came back to sit with me, breaking apart a roll and licking his lips with anticipation. 'Now, then, Mr—'

'Wait, please, Inspector. There's something I need to ask you first. Yesterday you said – I think you said – that it wasn't any accident that I got involved in that shooting; that that guy was gunning for me. Did I hear you right?'

'Oh, yes.' He sipped his coffee, shuddered, and stared accusingly at it. Apparently even policemen's stomachs had their limits. 'Pardon me, I must find the sugar.'

I waited until he resettled himself. 'Why do you say that?' I asked.

'Eh? Say what?' He was busy spooning in the sugar. One heaping teaspoon. Two.

'You said that gunman wasn't shooting at me by accident.'

'Oh, yes. But it's not I who say it, Mr Simon. I have a witness who says it; a waiter.'

'Who says what, exactly?'

'Who says that once Chastenet was dead – and that fact was all too obvious; his skull was shattered, his brains were – well, it was obvious. And then the murderer most definitely aimed at you, moving around the table for a better vantage. The waiter's quite certain of it; he was only a few meters away. You were very lucky. Some of the bullets intended for you lodged in Chastenet's body; others were stopped or deflected by the table or simply missed.'

'But . . . *uck*.' I had momentarily forgotten myself and sipped the evil stuff in my cup. 'But why would he be after me? I mean, it was Chastenet who had the secret. What do I know?'

'I was hoping that you might be able to tell me.'

'I don't have any . . . look, if he really wanted to kill me, what stopped him? I was unconscious. What could I do?'

Juneaux, having added the two rounded teaspoonfuls to the small cup of coffee, tentatively tried it and nodded, apparently finding it to his satisfaction. 'Well, you know, it's largely a question of time. One really can't stand in a crowded brasserie shooting off a gun all day long. After a while, people get upset. The police are called. Eventually one becomes uneasy and concludes that it's best to leave. That's one reason. Another is that he may well have been under the impression that he did kill you. I've seen your shirt. It was drenched in blood. Probably most important, however, he ran out of ammunition. His weapon seems to have been a nine-shot, nine-millimeter automatic pistol. All nine of the slugs have been recovered: four from the unfortunate Chastenet, three from the table, one from the floor, one from the wall.' With a smile he added: 'Happily, none from you.'

'Jeez,' I said.

Juneaux was a fast, eager eater, more or less flipping the food into his mouth and rolling his eyes with pleasure. He was already mopping up the last of his breakfast with one hand and reaching into his pocket for a cigarette with the other. He offered me the pack of Gauloises, got a shake of the head from me, and lit up with a smoker's happy sigh at the first drag of the day. This was a man, I thought, who enjoyed whatever simple pleasures life brought his way.

'Mr Simon,' he said, sucking in and exhaling a second lungful of smoke, 'I'm afraid I really do need to know exactly what brings you here. That is, to hear it from your own lips. I understand it has to do with your relations with your wife. I hope you don't think I'm prying.'

Well, I hadn't looked forward to it, but I'd known it was coming, and this morning I felt more able to make myself go through it one more time, to tell my troubles to one more stranger – one of the few remaining people in France who hadn't heard them yet, or so it was starting to seem.

'Four weeks ago,' I said with a sigh, 'Marcel Vercier knocked on my door. At the time, I didn't know he was my wife's father. In fact, I'd been under the impression . . .'

Two cigarettes later I was done. Juneaux had said hardly anything. He did make a few notes – in a decent leather-bound notebook this time and with a fountain pen – but I had the impression he was merely confirming information he'd already gathered. When I'd finished, he stubbed out his cigarette and smiled pleasantly at me. 'And so what are your plans today? Can you leave the hospital? Do you intend to go back to Veaudry?'

'Yes, I do.' I gestured at my ill-fitting shirt, my blood-spattered trousers and shoes. 'I'd really like to get back to my hotel and change my clothes. And I also want—'

I stopped. What I also wanted was to make arrangements about getting back to Barcelona as soon as possible to talk to Lebrun again, but I thought it better to wait awhile before mentioning this to Juneaux. He was just starting a murder investigation in which I was already involved up to my eyeballs, and it occurred to me that it might take a little sweet-talking on my part to get him to let me out of his sight. And I wasn't quite yet up to doing any sweet-talking.

'Very good,' he said. 'I must go to Veaudry too. You can ride with me. We can talk in the car. And I'll give you the grand tour of Melun on the way, if you think you can spare the time. But I must warn you. It may take all of five minutes.'

Chapter Fourteen

IT TOOK ALL of three. Like Paris some thirty miles to the east, Melun straddled the Seine. Like Paris, it had a medieval cathedral called Notre-Dame on an island in the middle of the river. But there the similarities ended. A midsize commercial and agricultural town, larger than Veaudry, it had been heavily damaged in the war, Juneaux told me. As a result, most of the central buildings had been rebuilt in the fifties in a style in which cost necessarily came first, architectural merit a distant second.

But what it did have that greatly interested me was an American Express office, up to which Juneaux pulled his black Citroën so that I could replenish my supply of cash. I'd had enough on me to pay the hospital bill before leaving, but only just barely. The money situation wasn't dire yet – I'd set aside twice as much in traveler's checks as I'd thought I might need in even the most extreme circumstances – but unanticipated expenses were starting to pile up. It wasn't only the hospital, but the unexpected trip to Veaudry in the first place, and now the upcoming return flight to Barcelona. I wasn't down to counting pennies, but the time had come to start counting dollars. I'd spent a lot of them so far, and if I was any closer to tracking Lily down than I had been when I started out from New York four days ago, I wasn't aware of it. It was true that I'd learned a great deal, though; I now had critical insight into Lily's makeup that I'd never even known I lacked. But would I ever get the chance to put it to use? Not unless I found her, and there I'd drawn a blank.

I'd expected that the inspector would want to interview me further on the short drive, but once we left the town behind he seemed to forget about me as he drove through the flat countryside, keeping occasional time to some tune in his head by tapping on the wheel with his fingers.

'Inspector?'

He looked over at me with friendly interest.

'Inspector, what you were saying about that gunman deliberately coming after me . . .' I shifted in my seat. This was not my favorite topic. I could hardly believe the words had come out of my mouth. Who, *me*? Still, I'd given some thought to what I had to say, and I went ahead and said it.

'Look, you're basing it on a single witness, right? A waiter who says the guy was shooting at me. But the whole thing only took a few seconds, and it was pandemonium in there. You know better than I do that eyewitness reports under conditions like that are next to worthless.' (I knew it because I'd heard movie detectives say it a dozen times.) 'I mean, this waiter wasn't just standing around and taking notes, was he? Unless he was out of his mind, he was ducking for cover like everyone else.'

'That's a good point,' he said obligingly. 'He may have been in error.'

Did he mean it, or was it just a polite way of declining to argue about it with a mere civilian and a foreigner to boot? But there was something else bothering me, and I pressed on. 'And also,' I said with what I hoped was proper diffidence to his station, 'I've been thinking about your idea that Chastenet was killed to stop him from talking to me. I'm not so sure it really holds up.'

'Doesn't it?' No detectable sarcasm; only mild interest.

'Well . . . look, I know I'm way out of my league telling you your business, but it's just that, if that's the way it was, then why wait to kill him at the Metropole, in a public setting, with witnesses all over the place? Why not do it the night before, at home? Or in the morning, before he left to meet me? For that matter, if they really wanted to kill me too, wouldn't they have been better off doing it in my hotel room, or on some dark, quiet street?'

He glanced over at me with what I thought was a look of approval. 'All right, let me see if I can allay your doubts.'

The killer, he explained, was almost certainly not from the neighborhood; probably a professional, most likely imported from Paris, maybe even Marseille. There had been a time, just after the war, when murder and murderers were not so uncommon in Veaudry, but it wasn't that way any longer. Now, it was better to bring in an assassin from outside, but one could not arrange that sort of thing in an hour or two. You had to talk to somebody who knew somebody who could maybe get somebody to do the job. This was because it was best if the person hiring the killer had never met him and didn't even know who he was, and the killer himself knew neither the person paying for his services nor the person he'd been hired to kill. I could see that, could I not?

'Yes, I guess so,' I said. 'That way there's no obvious connection between them.'

'Exactly. So let's say it took most of the night to make the necessary arrangements. That's very quick, but time was an important consideration here and they had to work fast. We'll say, therefore, that the assassin arrived early yesterday morning. We can assume that he had Chastenet's address and that he probably went there to do exactly as you suggested. But Chastenet wasn't there, you see. He was out shopping.'

I looked from the passing scenery to him. 'How did you come up with that?'

'Among other things, you told me. You said he had his shopping bag with him.'

'I did?'

That elicited another of Juneaux's silent, jiggling chuckles. 'In any case, the bag and its contents were still in the brasserie for me to see as well. To continue: the assassin had no idea where Chastenet had gone, but he did know about his appointment with you – we are assuming, after all, that that was at the root of his appearance here – so he went to the Métropole to wait. As soon as Chastenet appeared and sat down with you, our man came up to your table and did the business. Two birds with one stone. Very efficient.' He swung off a roundabout in the direction of the arrow pointing to Veaudry. 'That's the way it appears to me. What do you think?'

I thought it made a lot of sense, and I told him so. I also realized that I needed to revise the impression, made somewhere along the way, that Juneaux was a nice guy who wasn't very bright, who wasn't a very good cop. 'Thank you for explaining it to me.'

'Well, after all, you do have a certain interest in the matter. Tell me, how much do you know about Armand Chastenet?'

It took me a moment to answer. The switch in subjects was abrupt, and I was still a little dopey from the pain pill they'd given me at the hospital. 'Chastenet? Not much. Nothing, really.'

It came as a surprise, a humbling one, to realize that the man had been dead for twenty-four hours and I'd never even bothered to ask about him after my brief inquiry to Dr Grenier. Here was someone who'd still be living if not for me, who'd had his brains blown out because he'd tried to tell me something that he believed I might want to know, and I hadn't given him a thought. When had I gotten so wretchedly self-centered? I had my own troubles, sure, but that was no excuse. I hadn't been interested enough to find out how he'd earned his living, whether or not he'd left a wife and children, whether he was a good family man or—

'He was a sack of human shit,' Juneaux said, so matter-of-factly that I thought I'd misheard him.

'Come again?'

Armand Chastenet, he explained, had worked for a French movie company in Paris before the war, first as a lighting technician and then as a cameraman and film editor. When the Occupation came, he'd been offered a position with Continental, the German-backed film company that was then producing propaganda films for distribution to the French movie houses. Most of them were relatively harmless, lecturing the French on how happy they ought to be under German rule, and what a fine thing the Occupation was for France. Others, some starring well-known French actors (many of whom would be severely dealt with after the war), enlarged on not-so-harmless subjects: the punishment that would be meted out to those who shielded Resistance members and the horrible ends that awaited those who denounced 'France's selfless patriots' – i.e., collaborators – to the Resistance.

Chastenet had done what was asked of him and done it well. On the side he made himself even more useful and substantially richer, pimping for the German military among would-be starlets and providing officers with hard-to-get foodstuffs, goods, coffee, antiques – who knew how he obtained them? – that couldn't be found even on the black market, not at any price. He had made himself well-liked by his Teutonic masters, rising to become a production boss, a person with real authority, and, so a good many people thought, a full-fledged collaborator himself.

'And he never came up before the tribunals?' I asked as we left the highway at a traffic circle, following the arrow that pointed toward Veaudry. We were on the town's outskirts, an area of low warehouses and storage sheds. 'He was never tried?'

'Twice,' Juneaux said. 'Once by Donnadieu's tribunal, as a matter of fact, and then later by one of the motion-picture purge committees.'

'And?'

'And he was exonerated both times.'

'He was – I don't get it. Why?'

'Why? Because they concluded, correctly in my opinion, that he was a self-serving opportunist, a small-time shyster, no more. Hardly worthy of being called an enemy of the Republic.'

'But you just said—'

'Look at it this way, my friend. At the time, the Germans were the ones with the money, so naturally it was to them that he went. Where else should he go? And later, when the Americans came, he earned his living selling his services to *them*. And since that time he's been involved – well, until yesterday morning, I suppose we should say – in one kind or another of shadowy import-export scheme involving South America and Eastern Europe: wine, snails, tin, asphalt, who knows what else? Oh, once in a while he'd get caught doing something he shouldn't and have to pay the occasional fine, but never more than a slap on the wrist. He could afford it.'

'I see,' I said, wondering what it was that this shadowy and disreputable figure could have wanted to tell me. And why. 'Inspector,' I said slowly, 'you don't suppose this thing had something to do with the film?'

He glanced at me. 'The film?'

'Marcel Vercier's film, the one *he* was killed over, the one those thugs came looking for at my house.'

'I can't imagine—'

'Look, you said Chastenet was involved in making movies for the Nazis. *He* said he was a friend of Vercier's. This film of Vercier's –

isn't it possible he had something to do with it? Maybe he made it, or edited it, or something. He clearly said he knew something about it – quite a bit about it. Maybe there's something on it that implicates someone—'

'Implicates in what way?' It was the same question I had asked Charles Lebrun in Barcelona.

I shook my head. 'I don't know . . . maybe it shows someone collaborating, dealing with the Nazis? That would make sense, given Chastenet's situation, wouldn't it? And whoever it was, he killed Chastenet to protect himself.'

It was no more than a slight elaboration of Lebrun's theory vis-à-vis Vercier's murder, but it made more sense to me now than it had when I'd heard it in Barcelona a few days ago.

'Protect himself from what?' Juneaux replied. 'The general amnesty laws have been in effect for years. Unless the fellow worked for Klaus Barbie himself, no one's going to put him on trial now.'

'But don't people kill to protect their reputations too?'

'In books, sometimes.'

'Okay, forget about implicating someone. What about the possibility that there was something in the movie that absolved Vercier? Maybe somebody at the Grand Luxe didn't want that to come out, just the way somebody in New York didn't want it to come out.' It was all starting to come together, I thought excitedly. Two murders five thousand miles apart, one motive. 'Couldn't that be?'

Juneaux was ready with more cold water. 'If that were so, if there were such evidence, why would Vercier have kept it to himself all these years? Why would someone have waited so long to begin going around killing people? And why would Chastenet have demanded your assurance that Vercier was dead before saying whatever it was he had to say? Anyway, why should someone commit murder over such a thing? Why should it matter that much to anyone if Vercier was exonerated now, twenty years after the fact? Besides, well . . .' He shrugged.

'I know,' I said, nodding. Besides, what could any film possibly say that would exonerate him of the actions that were documented in his file, or of the smarmy nastiness of his fawning letter to the *Polizeimajor*? 'Well, it was a thought.'

'And one that we shouldn't dismiss out of hand,' he said kindly.

'No, it's a worthwhile notion. I can't claim to have anything better to go on.'

After a couple of kilometers during which the only sound was the steady whirring of the engine, he began to speak musingly. 'What do you think Chastenet's line of defense was at his trials? He declared that not only was he innocent of collaboration, but he ought to be considered a patriot because he routinely cheated the Germans, charging them outrageous amounts for fakes and inferior goods. And the thing is, it's true; he *had*, just as he later bilked the Americans and his own countrymen. An impartial swindler, treating all sides equally. He may have given plenty of people of all persuasions reasons to hate his guts, but he wasn't worth spending the energy of the justice tribunals on. There were more important people to deal with.'

He gave me a sudden happy smile as we turned onto Boulevard Clemenceau, Veaudry's main street. 'And now, happily, we too have more important things with which to deal. What do you say to a good cup of coffee? We can talk some more.' He patted his belly. 'We French, we believe in the virtues of a second breakfast, you know.'

Yes, but not less than an hour after the first one, they didn't. I was beginning to see how Juneaux had built up his considerable bulk. 'Could we stop at the hotel first?' I asked him. 'I'd like to wash up and put on some clean clothes.'

'Of course.' A moment later he had pulled up in the parking lot that the Hôtel Mercure shared with the railroad station. 'Would you like help getting out of the car?'

'No, thanks.' But I took care not to put any strain on my left side as I opened the door. Getting out and standing was slow going and I wasn't quite as steady as I'd thought I was. When I unthinkingly shoved the door shut with my left hand it resulted in a twinge that made me bite my lip.

Juneaux watched with concern and gently took my other arm. 'Here, I'll go in with you.'

Ordinarily I would have resisted, but I just nodded my thanks and let him keep hold of my elbow. My room was two elevatorless floors up, the banisters on the stairwell were less than substantial, and I preferred not to risk any more twinges. And so up we went, with

Juneaux attentively guiding me by the arm like a nursemaid, and me allowing it like the invalid I pretty much was.

I was going to bathe with the hand-held shower in the bathroom down the hall, but it seemed like too much trouble, what with keeping the dressing dry, so I just used a towel to sponge-bathe (no washcloths in the Hôtel Mercure) in a tiny, curtained-off alcove in my room that contained a sink and a bidet. I also checked my dressing for blood-spotting – there had been that twinge getting out of the car – and was relieved to find none. The plaid shirt they'd given me at the hospital, which smelled something less than laundry-fresh, went into the wastebasket, and after a moment so did my bloodstained trousers, which I knew I wouldn't ever put on again. The shoes, with only a few splatters on them, I wiped clean with the dampened towel. On the other side of the curtain Juneaux sat on the room's only chair, next to the room's only table, smoking and – I think – snoozing, as if he had all the time in the world, while I put on the softest, oldest flannel shirt I'd brought along (the kind of thing that Lily would have made me leave home if she'd been in charge of packing) and an equally disgraceful pair of woolen trousers.

'Inspector,' I called over the curtain, 'you said Chastenet was just a small-time crook, somebody they didn't think was worth worrying about – well, that sure wasn't the feeling I got at the Grand Luxe. Those people *hated* him.'

'Ah, yes, but, you see, that was because the talk turned to the period of the Occupation, which they are generally wise enough to stay away from. Most of the time they simply tolerate Chastenet and his cronies. They may not love them, they may not associate with them more than they have to, but they don't begrudge them their chairs or their glass of wine. And they get along with them when they must. If that wasn't the way it was, half of France would have murdered the other half by now. But when they begin to remember the war, the old animosities spring to life again. It's very sad.'

'I see.' But I didn't see, and I was shaking my head as I came out of the makeshift washroom. 'I guess it's hard for me to imagine that: hating someone one minute – with good reason – then getting peaceably along with him the next, and then hating him again the one after that. It doesn't seem like human nature to me.'

Juneaux looked at me the way a patient teacher looks at a favorite pupil, earnest but dense beyond all hope. Meditatively, he lit another of his pungent Gauloises and took a deep drag before speaking.

'Let me tell you about an old boss of mine, Rimeau, a chief inspector in Melun in the old days. He's a hero now; there's a memorial plaque in his honor; I should have shown you. And why is he a hero? Because, over two years' time, at terrible risk to himself, he helped almost one hundred Jews escape from the Germans. For this he was executed toward the end of the Occupation, when the facts were learned. But at the very time that the Germans took him out and shot him he was already marked for execution by the Resistance leaders of the Front National. Why? Because *they* had learned that he had had the opportunity, at *no* risk to himself, of warning an FTP unit of an impending Gestapo raid and had chosen to do nothing, letting twenty brave young *maquis* go to their deaths.'

He drew on his cigarette. The end glowed. I was silent.

'And why did he do nothing? Because he was a passionate anti-Communist and the FTP was, at that time, composed of dedicated Communists. But Communists or not, they were *maquis*. So you see, he was a traitor after all.'

'If this is supposed to be helping me understand—'

'Or was he a hero for saving the Jews? Should he be admired? Despised? Tolerated? Would you care to be the judge?'

'But Chastenet was a completely different case, wasn't he? How many Jews did he save? What did he—'

'*Everybody* is a completely different case, that's the trouble.' He slowly tapped the ash from his cigarette into a tin ashtray as he spoke. 'Once, a long time ago, my philosophy of human nature was that a person was either good or he was evil, and that most men were good. Then, when the war came, I began to think that down at the core, under pressure, perhaps everyone was rotten after all. Then, as I saw still more of life, I understood that things must be more complicated than that. People are too complex, they have too many sides, too many conflicting drives and ideals. To call anyone "good" or "evil" is to oversimplify to the point of absurdity. No one is totally either, everyone is partly both – in varying degrees, I grant you.' He looked up from his cigarette and smiled. 'So I thought then.'

'And now?' I asked.

'And now? Now I don't believe in having a philosophy of human nature anymore. I've seen too many good people do evil things and too many bad people do good things. Oh, I'm willing to say that there are a few truly good ones – Albert Schweitzer, Jesus Christ . . . no one else comes to mind at the moment – and some truly evil ones – Hitler . . . even Marcel Vercier, if it comes to that. But when it comes to making moral judgments about all the people in between, leave me out of it, I don't do that anymore. I don't worry about "good" and "bad," I just worry about the law. Break it and you're in trouble. That's my total philosophy of human nature.'

I shook my head. 'No, I'm sorry, I can't buy that, Inspector. When someone like Chastenet or Vercier goes out of his way to kowtow to the Nazis while his country is being—' I broke off as I felt the bruises at my temples burn; my face had flushed, sending a burst of blood to them. There I was, making righteous moral judgments again about 'human nature,' about how people ought to act in situations that I myself had never, thank God, had to endure. 'I should shut up,' I said humbly. 'I'm talking through my hat. I guess it's because when you're like me, when you haven't had to live through it, it's easy to see everything in black and white, not in shades of gray.'

I was thinking now of the emotional exchanges I'd heard in the Grand Luxe when the shouting had started, and of what Lebrun had said to me in Barcelona: everyone had had to compromise to some degree in order to survive. Grocers sold radishes to German officers, waiters served them their dinners, ticket-takers at sporting events took their tickets, and ushers showed them to their seats. What else could they do? There were obvious extremes, of course: Marcel Vercier and others like him had been evil; the timid grocer who sold radishes hadn't been. But where exactly did you draw the line between them, the line that, once crossed, made you an enemy of your people? Had an opportunist like Chastenet crossed it?

'No, it wasn't so much a question of black, and white, and gray,' Juneaux said. 'That's not the way I'd put it.' He was speaking slowly, thoughtfully. 'It was more . . .'

This was the first time I'd seen him struggling to put his ideas into words, and after a few seconds he gave up with a jerk of his head and a gruff shrug. 'Ah, who can explain it? So, are you ready? Shall we go? I'm in great need of that coffee.'

'Me too,' I said with feeling. The pain pill they'd given me at five-thirty was wearing off, or maybe it had been the stretching involved in washing up and dressing. Either way, I was ready for another, and I wanted some coffee to wash it down and boost it into my bloodstream.

I was pleased to find that I was steadier going downstairs than I'd been coming up, and although I kept one hand on the wall for safety's sake and took the stairs slowly, I could do it on my own. Juneaux, seeing this after the first couple of steps, removed his hand from my arm and offered no further assistance, which I appreciated.

After a slow, mute descent we reached the front door and stepped out into the Place de la République. It had been swept and hosed a little while before so that the cobblestones gleamed and little runnels of water glinted between them on their way to the drains in the center. It looked beautiful. And although I'd only been cooped up in the hospital overnight, the fresh winter air was like balm on my skin. It had warmed up a little, and there was even a wispy morning sunshine that felt so good on my cheeks that I wanted to weep with pleasure.

'I know a good café,' Juneaux said. 'I'll drive you.'

'If it's not far, I'd rather walk,' I said. 'It's nice to be outside.'

He smiled. 'I think you mean it's nice to be alive. No, it's not far; just across the square.'

I was concentrating on keeping my footing on the slippery, uneven stones and Juneaux, hunched into his coat, was submerged in his own thoughts, so that we were halfway across the square before either of us spoke again.

'No, it wasn't a matter of blacks and whites and grays,' he said softly. 'Well, it was that too, of course, but the main thing, you see, was that nothing during the Occupation was simple. Nothing. Especially in the early days, when we were all so dispirited and frightened. Everything, every activity, every transaction, every "good morning," was *complicated.* A person would say to his neighbor, "And how is your father this morning?" and all sorts of possibilities would arise. You couldn't simply answer with whatever came into your mind. You had to think it through before you said anything.'

I shook my head. 'I'm not sure I understand that.'

We had reached the middle of the square. Juneaux stopped to cup his hands around a match and get a cigarette lit. Then he began speaking again, so quietly that I had to strain to hear.

He himself had been a *gendarme* in Veaudry at the start of the war, he told me, already in his mid-thirties and settled in his family life and his career. Then, in the upheaval of 1940, when northern France was occupied and the south was placed under the Vichy government, he had remained at his job, even though the police were now technically under the command of the Nazis. What else was he to do? What else did he know? If he didn't provide for his wife and three children, who would?

It was an argument I was getting used to hearing, and it was hard to fault. The fact that those who joined the Resistance were heroes didn't necessarily mean that those who didn't were cowards or villains. A lot of people were just trying to get along the best they could.

Besides, he said, he truly believed then, as now, in the importance of order to society, Occupation or no Occupation. His job, as he saw it, was no different from what it had been before: the maintenance of civil order, the protection of ordinary citizens, and the apprehension of the criminals who preyed on them.

'But—' I hesitated, afraid of getting out of my depth again, then went ahead anyway. 'But you were taking orders from the German military. Didn't they ever—'

There was a gush of smoke from his nostrils. 'I was not taking orders from the German military,' he said, the first time I'd heard anything like harshness in his voice. 'The police here were not like the police in Vichy or in Paris, out-Nazi-ing the damned Nazis themselves. What went on at the higher levels I don't know, but it wasn't us they got to help them with their dirty work.' His mouth had set. 'I took no orders from them. I made things difficult for them every way I could.'

'I see,' I said, surprised (I suppose I shouldn't have been) and a little intimidated by his intensity. 'I'm sorry, all I—'

'Let me get to my point, dammit.'

Yes, sir, I thought.

He took a breath to restore his calm. 'Before the war, you see, I might see my friend the optician on the street and say, "Good morning, Henri, how are you today? Have you heard from your nephew Bernard lately?" and we'd have a pleasant chat and go our ways, and that was that.'

Road barriers swung down at the edge of the square, bells clanged, and an express roared through town, drowning out conversation for a few seconds, and then was gone in a swirl of dust almost as soon as it came. The barriers swung up, the bells stopped clanging.

'But in the Occupation it was no longer that way,' Juneaux went on, looking straight ahead as we walked. ' "Have you heard from your nephew Bernard lately?" I would say – the same casual question, no different from before – but for my friend Henri everything was changed. Was I just being friendly, or was there something more to it? Was Bernard perhaps suspected of being a resister and was I, as a policeman, trying to worm information out of Henri? Was I perhaps after all in the service of the Nazis? Was this a prelude to an interrogation? Or possibly I was giving him a veiled, friendly warning of an arrest to come and suggesting that Bernard disappear for a while? What did my inquiry mean? There was no such thing as a casual question between neighbors anymore. You could never be sure of what might result from your answer, of who might be tortured, or sent away, or killed.'

'I'm beginning to understand,' I said.

'Are you?' He flung the stub of his cigarette angrily onto the cobblestones and ground it out with his heel. His nostrils were flaring. This was a Juneaux I hadn't seen before. 'I was brought before Donnadieu's tribunal too. I suppose you didn't know that.'

'You?' I said, stunned.

'On 8 September, three days before Vercier's trial.' His head was down so that he was speaking into his chest. We had gradually been slowing down, and now he brought us to a halt altogether. Not knowing what to say, I just shut up.

'Things had gotten more complicated for me too, you see. In 1942 I had arrested a man in a brawl who, as it turned out, happened also to be a *maquis* leader. After he was jailed and sent to

Paris, the Germans came for him. He died in their hands. At the end of the war I was accused of collusion and arrested by the FTP.'

Jesus Christ, did this stuff just go on and on, tendrils within tendrils? 'What . . . what happened?'

'Oh, Donnadieu threw the case out,' he said as we began walking again. 'Several Resistance officers came forward to testify to the things I'd done for them. It was over in an hour, but not everybody accepted the result. There are still people in Veaudry who feel about me the way they do about Marcel Vercier or Armand Chastenet.'

'Look, I'm sorry I—'

His hand rested briefly on my shoulder. 'No, it's for me to apologize. I have no reason to be angry with you. Enough of ancient history.' His face lightened. 'Here we are. Let's go in and get that coffee.'

'Boy, am I ready,' I said, and then stopped when I saw where we were. 'The Brasserie Métropole?' I exclaimed. '*That's* where you want to have coffee?'

'Oh,' he said, looking at me with round, innocent eyes. 'You've heard of it?' And then he couldn't quite choke back a nasal, jolly whicker of laughter.

I told you he had an offbeat sense of humor.

Chapter Fifteen

He wasn't being morbid (he said); it was only that he thought that coming there might jog my memory. And it did. It took about two minutes.

We had just been served. Juneaux had ordered *café complet* – coffee, rolls, croissants; the same thing he'd had at the hospital. I had asked for *café au lait*, nothing else. The waiter wasn't the same one who'd been there yesterday. We were seated at a table along the wall, about ten feet from where I'd sat before, from where Chastenet had bled and died and I had bled but not died. There was no sign of any of that now. The entire place was sleek and gleaming, and the smell of floor wax was doing battle with the aroma of coffee and cinnamon. The linoleum shone, the walls had no ugly spatters or bullet holes that I could see (and I was looking hard), and a fresh, thick tablecloth covered the table that he and I had sat at. (Juneaux had blithely suggested that we sit there, but that was a little more than I was ready for.) No one else was using it either. For the time being, at least, it seemed to be for looking at, not for eating at.

People were staring at me too. I tried not to notice them, although I couldn't help overhearing one whispered exchange between two women as we sat down.

'But you said he was killed!' The speaker was aggrieved.

'He was,' said the other defensively. 'At least I thought he was. He should have been. He bled like a pig with its throat cut. I'm amazed he has any blood left at all.'

The eyes of most of the customers, however – and there were significantly more customers than there'd been yesterday, these things being good for business – kept drifting hungrily to the empty table. So did mine. And when they did for the third time or so, I sat up with a jerk.

'I saw his face,' I murmured.

Juneaux looked up from the croissant he was tearing apart. 'What?'

'I saw his face! I completely forgot! Damn!'

'But . . . are you sure? Everyone agrees he kept his face hidden. A hat, a woolen muffler – everyone says it was imp—'

'Yes, but when I was rolling around on the table and he was trying to brain me with his gun – did I tell you about that? – I got hold of the muffler without meaning to and pulled it away for a second. I was looking right into his face.'

'Can you describe him? Would you recognize him?' The croissant, half in each hand, was forgotten.

'Well, I was seeing him upside down, and I was scrambling around trying to get out of reach, but . . . yes, I might.' In fact, in my mind was a surprisingly clear picture of his face: squat features, squashed nose, mean little eyes. How could I have forgotten so completely about it?

'He was ugly,' I said.

Juneaux sputtered with laughter. For a cop on a murder investigation it seemed to me he did a lot of laughing and chuckling, not that it didn't have a certain charm. 'Ah, well, that narrows it down enormously,' he said. 'After all, how many ugly people are there in France?'

'All right, he looked like a toad.'

'A toad.'

'Wide mouth, wide-set nostrils, low forehead, sort of a flat face . . . I don't know. Like a toad. Short. Stocky.'

He went back to his croissant, tearing it thoughtfully into quarters. Flakes rained down onto the white tablecloth. 'We'll get some photos for you to look at. It may take a day or two. You'll be here awhile?'

'Uh, actually, I wanted to talk to you about that. I'd really like to go back to Barcelona, today if I can, but if you really need me—'

'No, don't concern yourself, just make sure I know where I can get hold of you there. And afterward as well. Are you sure you're up to traveling today?'

'Oh, I think so,' I said. 'If I take it easy. Wow, I'm glad I remembered about him. It's really a relief.'

His eyebrows went up. 'Ah?'

'Well, sure. Now I understand why he was trying to kill me. I saw his face, that's all.'

'And that's a relief?'

'Of course it is. You almost had me thinking there might be something deeper to it. But it was just an accident. He was upset that I'd seen what he looked like, nothing more.'

'I suppose that's one way of looking at it,' Juneaux said.

I looked up from my oversized cup; I'd been bathing my face in the aromatic vapor. 'And what's the other way? Or don't I want to know?'

'The other way of looking at it is that he's still at large. And if what you say is correct, he is no doubt *still* upset. That doesn't sound like much of a relief to me.'

'Thank you for pointing that out,' I said crossly.

'On the other hand, I could be wrong. I'm often wrong.'

I laughed. 'That's reassuring, I think.' I got out my vial of codeine pills, shook one out and downed it, and followed with a slug of coffee. 'Inspector, do you have any suggestions about what I ought to do?'

'For the moment I think that being somewhere else might be just the thing, and Barcelona sounds like a fine choice. And Mr Simon? Perhaps it would be best not to mention it to anyone.'

THE NEXT MORNING, for the second time in four days, I climbed the stairway of the Galeria Metropolitana. The steps were as dim and dusty as before, but big changes had been made in the showroom. No more half-opened packing crates or litter. The slate floor was clean and inviting, with beautifully lit coins, embossed medallions, and old jewelry displayed in head-high glass-fronted cabinets that covered three walls. The place looked downright classy. Maybe *Holiday* magazine had had it right after all.

Mrs Aguilar, however, was busy and distracted. 'If you're here to see Mr Lebrun, I'm afraid he has a client in with him at the moment.'

'I'll wait.'

'As you like.'

She returned her attention to the sheet of paper in her typewriter.

'Mrs Aguilar?'

She glanced up, eyebrows arched, fingers poised on the keys. I kept my voice down. 'I'd like to thank you for your help.'

'You're completely welcome, Mr Simon. It's been my pleasure.'

'I mean the note – you know? The note in my pocket. It was very helpful. I've just come from Veaudry.'

She frowned at me, shook her head slightly, and threw a glance at her boss's closed door. I was only making her nervous. After all, if she had wanted me to know who the note was from she would have signed it. 'Don't worry, I'm not going to say anything about it to Mr Lebrun,' I said. 'I just wanted you to know how much I appreciate it.'

'I . . . that's quite all right, Mr Simon.' She resumed her typing.

Behind me I heard the door to Lebrun's office open, and then a flood of animated conversation in German. When I turned I saw him standing in the doorway, all smiles and proprietorial good cheer, nattering glibly away with a distinguished-looking, well-turned-out older man with a perfectly blocked homburg in one hand and a beautiful camel's-hair-collared topcoat artfully gathered over his arm. A diplomat, I thought.

Lebrun saw me and actually looked happy about it. 'Mr Simon,' he chirped in French as I stood up, 'how nice to see you again.' Then something in German to the older man. I heard my name and '*Amerikanischer*.' Then back to French for my benefit. 'Allow me to introduce Herr von Feuerbach,' he said with great formality and a certain pride. I gathered I was seeing Charles Lebrun in action, 'buttering up' a client. 'Herr von Feuerbach holds an important post with the German embassy in Madrid.'

How about that, I'd actually figured out what the guy did for a living – working from mere surface appearances. Amazing. Louis would have been thrilled.

'*Wie geht es Ihnen, Herr von Feuerbach?*' I said, pretty much exhausting my German.

'How do you do?' he replied in silky-smooth English as we shook hands. 'Perhaps I should point out that Mr Lebrun is referring to the East German embassy, the GDR.'

I didn't know what he was expecting me to say to that, so I said 'Ah' and looked wise.

Lebrun cut in, addressing me. 'If you'd care to take a chair in my office, Mr Simon, I'll be in shortly. There are just a few more details to take care of with Herr von Feuerbach.'

'A pleasure to have met you,' von Feuerbach said to me. I thought he might click his heels, but no.

'My pleasure,' I said.

Lebrun's office too was quite orderly. Sitting upright on an easel beside his desk was a green velvet mat to which was pinned what appeared to be a necklace, a beautiful, gleaming thing full of pearls and rubies, with its centerpiece a dog, or sheep, or some such thing standing in profile on its hind legs.

I was standing there studying it when Lebrun came in, as jumpy as ever, but in a happy way this time, and stood beside me to gaze fondly at it, his hands clasped over his belly. 'Wonderful workmanship, don't you think? Look at the floral settings for the rubies. Herr von Feuerbach is very pleased. He's purchasing it for his home, you know – that is to say, his family castle – near Leipzig.'

'The Rearing Lamb,' I murmured tentatively, taking what was little more than a shot in the dark.

I heard a sharp intake of breath. 'You know this piece?'

'Merovingian . . . seventh century,' I said, scrabbling around in my memory for whatever crumbs I could retrieve about the necklace that, to all appearances, was the golden pendant I'd read about at the Forty-second Street library in New York the previous Saturday. Except that, according to *Holiday*, it was supposed to be occupying pride of place in the Tegucigalpa art museum.

'That's *right*,' a clearly impressed Lebrun said.

Clearly flustered too, I thought. I pressed on. 'Don't I remember hearing somewhere that this went to the Honduran Museum of Ancient Art?' I asked, as if I were very much up to snuff on such things.

'Why . . . yes, that's correct, but we, ah, got it back. It was . . . returned, you see. Too bad.' He managed to summon up an uneasy little smile. 'Won't you – won't you sit down, Mr Simon?

'We have a strict policy in this gallery,' he said more evenly when we were both seated. Being behind his familiar desk seemed to have replenished his self-confidence. 'If for any reason the purchaser is unhappy – perhaps they do not have the funds they anticipated – as was the case with Honduras – or perhaps there are insurance problems, or conservation issues at the location – we take back the work for the price paid and ask no questions.'

Baloney, I thought. I didn't know much about the fine-art world, but I knew, or thought I knew, that legitimate deals weren't closed and art objects didn't change hands until the funding, insurance, and conservation details had been worked out. So when a major piece was returned to the dealer by an institution, it almost certainly meant that there was something wrong with it, that its attribution had turned out to be faulty or uncertain, or that the – what do they call it – the provenance was suspect. The one truthful thing Lebrun had said was probably that the gallery was willing to take back works it had sold, no questions asked. As in any business, it wasn't good to have clients fighting you in court over a product that wasn't quite what you said it was. The sooner things were hushed up and forgotten the better. Especially if you could just sell it to the next sucker anyway.

Herr von Feuerbach, for example.

What do you know, Lebrun was a shyster. Had Vercier been one too? It looked like it. He had still been alive at the time the pendant had been sold to the Hondurans, so he'd have to have been in on it. Besides, having been a collaborator, how much of a leap was it to being an all-around crook?

Interesting, but I didn't see that it did me any good.

The intercom on the desk buzzed. Lebrun, eager to change the subject, jumped to punch a button. 'Yes?'

Mrs Aguilar's voice came on. 'It's Herr Eichendorf. He wants to know if the Transylvanian ten-ducat set can be shipped this afternoon.'

'Impossible!' Lebrun shouted into the machine. 'Is he crazy? Does he think we don't have other customers? Who does he think he is? Tell him not before Tuesday. Maybe Monday if we're lucky.' He punched the button again and looked at me. 'Some of these people. You wouldn't believe them.' Slowly, his feathers unruffled. 'So, Mr Simon, I didn't expect to see you again so soon.'

'Herr von Feuerbach,' I said. 'Herr Eichendorf. Do you have a lot of German clients?' I didn't know what I was probing for, but it was obvious that something here was making Lebrun edgy, and, considering the delicate nature of what I was there to ask him about – the sixteen-year-old Lily Vercier and her relationship to him – I thought that it wouldn't hurt for me to seize the moral advantage early.

'Well, yes, I suppose we do,' he said, as if he'd never thought of it before. 'We have, right from the start.'

He was uncomfortable, picking once or twice at his chewed-up fingernails. I held my tongue, waiting him out.

'You see,' he said at length, 'when Marcel first came to Spain after the war, he found that his reputation was known to many collectors in the, er, German community. They thought . . . that is to say, they assumed that, coming as he did from Occupied France, and having dealt with a number of high-ranking members of the German military . . . well, they assumed that he was on good terms with them.'

'And wasn't he?'

He colored. 'Only out of necessity,' he barked. Lebrun had a short fuse, and I had hit another sore spot. 'Marcel had a family. He did what he had to do.'

I looked down at my own fingernails. 'Our very amiable association and mutual esteem' – had that been required by necessity? What about looking forward to contacting Polizeimajor vom Steeg 'concerning the location of certain other art objects in which I am sure you will be interested'? Well, what the hell, Lebrun probably didn't know about that letter. He'd left without knowing about the tribunal, or so he said.

'In any event,' he went on, 'our earliest clients happened to be Germans. And we were grateful to see them walk in the door, I can tell you. They were customers and they had money to spend; were we supposed to ask them if they'd been Nazis? And turn them away if they said yes? All right, maybe some of them had been, but that was neither here nor there. The war was over. Now that I think about it, I suppose that they might have taken it for granted that Marcel, with his background was, shall we say . . .'

'Sympathetic to the cause,' I said.

Lebrun swelled up, snorting. 'Certainly not! I resent such an implication.' He managed to look genuinely offended. 'I can assure you that he has never implied such a thing, either by word or deed. Neither have I, I would like to point out.' He resettled himself in the chair, huffed a little, and continued.

What they, these wealthy German customers (who might or might not have been Nazis), assumed, he explained, was that Marcel Vercier must have had a large network of contacts with collectors in the occupying forces. ('Collectors' was his word. I'd have picked another.) And having access to this network, he would naturally have a known and trusted dealer's entree to the loot they now wished to sell. ('Loot' is my word. What Lebrun said was 'acquisitions.') Further, with the situation being what it was – 'the war and all' – these 'collections' would surely be available through the Galeria Metropolitana at attractive prices.

'*That* is what they assumed,' Lebrun said.

'And were they correct?'

He let a beat go by before answering. 'In large measure, yes, but mostly after the fact, in what one might call a self-fulfilling prophecy. You see, it wasn't long before other German collectors, émigrés to Spain, desperately short of money but not short of objects of art, heard about us and came to us with collections of their own to sell. We accommodated them.'

'At distress-sale prices,' I said, producing a narrowing of Lebrun's eyes. I wasn't trying to make an enemy of him on purpose, I just didn't seem able to help myself.

'This is a business, Mr Simon,' he said coldly. 'As in any other business, we try to pay as little as we can for what comes in and charge as much as we can for what we sell. That's the oldest rule of business; if you don't do it, you don't survive. It's simply a question of what the market will bear and not an ethical issue at all.'

That, to put it gently, was a matter of opinion. Even with Vercier's sympathies in regard to National Socialism aside, what the Galeria Metropolitana was obviously doing was knowingly, wholeheartedly profiting from loot plundered by the Nazis during the war. They were buying it from Gestapo officers, or Occupation bureaucrats, or others in that sleazy chain; individuals who now found themselves temporarily strapped for cash ('with the situation being what it was, and all'), and they were selling it to eager new buyers who didn't much care where it had come from or how it had been gotten and chose not to ask.

If that didn't involve ethical issues, tell me something that does. Lebrun might not be quite the piece of work Vercier had been, but he had to know what he was doing.

'What happened to your face?' he asked abruptly.

I managed not to touch my temple. 'I fell.'

'At your hotel?'

'Let me ask you something,' I said. 'Did you know that Vercier had been tried *in absentia* by a citizens' tribunal in 1944? And sentenced to death?'

Lebrun's bushy eyebrows jumped. His jaws worked for a moment before he spoke. 'I had no idea! To *death*?'

He was goggling at me with his mouth open, like a catfish flopping away on a deck. No, I thought, I'd been wrong in thinking he might have known about it; this was news to him. Either that or he was a hell of an actor.

'How can you know such a thing?' he got out at last.

'I've just come from Veaudry. I saw the tribunal records.'

He shook his head. 'To *death*,' he said again, wonderingly. 'But all he did . . . that is to say, he only . . .' He blinked; his upper lip jerked. 'They didn't . . . did they try me as well?'

'No. Well, not that I know of.'

Not surprisingly, that wasn't a good enough answer. 'Are you positive?'

'I told you, I don't know.'

'Because, you know, those people were so vicious, so filled with spite, they might do anything, they might even. . .' His mouth stayed open for a moment as an idea took hold. Then he leveled a quivering finger at me. 'I *told* you! It was they who killed Marcel, don't you see? They hunted him down like an animal and slaughtered him. My God!' And then, softy, sardonically, to himself. 'So his precious film didn't protect him after all.'

More likely it was his precious film that had gotten him killed; him and Armand Chastenet, and – almost – me. But what would have been the point of getting into that with Lebrun? No, it was time to gird my loins, so to speak, and do what I'd come to do: ask him the question I didn't want to hear the answer to.

'Mr Lebrun, that's not what I came back to Barcelona to talk to you about.' I breathed slowly in and out to get rid of the tremor in my voice. 'I'd like to know about the relationship that existed between you and Lily.'

I expected the question to bring on another of his ready flare-ups, but it didn't. He was calmer than I was. 'Relationship? What relationship? I already told you, I haven't seen her in twenty years. More than twenty years.'

'That's what I'm referring to – the relationship that existed twenty years ago.'

He looked at the ceiling. 'What is he talking about? Half the time I don't know what this man is saying.'

'Mr Lebrun,' I said, 'I was told in Veaudry that you and Lily had once been . . . close.' I held my breath.

'Is that so?' he said, and actually smiled. 'And who might you have been talking to?'

It was true then. I'd hoped against hope that it wasn't. And I'd told myself that it didn't matter if it was. I think I'd almost come around to believing myself too, but now I felt all hollowed out, emptied like an old potato sack. To think of Lily, fresh and innocent, living with this turd, even if he didn't look like a stuffed owl at the time . . . I didn't answer him; I'm not sure I could have. I just shook my head and waited.

'All right, then,' he said, lowering his head and looking me straight in the eye from under those eyebrows. 'She lived with me for a while in 1944 – five or six weeks, I think. I'm surprised she never told you. Why do you suppose she kept it from you?'

I stared woodenly out the grimy window, not wanting to look at him. 'Look, Mr Lebrun, I don't really care what went on then. All I'm interested in is where she is now.'

'Do you mean you think she might have come to me? Ah, I see. *That's* what you're asking. Well, I live upstairs. Would you like to go there now and see if you can find her? Even if I can't produce Lily I can offer you an apéritif.'

I thought it was pretty unlikely that Lily would have run back to someone like Charles Lebrun, but then, who knew anything anymore where Lily was concerned? But even if she had come to him, she certainly wasn't in his apartment at this moment or he wouldn't have invited me up. On the other hand, who was to say this wasn't a calculated bluff on his part?

Pretty doubtful stuff, but I didn't see that I could afford to pass up even the most improbable lead. 'Thank you, I'd be glad to have an apéritif with you.'

He jumped up. 'Very good. Come. Unfortunately, my wife is out this morning. She would have been delighted to meet you, I know. She was very fond of Lily.'

That stopped me. 'Your *wife* was fond of her?'

'Of course she was. Being a woman, and having no employment to take her away from home, she naturally got to know her better than I did while Lily was with us.'

With *us*? 'Wait a minute. You mean Lily stayed with you *and* your wife?'

'Yes, of course, what else—' It was only then that he caught the drift of my thoughts, and he climbed up on his high horse. The man had a remarkable ability to puff himself up like a blowfish. 'Why, what did you suppose?'

'I . . . I just . . .'

'Her mother was on her deathbed. Marcel couldn't care for her and also deal with a headstrong young girl; he came to us and asked us to take Lily in. Béatrice and I, we were glad to have her, a poor lost child. We did our best, we treated her like our own daughter. Even after her poor mother died, even after Marcel ran for Spain, we kept her with us as long as we could. And *you* thought— Really, sir!'

His expression effectively combined outraged decency and withering contempt, but I supposed he was entitled to it, and in any case I didn't mind a bit. I felt as if two hundred pounds had just been lifted off my shoulders.

'Mr Lebrun, I . . .'

'Besides,' he added icily, 'she was five months pregnant at the time.'

WHAM.

All I could do was to weakly shake my head. Things were coming at me too fast to cope with; I couldn't keep up. Considering that (according to Louis) I'd spent just about my whole life avoiding human complications, I was sure making up in a hurry for lost time. Lily pregnant . . . at sixteen! It wasn't so much the fact of the thing, although that was upsetting enough in itself to think about; it was more the idea that I could actually have gone all these years without knowing so important a thing about her, and that she could have gone all these years leaving me in the dark. I couldn't help wondering how many more things she'd kept to herself. How many other surprises were out there just biding their time?

'Pregnant by whom?' I asked when I was able to get out a near-complete sentence.

He jerked his head irritably. 'I didn't want to tell you about this at all, it wasn't my idea. Let's talk about it upstairs, where we can't be overheard,' he said with a glance at the door, on the other side of which sat the efficient Mrs Aguilar, audibly typing. 'I could use something to drink myself. Come.'

I was getting more apprehensive by the second. Europeans aren't like Americans that way. They don't invite new acquaintances into their homes at the drop of a hat, so why did I rate it? What new shocker was I being buttered up for?

Lebrun's apartment occupied the two floors above the gallery, the top floors of the building. To get there we took an elevator from the back of the showroom, a mahogany-paneled affair, much fancier than the public cage elevator below. As he was turning the key in his door, it was pulled open for us by a buxom woman wearing jeweled harlequin glasses, impeccably groomed and quite formidable in a fashionable belted woolen dress that emphasized her mighty bosom, with about a hundred cloth-covered buttons running down the front and a single strand of handsome natural pearls at her throat.

'What are you doing here?' she demanded crossly of Lebrun, in a voice as fluty as a society lady's in a Marx Brothers farce.

He was so surprised he jumped back, almost treading on my instep. 'Béatrice!' he cried in French. 'Isn't this your shopping day?'

'Renée wasn't feeling well, so we called it off. We'll go tomorrow. Everything's a mess in here. They're replacing the carpet pads. I expected you to be downstairs all morning. Now I find you're going to be barging in and out. It won't do.' She was more or less blocking the doorway, a figure to be reckoned with.

'Who's barging in and out?' said the aggrieved Lebrun. 'I merely—'

But I couldn't rein myself in any longer. Who cared where we talked? I just wanted to hear about Lily. 'Look, Mr Lebrun, if—'

Mrs Lebrun finally took notice of me standing out in the hallway. 'And who is this, may I ask? Or do you not plan to introduce him?'

Lebrun, looking as if he'd have infinitely preferred the second option, told her. Learning that I was Lily's husband immediately transformed her rather hard expression to one of sympathy and produced a long, appraising look – the sort of look that would have been delivered through a lorgnette if we were in that Marx Brothers comedy – one that I'm pretty sure translated as *Well, well, so this is the poor boob that Lily Vercier married.*

'I'm going to pour us some sherry,' Lebrun announced to end the uncomfortable silence.

'Go and sit down,' she ordered him. 'Use the living room, not the parlor. I'll be in to join you with the drinks.'

'There's no need—' Lebrun began, but she was already heading toward a sideboard at the end of the corridor. Grumbling, Lebrun motioned me to follow him.

The Lebrun living room was a largish, high-ceilinged space with draped windows, overstuffed furniture covered in floral chintz that matched the curtains, and an abundance of fat throw pillows. Some dried flowers, a big mirror over the sofa, and some old tinted photographs on the walls. No antiques. Mrs Lebrun was the interior decorator around here, I thought, and not her husband, an impression he confirmed by snatching up a couple of pillows from a corner of the sofa and tossing them onto the floor with an irritated grunt as he sat down. He indicated the other end of the sofa for me, but it seemed awkward to be looking at him sideways, so instead I took an armchair across from him, shifting the three pillows on it to make a little room.

'Go ahead and throw the damn things on the floor,' Lebrun said.

'It's fine the way it is.'

'Suit yourself. My wife will be right in with the sherry.'

I didn't care about the sherry, and I didn't give a damn about the pillows, I wanted only to hear what he had to tell me. 'Look, Mr—'

'Will you be going back home from here, Mr Simon?'

'Probably. I want to ask you—'

'If you have any trouble arranging tickets, ask Mrs Aguilar to help you. She's excellent with the airlines; knows the schedules by heart.'

'Thank you. Look, I really need—'

But I didn't make it that time either. Mrs Lebrun appeared with a tray. She set down a sherry glass on the coffee table in front of me, a second one next to a nearby armchair for herself, and a green bottle of mineral water and a glass before Lebrun. From a cut-glass decanter she poured the two sherries.

Lebrun gave her a black look. 'I wanted sherry too. I distinctly—'

'You'll drink mineral water. I don't want to go through another one of your attacks.'

'I think I should be the one—' But he quailed before he'd finished the sentence. He had noted that his wife, slit-eyed, was staring hard at the pillows he'd scattered on the floor. He knew he'd be paying for that later on and apparently thought he was better off not making things worse.

Mumble mumble, he finished.

Mrs Lebrun hadn't sat down yet. She stood there, feet apart, evaluating me through those harlequin glasses. 'Lily Vercier's husband, eh? And how is our Lily these days? Does she ever talk about us? About me?'

At last, we were going to get to Lily. 'Well, the truth is, I don't know where she is, Mrs Lebrun.' I didn't see any reason to keep this to myself. Lebrun would tell her soon enough anyway, if he hadn't already. 'In fact, the reason I'm here is that I'm trying to—'

But Lebrun cut me off, tossing a warning glance at his wife. 'Béatrice, Mr Simon doesn't know about what happened in . . . the old days. I was about to explain.'

'Aaah,' she said; a knowing sigh. This unexpected show of sympathy, while not exactly overwhelming, was so unsuited to her snooty demeanor that it shook me up more than I already was. I took a gulp of the sherry, hoping to fortify myself against whatever it was that I was on the verge of learning.

Relatively speaking, how bad could it be? I'd already found out that her father had been an enthusiastic collaborator, that she'd been pregnant at sixteen, that for seventeen years she'd steadily, convincingly lied to me about things big and small, keeping me out of the most important parts of her early life.

'Show him the picture,' she said. 'That's the best way.'

Lebrun shook his head so hard his cheeks wobbled. 'No, I think not, Béatrice.'

'What picture?' I asked with my heart thumping in my ears.

'There's no reason—' Lebrun began.

'If you won't, I will,' she snapped. 'He has a right.'

Lebrun hung his head and said no more.

I felt cold sweat pop out on my forehead. *Oh, Lord, what was coming now?*

Mrs Lebrun opened a wall cabinet and rummaged out of sight for a moment, then returned with a thin, tabloid-size newspaper. Lebrun, having apparently surrendered to her dominant force of personality, watched, sunk in edgy silence.

'It's the best way, Charles,' she told him again, putting the paper down in front of me with the front page up. It was a yellowed old paper, *Les Dépêches*, according to the masthead, and dated 20 September, 1944. I looked up at her. 'What. . . ?'

She gestured with her rounded chin at the black-and-white photograph that took up half the page. There was a brief caption in French beneath it: '*À Veaudry, la justice est servie.*' *In Veaudry, justice is served.*

The photograph showed a crowd scene in the square in front of the town hall, which was battered from bombs or shells, but still recognizable. Most of the people in it were men, some drawn-up and magisterial, others jeering at – and in some cases blatantly ogling – three dazed-looking, half-naked women huddled together in their midst. The photographer had arranged the participants so that the men were posed well to either side and there was a clear field of view to the women, who had been made to face the camera. The one on the left, only a teenager, had apparently resisted, so that the man nearest to her was pushing her chin up and around to make her comply. All three of them were bare to the waist, the bodices of their dresses having been pulled down around their hips. All were spattered with blood or filth, all had crudely shaven heads. The ones on either side had swastikas painted – no, tarred – between their breasts, and the one in the middle had a clumsily lettered sign hung around her neck: *We whored with the Germans.*

The one on the left, the teenager with that rough, hostile hand shoving her chin around so that she stared straight into the camera lens was, dear God in heaven, Lily.

Chapter Sixteen

HOW LONG I sat there staring at it I have no idea. I could almost hear the hiss and feel the heat as it seared itself into my brain, an image that will be with me every day of my life. That poor, scared, defiant child – she would have been sixteen in September 1944 – with her tiny new breasts like flower buds, and that shaven head, and that runny black swastika on her chest, and those leering faces . . . no matter what those men had been through, no matter what she was guilty of, how could people bring themselves to do something like that? And how guilty of anything could a girl that age be anyway? I didn't care if she'd screwed the whole German army, she didn't deserve this. Not for making love.

20 September, 1944. Only six months before she'd walked into my life in London. It was near-impossible to believe.

I sat up suddenly. 'The haircut,' I mumbled to myself. 'Oh, Lord.'

That appealingly close-cropped hair, that gaminlike bob that had made her so irresistible when I looked up and saw her waiting so charmingly at my desk – it was short because they'd forced her head down and publicly sheared all the hair off it in Veaudry only a little while before. And me, like a dumb puppy falling over its big feet trying to please, I'd told her a dozen times how terrific it looked, how unusual it was, how much I liked it. She'd managed to smile and look pleased, but every mention of it must have been like a knife in her heart.

If I'd been alone instead of with the Lebruns I probably would have moaned aloud, or kicked myself or at least smacked my forehead. As it was, I just stifled a groan, or maybe I didn't quite stifle it. How stupid I'd been, how utterly dense. Oh, sure, nobody could say it was my fault for not realizing. In England, where we'd met, the French punishment for 'horizontal collaboration,' as they called it, wasn't yet general knowledge, so there was no way for me to know, right? Besides, she was working at Free French headquarters; why would I associate her with collaboration, horizontal or otherwise? Later on, by the time I'd heard stories about shaven-headed women in France being paraded through the streets, Lily was part of my life; there was no reason to think about them in connection with her. And then even later, when she'd kept the same hairstyle through the years, I'd just associated it with the popular new Audrey Hepburn/Leslie Caron look. A lot of women looked like waifs.

Given all that, you can hardly blame me for not putting two and two together, right? Right. So why didn't it make me feel any better?

And why, I wondered now, had she never let her hair grow out over these many years? If it were me, I think I'd have done it at the first chance, the better to put those rotten memories behind me as much as I could. But Lily hadn't. Deep down, had she never gotten over her sense of guilt – or dishonor, or degradation, or self-hatred, or God knows what – so that even now she felt unworthy of having long hair? And – another sudden insight – was this where her unwillingness to have more children of her own came from?

Where the hell was Louis when I needed him?

When I turned the paper over so that I didn't have to see the photograph anymore and looked up at last, Mrs Lebrun had taken a seat beside her husband, and both of them were watching me, their drinks in their hands. For a moment it threw me to find myself still in that civilized, comfortable room. I had the feeling that I was returning to the real world, having somehow made it back from a journey to hell.

'Would you like to ask us anything?' Mrs Lebrun asked, gently for her.

I nodded, not trusting myself to speak. I felt awful, probably worse than I ever had in my life. It was as if I'd been violated myself, marched naked through the streets to be cursed and spat upon by any one who felt like it. *Let me find Lily*, I prayed silently. *Let me get down on my knees and apologize to her and ask her to forgive me*. Not so much for the things I'd done or said, although there was that too, but for the things I'd been thinking. My mind had been hardening toward her, I realized now. I'd turned smarmy and self-righteous, suspecting her of things she hadn't done, blaming her for things that weren't her fault, and – worst of all – seeing myself as the victim in all that had happened these last weeks.

But now, to see this . . . I couldn't understand how she'd been able to put it behind her the way she had. If it had been me, I think I'd have been a nut case today – a psychopath, or a paranoiac, maybe both. But all these years Lily had been – or seemed – unscarred, supremely normal, a wonderful, generous lover and companion. Where did I get off, me with my callow, painless, warless adolescence, criticizing that remarkable woman for doing everything she could to forget what they'd done to her and even to pretend to us both that it had never happened?

'What happened—' I cleared my throat to get the words out. 'What happened to her baby?'

'Ah, that's a sad story,' Lebrun began.

'She was stillborn,' Mrs Lebrun said. 'Such things were common at the time.'

She. A little girl. I shook my head. I don't know why, but somehow it made it worse that it was a girl. Jesus, poor Lily. 'And the father was German? Is that what it . . . this' – I pointed at the newspaper – 'was about?'

Nothing in this world could have made me look at it again, despite my having been staring so avidly at it only a few moments ago. I felt depleted, sucked empty of bone and muscle, as if it were only the chair that kept me from collapsing into a pulpy sack on the floor.

'Yes, all right, that's what it was about,' said Lebrun, 'but you must understand that it would be a terrible injustice to hold it against her. The Nazis, they were beasts, they forced many, many young women, and some not so young—'

'Charles, stop it,' Mrs Lebrun said severely, and to me: 'For Lily there was no question of forcing anyone to do anything, none at all.'

'Then—'

'It was young love, no more, no less,' she said. 'Werner was a private from Bremerhaven, far from home and not so very much older than Lily was. The world had turned to blood and ashes around them and so two young people found what comfort they could in each other. I hope you're not the kind of man to let such a thing affect your feelings about your wife.'

'No.' Once upon a time, maybe I would have been, but not anymore. The photograph had taken care of that. 'What happened to him – Werner?'

Lebrun answered with a shrug. 'Dead also. Killed in a munitions explosion a little before the baby was born. A shame. He wasn't one of the bad ones, not a little Hitler, just another soldier.'

The photograph swam back into my mind despite my effort to keep it out. I closed my eyes, not that it did any good. God, that poor, scared sixteen-year-old girl. Her mother dead, her baby dead, her lover dead, her father fled in disgrace, and then to be . . . to be . . . I shook my head; it was too appalling to think about.

I shivered. 'Why did you . . . what made you keep a picture like that? I would have burned it, I would have—' I was angry with them, I realized. If they hadn't kept it, I'd never have seen it.

'Well—' began Mrs Lebrun.

'We kept it,' said Lebrun, flushing, 'so that we would remember what they did, so that later on, when the lies and the denials started, we would *know*.'

I saw that half my sherry was left. I downed it in one swallow and sagged back in my chair, still trying to find my bearings. 'Mr Lebrun, why didn't you tell me about this before?'

'You never asked me. I didn't think it was for me to tell you.'

Mrs Lebrun looked at him disapprovingly. 'Charles.'

He glanced guiltily at her, then back at me. 'All right, the truth is, I was going to tell you the first time you came to Barcelona, when we talked in my office, but on second thought . . .'

'Second thought?' I said. 'Didn't you think it was important? Didn't you think that, with my wife missing the way she was—'

He cut me off. 'When I told you that Marcel had been accused of collaboration, you responded so violently, with so much emotion, that I didn't know how you'd react if you learned about Lily. I didn't want to cause you pain, that's all.'

'He means,' said Mrs Lebrun coolly, 'that he didn't want to cause himself pain. Charles isn't one for conflict or emotional scenes.'

Lebrun hunched his plump shoulders. 'It's true. I like peace, what can I say?'

It didn't seem to me that I'd responded so very violently, but maybe I wasn't remembering, and in any case I understood his point of view. I wasn't exactly one for emotional scenes either. 'I understand,' I said, 'but I'd appreciate whatever you can tell me now.'

Lebrun was reluctant, but under Mrs Lebrun's stern direction the story came out bit by bit. Lily had become pregnant by Werner in

December 1943, when she was fifteen. (*Fifteen!*) Not long afterward, her mother had come down with a serious, debilitating lung infection, and Marcel Vercier, unable to care for both his bedridden, terminally ill wife and pregnant, self-willed daughter (too busy pursuing his amiable association with Major vom Steeg? I wondered), had begged the Lebruns to take Lily into their care until Mrs Vercier's illness had reached its inevitable end, which was not long in coming.

'Poor, lost child,' he said, shaking his head. 'We'd known her since she was a baby. A good, gentle girl who had lost her way. How could we say no? Out of sincere affection, we welcomed her into our home with—'

'Sincere affection and the butter we got every week,' Mrs Lebrun interjected scathingly, 'and some rice, and even eggs. And a few other luxuries that you didn't mind making use of. Coffee! All provided by Werner.'

Lebrun's objection was weak, muttered into the back of his hand. 'That isn't really fair, Béatrice. Besides, I don't remember you objecting.'

'And soap, real soap, not that horrible green clay. And *fish*.' Mrs Lebrun had a dreamy look on her face, almost a smile. 'Do you remember little Marguerite's eyes when she saw fish on her plate after all those weeks of cold boiled chestnuts? And for dessert, a banana? She didn't know what it was. And *bread*! Bread by the loaf instead of a few stale slices a week. You're French, Mr Simon, and you know: we French can't taste food if there's no bread with it.'

Lebrun looked pleadingly at me. 'We're not bad people, Mr Simon. We would have taken Lily in in any case. Like everyone else, we were hungry all the time and we had an infant daughter of our own, so terribly thin. . . . If Werner wanted to help us in taking care of his Lily—'

His Lily. How strange.

'—then where was the harm? Did we steal food from our neighbors? No, these were German provisions. The soldiers would have gobbled them up if we hadn't.'

'I don't think you're bad people,' I said, not entirely honestly. 'I'm grateful to you for taking her in.' That part was true anyway. I looked down at my hands. 'The baby,' I said, 'had she named it?'

'Odile,' said Mrs Lebrun.

Odile. Her mother's name. 'Did she have it while she was with you?'

'In our house, in the bedroom. There was a midwife, but it didn't help.'

'You can imagine her state of mind,' Lebrun said.

I could indeed. My own wasn't in such good shape either. I nodded. 'Do you mind if I have a little more sherry?'

Mrs Lebrun got out of her chair to pour it for me, and added some to her own glass. They were both watching me.

I swallowed some of it and looked down at my hands. 'I'd like to know . . . can you tell me . . . I mean, the . . . the incident in the picture, how did it happen? Was there a tribunal, a trial. . . ?'

Was there any real reason I needed the details? No, but somehow I felt I had to know everything; a kind of obligation, I suppose. If she could bear living through it, I ought to be able to bear hearing about it, something like that. Or maybe it was more along the lines of self-punishment, a penance.

Lebrun barked with bitter laughter. 'A trial! No, my friend, there were no fancy tribunals for this kind of "crime." This was only a few days after "King Charles" strutted into Paris. This was the people's justice, the people's—'

'Charles, stop ranting,' Mrs Lebrun said. 'I'm sure Mr Simon is upset enough without your having one of your fits. Besides, it will make you ill.' She wet her lips on the rim of her sherry glass, put it down on the mahogany coffee table, and folded her hands in her lap.

'It was a week after the baby was born dead,' she said quietly. 'They came to the house for her, a mob of them—'

'With the bastard Goujon at their head,' Lebrun muttered. 'The great hero.'

'Yes,' said Mrs Lebrun. 'They already had poor Jeanne and Madeleine with them – the other girls you saw in the photograph – they were being pulled along with ropes around their waists – and now they wanted Lily. I explained that she wasn't well yet, but there was no reasoning with them—'

'All you had to do was look at their eyes to see how crazy they were,' Lebrun said. 'They shoved us out of the way, they threw a rope over her. She was crying. Goujon slapped her in the face, one side and then the other, bang, bang. They took her out the door. She fell down the front steps. They pulled her up. . . .'

I was hearing and not hearing at the same time, as if my brain, unable to absorb the horror pouring into it, was being dragged along unwillingly, far behind the words themselves.

'Goujon, did you say?' Only now, after hearing the name twice, had it registered. Claude Goujon, the grim sonofabitch with the creepy voice, the one who'd been making those insinuations about Lily in the café.

They looked at me, surprised. 'You know who he is?' Lebrun asked.

I didn't answer. I had remembered something. I reached for the newspaper with the photograph, the picture I had told myself I would never look at again, and looked at it again. And I was right. The man with his coarse, rough hand on Lily's terrified, defiant face, twisting her slender neck, was Goujon, all right, younger of course, but Goujon.

Until that moment, I'd never hated anyone in my life. Oh, I'd been under the impression that I had, for one petty thing or another, but I hadn't known what I was talking about. Now I understood what murderous, blazing hatred felt like. That miserable bastard – all I wanted to do was get my hands on him and twist his head around until his neck snapped. My hands were shaking. My head felt as if it were filled with steam under pressure, as if my eyes were about to pop out. I would go back to Veaudry, I would hunt him down, call him out . . .

'. . . made them get on their knees in the square and shaved their heads,' Mrs Lebrun was saying. 'Then they put those dreadful signs on them, and hauled them all the way down Avenue Carnot on ropes, while everybody . . . well, people were very vicious, very cruel. Many were sorry later.'

'Plenty weren't,' muttered Lebrun.

Mrs Lebrun shrugged. 'And that's the story, Mr Simon. They brought them back to the square afterward for the triumphal photograph.'

I had been taking deep breaths while she spoke, trying to calm my extraordinary feelings, but inside I was still raving, hatching homicidal plans for Goujon. After a few more moments, I managed more or less of a return to rationality.

'And then what happened?' I asked thickly.

'Happened? Nothing happened,' Lebrun said. 'Everybody went home.'

'No, I mean after everybody went home. What happened to Lily then? I met her in London only a few months later. How did she get there?'

Lebrun got a little squirmy at that, darting glances at his wife, but she stared fixedly back at him. *You* explain it.

'Well,' he said, 'she was very hard to control, you know, and it wasn't easy to support her with no more help coming from Werner, and, and, you know, the tribunals were forming, and there was talk, and so much confusion, and, and—'

'The fact is, we don't know,' Mrs Lebrun said when it appeared that Lebrun was never going to get there. 'We decided it was for the best if we – all of us – left Veaudry as soon as possible. Before the week was out, Charles and I went to Andorra and then came here to Barcelona. Lily didn't tell us where she was going.'

'She was sixteen years old,' I said slowly. 'Her head was shaven, she'd been frightened, and hurt, and humiliated, her mother had died, her baby had died, her father had left her . . . and you just let her go off on her own, to you didn't know where?'

'We had our own problems!' Lebrun said roughly. 'We had our own poor child to worry about! Lily wasn't *our* daughter. We'd taken her in as a favor, we'd fed her and clothed her—'

'Charles, be quiet,' Mrs Lebrun said. 'You see, Mr Simon, Lily stopped speaking. She wouldn't talk to us or to anybody after they . . . after the incident. We believe she may have gone to some relatives in Bordeaux, but we don't know for certain.'

'Bordeaux? I didn't think she had any family in B—'

I stopped myself. There were a lot of things that I didn't think, but that sure hadn't meant they weren't so anyway. Besides, I was out of questions that might conceivably be of help, or maybe I didn't have the will to ask anymore. I was full up on information about my wife's long-ago life, thank you, and didn't know how much more I could stand.

I stood up disjointedly, not feeling like the same person I'd been when I'd sat down. 'I appreciate your taking the time to talk to me,' I said.

'So what will you do now?' Lebrun asked.

'I don't know,' I said.

'Do you think you'll find her?'

'I don't know.'

Chapter Seventeen

THERE WAS A time, long ago, in another universe, when, so it seems to me now, I had been a fairly happy-go-lucky guy, taking things as they came and enjoying, or at least making the most of, whatever life tossed in my lap. Now dejection, fatigue, and pessimism were becoming my normal states of being, and I could feel my shoulders wanting to slump as I left the Lebruns' and slogged along the ancient streets through another gray, cold Catalonian day. But I was smart enough to understand that at least some of my depression of the moment was coming from my stomach. It was after one o'clock, and all I'd had to eat that day was the Hotel Carlota's standard breakfast of coffee and two slices of white bread with jam. And the sherry I'd had at the Lebruns' hadn't sat all that well.

So on the way back to my room I stopped for the sake of my spirits at a cheerful little restaurant with bright red tablecloths, situated on the Plaza del Rey. I took a table near the window, where I could look directly across the square at the monolithic old Palace of the Counts of Barcelona. Back in the days when Barcelona had been no more than an eventual holiday destination, this building had been number one on my sightseeing list, for it was there, on the worn stone steps leading up to the entrance door, that Christopher Columbus was greeted by the king and queen of Spain on his triumphant return from the Americas in 1493. And a little later, in the great hall, Ferdinand, Isabella, and the royal court assembled to hear the first account of the discovery of the New World.

From a Western historian's point of view, events don't get any more momentous than that, and I had hoped that sitting there in full sight of it, no more than fifty yards from the very same stones on which they'd stood, might give me a lift, but it didn't seem to matter. I didn't even feel any desire to walk over and stand on the steps myself and make the connection over time that I usually love. I just didn't care.

Lunch – the *menú del día*: salad, a bouillabaisselike fish stew, and cream custard for dessert – filled my stomach well enough but didn't do much for my mood either, and I sat there afterward, nursing my coffee and custard, feeling miserable. I was looking longingly not at the Palace of the Counts but at the rack near the door, on which hung my coat, in the inside pocket of which was an envelope that contained both of the letters that Lily had sent me. I'd gotten in the admittedly pathetic habit of carrying them around with me so that when the desire seized me to read them yet again – which was many times a day – I could either pore over them one more time looking for some kind of maudlin solace, or clues, or who knows what, or else deny myself the pleasure (if that's what it was), and thereby demonstrate to myself my rocklike strength and self-control.

As usual, rocklike strength was no match for maudlin solace, and after a few minutes I ordered another coffee, went to the rack, got the letters, and brought them back to the table, where I sat hunched over them and over the steaming little cup like a miser over his gold. By now I knew them by heart but I needed to touch the paper that she had touched. They'd been read so many times they were limp and parting at the creases. I smoothed out the first one.

My Darling Pete . . .

To my amazement, my eyes immediately filled with tears, the first time that had happened since the day she'd left, or rather the night of the day she'd left. Maybe it was the weight of the terrible things I'd learned from the Lebruns, or maybe I was still weak from my wound and the surgery afterward; whichever, it was clear that my resources – whatever inner strength I'd started out with – were just about depleted. I was out of steam, out of leads, out of hope, and I suddenly felt very lost and a long, long way from home.

The happy, effortless life full of laughter and love that Lily and I had had together now seemed like something I'd read in a book; the story of somebody else's life, not mine. It was hard to believe it had actually happened to me and no longer possible to imagine that someday it might pick up where it had left off. If she had walked through the door right then, I wouldn't have known what to say to her. I couldn't quite bring to mind the easy way we used to talk to one another.

I folded the letters up. I no longer wanted to look at them, I just wanted to go back to my room. I wanted to sleep, to have my mind empty for a few hours. I paid my bill and put the letters back in the envelope, muttering to myself a little when the second one, the cruelly brief 'Dear Pete' one, refused to fit in without an extra fold, a third one, at the bottom. It happened every time, and every single time I forgot and had to take it out to refold it. Why it irritated me as much as it did I didn't know, and why it wouldn't fit in a standard business envelope in the first place I had no—

With the letter half in, half out of the envelope, I froze. My brain, which had been sitting in my skull doing me as much good as a baked potato, was suddenly swarming with inferences and implications, all whirling around each other. For another minute or two I sat there, almost like an awed spectator watching my own mind at work, watching the conclusions line up in an orderly row.

'Damn,' I said softly.

I knew where Lily was.

SHE WAS RIGHT here in Europe and had been all along.

Fizzing with an energy I hadn't felt for days, I got up, slipped the envelope into my pocket, put on the coat, and strode – when was the last time I 'strode'? – out of the restaurant on my way to Las Ramblas and the España airline ticket office.

I was on my way to Corsica.

The evidence had been staring me in the face for days and all I'd ever done was grumble at the minor annoyance of having to fold that second letter an extra time whenever I put it away. It was that additional crease that was the giveaway, and I could hardly believe now that it hadn't clicked the first time I'd noticed it. Because, you see, there could be only one reason that a standard-length sheet of American typewriter paper would need to be folded more than twice to fit into a standard American business envelope, and that was that it wasn't really standard-length. Obviously. And what *that* meant – obviously – was that it wasn't really American. French business stationery, on the other hand, like most European business stationery, was a little narrower and a little longer than its American counterpart: about 8¼ by 11½ inches, compared to 8½ by 11 inches in the United States. Just long enough so it wouldn't fit into a regulation American envelope when folded the standard way, into thirds.

I no longer had the envelope that it had come in, but I remembered that it had arrived with only the usual two folds, which had to mean that the envelope had also been European-size, large enough to hold it. So how to explain the fact that it had been postmarked Washington, DC? Easy. She gave the letter to someone on the European side of the Atlantic who was flying to the United States – Washington probably just happened to be the destination – and asked him or her to mail it on arrival, thus giving it a US stamp and postmark and leading me to think she was still in the States. That seemed maybe a little implausible to me, even baroque, until I remembered that the letter had been dated 2 December, but the postmark on the envelope had been 4 December, two days later. And it certainly hadn't taken her two days to complete the fifty words enclosed (forty-six if you didn't count 'Dear Pete' and 'Love, Lily') or to find a mailbox.

So she had come to Europe. Of that much I was fairly sure. (True, I had no idea of the paper size in Asia or South America, or any other far-off continent, but I couldn't imagine a sequence of events that would put her in one of those places.) Now then: why Corsica in particular? Well, that took an additional leap or two of logic. The thing is, I was almost certain there was no place in Europe, outside of France, where she had any relatives or even acquaintances, and no place to which she had ever expressed attachment. That left only France, which was a strange choice to come down to, because the country she detested most of all was France.

Except for one atypical little-known corner of it, a rugged, mountainous, hundred-mile-long island out in the Mediterranean a little over a hundred miles from the mainland. Corse, as the French called it. Corsica, where Lily had spent those sweetly remembered childhood summers at her father's family's chestnut farm in the hills overlooking the sea near Calvi. I'd heard often enough how they were the dearest memories of her childhood, and how much she'd loved her old-country grandmother and grandfather, and the old stone farmhouse, and the herbal fragrances that rose from the hills on warm nights. Even her recollections of her father had been warm and loving when she'd talked about their times there.

So where else could she be but the family chestnut farm in Corsica? Well, a lot of other places, really, but this one made the most sense. Besides, I had a *feeling* about it. I didn't expect to have any trouble finding the place either. I knew the family name was Vercier, and I knew the farm was in the vicinity of Calvi, which wasn't exactly a giant metropolis. How hard could it be?

First, though, even before going to the ticket office to book a flight, I stopped at the post office to telephone the Gianinis, as I'd been doing every afternoon. I was so excited about Corsica I almost wished that there wouldn't be anything from her in Bensonhurst. Unfortunately, I got my wish.

At the airline ticket office, the one employee who spoke English was out for the day and I had a heck of a time arranging for a flight to Calvi, which would have been no easy trick to reach from Barcelona, even if I'd spoken the language. Flying from country to country in Europe is not the same thing as flying from state to state in the United States. In the end – after almost forty minutes – I emerged clutching not a single ticket but a little booklet of them. I would fly from Barcelona to Madrid, from Madrid to Paris, from Paris to Marseille, and finally from Marseille to Ajaccio, Corsica, from where I'd be on my own for the last fifty overland miles to Calvi. However, if I understood her right, the clerk believed she'd heard somewhere that there might be buses between the two. At any rate, there had been in the 1950s.

The earliest flight I could get from Madrid would leave the next morning, and I would arrive in Ajaccio twenty hours later, in the predawn, having caught what rest I could on the planes and during the layovers in Marseille and Paris. That was fine with me. I doubted if I could sleep anyway. Who needed sleep? I went back to my room to rebandage my incision, pack my things, count my money (things were getting tighter), and make arrangements for getting out to the airport.

But at the hotel there was a telegram from Inspector Juneaux: *Please call at once. Important.*

Not as important as my trip to Corsica, but what the hell, I had time enough to telephone him, so back out to the long-distance booth in the post office I went. He was in his Melun office waiting, and he was relieved to hear from me. 'Ah, I was hoping I'd reach you before you left for home. Can you come back to France?'

'You mean now? Inspector, I was on my way to Corsica. I think I know where my wife is.'

'Can it wait a day, Mr Simon? We think we have him, but—'

'Him? You mean the killer? Already?'

'They're detaining him in St-Germain-en-Laye, but they can keep him for no more than twenty-four hours without some substantiation. You're the only one who saw his face. I need you to look at some photographs.'

'You want me to come to St-Germain-en-Laye?' I wasn't sure where it was.

'No, no, we could do it in Veaudry if you like.'

'Well . . .' Naturally I wanted to do what I could to put that toad-faced bastard away. But right now I wanted to find Lily more. 'Look, couldn't we—'

'Will you be coming through Paris?'

'Well, yes, the airport, tomorrow at twelve-thirty—'

'Perfect. I'll have someone meet you and drive you here. It's only half an hour. Or we could do it in Veaudry, if you prefer. When you're ready to leave, we'll take you back.'

'Inspector, I only have a two-hour layover. I don't think I'd better—'

'All right, then, I can have someone meet you with the photo books. You can look at them right there, at the airport.' He was practically pleading. 'If you recognize him you could make out an affidavit to that effect on the spot. I'll have someone there who can certify it. You could be back in the air in two hours easily. You wouldn't have to leave the airport at all.'

But while he'd been talking, my mind had been working away on a tack of its own. It had taken me this long to figure out where she was; I could spare one more day. 'No, that's all right,' I said slowly. 'Actually, I'd like to go back to Veaudry' The skin on the backs of my forearms prickled. 'I have a little unfinished business there.'

BUT AS EAGER as I was to get my hands on the wretched Goujon, I wasn't up to facing the non-English-speaking staff at España Airlines to change my already-complex travel arrangements, so I took Lebrun up on his offer to make use of Mrs Aguilar's airline expertise. I really didn't want to see Lebrun again, so I was gratified when she handled the whole thing in the outer office inside of ten minutes, without Lebrun's even knowing I was there. But there was a further complication: the Marseille–Ajaccio flight was only a twice-a-week affair at this time of year; I would have to wait three days for the next one. Fortunately, the resourceful Mrs Aguilar came up with a perfect solution: I would spend the next day in Veaudry taking care of Juneaux's business – and mine – then take a 5 p.m. flight from Paris to Marseille in time to catch the overnight ferry to Corsica. Not only did the second-class ferry fare work out to be a whole lot cheaper than my original Marseille–Ajaccio flight, but it would be faster as well; the boat would dock at Calvi itself in the morning, probably before the Ajaccio–Calvi bus (if it still existed) could have gotten me there.

If I had things figured correctly, and if the logistics really worked out, and if, knock on wood, she was all right – something I refused to let myself doubt, although worry for her safety never stopped nibbling at the edges of my mind – I would be seeing Lily, talking to her, in less than forty-eight hours. Now that I was this close I was too excited to get much sleep during the night. And when I finally did drop off it didn't do me much good as far as having a restful night went; I had the damn Dream again, right up to and including waking up in the mental ward, tied to the bed.

TRUE TO HIS word, Juneaux had a uniformed *officier de paix* come and get me at the airport and drive me in a police car to Veaudry. An older man, tired-looking and short of temper – picking up visiting Americans was obviously beneath him – he had nothing at all to say, once having determined my identity. My questions were answered with shrugs, my remarks with shrugs plus grunts, so I spent the time looking out the window instead. The drive had little to hold my interest. The broad, beautiful Parisian boulevards were quickly left behind, giving way to miles of commercial thoroughfares in the working-class bedroom communities that ring the city, and then to sugar-beet fields and rolling countryside punctuated by look-alike villages, each with its central square of grass or cobblestones, its two-story railroad hotel, its stuccoed railroad station, and its somber gray Monument to the Fallen.

That left me free to dwell on bloody-minded thoughts of Claude Goujon. But did I really intend to find him and kill him? No, of course not. I mean, I know I did when I looked at that picture in the newspaper, and I *think* I did when I told Juneaux I was coming to Veaudry, but by now I realized that I'd been kidding myself; I wasn't the murdering type and I knew it.

All right, then, did I mean to physically assault him? Well, yes, actually, I did. I grant you, I'm not that type either, but, as Juneaux had said, nobody acts according to type a hundred percent of the time, and I thought I could make a good case for an exception in this instance. The wild, blood-hot rage that had pounded against the inside of my skull when I'd recognized him in the photograph had subsided as suddenly as it had come but had been replaced by something colder and deeper, like a frozen knife blade that I was carrying around, wedged deep inside my chest. He had the look of a tough guy and I was all too aware that I was nothing of the sort, but one way or another, I would get in my licks; I would make the bastard pay.

That photo was fixed in my mind, you see, more real than life. Every time I closed my eyes I saw it, and each time I was overwhelmed with a sense of . . . I don't know, guilt, I think; a horrible, hollow feeling that I had failed to protect Lily at the lowest moment of her life, that I should have been there when she needed me so terribly. It didn't make any sense, I know, but that's what I was feeling, and it sat inside me like a stone. When I found her I would make it up to her ten times over if I could, but I also had to do something now. I felt awful: guilty, frustrated, remorseful, vengeful . . .

And was punching another human being in the face, twenty long years after the fact, going to make me feel any better?

You better believe it.

Chapter Eighteen

THE POLICE STATION in Veaudry was a plain, narrow building between a greengrocer's and a pastry shop, so inconspicuous that I asked the officer if he was sure it was the right place, to which he replied with his usual economy of words, irritably tipping his head at an unassuming little brass plaque next to the door: *Sous préfecture de Veaudry*.

When I went in, I saw Inspector Juneaux seated on a high stool at a tall, angled wooden desk in a sort of bullpen area, a lived-in-looking space with a few casually arranged desks and lots of papers and charts thumbtacked every which way on the walls. It smelled like old coffee and old sweat, which, if I remembered correctly, was also the way the precinct house in Sheepshead Bay had smelled, so I guessed it was just the way police stations smelled. Amazing; after a lifetime of never having been in one, I was actually getting to where I could generalize about them.

Inside, there seemed to be some problem with the heating. It was freezing. Most of the people, women and men, were working in heavy, collared sweaters. Juneaux had put on a scruffy cardigan under his suit coat and wound a long, thin woolen muffler that had once probably been green around his neck. On his hands was a stubby pair of fingerless woolen gloves, the kind that always make you look colder (and more pathetic) than you already are. All the poor guy needed was a green visor and a pair of sleeve garters – well, and the loss of sixty or seventy pounds – and he could have passed for Bob Cratchit.

I cleared my throat. 'Hello, Inspector Juneaux, how are you?'

He looked up and smiled fondly. 'Ah.'

I pointed at a thin file folder on the desk. 'Are those the photographs?'

He nodded, opening it to the first two sheets and sliding over to make room for me. The pictures were pasted to loose-leaf paper, six to a page. Most, but not all, were prison photos, front and side views.

I riffled through them with my fingers. There were eight pages, total. 'Is this all? I thought there'd be more.'

'There are more if you wish, but first these,' he said. 'Forty-eight men are pictured here. One of them is the gentleman being held in St-Germain-en-Laye. See if you recognize him. If you're not sure about one, tell me and we'll set it aside to look at again.'

One glance at the first six and my confidence took a direct hit. The faces weren't that different from one another or, for that matter, from the picture I'd been carrying in my mind, which seemed suddenly to have grown a little fuzzy.

'You have to remember,' I said dubiously, 'I only saw him for a fraction of a second, and I was looking up into his face upside down, and everything was happening so fast – he was trying to bash me—'

Juneaux was as conciliatory as ever. 'Don't worry, if you don't see him, you don't, and that's all there is to it. It isn't your fault. For all we know, we have the wrong man in St-Germain-en-Laye. Any conclusions you come to, positive or negative, will be helpful.'

After six pages the only conclusion I'd reached was that French criminals looked alike: squat-faced, dark-haired, wide-mouthed, and dumb-looking. But then, when I'd just about given up, one of the pictures on the seventh page hit home. Maybe it was the way he'd posed, with his head thrown back a little, so that I found myself looking up into those same black, froggy nostril slits. To be sure, I turned the page around to give me the same bottom-to-top view I'd had from the tabletop. And there he was, Mr Toadface.

'Him,' I said, placing my finger on the space between his eyes.

Juneaux had been watching over my shoulder, quietly smoking. His face gave nothing away. 'You're certain?'

'It's him, all right. Bring on the affidavit.'

Now he smiled, a big, slow, close-mouthed grin. 'With pleasure, Mr Simon. And when that's done, what would you say to something to eat, courtesy of the Police Nationale? We French, we always like to have something substantial in the afternoon to get us through to dinner, as you know.'

I grinned back at him. 'That's news to me, but in your case I believe it.'

'Possibly they don't do it in Lyon,' he said.

THE NAME OF the man in the photograph was Georges Frévard and he was what Juneaux had said he might be: a freelance assassin, a Parisian killer-for-hire with a long history of detainments for 'suspicion' that had never materialized into anything beyond a few short jail sentences for minor offenses. There had never been any reliable eyewitnesses to his assassinations. Fortunately, Juneaux, relying on my 'toad' description, had concluded that Frévard might be the man he wanted and had let the nearby police departments know he was looking for him. So when he had been stopped in St-Germain-en-Laye, on the other side of Paris, for improperly exiting a traffic circle, the alert *gendarme* who had stopped the car had remembered and taken him in. The St-Germain-en-Laye *gendarmerie* had contacted Juneaux yesterday.

'Who hired him, do you know?' I asked. We were a mile or so outside of Veaudry, in Le Cheval Blanc, one of a chain of homely, institutional-looking roadside diners serving highway travelers in a hurry, the French equivalent of a Denny's or an International House of Pancakes. Juneaux had ordered the plate of the day for both of us without bothering to consult me. 'You'll like it,' he'd assured me.

'No, we don't know who hired him,' he said now. 'I haven't talked to Frévard yet; I'll do that later this afternoon. But of course he'll deny having anything to do with it and most likely provide a well-turned-out alibi to prove it. And even if he doesn't deny it he won't tell us who put him up to it. And even if he does tell us who put him up to it, he won't be able to say anything useful. It will just be another middle man who used a false name.'

I sagged. 'So what's the point? What have we accomplished?'

He was wounded. 'What have we accomplished? Plenty! We have a long-sought professional murderer in custody, and at long last we have a reliable eyewitness with whose help we should be able to lock him up for years to come.'

'You do? Who?'

Juneaux tilted his head and cocked an eyebrow at me.

'Oh,' I said after a moment. 'You mean me.'

'You did sign a deposition,' he said warningly. 'I hope you're not now—'

'No, I'll stand by it. And if you want me to, I'll back it up in court.'

He nodded, satisfied. 'Good, that's as it should be. As for the rest, all in good time.' His eyes lit up. 'Ah, look, here comes our order.'

He was right about my liking it. The daily special turned out to be like nothing ever seen in a Denny's: a round wooden cutting board set with big wedges of four kinds of cheese – Camembert, St-André, Reblochon, and aged, deliciously smelly, blue-veined Roquefort – and a thick slice each of a mousse-smooth *pâte de foie gras* and a coarse-textured *pâte de campagne* made from who knew what, but luscious all the same. All this with a basket of crusty bread and a bowl of *crudités* – carrot sticks, celery sticks, and those wonderful, rosy French radishes. The cheeses and pates were enough to stock a medium-size delicatessen, and we were expected, like those who came before and those who would follow, to eat as much as we wanted, leaving the rest for future diners.

Juneaux had a mesmerizing way of eating this kind of thing. A tiny sliver of cheese would be placed on a thin slice of bread and then, instead of putting it in his mouth, he would extend his tongue as a sort of plate on which the tidbit would be placed. The tongue would then be slowly withdrawn with its burden, and the result would be savored with great concentration, thoughtfully masticated, and eventually swallowed. It sounds disgusting, but it made the food look so good that it actually made me hungrier, and for some considerable time I came close to keeping up with him.

After a while, when I'd slowed down and my thoughts were beginning to drift, he suddenly spoke. 'You seem a little distressed.'

I looked at him, surprised. 'Well, of course I'm distressed. I mean, I haven't found my wife yet, I saw a man murdered the other day, I was damn near killed myself, I—'

He brushed this away. 'I wouldn't like to think you've come back to Veaudry searching for trouble.'

I blinked. Was I as transparent as that? I hadn't even been thinking about Goujon at the moment. 'No!' I lied. 'Of course not. What kind of trouble, what are you talking about? You asked me to come yourself, didn't you? I came to look at the pictures, what else?'

My blathering away like that, especially when delivered with such wide-eyed sincerity, didn't help my case. His suspicions hardened. 'And your "unfinished business"?' he asked.

'That? That was only—' I set down the mineral water I'd been drinking. What the hell, why shouldn't he know? I was pretty sure he'd be on my side on this, despite his expressed commitment to civic order. 'I was talking to this man in Barcelona,' I said, slowly rotating the glass on the table. 'He's from Veaudry originally – Charles Lebrun – and he told me—'

Juneaux almost dropped his wineglass. 'How do you come to know Charles Lebrun?'

'I wouldn't say I know him, but do you remember my mentioning the Galeria Metropolitana, Vercier's gallery? Well, Lebrun was Vercier's partner, so I needed to talk to him.'

'Lebrun and Vercier,' he said grimly. 'Now there's a team for you. So that's where he ended up, Barcelona. Is his wife still with him? The charming Béatrice?'

This last was said with a lip-curling sneer, something that seemed startlingly out of character in this generally easygoing man.

I nodded. 'They're still together.'

'Good, they deserve each other. A pair of bootlicking parasites. If there had been any real justice they would have sentenced him to— Pah!' He stopped himself with an expulsion of breath. 'Ah, why am I exciting myself? I'm as bad as the rest of them. What does it matter now, it's over and done.' He reached for a celery stalk and chomped angrily down. 'I'm sorry, Mr Simon, you were saying?'

But his reaction to the mention of Lebrun's name, so similar to what Claude Goujon's had been, and almost as vehement, had brought me up short. In Barcelona, Lebrun had told me that the reason he'd been disliked in Veaudry was that he'd been able to hold on to his civil service job under the Germans, creating jealousy among the less fortunate, and that he'd left France because there had been threats against him in the aftermath. He'd feared the possibility of a citizens' tribunal himself if he'd stayed. So he'd said, but now I was becoming increasingly certain that there had been more to it than that, and I wanted to know what it was.

'Hold on a second,' I said. 'Tell me about Lebrun. Did he – was he tried too?'

Juneaux seemed to debate with himself about whether or not he wanted to go into it, then, with what seemed a sigh of resignation, he made his decision. 'Yes, he was tried. Not long after Vercier's tribunal, as a matter of fact, also right there in the Café Grand Luxe, where *this* entire affair began.'

'The Grand Luxe? Didn't I read the trials were in the Palace of Justice?'

'Public buildings that were still standing were in short supply at the time. The Café Grand Luxe *was* the Palace of Justice.'

It made me think of those westerns where the carpet-bagging judge convenes court in the local saloon. Well, what better place for a citizens' tribunal? 'What did he do? What was he charged with?'

'The name Auguste Voyenne – is it familiar to you, Mr Simon?'

'No.'

'Well, I can't say I'm surprised. Voyenne wasn't what you'd call a larger-than-life character. He was, if the truth be told, an annoying old man, opinionated, set in his ways, not overly clean – but much beloved in Veaudry.' He permitted himself a slight smile. 'At least in memory he is much beloved.'

When the Nazis occupied northern France in 1940, Juneaux told me, Auguste Voyenne had been the head clerk at the city hall for as long as anyone could remember. The Germans had permitted him to keep his position, but had added a new responsibility: he was now to supervise the printing and distribution of *Le Matin*, yet another daily news sheet extolling the virtues of National Socialism and encouraging the right-thinking citizens of Veaudry to cooperate with the many Nazi edicts necessary for their own good in these difficult times.

The elderly Voyenne had accepted the new responsibility, but from the moment it began, the propaganda program was plagued with one inexplicable difficulty after another, rarely managing two days in a row without problems: the mimeograph ink had dried out, the rotating cylinder had jammed, the stencils hadn't arrived from Paris on time, the wax on them was defective, the horse that pulled the delivery wagon was sick. And then one day the Gestapo came and took Voyenne away; he had been denounced as a saboteur by a subordinate.

At this point Juneaux lifted his eyes from the much-reduced food on the table to look directly at me and gave an almost invisible shrug, as if apologizing.

'Denounced by Lebrun?' I asked. My voice snagged in my throat. I barely knew Lebrun and certainly had no particular affection for him, but I didn't want this to be true.

'Yes, by Lebrun. There's no doubt possible. The Germans recorded it. You can look at his file too if you want to. It's right there at the city hall.'

I shook my head. 'What happened to him? To Voyenne, I mean?'

'What happened to any of them?' Juneaux said with a shrug. 'They took him away, that was all we ever knew. He didn't come back to tell us.'

'That's awful,' I mumbled. 'I'm sorry.'

'Oh, there's more than that,' Juneaux said dryly. 'As his reward the helpful Lebrun was made the new head clerk, and from that time on, miracle of miracles, there were no more problems with dried-up ink or lame horses. *Le Matin* appeared every day, like clockwork, crammed with its wretched propaganda. There were no more silly grammatical mistakes that made the readers chuckle. And a new column appeared, more corrupt and poisonous than anything the Germans had written. It was called "An Honest Frenchman's Thoughts." It was anonymous, but . . .' He shrugged.

'You think Lebrun wrote it?'

'I *know* Lebrun wrote it. The German records are explicit. He was paid an additional two hundred and fifty francs over his salary for each column, if I recall correctly.'

'So he was a collaborator too,' I said heavily.

'He and his wife as well. Oh, you should have heard her crow while Lebrun held his important position. She made no secret of her enthusiasm for the plans of the Third Reich regarding France.'

I shook my head again. Much more of this and I would be subscribing to Juneaux's old philosophy of human nature – that, when the chips were down, everybody turned into a creep. 'And were they sentenced to death?'

'No, it was a close thing, but in the end their sentence was *indignité nationale*.'

That surprised me at first, but the more I thought about it, the more I could see that it applied to someone like Lebrun. *Indignité nationale* was a penalty invented by Resistance officials at the time of the Liberation to deal with acts that didn't quite come up to (down to?) the standard of treason or criminal collusion with the enemy, which were punishable by execution. Nevertheless, they were acts of willing collaboration deserving of punishment. The term isn't easy to translate into English; it's not quite what it looks like – 'national indignity.' 'National unworthiness' is the nearest literal translation, but 'national degradation' would probably be closest to the generally understood meaning.

A sentence of *indignité nationale* could run from a few years to life and meant, aside from the humiliation and debasement that went along with it, that the person so sentenced lost a great many basic civil rights, among them the right to vote, to serve in the military, to hold public office, to be employed in the fields of law, education, or government, to be part of the management of a company, even to belong to a trade union. In short, it wasn't death but it made it pretty hard to live.

'For how long?' I asked.

'For Lebrun, life. For his wife, five years.'

'Oh, jeez.' I rotated my head to work out some of the kinks that had been knotting up over the last few minutes. Life was funny, all right. For almost twenty years, Béatrice and Charles Lebrun had been living in a state of ultimate disgrace, shunned and despised by their countrymen – only they didn't know it, since the trial had been held in their absence. And so there they were, safe and snug and rich in Barcelona, still doing business with their Nazi cronies, same as ever. It was hard to find much justice, or much sense, in that.

'Well, I'll drop them a line and let them know about it,' I said. 'I can do that much anyway.'

'Let them know about what?' Juneaux asked. He was weary of the subject, I could see, and wanted to talk about something else.

'About the sentence. Or do you think they ought to go on thinking they got away with it?'

He frowned at me. 'I don't understand.'

'The *indignité nationale*. They don't know about it.'

'How could they not know about it?'

Juneaux seemed to have shifted into one of his obtuse moods. 'They were tried *in absentia*, Inspector. They weren't there to hear it.'

'The hell they weren't,' he said heatedly. 'They stood right there in the dock, right in the Grand Luxe – in the Palace of Justice – and heard the sentence read. Naturally, Béatrice tried to argue, she wouldn't shut up. They had to gag her.'

I was genuinely surprised. 'What do you know about that,' I murmured. 'I wouldn't have . . . they seemed so . . . he was so damn convincing.'

'Yes, he never had a problem with words,' Juneaux said dryly.

Damn. If Lebrun had lied to me about that – and had done it so well – then how much else of what I'd learned in Barcelona could I trust? Anything? I looked hungrily at the wine carafe, which I hadn't touched until then, but decided against it. Yes, I thought, there was one thing that could be taken at face value. The photograph in the newspaper, that had been no invention of Lebrun's, that I could trust. The details swam up in front of my eyes again, as clear as life.

'Thanks for telling me all that, Inspector,' I said, looking at my watch. It was four-thirty. Five o'clock had been the time that Goujon had reeled me in off the street and into the Café Grand Luxe the other day, where Donnadieu and the rest had been having their wine and brandy. And about matters like wine and brandy, the French were creatures of habit. My guess was that if I went there now, I would find Goujon, probably at the same table. And I dearly wanted to find Goujon.

'Unless there's anything else,' I said, 'I probably ought to be getting along. Thanks for the meal. Can you give me a lift back to town? '

'You haven't answered my question,' he said.

I was expecting that. 'My "unfinished business," you mean? Don't take this wrong, Inspector, but it's a personal matter, something I have to take care of by myself.' It wasn't a sense of manly taciturnity that had made me reconsider and keep my affairs to myself, but a fear that if he knew I'd come to start a fight he might feel duty-bound to interfere. And I didn't want to be stopped. The revulsion I felt toward Goujon and the anticipation of revenge were the nearest things to pleasure that I'd felt for weeks.

He sighed. 'You're not planning anything foolish, are you?'

I said nothing.

'I hope not. Whatever it is, I hope you'll be prudent. I'm not sure that, even now, you comprehend the depth of feeling in these matters.'

'I'm getting there, I can tell you that,' I said.

He used his knife to pry off one last bit of St-André from the wedge, swallowed it, wiped his mouth with a napkin, and stood up, searching in a pocket for the car keys. 'Take care of yourself, my friend,' he said solemnly. 'For my sake, if nothing else. I don't want to see anything happen to you.'

I was moved. 'Thank you, Inspector. . . .'

'You're a foreigner,' he explained. 'The forms . . .' He rolled his eyes. 'You have no idea.'

BUT PAPERWORK OR not, I had an account to settle with Claude Goujon, and I didn't intend to leave Veaudry without having done it. Juneaux let me off in the Place de la République, promising to have me picked up at seven-thirty that evening for the drive to the Paris airport, and I went up to my old room at the Mercure. I wasn't spending the night, but the Police Nationale had thoughtfully booked the room for me just in case, and it gave me a place to drop my luggage and change the bandage on my shoulder. The stitches had gone in almost four days ago now, and the flesh around the wound had gotten steadily healthier-looking. There had been no draining of fluid after the first day (and not much then), and the color had gone from a raw, puffy red to a more ordinary-looking black-and-blue. I redressed it with special care, adding extra adhesive tape and pressing it firmly down, feeling like a Roman gladiator ceremonially binding himself for battle in the arena.

And what exactly did I intend when I entered the arena? Nothing too well-thought-out, I can tell you that. There were times, in fact, when I asked myself what the hell I thought I was doing acting like the Masked Avenger, but then up would come the awful image of that bastard's hand pushing Lily's scared, dirty face around to the camera, and that tarry swastika between her naked little breasts, and that roughly shaven head, and Goujon himself sneering into the lens, so righteous and self-satisfied . . . and that was enough to stop my asking questions of myself.

I suppose the closest thing I had to a plan of action was a cinematic sort of scenario in which I would walk up to him and tell him why I was there. A silence would descend on the café as everyone turned to watch us. He would rise from the table to face me and I would say: '*À Veaudry, la justice est servie.*' I would slap him hard across the face. He would sink back to his chair in silent shame, unable to look me in the eye, his hands covering his face, and I would consider the account closed.

Even at the time I think I realized it was less a plan of action than an absurd fantasy, but it gave me immense satisfaction to imagine it all the same. And if he didn't choose to sink back into his chair in silent shame? Well, my imagination didn't get me beyond that point, so I supposed we'd just see where it went from there. In a way, I hoped he didn't cave in. I *wanted* to fight him. Oh, I didn't doubt that under ordinary circumstances Goujon would have been able to wipe up the floor with me, but it was impossible to believe that the tremendous weight of moral authority I was bringing with me could fail to carry the day.

As it turned out, of course, that wasn't quite the way it happened. To begin with, Goujon wasn't in the Grand Luxe when I got there, so the adrenaline that was pumping through me, ready for action, went to waste. Donnadieu was sitting at the same table, but with two men I didn't know. I nodded to him, but his vision wasn't good enough to see me, and it wasn't until I was five feet away that he stopped whatever he was saying and recognized me, squinting through his thick glasses. At a nod from him, the other two immediately got up with their glasses and went to another table.

'Sit down, Mr Simon,' he ordered. 'Welcome back to Veaudry. Did you want to see me?'

I remained standing. 'No, I'm looking for Claude Goujon. Do you know where I can find him?'

'He'll be along soon. He doesn't miss many days.'

That was good. My precious scenario wouldn't play out nearly as gratifyingly in private. I took a chair that faced the entrance and ordered a black coffee.

Donnadieu's palsy seemed worse than the last time, and with a grunt of annoyance he hid his hands under the table. 'Are you sure I can't help you?' He was speaking softly. This conversation, unlike our previous one, was not for general consumption.

'No, thank you,' I said. 'It's Goujon I need to see.'

'To settle a score, I suspect.'

I stared at him. What was this anyway? How come everybody took one look at me and knew what I was thinking? This was getting extremely irritating. 'Yes, it's to settle a score,' I said coldly, not really meaning to talk about it to Donnadieu at all, but there was all that adrenaline bubbling around inside, clamoring to be let out in one way or another. 'I saw a picture in a newspaper. Goujon was in it. So was Lily Vercier. I'd like to discuss it with him. He—'

' "In Veaudry, justice is served." Am I right?'

Yes, he was right, but that was supposed to be my line, dammit. I had the feeling I was losing control of things here. 'That's right,' I grumbled, but I wasn't really surprised that he'd remember the photo. That must have been a big day in Veaudry.

Donnadieu took one of his milliliter sips of brandy and set the glass down, growling with exasperation when his tremor made it clatter against the table. 'I wonder if there aren't a few things you should know about that before you . . . discuss it with him.'

'Mr Donnadieu,' I said hotly, 'I don't mean to offend, but I don't want to hear any more stories about Lily. Not from you, not from—'

'This is not about Lily. It's about Claude. I think it may affect your attitude toward him.'

'Go ahead,' I said with a shrug, glancing at the door, hoping to see Goujon come in. I wasn't there to listen to Donnadieu, I was eager to confront Claude Goujon. 'But you can forget about affecting my attitude.'

'That may be so,' he said equably. 'I can only try. First, I wonder if you're aware that when they were both very young, Claude had feelings for Lily.'

'No, but I'm not surprised.' I was keeping one eye on the door, barely listening. So he'd had a crush on her, big deal.

'They were not reciprocated, however. Lily was little more than a child.'

'That shows she had good taste even then,' I muttered. I think that maybe a part of me was afraid that somehow, against all odds, Donnadieu *would* say something to water down my antipathy toward Goujon, and I didn't want that to happen, so it was important to hang tough, to keep that hard knot in my stomach.

'Your coffee is going to get cold,' Donnadieu said.

'It doesn't matter.'

I didn't know why I'd ordered it. I was already on edge enough to sense an uncomfortable pressure from my bladder and I didn't want to encourage the feeling. For one thing, I knew all too well the kind of primitive, hole-in-the-floor affair that I was likely to find at the back of a small-town workingman's bar. But mainly, being in the toilet when Goujon came in didn't at all fit the picture I had in mind. I preferred—

'Young man,' Donnadieu said with a sudden increase in crispness, 'if I were you I'd pay attention to what I have to say. Now, when he was in the Resistance—'

'Look, Mr Donnadieu . . . Colonel . . . no offense, but I'll tell you right now, I don't give a damn how brave he was, or how much he suffered, or how many Germans he killed, or anything else. None of it makes any difference, not to me, not about this.'

Chapter Nineteen

WRONG AGAIN.

When he was in the Resistance, Donnadieu told me, Goujon had been a near-legendary, Zorro-like figure, famous in the countryside and feared and hated by the Nazis. In an effort to learn where he was, they had twice taken his father into custody and tortured him. The second time, the old man had died. Goujon's only remaining close relative, an older brother, also a *maquis*, had been blown to pieces during a disastrous raid on a German convoy near Bobigny not long after. Before that, at the very start of the Occupation, Goujon's young wife had been caught by accident in the crossfire between a German staff car and a lone sniper. She had bled to death on the street in Veaudry.

Donnadieu paused and looked at me with a slight tilt of his bald head. *Bad enough for you?*

'All right, what happened to him is terrible,' I said, 'and I never thought he was anything but a brave fighter, but that has nothing to do with what he – what all of them – did to Lily. She was sixteen, for God's sake. It doesn't excuse it.'

That's what I said, but I could already feel my hoarded, cherished determination to drive my fist into this guy's teeth beginning to dissolve. And what came next finished it.

Had I noticed Goujon's rather strange voice? Donnadieu asked. He hadn't always sounded like that, I was to understand, but near the end of the Occupation he was arrested by the Germans in Paris and taken to their principal torture chamber on the Avenue Foch. They suspected they had a Resistance sympathizer but luckily had no idea it was Claude Goujon himself. However, among the things they did to encourage him to provide whatever information he might have was to apply an electric prod repeatedly to his throat. And to other parts of his body, to additional ill effect. They got nothing out of him, but when they let him go he no longer had a human voice, he had lost the ability to father a child, and his sex life was over. At the age of twenty.

'All this had happened to him,' Donnadieu said. 'Now try to imagine how he felt when the purges began. For three years he had risked his life against the Nazis every day. His family was dead, killed by the Germans, and he himself was scarred and mutilated, no longer a normal man. His young wife had been lost to him forever. Now—'

'All right,' I mumbled, defeated, 'I get the picture.'

He plowed ahead anyway. 'It was the time of reprisals. Vengeance was in the air. Everyone could feel it; those who weren't trembling with fear were trembling with anger. And there was Lily, a charming, pretty girl whom Claude had once dreamed about. Her father a notorious traitor and she herself the concubine of a German soldier, living a life of ease under his protection while so many, many others—'

I held up my hand. 'It's enough, no more. Please.' I was staring at the table, my thoughts and emotions an unsortable jumble. Mostly, I think, I was frustrated; angry with Donnadieu for spoiling my big scene. But I was also a lot of other things: ashamed, contrite, humbled. And for sure, the adrenaline had long since stopped pumping away. I was wrung out.

That was when I saw Goujon come in. 'Thank you for talking to me, Colonel,' I said, getting up.

And when I walked past Goujon on my way to the door, I was the one who couldn't raise my eyes. I never did look him in the face. All I wanted to do was get the hell out of there. I was rapidly coming around to Juneaux's current philosophy, or rather nonphilosophy, of human nature: When it comes to making blanket moral judgments about people – please, leave me out of it.

At the same time, I understood that something good, something positive, had just happened to me. A corner had been turned. I was all through rooting around in the stale, smelly dregs of the past. That was it; no more Nazis or collaborators, no more torture, trials, purges, revenge, spite. From this point on I was looking forward, not backward. The Second World War was over and done.

Tomorrow, Corsica. Tomorrow, at long last, Lily.

UNFORTUNATELY, THERE IS usually a good reason for rock-bottom prices, and the fare that Mrs Aguilar had gotten for me going from the French mainland to Corsica was no exception. As my Uncle Sol would have put it, a picnic it wasn't.

Like my fellow second-class travelers, I'd started out in the passenger lounge, squirming around in one of the nonreclining torture-rack seats, trying to find a position in which sleep was possible, if not probable, while keeping one hand (or one foot) on my bag. My fellow voyagers all appeared to be Corsicans, generally in family groups, returning home after a trip to the mainland, most of them with at least one frowsty, fussy baby. By three-thirty in the morning I'd come to the conclusion that getting any sleep just wasn't in the cards. The glaring lights had never been lowered, and everyone was either noisily restless, noisily snoring, or noisily throwing up. The atmosphere had gotten pretty bad by then, what with the mingled smells of leftover picnics of cheese, red wine, and garlic sausage (both going down and coming up), and the musky odor of a hundred cooped-up, fully clothed, imperfectly washed human beings.

So up I got and staggered out onto the deck under a moonless, starless sky, found a metal life-jacket hamper that doubled as a bench, used my sleeve to wipe away the heavy dew, zipped up my coat, and lay down with my cheek cushioned on my forearm, all scrunched up against the cold to wait out the four hours until we docked as best I could. At least the air was breathable, no small improvement.

To my surprise I fell asleep, not waking up until I became aware of a shaft of light against my eyelids. I jumped, caught in a dream fragment in which a powerful light – a prison searchlight? – had suddenly flicked on, catching me in some furtive, shameful deed, but when my eyes popped open I found myself looking at the fiery orange rim of the sun just coming up over the peaks of a gloriously rugged range of mountains, richly green at their base, hidden in lilac-colored morning shadows along their flanks, and snow-covered at their tops. I could feel the sun's warmth on my forehead, and for a minute or two I just sat there basking thankfully in it as it rose higher. I'd been so centered on finding Lily that I'd given little thought to where it was I was going – the Mediterranean, where the sunlight would have some palpable heat in it, even in December. After the string of gray, chill days in Veaudry and Barcelona, and before that in New York, it felt like heaven. No wonder so many of the old religions had the sun as their number one benevolent deity.

When I'd thawed out enough to open my eyes again, the ferry had turned to enter the bay of Calvi, a wonderful sight on this clear morning with its flawless, curving beach and small-boat marina to the left, the pretty little town itself, all cheerful, red-tiled roofs and winding streets, in the center, and, forming the right-hand margin, looming over everything on its own rocky promontory, the stupendous old *citadelle* surrounded by its sweeping ramparts. Back in the 1400s it had been the proud heart of Calvi, but now the citadel held only a few shops and cafés near its entrance, at the isthmus where it connected with the town. Otherwise it was empty and decrepit, a humped, moldering warren of thick-walled, pockmarked ocher buildings, steep, cobbled streets, and ruined stone towers. But imposing as hell all the same.

As a historian I knew something about its past. The pockmarked walls and blasted towers were leftovers from two terrific sieges. In 1553 it had been bombarded with eleven thousand cannonballs by a French–Turkish armada. And over two hundred years later, in 1794, it was attacked by a British fleet commanded by Admiral Nelson and bombarded once again, according to reasonably reliable records, with another eleven thousand cannonballs. That's the sort of thing that sticks in your mind, or in my mind anyway, which is probably why I remembered it. It's also the sort of thing that raises oddly persistent questions (e.g.: Why eleven thousand? And who was counting?). At any rate, if the people of Calvi had an unlucky number, I was pretty sure I knew what it was.

A young couple I hadn't seen before – first-class passengers, I supposed, judging from their enviably spruce, well-rested look – came out to stand beside me as the ferry began its docking process. They were from London and they were on their honeymoon, the young man told me proudly, having first established that I spoke

English. It was the first time they'd traveled outside of Great Britain, and did I have any idea what that wonderful old fortress above us was called?

I told them what I knew about it, also remembering for their edification that the fracas in 1794 was the battle in which Admiral Nelson had lost his eye – not in a sea battle but on shore, where he'd been commanding a battery and had been struck by flying stones from an explosion. It was also Nelson's troops that had destroyed the supposed house of Columbus's birth there within the citadel too, although quite a few other cities in other countries also claimed Columbus as their own, and Calvi didn't really rank very high on the list of probables, because, well—

I stopped my lecture in midsentence, partly because the poor kids had gotten more than they'd bargained for and were making edging-away motions, but mostly because it occurred to me why I was babbling on like that. It was because I'd suddenly been hit with a first-rate case of cold feet. Now that I had actually arrived in Corsica I'd lost all confidence in what I was doing. The lovely optimism that had kept me going for the last two days was stone cold dead. What made me so sure that she was in Corsica? A piece of paper that happened to be a quarter of an inch longer than usual? That seemed ridiculously tenuous now, little better than self-delusion. Besides, what made me think her grandfather's chestnut farm was still there, or that he still owned it? Or that he was still alive, for that matter? She hadn't seen him since before the war. He'd been an old man then, and a lot of things had happened since. The Nazis had come to Corsica too, and there had been heavy resistance, reprisals, and destruction.

And even if the farm was there, and Lily was on it and had come to no harm, what then? Where did we go from there? On sober reflection, the gauzy happy reunion that I'd blithely dreamed up hardly seemed like a sure thing. By the time I got my bag off the ferry and stepped out onto the sunny cobblestoned square at the foot of the citadel I had practically talked myself into turning around, getting back on board, and going home.

Well, not really. I was down in the dumps, all right, but I knew there were plenty of non-Lily-related reasons for that. I'd just had a lousy night's sleep, I was hungry, thirsty, grubby, and unshaven, and

I was standing in yesterday's too-warm, not-so-fresh clothes, with my money running out, in a strange city where most of the locals spoke a dialect that was peppered with old Genoese words and inflections and hard to understand, and even the French itself had a sinister, alien ring. As a fairly seasoned traveler I knew that these were not conditions conducive to high spirits, and the best thing I could do was to remedy them to the extent I could. Since there was nothing to be done about the grubby, tired part at the moment, that meant getting something to eat and drink.

Fortunately, the little town was well supplied with seaside cafés, most of them serving coffee and pastries on tented outdoor terraces, which seemed a wonderful thing at this time of year. As small as it was – only a few blocks square, excluding the citadel – Calvi was a more cosmopolitan, international-looking place than I'd expected. There were sleek, expensive-looking yachts in the marina, and the cafés had plenty of visitors in them – trendy, fashionable Italians and French, mostly – who all appeared to have two words on their lips: 'Sophia' and 'Loren.' It seemed an Italian-American movie company was filming there, and everyone was engaged either in talking about where she'd supposedly been seen last or in swiveling their heads in hopes of catching a glimpse of the great lady right then.

The cafés looked nice, but I had some questions to ask and I didn't think I'd find the answers in the tourist spots, so I hauled my bag two blocks up the road from the harbor to rue Clemenceau, a twisty old street with a few of the more decrepit souvenir shops, not open for the day's business yet, and some dim, small bars and cafés that were clearly not there for the tourists I'd seen at the waterside.

I walked into the first one I came to, a nameless bar with a lap-top counter at which five or six workingmen stood smoking, chatting, and knocking back coffee or hot chocolate, croissants, and some kind of plum-colored liqueur served in shot glasses. The tables, which cost a few francs more to sit at, were empty except for one elderly German couple who looked as if they'd wandered in by accident and were trying to figure out how to leave gracefully. I went up to the counter and nodded at the men on either side of me, receiving curious but courteous enough tips of the head in return, then ordered a *café au lait* and a couple of chocolate-filled croissants (asking for the chocolate was a sure sign that I was feeling low, if I hadn't already known it), and dug in. The *café au lait* came in one of those soup-bowl-size cups that you need two hands to lift, big enough so that I could practically stick my face into it, which I did, more or less, gratefully inhaling the aroma and feeling my spirits revive as I gulped a third of the rich, milky stuff down. A couple of hunks of the chocolate croissant and my feet were solidly on the ground again. The world was a brighter place, full of hope and possibilities.

'I'm from America,' I announced to the bartender in French, loud enough for all to hear. 'I'm looking for the family Vercier. They live around here, or at least they used to. They had a chestnut farm.'

To my surprise, this created a lively debate around me. Yes, there were some people named Vercier who had a chestnut farm, up in the hills above Capu di Bestia. No, that was in the old days; they'd sold it, hadn't they? No, they hadn't sold it, they'd turned it into a restaurant, La Castagna. No, they—

'That's right,' I exclaimed, 'La Castagna!' That was the native Corsican term – the Italian term, really – for 'chestnut,' as opposed to the French *châtaigne*, and I remembered Lily telling me that that was what they'd named the farm: La Castagna. Had I actually struck oil on my very first try? 'Where can I find it? How do I get there?'

But nobody was paying attention to me. The argument went on. No, no, not a restaurant, but an inn, declared a wiry, black-haired man in a beige duster streaked with flour. He knew because he made deliveries there every morning, didn't he? Sometimes he talked to the housekeeper, so he was able to keep up with things. What they'd done was sell off most of the land and use the money to install indoor plumbing in the farmhouse and generally fix the place up for business, but it wasn't doing so well, and anyway, it was closer to Bocca di Melaja than Capu di Bestia, because to get there you had to turn in from the coast—

'You go there every day?' I interrupted.

He addressed his friends. 'Isn't that what I just said?'

'You're going today?'

He looked at me. 'Is today a day?'

'What I mean is, could you possibly take me with you?'

He hesitated, began to shake his head.

'I'll be happy to pay.'

Oops, wrong approach. I'd forgotten the stories I'd heard about the pride of the Corsicans. Down here, you didn't take money for favors, and you didn't offer any either. His face closed. 'It's not a question of money.'

The others muttered their agreement. *Mumblegrumblemumble.*

'The Verciers are my wife's family,' I blurted, appealing to anyone within range. 'Her father came from Corsica, he grew up on the farm before the war . . .'

It made all the difference. Suddenly I wasn't an intrusive outlander, I was kin, or the next thing to it. There was a barrage of questions about Lily's father from men who wondered if they might have known him (none of them had, although one or two believed their fathers or grandfathers had spoken of him as a young man).

'Okay, you can come with me,' said the man in the duster, noticeably more friendly. 'But I go in five minutes and I'm not waiting around.'

That gave me time to ask if there was someplace I could leave my bag and winter coat for a while; if I actually found Lily, I wanted everything to be as right as possible, and for me to be lugging a suitcase and a bulky New Yorkish coat when I saw her would have added a bungling, comic quality that was the last thing I wanted. The bartender told me that I was welcome to leave them in the storeroom in back, which I did with thanks, but I could see the question in their eyes: *He comes all the way from America to visit his wife's family, but he doesn't plan to stay the night with them?* This too apparently went against Corsican notions of honor, or rather of hospitality. Clearly, I wasn't making the best of first impressions.

My driver gulped the last of his liqueur, ground out his cigarette stub in an overflowing ashtray, and jerked his thumb toward the door. 'Let's get going.'

His name was René Benedetti, and he delivered bread from Calvi north along the coast road to Ile Rousse, then back via the mountains through Belgodère and Muro. La Castagna was one of his early stops, not far from Calvi. So as it turned out the final leg of my journey to find Lily – if she was really there – was to be made in an ancient, rackety red panel truck that said *Boulanger* on the sides, with a rifle jiggling in a rack behind my head ('You never know when you're going to come upon a boar'), and munching a warm baguette that René had generously offered me, and which I knew enough to accept, and for which I knew better than to offer payment.

Naturally, the first thing I asked him was whether he had seen Lily there – that is, whether a woman in her thirties had appeared in the last ten days or so – but he wasn't able to help. Generally, he left his loaves in the mailbox at the bottom of the road up to the farmhouse, and didn't see anybody at all, except maybe the housekeeper. There were some people staying there, that's all he knew, because they were taking eight loaves a day, instead of the two they took when there weren't any guests.

So I settled restlessly back to wait, chewing on the fragrant bread while Benedetti pointed out the sights, or so I think he did; I was too wired up to listen. We stopped for a few deliveries at little grocery stores on the outskirts of Calvi, then turned up into the hills, driving through a landscape of rocky outcroppings and scrubby but densely packed bushes – the famous near-indestructible native *maquis* of Corsica, from which the *maquis* of the Resistance had taken their name.

After a while we passed through a stony, near-deserted village – San Croce, Benedetti said – of roughly cut granite blocks. No gardens, no bushes, no trees, except for a manicured plot of land, in the very center of the village, on which sat an ornate Pisan church painted pink, its fancy Baroque curlicues embellished with white; it was the one spot of brightness and color in this otherwise harsh, gray setting. The only people we saw were some melancholy-looking old men drinking coffee and playing a board game in a bar, and a few women – old or young, it was impossible to tell – trudging along in black shawls and long black dresses and carrying well-used cloth shopping bags. We were no more than seven or eight miles from lively, trendy Calvi with its fancy yachts and well-heeled tourists, but here we seemed to be in another century.

Not far beyond the end of the village, Benedetti stopped the truck in front of a rickety row of mailboxes at the foot of a steep, rutted road running up into a copse of oak and chestnut trees and disappearing after about fifty feet around one of the many outcroppings of rock that studded the countryside. 'Here we are, my friend,' he said as he went around to the truck's back doors. A handpainted wooden sign, LA CASTAGNA, was nailed to the framework supporting the mailboxes. A painted arrow pointed up the road.

I didn't move. Suddenly I wasn't ready for us to be there. Those cold feet had come back with a vengeance. Let's just say I'd been right about the paper size and she was here. What then? How did I approach her? What would she be like? The old Lily? The new Lily? How would she feel about seeing me walk in on her like this? Above all, what the hell did I say to her? I'd played the scene over in my mind a thousand times but never worked out what I was supposed to say. Things had changed so much – I'd learned so much, in so short a time – that I was having trouble getting a fix on who she was. And I was worried that my own resentments would come boiling to the surface: Why had she run away like that without warning me? Why hadn't she told me where she was? How could she do that to me? How could she not trust me?

'Here,' Benedetti said, holding out an armful of unwrapped loaves. 'It's not far. You take these up to them. A man with a loaf of bread is always welcome. With eight loaves, they'll love you.'

We shook hands and I nodded my thanks and started trudging up the hill with my arms filled with bread and my mind strangely unfocused, almost floating. The brushwood growing beside the road, I thought bemusedly, seemed familiar, almost as if I'd walked up that road many, many times before. That added a surreal element to an already dreamlike situation. It was almost as if—

As I came to the jumble of boulders I remembered why it was I knew this countryside. It was vegetation like this – heather, myrtle, thyme, rosemary, other exotic things I didn't know the names of – that surrounded me in the Dream, when I lay hidden near the old farmhouse, watching the Sphinx-lady with the basket. How curious. Was it possible, then, that the dream took place in Corsica, not mainland France? But how would I have known what Corsica looked like? And anyhow, dreams didn't 'take place' anywhere, did they? They were inventions: bits and fragments and mixed-up pieces of nobody knew what, patched together from things one had read, or heard, or dreamed before. . . .

Still, the association was enough to bring out a sweat on my forehead and slow my steps down to an irresolute crawl, and when I rounded the outcropping and saw what lay before me I stopped moving altogether, and probably stopped breathing as well. There, thirty yards in front of me, unmistakable in the clear, slanting morning sun, was the house.

Or rather, the House. As in the Dream.

In the movies it's common to show astonishment by having actors drop things. Supposedly startled people are always losing their grip on trays of food (crash!), books, pencils; cigarettes or pipes fall out of their mouths. But to me it had never seemed very believable. I mean, why would you let go of something when you're surprised? Wouldn't the natural tendency be to flinch, to contract your muscles and thus grip things tighter, not to relax them and lose hold?

Well, no. I don't know when it was that I'd let go of the loaves, but there they assuredly were, scattered at my feet on the stones like pickup sticks. I could make no sense of what was in front of me. Stupefied, I continued to use what I'd seen at the movies as a guide: I blinked, I shook my head. But the stark two-story house remained, complete in every detail, and as real and solid as . . . well, as solid as a stone farmhouse.

No, not quite in every detail, I realized as my mind slowly unfroze itself and the gears began to turn again. True, ninety percent of it was the same. The rough-plastered whitewashed walls with the underlying gray stone showing through here and there; the picturesque, steeply pitched slate-tiled roof; the fieldstone chimneys at either end; the two doors, one full-size and one only about three feet high (for farm animals in the old days, I had always supposed); the off-kilter, uneven windows – all these things were as I remembered them. But the window shutters – in my dream they were green; now they were red.

If anything, the discrepancy made it all the weirder. Why would I have everything right but the color of the shutters?

But mistaken colors or not, it was without question the same building, the place I'd dreamed about. All it needed now was the Woman Without a Face. I was shaken enough so that it was with a hollow feeling in my stomach that I made myself look toward the corner of the house, where she was usually standing near a clump of gnarled bushes. To my relief she wasn't there (the bushes were, however). I began to untense a little, but as I did, the full-sized front door opened and out She came, down the two stone steps. Not in the familiar long blue dress with a basket on her hip, but in a short-sleeved, square-throated blouse and a pair of red pedal pushers, and with an envelope in her hand.

It was, of course, and always had been, Lily.

Chapter Twenty

HER EYES WERE fixed on the rocky, uneven footing, so she saw the bread strewn across the path before she ever saw me. She stopped, puzzled, and glanced up, and there I was, once again looking into those deep, clear, lovely cornflower-blue eyes, only fifteen feet away. 'Lily—'

She was extravagantly startled to see me, that much was apparent. What else she was feeling I couldn't tell, but speaking for myself, I was reduced to jelly, as stricken as I'd been the first time I'd seen her, back in London so long ago, when she'd walked up to my desk, also carrying an envelope.

Don't blow it, I warned myself. *Shut up, don't start chattering away. Don't frighten her, don't reproach her, don't drown her in sympathy. Don't ask a million questions. She seems all right, thank God, that's the important thing. Take it slow, give her a chance to react, let her say something first.*

She stared uncomprehendingly at me, squinting as if to make sure I was real. 'Pete. . . ? But how did you . . . how did you. . . ?'

I came a couple of nervous steps closer. 'If that letter's for me,' I said, 'I can save you the postage.'

Was it supposed to be a joke? Don't ask me. I think I was just trying to say something mundane, something silly, to decrease the extraordinary tension.

In any case, I don't think she heard me. She just kept staring, her mouth working, and then the letter fell from her hand (I'll never sneer at movie conventions again) and she took a jerky step back. I could see that she was going to run back to the house.

'No, don't do that,' I said, reaching for her with both hands as she started to turn and managing to get my arms around her and gather her in. It was like catching hold of a terrified bird. She seemed more fragile than I remembered, and I could feel her heart fluttering against my chest. She was pushing rigidly away from me, straining backward, both tightly clenched fists raised between us. To feel her struggling like that – against *me*, as if I were some kind of monster – was horrible, but I held her tighter still, pressing her head down against my shoulder and putting my lips to the familiar, velvety pelt of her hair.

'Lilylilylilylily, shhhh, shhhhhhh . . .'

For a second more she remained stiff and resisting, her muscles like wire, and then I felt them slacken a little. She let out a shuddering sigh.

'Lily, Lily, Lily . . .' I rocked back and forth with her.

Slowly, slowly, like an ice sculpture thawing, her body relaxed, her fists unclenched, and her arms came down and wrapped loosely around me. After another moment they tightened. I closed my eyes, knowing that I was happier than I'd ever been in my life or was likely ever to be again. If I'd been offered the opportunity to spend the rest of my time on earth standing there with her just like that, I'd have taken it without hesitation.

'Pete,' she murmured into my shoulder, 'I can't believe it's really you. I'm so sorry about everything. I've made such a mess. . . . I just didn't know how I could . . . Pete, darling Pete, there's so much about me you don't know.'

I stroked her hair, over and over. 'Lily, I do know. I know about everything. I know what your father did during the Occupation, I know about . . . about what they did to you—'

'Did to me?' she whispered. She had stopped breathing.

'In Veaudry,' I said gently, keeping her face against my shoulder. 'I know about Werner, I know about your baby girl. How could you think it would make any difference to me? It only makes me love you more, if that's possible.'

She began weeping freely into my shoulder now, so that it was hard to understand the words that came pouring out of her. 'Pete, I thought . . . I thought you wouldn't want to touch me . . . Oh, darling, I know you love me, but I thought . . . I thought . . . even you wouldn't be able to forgive me—'

'Forgive *you*—!' I cried and was unable to say more.

'But my father – he was so . . . such a—'

'Honey, I don't care, it doesn't matter. You're not your father.'

Her head came up now, so that we were looking earnestly into each other's faces. Her blue eyes were tear-washed and luminous. 'But it's me too, Pete. I'm my father's daughter, isn't it obvious? I was so selfish . . . so greedy. The things I did—'

'Lily, you were *fifteen*. Look, think about Natalie for a minute, will you?'

'What? About. . . ?'

'Natalie.' Natalie Gardener was one of the kids that Lily counseled at the school, a fifteen-year-old girl who had been in Juvenile Hall twice for soliciting. 'Would you call her a bad girl, an evil girl?'

'No, because it's not her fault, she's only a child. Her father . . . Oh, I see what you mean.'

'Well, you had it a whole lot worse than Natalie ever did.'

She shook her head, her teeth clenched. 'But look at what I did, Pete. Werner was a *German*, the enemy; he was occupying my country, starving my people, and I . . . sweetheart, I thought, if you knew about us . . . if you knew, you wouldn't ever be able to look at me again without . . . without a picture in your mind of . . . of . . .'

There was a picture in my mind, all right, but Werner wasn't in it – only a scared, defiant, half-naked child with a shaven head and a tarred swastika between her breasts, surrounded by a mob of closed, unforgiving faces. And no one to defend her.

'Now you listen here, my girl,' I said, 'you just damn well better get used to the idea that I'm not that easy to get rid of. I'm afraid you're stuck with me, like it or not.'

To my surprise and my deep pleasure, she smiled. *Why, you look like the old Lily*, I thought with a surge of pure joy. She touched my lips with an exploring finger, looking at my face as if she'd never seen it before, the way she did sometimes. 'Pete, Pete,' she said, sighing, 'I can't tell you how glad I am to see you.' Her brow contracted in the tiniest of frowns, making her eyes seem even clearer and deeper. 'Everything's going to be all right, isn't it?'

I kissed her fingertips and laid her cool, smooth palm against my cheek. 'It already is, honey. We're together again.'

*

BUT OF COURSE it wasn't as easy as that to sort things out, and we spent the rest of the long day talking, and talking, and talking. We had lunch in the village, a garlicky soup thick with potatoes, beans, and ham bones, and then she took me back up the hill to a stone fence beneath an oak – the ruins of a stone fence, rather, built nobody knew how many eons ago, by the Phocaeans, or Romans, or Tuscans, or any of the dozens of other peoples who had come to Corsica and long ago gone from it. And there we sat almost the entire day, sometimes on the wall, sometimes lazily lying on the grass with our backs against it, looking out over the mountain flanks toward Calvi and the coastline.

Lily was cautious at the start, wanting to determine if I really did know everything, but then she opened up and began to speak freely about how it had been; about her father's Nazi connections, about Werner, about the baby, about everything except that awful day in Veaudry, the day of the photograph. A little, yes – 'They were quite harsh with us; they shaved off our hair' – but no details beyond that. And that was fine with me; better than fine. For my part, I didn't tell her – and never will tell her – that I'd seen the picture of her in the extremity of her humiliation. Louis would cluck his disapproval at my withholding it, I suppose, but as far as I was concerned, there were things in a relationship that came before unfettered, no-holds-barred deepness and authenticity. Anyway, Louis was never going to hear about the picture either.

It was Lily who did nearly all of the talking, which was as it should have been. I restricted myself mostly to a running commentary of matter-of-fact, commonsense observations meant to reassure: a fifteen-year-old girl who has an affair with a German soldier in the middle of a horrible war is not a criminal or a traitor, and the actions of a crowd caught up in the fierce exhilaration of release after a long, brutal subjugation don't make her one. And the behavior of a father, however repulsive, is his responsibility alone; it doesn't pass down through the genes or the blood to taint his offspring. And so on.

Platitudinous as they were, they seemed to fill some void in her. She listened hungrily to them, almost visibly soaking them up. *The healing process is starting*, I thought. *Maybe we can come out of this whole, after all.*

The story of the baby, Odile, was hard for her to tell me, of course, but I think that talking about it after bottling it up for so many years brought home to her what a long time ago it had been, and how much had happened in her life since then. After the first couple of hesitant sentences she was calm, thoughtful, factual, pouring it out not in a torrent, but in a peaceful, steady stream. While she talked I held her hand. *She's starting to put it behind her*, I thought gratefully. *At last.*

'What else would you like to know about, Pete?'

'Well, I'd like to know where you went after the baby, after you left Veaudry – if you feel like talking about it. How did you wind up in London?'

From Veaudry she had come here, to La Castagna, she told me, where her wonderful grandparents had willingly taken her in. And La Castagna, as it turned out, was a meeting place for members of the *maquis*, which her grandfather ardently supported. One night they'd been briefed by a woman member of de Gaulle's Free French Forces who had come to the island by ship for the purpose of coordinating the Resistance's mop-up operations. She'd stayed at the farm for a few days and had gotten to know and like Lily, and before she left she'd asked her if she'd be interested in working at Free French headquarters in London. Lily had hardly known who de Gaulle was, or what the Free French Forces were, but she'd jumped at the chance to get away from France, and when the woman boarded her ship bound for England, Lily was with her. Four months later she'd walked into Captain Hendricks's office on Grosvenor Square with her envelope – and there I was, the cutest GI she'd ever seen.

'Lucky for me,' I said. 'What if I'd been out of the office or something? Good God!'

She smiled and dropped her eyes. 'Do you . . . do you want to hear about Werner?'

'Yes.' *I want to hear about anything you want to tell me about.*

'Werner Leuschner. A sweet, lost boy. He was fifteen too, you know, born the same month I was—'

'No, I hadn't known that.' *So they were both children.*

'He was from Bremerhaven,' she said dreamily, staring out at the bay, out of which the ferry was steaming, just rounding the point of the promontory and heading south, toward Ajaccio. 'A music student. He played the piccolo.'

'The piccolo?'

She nodded. 'He'd actually managed to buy one in Paris – he was so excited – but then he broke his glasses almost the next day and couldn't read his music.'

I came perilously close to bursting into laughter, which probably shows how worn out I was and how tattered my self-control. But the thing was, you see, that I had conjured up this image of her lover as some kind of blond Aryan god, and now to find out that he was a fifteen-year-old piccolo player who couldn't see his music without his glasses . . .

'He was a good-hearted boy. The last thing in the world he wanted was to be a soldier. He never wanted to leave Germany. They conscripted him. All he ever wanted to do was to be allowed to study the piccolo.' She was smiling a little. 'You would have liked him, Pete.'

'I'm sure I would have,' I said.

Not long after that we seemed to have talked ourselves out, and so for a long time we just sprawled contentedly, shoulder to shoulder, with our backs against the warm, smooth stones, looking down on the white sweep of the bay and the citadel, so insignificant when seen from here, and catching the occasional glint of a car on the streets of the town.

'Maybe we should be getting back,' Lily said. 'It's close to dinnertime. You must be starving. I know I am. All this talking really takes it out of you.'

'Uh-huh.' I nodded but didn't move. I was too comfortable, too at peace. The wonderful Mediterranean sun was warm on my face, my hands were loosely laced on my abdomen, my arm was against Lily's arm. Above all, Lily and I were back in synch or well on the way to it. I couldn't imagine feeling a more perfect sense of repose, and I didn't want it to end. And Lily, despite her suggestion, must have felt the same; she hadn't moved a muscle either.

'How's Grandfather Vercier?' I said idly after a time. 'How does he like being an innkeeper?'

'Grandfather? Oh, he died long ago; I thought I told you that. I don't know the people who own La Castagna now. I just came here because I always loved the place and I didn't know where else to go. And I did have to go somewhere, Pete. I couldn't stay there in Brooklyn. It was almost as if my life with you, my whole wonderful life with you, had been a movie, and I'd been an actress playing a part the whole time, and now it was over, and I had to go back to being me, the real me, and . . . and . . .'

'I understand, honey. I really do. I just wish you'd trusted me more.'

'Oh, so do I, but I was really a mess, Pete. I thought my head was going to come off.'

'Poor kid. Better now?'

'Yes.' Her hand reached over to graze lightly over my forearm. I felt the hairs stand up. 'Since *you* came, definitely yes.'

Purrrr. 'I can understand why this was the place you came to,' I said, turning on my side toward her. She lay face up with her eyes closed. 'There's something about the old house – peaceful, solid, enduring . . .'

'Yes, that's what you said before.'

'Mm.' I was pleasurably engaged in the contemplation of her profile – lying face up, with her eyes closed, she *did* look a little like Leslie Caron – and I was about to put my finger on that charmingly upturned nose in hopes of making her laugh – when her words finally made it to my higher nerve centers.

'I said *what* before?'

'The same thing, the same words – about the house. Enduring, solid—'

I was up on one elbow. 'I said that about the house?'

'Well, sure.' She opened her eyes. 'What are you looking so confused about?' A little furrow of anxiety had appeared between her eyebrows. 'What's the matter?'

'No, no, no, nothing's the matter. It's just that – Lily, that's the house that's always in my dream.'

'Is that so? Why didn't you ever tell me that?'

'Well, I didn't— Are you telling me I've seen it before? How could I have?'

'In that picture, don't you remember?'

'What picture? No!'

We had both sat up now, backs against the wall. 'Yes, you do. Grandpère sent it to me years ago, a big one, hand-tinted. It looks exactly the same now, except the woodwork's not green anymore.'

I shook my head. 'Lily, I don't—'

'Yes, you do. It's in our scrapbook, Pete. For goodness' sake, you—'

'Do you mean the one of you as a little girl? With the knee socks?'

'Yes. I was eleven.'

'Of course I remember that one. But what's it got to do with the house?'

She smiled. 'What am I doing in the picture?'

'Nothing. Just standing there looking gawky, with legs like a pair of chopsticks.'

'Thank you.'

'But cute, cute as a button.'

She laughed. 'And where was I standing, with my legs like a pair of chopsticks? Think.'

'I don't remember. On the grass, in front of . . . in front of . . . damn, you're kidding me. Was it in front of the old farmhouse?'

She tapped her temple. 'Aha.'

So, another mystery solved.

WE HAD A simple, satisfying dinner of cheese-stuffed cannelloni, fried sardines, and little doughnuts – *beignets* – made with chestnut flour, in the inn's dining room, a big, pleasantly rustic room with a wood-beamed ceiling, an unglazed tile floor, and a huge unlit fireplace. Only two of the other five tables had occupants – a scowling older man who sat as far from the rest of us as possible and used his fork like an unnatural instrument, thumb on one side and four fingers on the other, and an exuberant, self-absorbed family of three so we had it pretty much to ourselves.

A pottery jug of local wine, sweet, strong, and amber-colored, had been placed on each table (we noticed the ten-year-old boy swigging away with his parents; could that have been why they were all so exuberant?), and we each had a glass while waiting for the food to be served. It went quickly to our heads, making us both a little giggly, so that we agreed to a moratorium on serious talk.

Instead, Lily rambled pleasantly on about the old days at La Castagna – how, as a little girl, she had once helped her grandmother roast an entire goat in the big fireplace, back when the whole ground floor was a single room with a primitive open kitchen tucked into one corner; how her grandfather had made with his own hands, out of chestnut wood, the two chairs that still stood along one wall in what was now the anteroom; how her grandmother used to send delightful chills down her spine with earnest warnings of dead spirits who announced their presence with an otherworldly humming that only those about to die could hear. Of her father, and their walks together, and the rainy-day stories he told her in the root cellar, she spoke not at all, and I didn't press her.

We took our coffee in the anteroom, sitting in the chairs her grandfather had carved, and now it was my turn to talk. I told her about my adventures in searching for her. She was, I think, embarrassed but also mightily pleased at all the trouble I'd gone to to find her – except, of course, when it came to the shooting in Veaudry and my getting nailed with the chunk of wood. I tried to play it as lightly as possible, and even for laughs when I could, but she was obviously shocked, and there were many warmly gratifying expressions of concern and solicitude, so many and so warm that I was grateful that I'd been shot, or speared, or shrapneled, or whatever it was I'd been.

By the time I finished we were both exhausted and falling asleep, so we headed upstairs. Lily said she had asked for and gotten the corner room, which had been hers when she was little, although now it was smaller, as all three of the original bedrooms were, to make room for the creation of two additional ones. As I closed the door behind us, Lily turned to me, put a hand gently on each of my shoulders, and dropped her eyes. I got nervous. What was coming now?

'Pete, I'm not sure if . . . I mean, everything is going so well now . . . I don't know if it would be a good idea for us to . . .'

'Me neither,' I said in all honesty, and much relieved that that was all it was. 'There's plenty of time. Let's get to know each other again first.'

And so, with no more talking, we fell asleep in each other's arms, as chaste as a pair of infants (not as easy as I'd thought, since my luggage was sitting in a bar in Calvi and I was sleeping without anything on). In the morning I awakened on my side to find Lily studying my face from three inches away, our foreheads almost touching on a single pillow.

'Hi,' I said. 'Do I know you?'

'Hi.' Her voice was sleepy, tranquil, a joy to hear. 'Pete, isn't this nice?'

'Not too bad.' I pressed the tip of her nose and she laughed on cue. 'Listen,' I said, 'let's be serious. I'd say we know each other pretty well by now, wouldn't you?'

She opened her arms to me. 'It's amazing. I feel as if I've known you for years.'

Chapter Twenty-One

BY THE TIME we got out of bed, my luggage, having been picked up in Calvi by Pascal, the inn's busboy-waiter, on his way to work, was outside the door. That meant that for the first time in three days I was able to shave and put on fresh clothes, which I'm sure Lily appreciated as much as I did.

'You know, I don't think I realized how seedy you were looking,' she said as we sat down in the spare little walled garden behind the house, where a few tables had been set out in the sun for those hardy enough to breakfast outdoors in the 'wintry' morning temperature of fifty-five degrees or so.

'That's because you were so happy to see me.'

'Yes,' she said seriously, 'it is. Pete . . . darling . . .' She reached her hand out to me across the table and I took it. 'I don't know how to tell you how sorry I am for . . . for the stupid way I've been acting. The last thing in the world I wanted to do was to hurt you. I just couldn't—'

'Now come on, Lily, enough already. We've been all through that. It was me. If I hadn't been so self-centered all this time, so damn dense—'

'No – oh, no – you've always been wonderful. You're the best thing that ever happened to me.' Her fingers kneaded my palm. 'That was another thing, Pete – I was so terribly afraid something would happen to you.'

'To me? But why to me?'

'Because you'd try to protect me—'

'Of course I'd try to protect you. It's in the contract, I believe.'

'Yes, but after I saw those men, those thugs . . .' She shivered. 'I was afraid that whatever was happening wasn't done yet, that more awful things were going to happen, and I didn't want you involved. It's not that I didn't think you could handle things, I just wanted you to be safe. It was my responsibility, not yours, and I wanted to take it away with me. Can you understand that?'

'Hey, we're in this together,' I said softly. 'For better or for worse, remember?'

She looked at me, her eyes huge and bright.

'Look,' I said. 'The only thing that matters is that you're all right – and that we're back on track.' I gave her hand a solid squeeze. 'Right?'

She nodded. 'Thank you for coming after me,' she said softly, with her eyes lowered, then looked up, smiling. 'And that's the last I'll say on the subject.'

'Good, I'm glad to hear it. Let's eat.'

Breakfast was the same as it had been at the stand-up bar in Calvi: coffee or hot chocolate and croissants, either plain or chocolate-filled. We took a basket of plain croissants and coffee – *au lait* for me, black for Lily, as usual – and once we'd had a few swallows our talk turned to the unanswered questions that were still rattling around out there. Why had Chastenet been killed in the café in Veaudry? What had he been going to tell me? Why had her father been killed back in Brooklyn? Who was behind the murders? What was on Marcel Vercier's precious film that had apparently gotten two people killed? Why had he been so insistent that Lily see it? On these perplexities we got nowhere that I hadn't already gotten with Sergeant Kovalski or Inspector Juneaux, which is to say not much of anywhere.

What was troubling me the most, but what neither of us wanted to think about, let alone talk about, was something Lily had already mentioned: the knowledge that whatever was going on probably wasn't over yet. That other copy of the film, if it really existed, was still out there somewhere, and someone was presumably still after it. And, according to Lebrun's cleaning lady, Lily was supposed to hold the key to its location. Did the killer believe that too? There was no way of knowing, but it meant we couldn't count ourselves out of the woods yet. It was something I was reluctant to frighten Lily with, but I knew it had to be brought up.

'There's one other question, Lily,' I said as casually as I could after Pascal had brought us second cups of coffee. 'You remember there's supposed to be another copy of that film of your father's?'

'How could I forget? Those two creeps.'

'Well, Charles Lebrun said something interesting to me when I was in Barcelona.'

At the mention of his name her mouth turned down. 'I wouldn't put too much stock in anything Uncle Charles said, Pete. He was as bad as my father. Well, almost as bad. Anything that man told you, he told you for his own good, not yours, believe me.'

'Don't worry, I'm aware of that. But what he told me was kind of intriguing – if it's true. He said that your father said you'd know where it was.'

'I'd know where the film was?' She looked up from lathering a piece of croissant with strawberry jam. 'My father told him that?'

'No, according to Lebrun, your father said it to their cleaning lady, and she told Lebrun.'

She was shaking her head. 'It's not true. How could I know anything about it? I never heard of it until he showed up out of nowhere and pushed it at me that morning.' She went back to applying jam. 'And I don't want to know.'

'No, that's not what I thought Lebrun was saying. When the time came, you'd know where to find it – that's what he said. It was supposed to be an insurance copy that your father hid away. And what I thought Lebrun meant was that you'd be able to figure out where to look, if it ever became necessary, that it was someplace only you'd be likely to think of.'

'But that doesn't make any sense, Pete. How would he expect me to know there was another copy hidden away somewhere, let alone where to look for it? Or when it "became necessary," for that matter? Do you see what I mean? I hadn't heard a word from him since 1944. Unless he let me in on the secret, how could I possibly—' She put down the butter knife and croissant. 'Oh, boy.'

'Lily, what is it?'

'Pete . . . he wrote me a letter.'

'A letter? You never told me that.'

'I didn't open it. It came the day after he was killed, the morning after those awful men broke in. I just tore it into a thousand pieces the minute I saw it was in a Hotel St George envelope. You don't suppose that's what it was about?'

'Could be,' I said with a sigh. 'You wouldn't still have the pieces somewhere, would you? At home?'

'Ugh, no. I didn't want anything of his in the house. I'm really sorry, honey, I was just so . . . Wait a minute,' she said slowly. 'Someplace only I would be able to think of? You don't suppose . . .'

I waited, holding my breath so as not to distract her.

'Our secret place,' she whispered, more to herself than to me. 'We used to spend whole, wonderful afternoons there. He used to tell me stories—'

'You mean the old root cellar? Right here on the farm?'

'Yes, that was our special place. Nobody else had used it for years, maybe for centuries.' She clapped her hands. 'There's a kind of natural vault in one of the walls, where some of the stones were loose. We used to put our treasures in it – a rabbit bone, a piece of Etruscan pottery – and cover it up again with the stones. Pete, you don't think—'

'Well, let's find out.' I gulped down the rest of my coffee. 'Where is it, under the house?'

She didn't answer. Her excitement had died down now. There was a doubtful frown on her face, as though she were reconsidering whether or not she really wanted to find it. 'I'm not even sure the place is still there anymore. They've probably filled it in.'

'Lily,' I said, 'I don't give a damn what's on that film. All I want is to have it found and out in the open. Listen to me. There's someone out there who's already shown he's willing to commit murder over it. And if there's any possibility that he thinks you're the one who stands between it and him . . .'

She shuddered. 'I understand. All right, let's go see. It's not under the house, actually, it's built into the hillside up above, more like a cave than a cellar, really. It—'

We were interrupted by a frightened yelp from a woman several tables away – the mother from the family of three that had been at dinner the previous night. Sitting alone with the boy this morning, she had just yanked the ten-year-old roughly to his feet, upsetting a pitcher of milk onto his trousers. 'Come! Run!'

'Bandits!' somebody else shouted.

'Stay there! Nobody move!'

The brusque command, in a Corsican dialect that I could barely understand, came from behind me, where I also heard a churning of gravel. I spun in my chair to see four men running toward us at full tilt. The two on the outside brandished ancient-looking rifles with canvas slings, much like the one that had been in the cab of Benedetti's bread truck. Behind them, in the parking area, dust still rising from its tires, was a battered, rust-streaked minibus with the side door ajar. Before I could do anything but start to get up, they were on us. One of the ones with a rifle shoved the muzzle into my belly, pushing me back down, then kept it trained on my forehead. It was the second time in less than a week that I'd looked into the barrel of a gun, I thought distractedly. How was it possible that anyone's life could turn around so much?

'I—'

'Shut up! Be quiet! If you move, you're dead.'

'What do you—'

But I didn't have to ask what they wanted. They wanted Lily. One of the ones without the rifles gestured roughly at her: *get up*. She looked wildly at me, but before I could respond (and what was I going to say?) he had jerked her out of her chair by the arm.

She struggled to pull away from him, and I started up again, but the man who had her produced a knife from somewhere – an evil, scimitar-shaped thing, probably a hunting knife – and inserted the wicked point deliberately into her ear, staring straight into my face all the time. Lily and I both froze. Even her eyes stopped moving and went unfocused.

'Sit, you,' he hissed at me. Wolfish and snaggle-toothed, with nervous, crazy eyes, he looked as if it wouldn't take much to put him over the edge.

I sat quickly, holding both hands out in what I hoped was a conciliatory gesture. 'Look, I don't know what you want, but you've made some kind of mis—'

One of the others jerked his head toward the minibus. 'All right, all right, we have her. Come on, let's get out of here.'

'No, wait!' I yelled, starting toward them. 'At least take me too! Take me instead! Please, just let me go with her!'

For an answer I got the butt of the rifle in the middle of my chest, sending me back into the chair and tipping it over in the process. By the time I untangled myself from it and scrambled up, the van door had been pulled closed, the tires were screeching, and they were rocketing down the driveway with Lily inside.

The whole thing had taken maybe thirty seconds.

Chapter Twenty-Two

NOW, NOW, I don't think we have to involve the police in this,' Mr Salvini, the innkeeper, said placatingly, meanwhile inserting himself between me and the telephone on the wall beside the reception desk. 'My advice is to wait and see what happens.'

'Are you out of your mind?' I yelled, trying to elbow by him. 'They have my wife! They just walked in and took her!'

'Yes, but you're not from here, you don't understand the way things work here.' We were jostling each other in what might have been a comical-looking encounter at any other time. Both his hands were on my chest, trying to hold me off. 'Calm down. Believe me, they won't hurt her.'

So I hoped with all my heart, but I wasn't going to take his word for it. 'God damn you, get the hell out of my way!' I screamed into his face, and I guess I looked formidable enough (or hysterical enough) to scare him, because he gave up and stepped meekly aside.

It was an old-fashioned telephone with a handle. I cranked it a couple of times and picked up the earpiece. 'What's the number?'

Salvini shrugged.

'You have to ask the operator,' volunteered young Pascal, who'd been slouched in a corner watching absently, silent until now except for the steady cracking of his chewing gum.

'IS EVERYBODY HERE crazy?' I said hoarsely to Brigadier-chef Jean Chambray, the benign, phlegmatic policeman who had come up to La Castagna from the *sous-préfecture* in the village in response to my call. He had just finished giving me the same incredible advice I'd heard from Salvini: calm down, don't do anything; wait and see what develops.

'What kind of policeman are you?' I shouted at him.

'Sit down, don't get so excited. Would you like a cigarette? A Coca-Cola? Pascal, bring Mr Simon a Coca-Cola.'

'All I want is my wife,' I said, leaning on the table at which he sat, calmly smoking a smelly black cigarillo. My jaws hurt from clenching my teeth. I felt unutterably frustrated and befuddled, caught in some kind of nightmare quicksand I couldn't claw my way out of. 'How can you just sit there? Don't you understand?'

'If you'll sit down again, I'll try to explain,' he said with a long-suffering sigh, as if this were a daily occurrence here, unfamiliar only to ignorant strangers. 'Take my word for it, Mr Simon, carrying on like this isn't going to get us anywhere.'

'I don't believe this,' I mumbled, slumping back into my chair. We were at one of the tables in the inn's dining room.

'There, you see? Isn't that better?' he asked.

'No, it's not better. Who knows what they're doing to her?'

His crumpled features relaxed into a benevolent smile. 'They're not doing anything to her, I assure you. Let me explain.'

I was half out of my chair again. 'How can you possibly— All right, all right, go ahead, explain.'

'That's better.' He took a last, slow drag on the cigarillo and placed it in an ashtray. 'Now. How familiar are you with the bandits of Corsica?'

'A lot more than I want,' I said impatiently. This sounded like the start of a lecture.

A lecture it was. Corsican banditry had a long tradition, dating back at least to Genoese times, Chambray told me in his affable, leisurely growl. Today's bandits could be divided into two strains. The first were common, vicious brigands who preyed on the innocent. But the ones we had encountered that morning were not of that category. They hadn't actually hurt anyone, had they? They hadn't robbed those present at gunpoint, had they, even though they had had every opportunity? No, they had come with a single, well-formed purpose in mind—

'Yes, to get Lily.'

—had efficiently accomplished it, and had gone on their way, harming no one.

'The hell they didn't—'

The other strain, to which these men clearly belonged, were descended from the *bandits d'honneur* of the last century, men who had taken to the *maquis* to hide from the authorities in the course of a bloody but honorable family vendetta. There they could and did live off the land, sometimes for decades. They did not rob or harm innocent people, but only the enemies of their families or of Corsica itself. These brave, primitive men had all but died out by the 1930s, but when the Nazis came, a new generation took to the mountains to wage guerrilla war on the occupiers; men of honor, men of purpose. After the war, for one reason or another – the accidental killing of a neutral bystander, the continuing enmity of those who had collaborated with the Nazis and were still in positions of power – a few bands remained in the hills, living the old life.

And there they still were, not model citizens, no one would make such a claim – they often resorted to ransom and extortion – but not a danger to the average Corsican or the well-meaning tourist, only to those who had good reason to fear—

'What are you talking about?' I exploded, unable to sit still any longer. 'They just dragged off my wife. They did it with guns. They threatened her with a knife.'

'Yes, and that's a question I was coming to. Why should they choose Mrs Simon? Did she have reason to fear them? Did you?'

I opened my mouth to dismiss the idea, but snapped it closed without saying anything. Why had they chosen Lily? Did we have reason to fear them? Were they after the film too? But how would these mountain men know anything about that? More likely, this was some kind of belated revenge for her father's activities during the Occupation – or even against Lily herself for her sin of 'horizontal collaboration.' My stomach turned over. *At La Castagna, justice is served.*

But how would they know about what had gone on in France during the war? Or even if they did know about Vercier, who after all was a native son, how would they know who Lily was?

I probably should have shared it all with Chambray, but I kept it to myself. For one thing, I was deathly sick of telling strangers about it. But mainly, from the way he was going on about these 'men of honor,' I wasn't sure whose side he was on.

'What will they do to her?' I asked dully.

'Do to her?' He seemed surprised, almost offended. 'I told you. Nothing. They wouldn't harm a woman, in any case. No, no, clearly they are holding her for ransom. A business transaction, that's all.'

I prayed that he was right.

'Why they would choose her in particular, I don't know,' he continued. 'Are you a rich man, Mr Simon?'

'No. I'm a teacher. Now look—' I was trying my hardest to sound reasonable and unruffled. 'Surely you can't mean we just sit here until we hear from them? Shouldn't we be trying to find them, or at least find out who they are, or – or something?'

Slowly shaking his head, he lit another of his crooked cigarillos. 'Listen, let me tell you what would happen if we found them. Immediately, it would be out of my hands; the divisional commandant would take charge. Fifty policemen would descend on them with vans and cars. There would be a standoff. The police would go in shooting. Your wife might easily be killed. Believe me, I've seen it happen before. Better to wait.'

'For what? Until *when*?'

'Oh, I'll be very surprised if we haven't heard from them by this time tomorrow.' He pushed back his chair and rose, smiling. 'And then we'll put our heads together and see what's best, eh? That's my plan.' A friendly, encouraging hand patted my shoulder. 'And that's the best way, Mr Simon.'

BRIGADIER-CHEF CHAMBRAY left me in a tumult of bewilderment and dismay, unwilling to accept his 'plan,' but unable to come up with anything workable on my own, although my mind never let it alone. I thought of going to higher levels of policedom – perhaps the commandant that Chambray had spoken of, or the prefecture in Calvi – but Chambray had struck fear into my heart with his talk of a shootout. I buttonholed the other guests – what had they seen? What did they think? What should I do? But they either agreed with Chambray and Salvini or shook their heads and scurried off, unwilling to become involved.

It might have been grasping at straws, but I thought that

Inspector Juneaux might be able to do more from the mainland than the locals were ready to do here, and I was heading for the telephone in the anteroom when Pascal, the young waiter and busboy, stopped me as I passed the swinging doors to the kitchen.

'That cop was full of shit,' he said. 'He doesn't know anything. You want to find your wife?'

I stared at him. Pascal was the one person in the place I hadn't thought of talking to about the kidnapping. He was a skinny, unappealing youth of eighteen with a bad complexion, a slouching manner, and no traits of note other than his gum-chewing (unusual for a European), his passing resemblance to James Dean, of which he was clearly aware, and his ability to spit a good six feet with no apparent ejaculatory effort (a skill I would have sold my soul for when I was twelve), and it simply hadn't occurred to me that he might have anything useful to contribute.

'What did you say?' I whispered, hoping I'd heard him right.

'Meet me in back in five minutes. It's my break.'

Fifteen minutes later, as I paced up and down the worn grass behind the house, close to bursting with impatience, the kitchen door finally opened and Pascal sauntered down the stone steps, drying his hands on his apron.

I practically grabbed him by his shirt collar. 'You know where my wife is?'

'I know who those guys are,' he said carelessly, pleased with the reaction he'd gotten. 'They know me too.' He leaned back, resting both elbows on the stairs' iron railing. 'I did stuff for them in the old days, when I was a kid. They trust me.'

I doubted it, but I was in no position to pass up anything. 'Who are they? What do they want?'

'Pascal!' Salvini's voice came through the partially open kitchen window. 'Look at this place. There's not one clean saucepan in here. You don't like your job anymore? You suddenly got independently wealthy?'

'Five minutes!' Pascal yelled over his shoulder, and then, more quietly: 'Old fart.' He took me familiarly by the arm and walked us a few yards up the hill, to stand beside an old, slate-roofed stone hut built into the hillside. *The root cellar*, I thought absently. At this point I didn't much care.

'Tell me,' I said.

They were called the Ozouf gang, Pascal said, a group of former *maquis* led by a one-time Resistance captain named Raoul Ozouf. Like the other Resistance groups they had come down from the mountains after the war; unlike them, they had continued as a clandestine organization of Nazi-hunters, ferreting out islanders who had trafficked with the occupying Germans but had escaped trial or had not, in Ozouf's opinion, been properly brought to account by the law. Ozouf and his people would hold kangaroo courts, complete with the testimony of victims, and mete out their own punishment. The worst offenders were killed, sometimes brutally; others were beaten, or held for ransom from their families, or frightened off the island one way or another.

These acts of revenge – a sort of patriotic vendetta that brought to mind the *bandits d'honneur* of the past – naturally made them heroes to much of the populace, but after a grace period that lasted a full decade, the local authorities, pressured by the police high command in Bastia, had begun going after them. Warrants were issued. Arrests were made. With some of his men, Ozouf had taken to the hills again. That had been six years ago. Since then they had existed entirely outside the law, living mostly by blackmail and kidnapping, but they had remained on the good side of the locals by limiting their misdeeds to unpopular citizens as much as possible – former Nazi sympathizers, corrupt politicians, and the like. There were some unavoidable exceptions, of course, especially when they hired on to carry out occasional jobs for outsiders, usually involving some kind of intimidation, or extortion of one kind or another. But they only rarely killed anyone nowadays.

'Only rarely,' I echoed dismally. 'Great.'

'Well, there was this one guy from the mainland a couple of years ago, and he put up a fight, you know, and, well—'

'And?'

'And it didn't end so good.' He shrugged. 'But you don't have to worry, they'd never—'

'Hurt a woman,' I finished for him. 'I know. I hope you're right, Pascal. Look, can you really put me in touch with them?'

'Maybe. What would you do if I did?'

'Reason with them. Explain that they made a mistake.' I hesitated, then, wanting him on my side, went on, 'You see, Lily's father comes from here, right from La Castagna, and he was a collaborator during the war, and I think that they must believe—'

But Pascal was laughing at me. 'Forget it, Mr Simon. You'd better just pay them what they want. Maybe bargain a little – they're pretty reasonable. Otherwise, you know . . .'

I nodded grimly. Otherwise, that famous, unbreakable Corsican bandit code of never hurting a woman might turn out to be flexible after all. 'The one with the knife, was that Ozouf?' I asked, hoping the answer was no.

'No, he wasn't with them, but I recognized his men – Prosper, Giorgio – he was the one with the knife. That guy is a lunatic. The other two I didn't know. I think maybe one is named André.'

'How do I find them, Pascal?'

He shook his head. 'Are you joking? You'd never get in. I could take you, though. You want me to? Could be dangerous – these guys are crazy.'

No crazier than I was at the moment. 'Of course I do. Now?'

He studied me, cracking away at the gum. 'How do I know you wouldn't go to the cops later? You already did once.'

'No, no cops. Pascal, all I want is my wife. If I get her back, that's the end of it, I promise. There won't be any trouble.'

Did I mean it? I didn't know then and I don't know now. On principle, I'm dead set against negotiating with terrorists or kidnappers. But right then principle wasn't high on my list of priorities. 'Can we go right now? You can trust me.'

He shook his head as if rethinking it. 'I don't know, Mr Simon. I'd be taking a big chance. Those guys would come after me if something went wrong.'

'Nothing will go wrong,' I said as if I had some idea of what I was talking about. 'And I'll be glad to pay you for the risk.' I thought Pascal might be an exception to the no-money-for-favors rule, and I was right.

'How much?'

There I was at a loss. What was the going rate for this kind of thing? 'How much would it take? I don't have a lot of money.'

He took a long, gum-chewing look at me. My old pants and grungy jacket must have convinced him I was telling the truth. 'A hundred francs?' he asked, not with much hope.

Twenty dollars. 'I'll give you two hundred if you really get me to them.'

'Pascal, damn you!' shouted Mr Salvini.

'Old fart,' Pascal said again. 'Okay, four o'clock. I'm not working dinner tonight. I'll meet you down at the mailbox. And don't worry.'

Right.

ONCE I FIGURED out where to put my hands and feet (respectively, on Pascal's ribs and on the chrome rear wheelguards on either side), and learned to keep my shoulders and head tucked in and centered above the bike on the curves, I began to think I might actually make it to wherever we were going without falling off the back of Pascal's motor scooter. We zipped through San Croce without pausing at either of the two stop signs, then swung down the looping road to the coast highway, where Pascal pointed the scooter toward Calvi some four or five miles away, and we scudded smack into the wake of a lumbering truck that was belching foul, sooty exhaust. Rather than falling back into cleaner air, Pascal stayed right behind the truck, about twenty feet away.

'Cuts down the wind resistance,' he explained, squinting through the grit.

Only when the truck pulled off at an intersection did I dare draw enough breath to speak again. 'I thought we were going to the mountains,' I shouted into his ear.

'No, the citadel. That's where they are now.'

'They're hiding out in the citadel? And the police don't know it?' Oh, the Calvi police knew, all right, he told me, but there was an understanding. As long as the several gangs that intermittently used the moldering, otherwise empty old fortress as a temporary base didn't bother anyone in Calvi, the local cops were happy to look the other way. Every once in a while, some gang would violate the rule – stupidly shoot up a bank right there in the town or kill some local citizen in one of the bars on Rue Clemenceau – and then, just as the *brigadier-chef* had said, in would come the cops, all barrels blazing. And the gangs had no shortage of weapons, so it would be like a small war. Once, a couple of years back, the police had even brought in a tank with a cannon. They'd fired back and forth for two nights and a day, a wonderful show.

With this happy memory lighting Pascal's features, we turned onto the Avenue de la République and entered the outskirts of Calvi. A mile ahead, atop its promontory jutting out into the sea, the sloping bulwarks of the citadel glowed golden in the afternoon light, like the walls of a fairy-tale castle.

Chapter Twenty-Three

SEPARATING THE THRIVING modern town from the brooding fortress was a sort of no-man's-land on an isthmus at the base of the great rock on which the walled citadel had been erected five hundred years before. Once, apparently, there had been structures on the narrow, flat neck of land, but all that was left now was some broken masonry and concrete in what was otherwise a hard-scrabble landscape of sand, gravel, and junk. A few cars and scooters were parked at one end, near the wooden bridge – once upon a time a working drawbridge, no doubt – that led to the entrance, and Pascal left the scooter among them, chained to an iron ring embedded in an ancient stone block.

'So, here we are,' he said, and for the first time I thought I caught a whiff of nervousness, of counterfeit cheer, in his voice. 'You want to go up now?'

'Absolutely,' I said, matching false optimism with false confidence. 'Lead me to them.' *Walk unarmed into an abandoned Genoese fortress to negotiate for my wife's life with a gang of Corsican bandits? Sure, what's the problem?*

Everyone had been assuring me that Lily would be unharmed, and I'd succeeded in making myself believe it – well, three-quarters believe it – but now, cricking my neck to gaze up at the massive wall that rose in a smooth, buff-colored inclined plane directly from the ground at our feet, a cloud of black, hollow fear seemed to swell up in me. Lily and her father had both been branded as collaborators in France, something I assumed the bandits knew (why else choose her?). Did that change the equation? Did this much-talked-about code of honor concerning women apply to supposed ex-Nazis, as far as the Ozouf people were concerned?

'Don't let them hurt her,' I mumbled to whomever it was I was praying to. 'Please, let her be all right.' Surely, neither fate, nor justice, nor God would have permitted me to find her whole, only to lose her again the next day.

'Let's go, let's go,' Pascal said, jerking at my arm.

'Right, yes,' I said, wishing heart and soul that I knew what the hell I was doing.

TO GET INTO the old fortress-city we had to cross the short wooden bridge that ran over the dry moat, then walk up a curving ramp that took us to a dark, high-ceilinged rock-and-masonry tunnel with an abandoned stone guard station on either side. Once through this musty but still intimidating entryway we were within the ramparts, inside the citadel itself. To my surprise, there was a cluster of four or five bright little bars and awninged cafés at the foot of a winding, cobblestoned street, most with a smattering of customers who looked neither like bandits nor like people who were worried about bandits. In the open front of one of them, two sleepy, cigarette-smoking guitarists sat playing a forlorn tango.

Pascal, silent now, led me past these pleasant, ordinary-looking places and up the steeply rising street, the character of which soon changed completely. No more cafés, no more people strolling unconcernedly about; just a deserted passageway between long rows of three- and four-story buildings, derelict and blank-windowed, that ran ahead as far as I could see.

At one point the curving, climbing street became a cobblestoned stairway – the kind that horses could negotiate, with shallow four-foot-wide steps – and at the top of this incline, where it angled to the left, three lean, dark young men, not much older than Pascal, lounged at a table playing cards in the shade of stucco wall behind them. When they saw us they stopped to watch us mount the steps toward them. None of them got up or even changed his position. They still held their cards. There were two rifles just behind them, propped in a corner of the wall.

'Don't worry,' Pascal said, licking his lips. 'I know these guys.'

I hunched my shoulders. *What, me worry?*

'Eh, Pascal, how goes it?' one of them said lazily when we reached them. That much was a relief anyway. They really did know him. 'Who's this?'

'Don't worry, Léon, he's all right. He's not from around here. He's staying at the inn. He's just some kind of professor.'

For some reason this removed any lingering fear of me on their parts. 'Is that so? What's he want?'

'He wants to talk to Raoul.'

'What about?' Léon scratched his upper lip with his fan of cards while he yawned.

'That's his wife that Raoul's got,' said Pascal, with the pride of a bringer of important news. 'He wants to get her back.'

'Hey, make up your mind, Léon,' one of the other players said. 'You want a card or not?'

'All right, go ahead,' Léon told us, turning back to the game. 'He must be crazy, though.' All three laughed.

The citadel was even bigger than it appeared from outside; bigger and higher. Streets and alleys spiraled and doubled back confusingly on one another as they rose, crossing and recrossing each other, creating arched stone passageways. The higher we climbed the rougher the paving became, going from cobblestones to river rocks, to smaller, more irregular stones mixed with brick fragments, to scattered stones barely set into the dirt. The empty buildings with their broken, sagging shutters were constructed either of rough-hewn granite blocks or ocher stucco over brick. Some of the numerous holes in the facades (Nelson's work?) had been repaired with bricks, mortar, rubble, mud, and straw, with varying success.

Wherever buildings had been completely destroyed, and many had been, there were now stony plots of grass and weed, with the outlines of the nonexistent buildings still clearly visible on the ones on either side. There was nothing living to be seen. I was starting to feel like a ghost myself, as mutable and insubstantial as smoke.

'There!' Pascal said.

We had emerged from the coiled, constricted streets that formed the central bulk of the citadel, coming out onto a flat, triangular space high along the walled perimeter. This was, I saw, the north-western-most corner of the fortress, a prowlike extension with a commanding view of the bay and the sea beyond. At its point a rounded, ruined bastion faced the water and a couple of long, shoulder-high crumbling stone chambers – ammunition storerooms? – stood nearby in the weedy gravel. At the base of the triangle, overlooking it, was a single three-story building, in no better condition than any of the others except that its slate roof looked whole. And parked higgledy-piggledy in front of it were three automobiles: two old sedans . . . and the rusty gray minibus in which they'd taken Lily away. She was here.

NEAR THE VERY point of the prow a couple of men stood beside the ramparts, which at this, the highest level of the citadel, formed a thick, waist-high wall. One wore a wide-brimmed straw hat and was talking and gesticulating. The other was a shorter man, bareheaded, listening with his head down and his arms folded, and it was to these two men that Pascal was pointing.

'That's him right there,' he said, awestruck. 'That's Raoul. The other one, that's Giorgio, you remember him.'

They saw us at the same time as we saw them and turned to face us as we approached over the gravel and broken stones. Since I recognized the man who'd been doing the talking as the wolfish, broken-toothed, crazy-looking one who'd stuck the knife in Lily's ear (hardly a face I was likely to forget), I knew that the other had to be Raoul Ozouf, and he came as a surprise. I suppose I'd been expecting some flamboyant character in a bandanna, with flashing eyes and a devil-may-care laugh. But Ozouf was no Douglas Fairbanks; rather a slightly built, stooped, fragile-looking man who appeared to be a prematurely aged fifty. The set of his mouth made me think he might be in some kind of pain.

Pascal practically fell to his knees when we reached him and immediately started blabbering. If he'd had a hat he would have been twisting it in his hands. He'd slipped deeper into the local dialect and was stammering with excitement besides, so much that I couldn't follow what he was saying. Neither could Ozouf, who stopped him after a few seconds.

'Pascal, slow down. Start over. This man, who is he?' His voice was surprisingly quiet, with the words delivered a little mush-mouthed.

I heard Pascal say my name, then something about 'the woman.'

Ozouf looked directly at me for the first time, and I immediately revised my first impression of ordinariness. Frail-looking he was, but with freezing, arrestingly intense ice-blue eyes, the strange eyes of a Siberian husky.

Having looked me over, he turned back to Pascal. 'No – he wants to pay to get her back?'

Clearly, the idea surprised him. Which meant, obviously, that she hadn't been kidnapped for the purpose of ransom, as everyone else seemed to think, but for some other reason. That left two possibilities, both of which I disliked extremely: (a) she'd been taken to 'punish' her for her supposed wartime transgressions, or (b) Ozouf was in the pay of whoever was after that cursed missing film – Pascal had said the bandits sometimes hired on with outsiders – and she had been abducted to get the location of that film from her. She'd been in their hands now for something like five hours, and if it was the film they were after, I just hoped that she'd come out and told them where it was and not been stubborn. If she hadn't, I'd tell Ozouf right now; he was welcome to it. In fact, I'd thought about bringing it along just in case, but concluded that I'd be in a better position to get us both out of there alive if I didn't have it right there with me.

If it harked back to the war, on the other hand, I was going to have a hard time of it.

'You're the husband?' Ozouf said with interest, working his tongue around the inside of his cheek. He had a toothache, I realized; that was what was hurting him. Good dental care was no doubt hard to come by in the mountains. His cleanly shaven face showed the effects of the years he'd spent in sun and wind, and his graying hair had been pulled back into a short ponytail. He wore the same kind of unremarkable clothes as his men: a dark, shapeless turtleneck sweater that hung loosely on him, and baggy corduroy pants. The only concession to the bandit garb of yore was the broad, falling-apart leather belt into which were stuck two long-barreled revolvers, one on each side.

'Yes,' I said, 'and whatever you've heard about Lily is all wrong. She—'

He shook his head: never mind all that. 'How much is she worth to you?'

Deep inside my chest there was a piston-thrust of excitement, like an engine suddenly turning over. *How much is she worth to you?*

If nothing else, that was proof positive that she was all right, wasn't it? I made myself speak evenly. 'I'm not talking about it until I see for myself that she's all right.'

He thought about that, poking away inside his mouth with his tongue, and I worried that I'd come on too strong, or too soon, or something. I was, after all, steering by the seat of my pants in a situation in which I had no comprehension of the rules, but to my relief he finally shrugged and said, 'Sure, why not?' no differently than if I'd asked to inspect a used refrigerator he had for sale before making an offer.

He turned to the building behind him, where another man – not one of the ones who'd been at La Castagna – was watching us from an open window on the second floor, his foot resting on the low sill.

'Eh, André, bring her over there for a minute.'

The man dropped back out of sight and an instant later there was Lily, framed in the casement and bathed in the sun's rays like a saint in a fifteenth-century painting. She looked scared but unhurt. I felt like singing.

'Pete!'

'Lily, are you okay?'

'Yes, they—'

But at a sideways tip of the head from Ozouf, she was whisked back out of sight.

'How much?' he asked again. You know how, in those cartoons, when Elmer Fudd gets offered some phony deal by Bugs Bunny, you see dollar signs in his eyes? Well, that's what Ozouf's remarkable eyes looked like.

How much. I didn't give a damn how much, all I wanted was to get her out of there. Only how did I go about it, what did I offer, how was this game played? I looked at Pascal, hoping for guidance – why hadn't I asked him before? – but he was still gaping slack-jawed at his hero. Giorgio too was watching silently.

'Well . . .' I said.

At which point the door to the house flew open and a rumpled man dressed incongruously in a business suit and tie barreled down the stone steps, his heavy thighs churning. 'Hold on, hold on!'

I stared at him, astounded. '*Lebrun!*' I exclaimed.

Chapter Twenty-Four

SINCE THE TIME Lily had been taken I'd come up with a dozen potential scenarios, and in some of the crazier ones Lebrun had figured in an auxiliary role. But to see him here in Corsica, in the heart of Ozouf's stronghold? *Charles Lebrun?*

All I seemed to be able to do was stammer away. 'How did you . . . what are you . . .'

He barely looked at me. 'What story has he been telling you?' he demanded, catching at Ozouf's arm.

Ozouf fixed him with those penetrating eyes, which would have been enough to rattle anybody, and waited for the hand to be removed from his arm, which was quickly done. 'He says that's his wife in there,' Ozouf said calmly. 'And he says that whatever I've heard about her is all wrong.'

I looked at him, surprised. I'd thought that had gone right by him while those dollar signs were clanging away behind his eyeballs.

'Well, of course that's what he'd say,' Lebrun said. 'What do you expect? He's married to her, he wants to protect her, he, he—'

'What the hell is going on here, Lebrun?' I said, able now to manage a complete sentence and a complete thought. 'What are you after, the film? Is that what this is all about?'

'Yes, the film, of course, you idiot, the film! But she – no, wait, let's look at this reasonably.' He made calming motions with one hand, as if everyone else were overexcited and he was the only one who was composed. 'Look, my friend,' he said to me with a sick smile – he was going into his buttering-up mode. 'The truth is, I'm glad to see that you're here. I hope you can persuade Lily to be cooperative and save all of us unnecessary grief and trouble. As you say, I'm here for one thing only – the film, and what's that to you? Or to her? Once I have it, I'll go my way, you'll go your way, and everyone will be happy. What do you say, am I right?'

'The hell with you, Lebrun,' I answered and spoke instead to Ozouf. 'Listen, let me tell you something about this guy. They tell me you hate the Nazis. Well, do you have any idea who you're dealing with here?'

Ozouf frowned and began to say something, but Lebrun cut in with a laugh. 'I see you're up to your old tricks again, aren't you, Mr Simon? Now you listen to me.' The buttering-up phase, brief as it had been, was over. 'So far I've been reasonable. Your wife has not. Believe me, I don't want to have to have these gentlemen hurt her. I've always been very fond of Lily.'

There were now six of us standing out in the sun: Ozouf, Lebrun, Pascal, Giorgio, me, and one of the other men, Prosper, who had sauntered out behind Lebrun. Until this point, everyone had been watching Lebrun and me in nonchalant, bemused silence, almost as if idly looking at a couple of actors in a street play, but now Ozouf spoke warningly to Lebrun.

'There will be no hurting of the lady. I've told you this before.'

Why, he doesn't like Lebrun, I thought. That much was good, anyway.

Giorgio, the gap-toothed, crazy-looking one who'd had the knife, suddenly grinned. 'We could always hurt *him*, though,' he put in helpfully, 'if it would do any good.' *Him* was me, of course. The better acquainted I became with the Corsican bandit honor code, the more flaws I saw in it.

'There's not going to be any hurting of anybody,' Ozouf said, following it, after a richly meaningful pause, with: 'Not yet. Now,' he said to Lebrun, 'tell us about this film.'

Lebrun threw up his hands. 'Oh, for God's sake, I told you all about it. You've already been paid.'

Ozouf shrugged. 'So? Why not tell me again? Are we short of time?'

'Very well, why not, what else do I have to do?' Lebrun said sarcastically, and then launched into a glib, fantastic tale about how he was part of a covert European organization, the Armée Secrète, dedicated to hunting down ex-Nazis who had escaped justice –

much like Ozouf's group, but on an international scale. Knowing of Ozouf's similar sentiments, he had contacted the outlaw group for assistance in this important matter.

'*What?*' I was flabbergasted. The idea that a parasitic crud like Lebrun – Lebrun, of all people – would have the nerve to come up with a story like this . . . 'Wait a minute, this, this—'

'Quiet,' Ozouf said harshly, turning his unsettling eyes on me. 'I'll tell you when you can speak.' *Damn*, I thought, *he doesn't like me either*. 'Lebrun, go ahead.'

'The film was in the possession of her father,' Lebrun continued smoothly, sensing that he was a leg up, 'the notorious collaborator Vercier. We think it may provide the only existing proof of treason on the part of certain associates of Vercier's, high-ranking figures in Paris and Rouen. But she refuses to help us.'

Good for her, I thought impulsively. Five minutes ago I'd been hoping just the opposite. And I wasn't going to help Lebrun either, not unless it came down to a matter of Lily's life or health.

'But why?' Ozouf asked. 'Why should it matter to her?'

Lebrun cast a darting, uneasy glance in my direction, then edged a couple of steps away from me. 'You know what she is,' he told Ozouf out of the side of his mouth. 'You know what she was in the war, you saw the newspaper.'

So the squalid, overstuffed sonofabitch had shown them his precious picture, had probably brought it with him from Barcelona for just that purpose: to help win them over to his side. I felt the blood come to my face, but I couldn't tell if it was from anger, frustration, or humiliation. When I looked around me, there were no leers, no suggestive exchanges of glances, only impassive, disinterested observation, and for that I felt something close to gratitude toward these wild men.

'Why should it be surprising that she still protects her old friends?' Lebrun went on slimily. 'As the father was, so is the daughter.'

'You miserable bastard,' I said, unwilling to be quiet any longer. 'You know damn well that's not true.'

Lebrun continued to address the others. 'And we all know what her father was, don't we? He—'

'Yes, your partner!' I shouted over him.

At this Lebrun shook his head and laughed at the drollness of it. 'Ha, ha, ha. I'd hardly say "partner," ' he said, eyes twinkling as if correcting an amusing error. 'Naturally, I had to conduct some business with him; that was part of the plan. I already—'

'For twenty years,' I said.

His face darkened. 'Not . . . true,' he declared, glaring at me. 'That is a despicable lie, and you know it very well.' He turned to Ozouf and the others, trembling with emotion. Despite the bombast, the guy was a better actor than I'd given him credit for. He could turn it on and off at will. 'Do you know who this man is? Do you know? First, he's not a Frenchman at all, despite what he wants you to think. He's an American who *ran* from France. And of course he's going to side with his wife and his father-in-law. As the wife is, so is the husband, isn't that so too?' He aimed his finger at me. 'This is Pierre Simon, a professor of European history, famous in America for his revisionist lectures condemning our great heroic French Resistance. I can show you the newspaper articles.'

'I don't believe this,' I muttered, but as I did I became aware that there had been a change in the atmosphere of the little knot of men around us. No longer looking on casually, they were now following every word. Prosper and the feral Giorgio were staring fixedly – threateningly? – at me. Ozouf was leaning against the wall, looking down at the cigarette stub he held in his fingers as he expelled a lungful of smoke, but his taut posture radiated a tension that hadn't been there before. Even Pascal's mouth had hardened.

This was not a good feeling. Had Lebrun, with his farcical claims, turned this into one of Ozouf's kangaroo courts? Was this no longer about Lily but about me? Was I on trial? Was Lebrun the prosecutor – speaking for the noble, nonexistent 'Armée Secrète' – and I the witness in my own defense? I looked again at Pascal for a clue, but he was in his own version of paradise, oblivious to everything but the joy of being in on the inner workings of the gang.

There was something else that I realized only belatedly. The isolated patch of weeds and gravel on which we stood could hardly have been more perfect for dumping a body. All alone at the seaward tip of the deserted citadel, where no one could possibly see us, with the town far behind us and out of sight, and nothing but the Bay of Calvi in front. The citadel's wall, against which some of the men were leaning while they smoked, was waist-high and about three feet thick, and the top surface angled down and away, probably to make it easier to repel invaders, although it was hard to imagine how anyone could have gotten up the sheer, almost vertical outer face of these ramparts from the rocky coastline a hundred feet below. It would be the easiest thing in the world to tip a corpse – or a living person, for that matter – onto the slanting top of the wall and watch him roll down off it to plunge either into the ocean itself or onto the shoreline rocks, where the next tide would soon carry him out to sea.

What if that were me? What would happen to Lily then?

'And what do you say to that, Mr Professor?' Ozouf asked, bringing me back to reality with a bang.

Instinctively, I moved away from the rampart. 'I'm no revisionist,' I said, feeling the way you do when you're going through Customs with nothing to declare – you know what I mean; guilty-looking and unconvincing as hell even when there's nothing to feel guilty about. 'But there are obviously a few things you don't know about Mr Lebrun.'

'Watch out, everybody,' Lebrun said with a laugh. 'Here comes some more revisionism.' Ozouf told him to be quiet.

I told them what I'd learned from Inspector Juneaux: how Lebrun had betrayed the old patriot Voyenne, his predecessor at the Veaudry city hall, in order to take his place, how he'd willingly written and been paid for his pro-Nazi 'Honest Frenchman's Thoughts,' and how in the end he'd been sentenced by the tribunal to *indignité nationale* for life.

While I spoke, Lebrun had been doing his swelling-up trick, huffing away with outraged virtue. 'What a contemptible pack of lies!' he cried, broken-voiced. 'A fabrication from first word to last. Can't you see what he's trying to do? *He's* the one—'

'You can check the records,' I told Ozouf. 'They're in the city hall in Veaudry.'

'That's simply not true,' Lebrun protested to Ozouf, thrashing his arms. 'Oh, I grant you, there was some small difficulty, but that was just an old enemy trying to settle a personal grudge; we can all remember how common that was then. In any case, what difference does it make? The general amnesty laws make everything moot.

He's trying to bargain for time, that's all, isn't it obvious? He knows it would take days for you to verify it especially because there *was* no such sentence, so the records don't—'

'It wouldn't take days,' I countered, feeling the first real prickle of hope that I might actually be able to turn things around. Unless I was mistaken, Lebrun's sham agitation had become the real thing. He'd had no idea that I'd learned about his sentence, and it had knocked him off-balance. And my impression, from the way Ozouf was regarding him, was that the bandit leader was thinking something similar. The other two I wasn't so sure of. I pressed on. 'It wouldn't take more than a few minutes. A telephone call to Inspector Juneaux in Melun.'

'Who are you going to believe?' Lebrun said with an angry thrashing of his arms. 'A fellow Frenchman, or an American so-called professor who married an SS colonel's whore?'

Poor nearsighted, piccolo-playing, fifteen-year-old Werner, I thought, almost smiling, would have been gratified to know that he'd been promoted to colonel. In the SS, no less.

'I have the inspector's telephone number,' I said. 'You could call from Calvi. And if he's not in his office—'

'There's no end to this!' Lebrun said impatiently, and he was back to his play-acting now, doing a pretty good rendition of fed-up contempt. 'Why are we wasting our time with him? Listen to me: not only is he the acknowledged friend and son-in-law of the traitor Vercier, whose sentence of execution my organization is proud to have carried out. There's more. Ask him *why* he was in Veaudry a few days ago. It was to meet with the traitor Armand Chastenet. How do I know this? Because' – and now that plump, accusatory finger jabbed at me again – 'at the very moment our people carried out Chastenet's execution, he was in secret conference with him – ask him if he wasn't! See what he answers!'

So Lebrun was admitting to both murders, I thought. Nice to have it confirmed, but my problem at the moment was saving Lily's and my necks, and I was having trouble making much headway at it.

'I'm sick of his endless dirty allegations, his vile theories,' Lebrun raved on. 'They'll never stop.' He faced Ozouf squarely. 'Raoul, I think you know in your heart that we'd all be better off with this man dead.'

I started to speak. 'Now, let's just—'

'Be quiet,' Ozouf said. Returning to Lebrun, h hook his head. 'Kill him? I don't know, that's not what we contra for. Murder, that's risky, that annoys the authorities.'

'I'm aware of that,' Lebrun said. He pretended to w matters. 'I believe my organization would be willing to double fee. I think I can speak confidently for them. Forty thousa ncs. That's a great deal of money, Raoul.'

My hopes, such as they were, took a sharp downturn. The might very well hate Nazis, but they were also outlaws, and money came into play I suspected that principles took a backs And as far as money went, I was out of the running. It wasn't an high-minded aversion to negotiating with kidnappers, either; that had gone out the window. But forty thousand francs was eight thousand dollars, more than I could possibly get my hands on without going back to the States, and even then I'd have had to borrow it. Obviously, Ozouf and his people weren't going to go for that.

'So much money – you have it with you?' Giorgio asked, smiling. Even his smile was like a wolf's. You could see all the way to his back teeth.

'No, of course not,' Lebrun said hurriedly. 'I never carry much on me. It's back at my hotel. In the safe,' he added.

'No, I don't think it's worth the risk,' Ozouf said. He'd been stroking his chin and staring out to sea, but now he turned to look at Lebrun with a faint smile. 'Perhaps if it was possible to triple it. . . ?'

That did it. I was as good as dead. I started looking for ways out. Grab Lebrun and use him for a shield? Snatch a gun out of Ozouf's belt? And then what? Nothing seemed very promising, and the terrible question remained: what would happen to Lily afterward?

Lebrun did some more mock-weighing of his 'organization's' resources, and hunched his shoulders in defeat. 'All right,' he said glumly. 'Sixty thousand francs.' *The bastard's as happy as a clam*, I thought bitterly.

Ozouf, working his tongue in his cheek, nodded thoughtfully – even a little sadly – and pulled one of the old, long-barreled revolvers out of his belt. I think I tried to say something, but I don't remember what, if anything, came out of my mouth. A croak, probably. I know I flun[illegible]p one hand as if to block the bullet. I wasn't afraid so much as [illegible]unned. How had it come to this?

Ozouf pulled [illegible]ck the hammer with both thumbs, raised and extended his [illegible], turned slightly, and shot Lebrun in the throat.

Chapter Twenty-Five

LEBRUN MADE NO cry, expressed no surprise, or pain, or horror, had no reaction other than emitting a little sigh and shutting his eyes. His hands remained at his sides. After a second, as a bubble of bright blood appeared on his collar beside his tie, his head jerked, his knees gave way, and he began to tip slowly over to one side, but before he reached the ground Giorgio and Prosper swooped down on him, plucked him up by either arm, dragged him a few steps – some still-living reflex center low in his brain made his feet shuffle clumsily along – and tipped him backward onto the top of the thick wall. The smallest of shoves from Giorgio to help him along, and Lebrun's body rolled and skidded down the sloping top and into space, taking a few loose stones with it.

The rest of us stood perfectly still, waiting for the sound as he struck the sea or the rocks, but the surf made it impossible to hear. Prosper walked a few yards to the side, from where, leaning over, he had a view of the rampart's base. 'He's on the rocks, half in the water,' he said matter-of-factly. 'The tide's coming in. He'll be gone in half an hour.'

Ozouf thrust the pistol back into his belt with the appearance of a man well satisfied with his day's work and looked at me with mild amusement. 'So, are you all right?'

'What . . . what will happen to my wife?' I said. I still felt stunned, like a slaughterhouse cow that's just been whacked in the forehead with a hammer but is somehow still alive, more or less.

'You'll take her with you. No charge; we've already been paid.'

'But why did you – how did you know he was lying? How did you know I was telling the truth?'

'I used my judgment,' he said with a shrug. Then, as we began to walk back to the house with an ecstatic, goggle-eyed Pascal in tow, he added something else, but the wind carried it off.

'What?'

'He's asking you,' Prosper said, 'what the hell are these general amnesty laws?'

WE FOUND THE missing film right where Lily had said it would be, encased in its canister, tied up in rotting green oilcloth and tucked into a hidden niche in the stone wall. There was a little stone bench along the opposite wall, at which Lily looked with pensive melancholy, even running her hand along it. I knew that it must have been the spot where her father had told her those rainy-day stories of doomed lovers so long ago, but neither of us said anything, and by the time we came out again into the sunlight she was over it.

Watching the film proved to be a problem because it was in 35-millimeter format, the gauge used in movie houses, and thus required a real theater projector. I suppose we might have found a movie theater in Calvi that would have shown it to us if we'd looked hard enough, but Lily had decided she didn't want to watch it, and I was in no pressing hurry either. I intended to see it all right, but I didn't feel up to dealing with whatever was in it yet. I guess we both just needed to decompress.

By the same token, for the remaining day and a half we had to spend in Corsica before we could get a flight home we talked (and talked) about everything under the sun *but* the long, strange train of events that had culminated at the citadel. It wasn't that we purposely avoided them; we simply had other things we were more eager to talk about: ourselves, for example. And the future, not the past. Only once did the forbidden subject arise, and that was in the form of a discussion of what we were to do when it came to informing the police about Lebrun's death. Lily and I both think of ourselves as law-abiding people, so we each started out a little defensively, with labored arguments meant to convince the other that it was better to leave the Corsican police out of it and simply let things lie. But we soon realized we were on the same side, for the same reasons: (a) Considering that Lebrun had been behind two murders, had done his best to get me killed up there in the citadel, and would almost certainly have murdered Lily in the end as well, he had gotten what he deserved. (b) Ozouf had saved our lives – certainly mine – to his considerable financial disadvantage. What kind of gratitude would it be to set the police on him for murder? (c) Would the police pay any attention anyway? (d) And if they did, what good or useful purpose would be served?

And so, kicking my once-cherished principles under the rug one more time, I let the matter rest, considering it one more example of justice in the raw. I did at least resolve that when we got back I would call both Inspector Juneaux and Sergeant Kovalski to tell them that it was Lebrun who had engineered the murders and that he had been dispatched by bandits in Corsica; we didn't want either of those good men to go on hunting a man who no longer existed. And there we let the matter rest. Aside from the twenty-minute conversation that resulted in those decisions, we stayed away from Marcel Vercier, Charles Lebrun, and everything related to them.

Ditto for our long trip home via Air France, during much of which Lily slept with her head on my shoulder and my arm around her, so that when we got off the plane at Idlewild I hadn't moved for four straight hours for fear of waking her up. I felt like the Tin Man before the oil can was applied.

That night, back in our own bed, we slept the restless sleep of the travel-lagged. In the morning Lily awakened early and hungry, went down to the kitchen to forage, and returned with a puzzled look on her face.

'Pete, what in the world were you living on while I was gone? Flour? Tomato paste?'

'I don't know,' I answered truthfully.

We decided that what was called for was a real Brooklyn breakfast – pastries and coffee at the big Dubrow's Cafeteria on Kings Highway – and drove there through the gray slush of a day-old snowfall. And it was there, in a safe, warm, brightly lit atmosphere redolent of cinnamon and almond paste, over cherry-cheese blintzes and hot apple danish, that I thought it might be time to return to our unfinished business.

'Lily, I made a couple of calls while you were showering and getting dressed. One of them was to Stanley Kessler. He's going to run the film for me this morning, before the matinee starts. Are you sure you don't want to come?'

Stanley Kessler was one of my boyhood friends, the only one of the gang I ran with, to my knowledge, who had achieved his life's highest ambition, the one he'd solemnly vowed to reach on the day of his twelfth birthday: Stanley was now the projectionist at Loew's Pitkin, the grand art deco movie house that was the pride of Brownsville.

'No, I don't want to come.' She shook her head, toying with her danish. 'There's nothing he could say that I'm interested in hearing. Besides, the things I want to know aren't going to be in any movie.'

'Things like what?'

'Well, if it really was Uncle Charles who had my father killed—'

'Oh, it was. He flat out said so up at the citadel. Chastenet too – the one in Veaudry.'

'—then why did he wait until my father came to New York? Why didn't he do it long ago in Barcelona?'

'I know, I've been wondering about that too, and I think everything goes back to the film, Lily – or rather the two copies of the film; Lebrun was after them both. He knew your father had one copy in a vault here in the States, so he had to wait until he came here and got it out.'

She rocked her head slowly back and forth. 'What could be on it that was so important to him?'

'Whatever it is, I'll find out soon enough. Whether or not I'll understand is another question.' I looked up at the wall clock. 'Time for another cup of coffee before I head for the Pitkin. Want one?'

She nodded, and I went back to the counter, got two refills, had the ticket punched again, and returned to the table. Lily was deep in thought, rolling tiny balls of dough with what was left of a danish.

'The other copy of the film,' she said deliberately, working things through. 'That's the one we brought home from Corsica, the one I was supposed to know where to find, right?'

'Right.'

'So if I was supposed to know where it was all along, why did Uncle Charles wait weeks, until I was in Corsica, to come after me?

Why didn't he do it right away, after he killed my father?'

As it happened, I actually knew the answer to that. 'Because he didn't know it then.' It was Lebrun himself, I told her, who had told me that he'd only heard about the 'insurance copy' from his cleaning woman just before I'd called him from home. By that time, of course, Lily had already left, so he had no more idea of where to find her than I did.

'But how would *he* have known that I'd left?'

'Because Kovalski told him, or rather Officer Ramirez did.'

I explained that the other telephone call I'd made that morning had been my promised call to Kovalski. One of the things he'd told me was that Lebrun, in one of his conversations with Ramirez, had asked, reasonably enough, after his partner's daughter, and had been informed of the situation. The 'ask your wife' he'd flung at me on the telephone had been nothing but a malicious joke. He knew he wasn't taking a chance on my getting hold of the film because I didn't know where she was either.

'But then,' she said, 'when you were in Barcelona, you told him you were looking for me—'

'I'm afraid so,' I said.

'—and he had you watched because he figured that you had a better chance of locating me than he did on his own? Is that the way it worked? He hoped you'd lead him to me, and I'd lead him to the copy?'

'That's what I come up with. I think he had someone reporting to him from Veaudry – if I had to guess about that, I'd say that it was the head clerk at city hall, the guy who was in Lebrun's old job, but who knows? It could have been anyone. And then when I went back to Barcelona, I was dumb enough to ask his assistant, Mrs Aguilar, to get me a ticket to Corsica. She must have told him, and he must have thought: what other reason could I have to go to Corsica other than that I believed you were there? So out he came too, maybe on the same boat.' I shrugged. 'That's it. What do you think?'

She looked at me with her head cocked while she processed the whole complicated mess. 'Whew.'

'You're telling me,' I said. 'Well, it's movie time for me. I'll drop you off at home on the way.'

I really wasn't much more eager than Lily was to watch whatever was on the wretched film, but an hour after I left her at the house I was back, dashing headlong up the front steps and bursting in on a startled Lily. I grabbed her by the wrist. 'Come on!'

'Where? What's—'

'Back to the Pitkin,' I said. 'Lily, you have to see this!'

LOEW'S PITKIN IS one of those astonishing old neighborhood theaters built in the thirties, when movies had nothing but good times ahead: gilded classical reliefs, plush carpets, chandeliers, a grand staircase, a glittering lobby the size of most of today's entire movie houses. And uniformed ushers complete with double rows of brass buttons on their tunics and plug hats held on with elastic chin straps. When I was a kid, it was always a special treat to get taken to a picture show there, especially on a weekend evening, because there was an eight-act vaudeville show that went along with it instead of a second feature.

Following Stanley's instructions, we showed up at the same side door I'd come to before. This time when he opened it he looked positively furtive. 'We have to hurry,' he whispered, although the place was empty. 'You're pushing it. Kids' matinee. They start setting up at noon. You'd better sit upstairs. Be careful, I don't want to turn on the lights.' He shook his head. 'How did I let you talk me into this? You owe me, Pete.'

'I think he's a little nervous,' I said as Lily and I found our way in the dark to the last row of the balcony, just under the projection booth, while Stanley set up the projector. 'I'll make it up to him.'

She turned to smile hesitantly at me as the projector whirred on and a beam of pale blue light shot through the floating bands of cigarette smoke that still hung about the ceiling from the previous evening. 'I'm a little nervous too.'

'I'll make it up to you too.' I put my arm around her shoulders, kissed her on the temple, and drew her toward me. We might have been a couple of teenagers settling back for a session of necking in front of the silver screen.

The film, in what seemed to be professional-quality black-and-white, had no title or credits. Once the numbers finished flashing backward we were into the meat of it. It was thirty-five minutes long and was shot in one take, as far as I could tell. It showed no secret conferences, revealed no Frenchmen betraying their nation. It showed nothing but a single person, a lone man working quietly at his craft and explaining what he did as he did it.

The craft was counterfeiting, and the man was my father-in-law, Marcel Vercier.

Chapter Twenty-Six

'GOOD DAY' I felt Lily's arm jump at the sound of his urbane voice coming from the big speakers, so unlike the shrill screaming on our doorstep. 'I am Marcel Vercier of Veaudry, and I have for you a salutary fable of good and evil, and of the error of trusting too much to appearances.'

'You should know,' Lily said under her breath.

'Today is 29 October, 1943. We are in the third year of the German Occupation of northern France.' The sound quality wasn't up to modern standards, but it was easy enough to understand him.

He slipped on the metal-rimmed glasses, looked down at the sheet of paper in his hands, and read aloud from what appeared to be handwritten notes. 'When these evil days are over, there may come a time of terrible retribution. In the event that such a time should indeed come upon us, I now make this visual record as proof that I never betrayed my country.'

'*Menteur*,' Lily said to the screen. Liar.

'Shh. Watch.'

Vercier folded up the paper and slid it aside, then smiled into the camera with a puckish charm that had surprised me the first time I'd seen it. 'Naturally, it goes without saying that if by chance the Germans should win the war, nobody will ever see this – including you.'

At his nod the camera panned down to the tabletop to show a framed rectangle of silk fabric into which were set three large, old-looking coins. 'Now. Here in front of me are three ancient silver coins of considerable value – Syracusan decadrachms from approximately 450 B.C., during the time of the Greek colonialization of Syracuse.' He removed them gently from their mat and placed them on the table side by side, describing each one as he laid it down.

'The relief heads they bear are those of Hieron the Tyrant, the nymph Arethusa, and Mithradates VI of Pontus.'

'They were in the tribunal records,' I told Lily. 'They went to Goering himself.'

I don't think she heard me. She was focused rigidly on the screen, breathing through her mouth.

'They are the property of the widow Françoise Denier.' Vercier was still smiling. 'In a few days, I will inform my esteemed associate Polizeimajor vom Steeg of their illegal possession – by a Jew, no less – and Major vom Steeg will see to it that they are removed to more appropriate Teutonic lodgings.'

'I want to go,' Lily said, starting out of her seat. 'Why did you—'

I held her back. 'Will you wait? Sit. Give it one more minute, you'll see.'

'Unfortunately for poor Major vom Steeg,' Vercier went on equably, 'what he will come away with are counterfeits; counterfeits of the highest quality, to be sure, but counterfeits all the same. These' – he gestured at the coins – 'the originals, will go back to the widow Denier with my compliments, and, let me point out, at no cost whatever to that good woman.'

'What?' Lily whispered to him as if he could answer her. She stopped struggling, looked wonderingly at me, and silently sank back into her seat. I put an arm around her again. I could feel her shivering.

'For some time now,' Vercier said, looking at his folded hands, 'our German masters have been the recipients of my assistance in securing for them various objects of value that had been in the possession of Jews and other undesirables who lack property rights under the current regime. Our masters have been happy to pay me – pay me quite generously, I may say – and I have been more than happy to take their money.'

He stared suddenly into the lens – right into our eyes – and for the first time looked a little like the intense, determined old man from our doorstep. 'In every case – every single case – the objects they received have been counterfeits created by me. I swear before our good Lord that I have never put into their hands a single authentic object that had been the property of a citizen of our country; not once. Whenever possible the original pieces went back to their owners—'

'I don't believe you,' Lily murmured, but without conviction.

'—who could then rest easier, being able to show receipts from the German authorities confirming that the objects had been confiscated, as required by law, and were no longer in their possession. When even this was impossible for them, I myself paid them all that I honestly could for the objects and kept the originals myself for future use. This I swear before God almighty.'

Lily turned from the screen to me. 'Pete, you don't suppose it could be true? That he – but why—'

Vercier reached to one side and pulled into the field of view a tray holding a mallet and some metal implements. Setting them beside the coins, he folded his shirtsleeves neatly to the elbow. The camera zoomed in so that the tabletop and Vercier's delicate, graceful hands filled the screen. From the tray he took a metal tablet about an inch thick and four inches on a side and placed it in the center of the table's visible workspace. Laid flat on top of that was a slightly smaller metal tablet with a circular depression in the center.

'My profession is that of restorer of and dealer in ancient coins and jewelry,' he said as he arranged the items. 'As it coincidentally happens, the skills required are also those of a counterfeiter, and it is one of these skills, the making of counterfeit coins, that I shall now demonstrate. Here before me' – one hand indicated the two metal plates stacked on one another – 'resting on this anvil is the lower die, the die that will strike the reverse side of the coins. And here' – he held up three eight- or ten-inch-long metal cylinders, each about an inch in diameter – 'are the upper dies to strike the obverse sides of the coins. Permit me the small vanity of pointing out that, unlike so many of the present day's negligent and unskilled copiers, I do not cast my finished products in molds or use any mechanical means of reproduction; I strike them, as you shall see, using dies which I myself engrave by hand. The hardest part of the process, the engraving of the dies, which took several weeks in this case, has already been done. Here are the results.'

One at a time he held the dies up to the camera, ends forward, so that the images that had been cut into them were visible: two classical heads in profile, one full-face.

'And these,' he said, holding up one of several plain, lens-shaped metal disks, 'are the silver blanks, from which I will strike the new coins. Observe.'

Vercier took one of the blanks, set it into the circular depression that had been cut in the lower die, into which it fitted perfectly, placed one of the cylindrical upper dies squarely on it, like a chisel, and gave it two sharp taps with the mallet. The disk was removed and the operation repeated twice more, using the same lower die but the other two upper dies and fresh disks. The three newly made coins were then laid out on the table beside the originals. To my eyes, at least, they seemed identical.

'You will note,' he said with obvious pride, 'that each coin is complete to the smallest detail, even bearing the name of the engraver, Eukleidas of Syracuse, in Greek letters, along the rim. As to the reverses, unfortunately here I was forced to bow to the exigencies of time.' He turned the counterfeit coins over. Each of the other sides had the same simple square cut into it – the design that had been impressed on it by the lower die. 'While these incuse squares were common on early Greek coins, by 450 B.C. the reverses had become more elaborate and individual, as you can see here.' He turned over the authentic coins to show three different, complex scenes showing groups of people; the images were too small and detailed to see clearly. 'Ah, well, that's as it must be. However, I feel reasonably safe in making the assumption,' he said dryly, 'that neither Major vom Steeg nor Herr Goering is likely to have a particularly close acquaintance with the precise chronology of the evolution of Greek colonial coin design. They will be content, I think, with their incuse squares.'

The camera pulled back so that we could see Vercier's face again. He talked on a little more, clearly enjoying himself and roguishly pointing out that his bronze dies were good for about ten thousand stampings each ('After all, there are already so many inauthentic Greek coins in existence, what are a few more?') and explaining his 'exclusive, highly technical process' for artificially aging coins. (He put them in a box filled with iron filings and stuck the box in the axle housing of the village milk wagon for two days.)

'The widow Denier will get her possessions back,' he said. 'The Germans will have three beautiful coins to rub their hands over, with the added joy of having legally stolen them from a Jew. And I will get my money for my humble assistance. Everyone will get what they deserve, wouldn't you agree? All ends well.'

He nodded again to someone unseen on one side of the camera lens, this time as if he'd been signaled that it was time to conclude.

'Ah . . . I would like to say one more thing,' he said, hurrying a little and for the first time looking unsure of himself. His eyes went down to his folded hands again. 'I believe that I am not known as a particularly generous or charitable man. The question then is sure to arise: why would I engage in this dangerous, painstaking effort to fool the Germans? Why go through all this work when I could collect the same fee from them by simply informing them of the location of the authentic objects and ridding myself of the matter?'

He spread his hands, palms up. 'That is something I have asked myself frequently, without ever arriving at a completely satisfactory answer, but I will tell you what I think. I think it's simply that . . . well, that these high-handed, brutish confiscations are so hateful, so unjust, that I feel I must do whatever I can to help the victims. How could I not?'

He looked suddenly back up into our eyes. I had the impression that he'd embarrassed himself, but then, with a shrug, that dry, puckish smile was back in place. 'My better judgment has been warped, you might say. Aside from that, there is the considerable artistic satisfaction of duping these Nazi "connoisseurs," and the pleasurable irony of being paid by them for performing a service for the Jews. And then, of—'

The film ended with a clatter and the screen went to blank white, then to black as Stanley turned the projector off. I had kept my arm around Lily the whole time, and now I squeezed the back of her neck. 'Some movie, huh?'

'Can it be true, Pete?'

'It sure looks like it to me. As far as those coins go, he did it right in front of us.'

'So he – I can't—' She shook her head incredulously. 'He didn't really collaborate with them then.'

'Apparently not.'

In the sudden darkness I could hardly see her, but I knew she was crying. 'Oh, Pete . . . I feel so horrible . . . the way I treated him, and he was only . . . only . . .'

'Now wait a minute, honey. Remember, he wasn't any prize as a father. He pawned you off to Lebrun when things got hard, and then he ran to Spain and left you alone in France and never looked back when you were a sixteen-year-old kid carrying a German's baby, and for twenty years he never even bothered to find you, and besides that, don't forget that he and Lebrun had no problems dealing with old Nazis in Barcelona.'

'Yes, but he wasn't a collaborator, not during the war.' She turned to look at me, her eyes gleaming in the darkness. '*My father wasn't a collaborator.*'

I touched her cheek to brush away a tear track with my fingertips. 'No, he wasn't a collaborator.'

'Now get the hell out of here, will you?' It was Stanley, leaning urgently out of the projection booth and pushing the film canister down at me. 'The show's over. I gotta set up Bugs Bunny.'

'Da show's ovuh,' Lily whispered to me in a pretty good imitation of Stanley's Brownsville accent. 'I godda seddup Buhgs Buhnny.' And then, exactly why I couldn't tell you, we burst into laughter that was like honey on our throats.

BUT ON THE drive home the unanswered questions started crowding in on us. Every time one of us would ask something, the other would answer with a new question. 'Why had Marcel Vercier been silent all this time, why hadn't he used the film to try to clear his name with the authorities years ago?' I would ask. 'Never mind the authorities,' Lily would answer, 'why would he let me go on thinking he was a traitor? His own daughter?' And on and on. What was there in the film that was so important to Lebrun? Why had Mrs Aguilar, his secretary, surreptitiously slipped that note into my pocket telling me about the tribunal records at the city hall – what was her interest in any of this?

It was only on that last point that we arrived at any kind of answer, and that came while we were waiting at the endless stoplight at Bay Parkway and McDonald Avenue.

'I think I understand what Mrs Aguilar's part was,' Lily said suddenly.

'You do? What?'

'Nothing. She never put that note in your pocket.'

'No, that can't be. I thanked her for it later, and she—'

And there I stopped. What Mrs Aguilar had done, now that I thought about it, was to say 'you're welcome' nervously and noncommittally and return to her typewriter as fast as she could. In other words, she had acted like a polite, busy person who didn't know what I was talking about and wasn't eager to strike up a conversation with a crackpot who insisted on thanking her for something she hadn't done. Lily was right.

'But . . . if it wasn't her, then who . . .'

'Uncle Charles.'

I shook my head. 'That's crazy. Why would he want me to go to Veaudry and see the tribunal records? And even if he did, he could've just told me, not gone through the rigmarole of getting a secret note into my pocket.'

'I don't think so,' she said. 'See, he would have wanted to keep alive the impression that they'd been dealing in old Nazi loot because that's what brought the shop its customers – you told me that yourself – but at the same time he wouldn't have wanted you to think that he himself was *knowingly* making a profit on what the Germans had stolen during the war.'

'Why wouldn't he?'

'Because then you might have been outraged enough to bring the law down on him.'

'That's true enough. If I'd thought—'

'So instead he wanted you to see the record of my father's trial, which Uncle Charles – supposedly – knew nothing about. That would strengthen the story about my *father's* Nazi dealings, but leave Uncle Charles innocent and above it all. Are you following this?'

'Just barely, but you know, Lily, I think you're right.'

At that point, the light having changed a quarter of a second before, the driver behind us pounded on his horn and that was as far as we were able to get. But a few minutes later, as I stepped out to open our garage door, along with the blast of chilly air came another glimmer of light. I began to see what I thought might be a way to finally arrive at the rest of the answers.

'I have to make a phone call,' I said as we got out of our coats in the foyer.

'Now? This second?' said Lily, still deep into trying to puzzle things through. 'To whom?'

'To Tegucigalpa,' I said.

Chapter Twenty-Seven

IT TOOK A few minutes to get hold of someone at the Honduran Museum of Ancient Art who could speak to me in English.

'Yes, how may I help you?' said Señor Carías, the curator of jewelry and ornaments.

'I'm calling about the Rearing Lamb, the seventh-century Merovingian pendant that you acquired a few months ago?'

'Ah, yes, and what would you like to know?'

'I believe I heard somewhere that you returned it recently to the Galeria Metropolitana.'

He replied with a melodic Latin laugh. 'No, sir, you heard incorrectly. I assure you, it's still very much with us, in our center gallery. I hope that you can come and see it soon.'

'Thank you, I'll certainly try.'

I'll be damned, I said to myself as a good many things clunked into place. The glimmer of light had opened up into a sunburst. I hung up and walked into the kitchen, where Lily was putting up some coffee for us.

'*Voilá*,' I said.

What had the call to Tegucigalpa told me that was so important? It had told me that Charles Lebrun had lied about the Rearing Lamb's having been returned to the Galeria Metropolitana. It had never been returned; it had been in Honduras all along. Which meant, and this was the critical part, that there were two – at least two – Rearing Lambs: the one I'd seen in Lebrun's office in Barcelona, and the one that had reposed all along in the Honduran Museum of Ancient Art. Which meant, in turn, that one of them – at least one of them – had to be a fake.

That much was certain. From there on, things necessarily got more conjectural. Lily and I were willing to conjecture, however – what else could we do, with Vercier and Lebrun both dead? – and over a pot of coffee and a package of stale peanut butter cookies that I'd somehow overlooked during her absence, we did just that, working from this newly learned fact and piling inference on surmise on speculation. But in the end we sat back with a feeling of closure, satisfied that we'd made as much sense of things as anyone was ever going to make.

First, the Galeria Metropolitana was a scam. Well, it probably conducted some legitimate business, but it was first and foremost a forgery mill. When they got hold of a particularly good coin or piece of jewelry from one of their ex-Nazi pals – the Rearing Lamb of Merovingia, for example – the talented Vercier would knock off a copy or two. Then they'd have two, or maybe three, highly profitable sales to make instead of one, a safe enough gamble if they made sure they placed the pieces in widely separated markets. And in the case of the Rearing Lamb, they couldn't have been much more separate: a little-known museum in Tegucigalpa, Honduras, and the family castle of Herr von Feuerbach, a private collector in Leipzig, East Germany, behind the Iron Curtain. Obviously, there was a lot of money to be made from this kind of shenanigan; the Honduran museum had paid them one hundred thousand dollars, if I recalled correctly. What von Feuerbach paid on top of that I didn't know.

A lot of money. And that, we reasoned, was why Lebrun had been so desperate to get his hands on the two copies of the film. He knew that if the beans were ever spilled about Vercier's being a skilled forger it would mean not only the end of their lucrative gallery operation, but a probable spell in jail and a life-crushing load of debt from court judgments that would be sure to go against him. So the films and their content had to be destroyed and Vercier along with them, since he was now showing clear signs of wanting to spill the beans. And if I or Lily had to be gotten rid of along the way, well, that was too bad.

And why Chastenet? That was something no one would ever know for sure, but given what we already knew, we could make a pretty good guess. Chastenet had been a filmmaker. He had also been a friend of Vercier's. He'd said that he'd known what was on the film – very likely he'd been the person behind the camera – and if that was what he'd been going to tell me about that morning, then obviously he had to be taken out of the picture too. Which he was, and me almost along with him.

That left us with the most mystifying aspect of all. If Chastenet knew what was on the film, then why hadn't he brought it to light years before in an effort to clear his friend? Why wait until the very day he learned (from me) that Vercier was dead? And, more to the point, why had Vercier himself never tried to clear his own name? Why make the film at all if he wasn't going to use it? Why, for twenty years, had he permitted his daughter to despise him for something he'd never done?

It was Lily who came up with the explanation, and it was the same one we'd come up with for Lebrun, the simplest of all motives. 'Money,' she said after we'd thought about it for a while, silently dunking rock-hard cookies.

I looked at her. 'I don't follow.'

'Well, look. Father was making a lot of money, the same as Uncle Charles was. What would happen if he'd gone ahead and used the film to clear his name? The word would be out that he was a forger, and that'd be the end of their business. I hate to say it, but somebody like my father would be much more interested in the business than in his reputation back home. In fact, as long as he was safe in Barcelona, I doubt if he ever bothered to give it a thought. So he set the two copies aside – just in case they ever came after him – and went on happily raking in the cash, hoping the situation would never arise. And he told Chastenet to keep it to himself, which he did, right up until the time he heard my father was dead.'

'But not to tell *you*? To just let you go on thinking—'

She gave me a wistful smile. 'As you said, he wasn't much of a father. I'm afraid that just wasn't his thing.'

'Yes, that all makes sense,' I said, nodding. 'Unfortunately. And you think he had a change of heart when he found out he only had a little while to live? He didn't want to go to his death with you believing that he'd been a traitor?'

'Yes, that's just what I think.' Her eyes suddenly welled up with tears again. 'And I was so awful to him, I wouldn't even let him—'

'Lily?' I said softly. 'We actually have some vacation money left in the bank, enough for a couple of days, anyway. What do you say we go up to the mountains, the way we planned? And forget about all this for a while? How does that sound?'

She wiped at her eyes with a tissue and summoned up another smile, more wholehearted this time. 'Fabulous,' she said.

WE WERE ON the George Washington Bridge, high over the Hudson River, on our way to the Catskills. Manhattan was behind us and the snow-flecked Palisades lay ahead. I was driving and Lily was leaning back in the passenger seat with her head on the headrest, looking out the window and watching the gray steel superstructure of the bridge whiz by. We were both happy and relaxed.

'I just had a funny thought,' she said lazily.

'Uh-huh.'

'The murders, the whole sorry mess – it was all for nothing. None of it had to happen. All Uncle Charles had to do was leave well enough alone and everything would have worked out for him. Nobody would be dead. Nobody would have killed anybody.'

'Huh? How do you figure that?'

'Well, look, I wasn't going to watch that film no matter what my father said, right?'

'I guess not.'

'And I certainly wasn't about to go to Corsica to locate the copy. I wouldn't have walked around the corner to find the copy. I didn't even know there was one. If Uncle Charles hadn't panicked and had my father murdered, and then sent those thugs to our house, and gotten Sergeant Kovalski involved, I'd have gotten over seeing him in a few days. My father would have given up and gone back to Barcelona without showing it to anybody. I'd never have left home. You'd never have gone to Veaudry. Chastenet wouldn't have been murdered because he never would have made that speech in the café. You wouldn't have had to follow me to Corsica, and I wouldn't have been kidnapped, and Uncle Charles wouldn't have gotten himself killed either.'

That was a lot of theorizing. We had turned off the bridge and headed north on the Palisades Parkway before I finished digesting it and coming to the conclusion that she was exactly right on all counts.

'Damn, that's a funny thought, all right.'

'One good thing came out of it, anyway, I suppose. We got rid of some old skeletons that'd been cluttering up my closet for a long, long time.'

'Make that two good things. I'm betting I've had the Dream for the last time. I know who the lady is now, and there's no mystery.'

She smiled and laid her hand lightly on my knee. 'No, there's no more mystery. We know each other even better than we did before, don't we?'

I smiled back. 'Not just each other. Ourselves.'

WE STAYED AT the Concord Hotel for two days and nights. We listened to Connie Francis. We danced to Xavier Cugat and Abbe Lane. We rented skis and took advantage of such skiing as the Catskills allow. We slipped, and slid, and laughed on 'the world's largest artificial ice-skating rink' and played in the heated Tropical Indoor Pool. It was wonderful. Nothing whatever of importance happened.

Except . . .

On the second night, as we were preparing to go downstairs for dinner and Lily was blotting her lipstick at the mirror over the bureau, she paused to study her reflection.

'Pete,' she said slowly, 'how would you feel about me letting my hair grow? You've never seen me with long hair, and I think maybe it's time for a change.'

It took a minute for my throat to unthicken enough for me to speak, and even then I had to turn away so she wouldn't see the contortions I suspected my face was going through.

'Oh, I like it fine the way it is,' I said as casually as I could. 'But maybe it is time for a change.'

'HI, SHARON. YES, fine, how's your holiday been?'

It was the morning after we got back from the mountains, and Lily had just picked up the telephone. I went out to shovel the small dusting of fresh snow off our steps, and when I came back she was just ending the call. 'Let me call you back,' she said, and turned to me with a quizzical expression on her face.

'What's up?' I asked

'That was Sharon at the school. Would you have any idea what she was talking about? Minot, North Dakota? The new baby?'

'Oh, yes,' I said, 'Minot. Um, well, it's like this. . . .'